# The
# *Getaway*
# List

## Also by Emma Lord

*Tweet Cute*
*You Have a Match*
*When You Get the Chance*
*Begin Again*
*The Break-Up Pact*

# The
## *Getaway*
# List

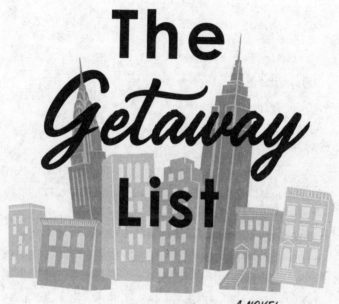

*A NOVEL*

## *Emma Lord*

WEDNESDAY BOOKS
NEW YORK

*To Janna and Alex for being in my corner from the very start. I might have moved to New York without my own "Getaway List," but thanks to you I have crossed off more dreams come true than I ever dared to write down.*

Published in the United States by Wednesday Books, an imprint of St. Martin's Publishing Group

THE GETAWAY LIST. Copyright © 2023 by Emma Lord. All rights reserved. Printed in the United States of America. For information, address St. Martin's Publishing Group, 120 Broadway, New York, NY 10271.

Excerpt from *The Rival* © 2024 by Emma Lord.

www.wednesdaybooks.com

Designed by Jen Edwards

The Library of Congress has cataloged the hardcover edition as follows:

Names: Lord, Emma, author.
Title: The getaway list : a novel / Emma Lord.
Description: First edition. | New York : Wednesday Books, 2024. |
Identifiers: LCCN 2023036257 | ISBN 9781250903990
    (hardcover) | ISBN 9781250904003 (ebook)
Subjects: CYAC: Friendship—Fiction. | Interpersonal relations—
    Fiction. | New York (N.Y.)—Fiction. | LCGFT: Romance
    fiction. | Novels.
Classification: LCC PZ7.1.L676 Ge 2024 | DDC [Fic]—dc23
LC record available at https://lccn.loc.gov/2023036257

ISBN 978-1-250-90401-0 (trade paperback)

Our books may be purchased in bulk for promotional, educational, or business use. Please contact your local bookseller or the Macmillan Corporate and Premium Sales Department at 1-800-221-7945, extension 5442, or by email at MacmillanSpecialMarkets@macmillan.com.

First Wednesday Books Trade Paperback Edition: 2024

10  9  8  7  6  5  4  3  2  1

# Chapter One

If you think about it, getting rejected from all ten colleges I applied to is quite the feat. I did that whole thing where I picked three "shoo-in" schools, three maybes, and three reaches—even threw in a cheeky application to NYU, just in case a rich distant relative died and left me a zillion dollars for tuition—and got back a slew of "Thank you, but" emails and very thin envelopes addressed to one Riley Larson. Sure, our poor mailman hasn't looked me in the eye since April, but you know what? Statistically speaking, it makes me kind of a big deal.

My mom is not especially pleased that I turned the rejection letters into a paper-mache collage and stuck it on my graduation cap, but I've been a mostly model kid as of late. Not to mention I just conceded my entire summer to helping her at the coffee shop. I'm entitled to a little teenage rebellion. Plus after four long years of sleep deprivation, GPA-related tears, and enduring the humiliation of having a literal earthworm as a school mascot (don't ask), the students of Falls Creek High deserve some comic relief. I'm only doing my part.

I slide past my classmates toward my seat with the rest of the *L* last names, sandwiched between an already tipsy Elle Lake (in-state school) and a very grim Chet Lawrence (Harvard, the nerd). The school has apparently placed tiny packs of gummy worms on our seats. A little on the nose, but after I unwrap mine I raise a bright green worm and say, "To getting the hell out of here."

A good number of classmates join me in this nonsense toast, though for me it comes with a slight bitter taste even a lime-flavored gummy worm can't wash down. Most of them *are* getting out of here. Far as I know, I'm going to be stuck in Falls Creek until I Falls Croak.

Before I can indulge in another pity party I scan the crowd of parents behind us for my mom, who in true mom fashion somehow got here before I did. She'll be somewhere in the front row and because of that I've already texted her a list of kids a mile wide who have asked her to record them walking across the stage. She's happy to do it. Nobody loves a mission more than my mom does. Hell, she'll probably just do the whole five-hundred-kid graduating class "just in case."

Before I can find my mom my phone hums to life in my lap with a message from, of all people, Tom.

They're livestreaming this. Don't fuck up.

My face blooms with an immediate warmth, a smile tugging at my lips. Tom is my all-time best but also worst friend — best because we would literally die for each other, and worst because in the last year he's texted with the frequency of a prehistoric rock.

> Does the blue of this graduation gown
> make my existential terror pop?

Tom's reply is instant: Not as well as a standard black might have, but well enough.

I know there's no way Tom can actually see me, considering the camera is trained on the stage, but it feels like he's in this stuffy gym with us just the same. Hell, he would be, if it weren't for his mom, Vanessa, abruptly moving him up to Manhattan the summer after freshman year of high school in a bold attempt to ruin both of our lives. (All right, it was for her enormously cool job as a scriptwriter and director—her debut indie film became a cult-classic, Oscar-nominated hit—but the other point still stands.)

What happened to the entirety of NYC that you're bored enough to be watching this? Thought you'd have a whole gang of Columbia nerds to hang out with by now, I text back.

The principal shoots me a pointed look from the stage. I aim my cheekiest grin at him but don't bother trying to hide my phone. What is he going to do, suspend me again in the last five minutes of my high school career? Been there, permanent recorded that.

> So plot twist I think I'm taking a gap
> year? Anyway NYC's hottest club
> is virtual graduations in Virginia.
> Keep up with the times

I blink at my phone screen and let out an audible "Huh." Last I checked Tom was all gung ho on the whole Ivy League scene. Hence the mug I got him off Etsy with the Columbia logo on one side and the words "nerd juice" on the other.

Excuse you sir?? What are you doing with a gap year??? And then to soften the assault of my many punctuation marks, I add, If you're joining the circus and didn't invite me I'm about to make you dearly regret it.

Tom doesn't answer immediately, but this is to be expected. Lately anytime I ask Tom a personal question it takes him three to 314 times as long to answer. I settle in with my gummy worms and allow myself the indulgence of completely and utterly dissociating through all five graduation speeches by reading the latest fantasy novel I've got downloaded on my phone, only to get bodily yanked by Elle when it's finally our row's turn to cross.

A lot of things occur to me as I take the steps up to that stage. Largely unhelpful things—like for instance, I still have no idea how to write out a check even though the lady at the bank recklessly gave me a whole box of them when I opened my account on my eighteenth birthday last month. Or that I have never successfully cooked anything that didn't have microwave instructions. Or that I have no idea what I'm planning to do with my life, or what I'm doing beyond this summer, or even a solid enough sense of my own hobbies and interests not to immediately fail even BuzzFeed's most ironclad "Build A Pancake Breakfast And We'll Tell You Your Future Career" quiz.

All too soon Elle is walking ahead of me, beaming her best "I definitely did not sneak sips from my mom's boxed wine" smile as she crosses the stage. I feel the outline of my phone in my pocket take a deep breath, buoyed by a sudden calm. Tom's here. Or as *here* as Tom can possibly get. It doesn't matter how much time passes—I always feel like the bravest version of myself when I've got him near.

The lights are so bright when I cross the rickety stage that I can barely find the camera livestreaming the event but manage to clock it just in time. I take my diploma from our principal—who could maybe do a better job of not looking so happy to see me go—and when he extends his hand for me to shake I look right at the camera and make a quick series of gestures with one of my hands that ends with me making a trumpet with my fingers against my nose.

The student section erupts in laughter. I blow a kiss for good measure, immediately catching sight of my mom with a palm to her forehead but the camera still diligently held up in the air with the other hand.

Tom's already texted before I get back to my row. Congratulations, you absolutely ridiculous person. Alongside it are a jumble of hand-gesture emojis that approximate the handshake I just did a short one-sided version of onstage, the silly one we made up in fifth grade.

The smile on my face aches a little, thinking of how far we are from those little ragtag, rowdy kids now.

Now please explain to me what you did to that unsuspecting graduation cap, he adds.

I ease back into my seat, taking the cap off and settling it into my lap to look at all the rejection letters, glossy with glitter glue. Tom knows about the rejections, of course. I text him at least once a week with updates and questions about what he's up to, even if half the time it's a bit like talking to a wall. I know he'll get a kick out of my little art project, but before I can take a picture of it I flip the cap over to look at the inside, feeling like I'm flipping over some tender underside of my heart.

There's another piece of paper taped precariously underneath. This one is handwritten, and something only Tom would recognize—"the Getaway List," we dubbed it after Tom moved away. It's made up of adventures we never went on—an interactive writing class in Manhattan we wanted to take the summer after freshman year before my mom got promoted and needed me to help take over shifts when they were short-staffed at the coffee shop. A camping trip we tried to orchestrate with some friends sophomore year that fell through. A part-time job I wanted to get last summer at the same bike-messenger service where Tom works in the city so we could relive the glory days of spinning our wheels all over this town, but my mom had me indefinitely grounded for the infamous suspension.

The idea was that when we met up again we could do everything on the list to make up for lost time. The problem is we just kept losing more of it. The list started as a denial that we were apart, but over time just became an acceptance that there was nothing we could do to change it. An acceptance that's led me to this absurd moment now, when it's hitting me with a fresh ache that I haven't seen the person who knows me best of anyone in the whole world in almost three years.

It feels like a risk reminding Tom, because neither of us has mentioned it in months. I'm worried it would almost feel like admitting defeat. Only as I'm sending Tom a photo of it and feel an uncharacteristic shiver of nerves do I understand the truth—part of me is still hopeful we could do some of it, and another louder part of me is scared that we're so far removed from the kids who started that list that Tom wouldn't even want to anymore.

Tom doesn't reply right away, but I do get a text from my mom that says Can't wait to show this to your grandparents, along with a photo of me grinning like a jackal onstage with my thumb jammed against my nose. I snicker and tuck my phone away for the rest of it, trying to put the anxiety out of my mind.

It feels like someone pressed fast-forward on the whole morning after that, because before I know it the principal is congratulating the graduating class and rickety chairs are squeaking as we all clamber to our feet. Graduation caps and gummy worms are flying through the air, kids are yelling like they've suddenly grown a third lung, and I feel the electricity of the room like it's buzzing in my bones.

No, wait. My phone is literally buzzing against my hip. I pull it out and see the belated response from Tom.

> I miss the shit out of you you know. Every day. I'm sorry if I've been bad at keeping in touch so I just wanted to say that.

I blink at the text, my throat tight. Caps are still flying and students are jostling each other and hollering and setting off confetti poppers and I'm standing in the middle of it all, staring at my phone screen and typing out the words I miss the shit out of you too.

"Riley!"

I snap my head up to see Jesse half jogging over to me. His robe is already wide open, his ripped black jeans and faded band T-shirt a sharp contrast to everyone else's spiffy graduation best, including the upsettingly traffic-cone-orange sweater set of my mom's I'm wearing now.

I'm half considering demanding he trade outfits with me—those few months we dated sophomore year we swapped enough clothes that there's actually no guarantee that isn't my shirt he's wearing—but he's already spilling over with excitement, his mop of dirty blond curls lifting as he runs over.

"Dude, high five."

I oblige Jesse, who doesn't just high-five me but grabs my hand and holds it up like I'm a champion prizefighter. His eyes look like someone backlit them with neon.

"Look at us, actually going out there and following our *dreams*," he says, emphasizing the last word with another squeeze of my hand.

"Getting a McFlurry and napping until August?" I ask.

Jesse is even more absurdly enthusiastic to be alive than usual, because he spins and releases me like a clunky ballerina.

"Nah, I mean saying 'screw the establishment!' and going our own way. You know we're among the select few cool kids without colleges next to our names in the graduation program?" he says, proudly holding one up.

I did not know there was a program in the first place, let alone one that tattled on us. Jesse tucks his carefully into his robe the same way he always does with flyers and knickknacks from events, collecting mementos like a tall magpie.

"Huh. Well, I'm not really yelling anything at the establishment," I admit. "I'm probably just going to start taking community-college classes in the fall."

Jesse's grin wilts like he wasn't expecting such a boring thing to come out of my mouth, and to be fair, I wouldn't have either. He recovers quickly and says, "Well, maybe you'll have to come up to New York. You can crash with the Walking JED anytime."

"The band is moving to New York?"

I'm more surprised that I didn't know than I am at the idea of them moving. The Walking JED (so named because their names are Jesse, Eddie, and Dai, and all three of them are painfully obsessed with zombie lore) are so ridiculously talented that it's kind of a wonder they didn't all get Walking GEDs and ditch this Popsicle stand years ago. Jesse's the lead singer and writes most of their songs, and between his delightfully offbeat sense of style and distinctly sweet and smoky voice, it's only a matter of time before someone is shoving a record deal in their faces.

Jesse nods, every inch of him thrumming with energy. "Bright and early tomorrow morning!"

There's no ignoring the pang between my ribs this

time—the one that's been aching just under the surface for months. Truth be told I don't really have any designs on college, so it's not getting left behind in the literal sense. More like the figurative one. I look around and everyone has some kind of plan. College. Pursuing a passion. Seeing the world.

I've got the McDonald's drive-through and then just a giant blank slate of "???" on the other side. I feel a surge of irrational fear, like I've just stepped too close to an edge I didn't realize was a cliff.

But then I feel two firm arms wrap around the back of me and my mom's familiar minty breath saying into my ear, "Well, if it isn't my newly graduated hellion."

I lean in as she kisses me on the temple and gives me an extra squeeze before letting me go.

"Look," I say, handing her the diploma. "Free kindling."

But then she gets all misty-eyed and says, "I bet we can find a decent frame for this. Put it up somewhere in your room?"

I'm about to object to the idea of disrupting the vibe of any place in the apartment with a reminder of the most monotonous years of my life when Jesse squints at us and says candidly, "Yeesh, I always forget how alike you look."

He's not wrong. This is partially due to the fact that I am a carbon copy of my mom, to the point where the dad I've never met might as well have just hit Control + C, Control + V on my mom's internal keyboard and walked away. We have the precise same honey-brown curls, the same hazel eyes, the same tall, wiry frames and even, somehow, the precise same freckle under the right side of our lower lip.

But the alikeness is even more exaggerated by the fact that my mom is only nineteen years older than I am, and people assume she's my sibling as often as my parent.

"Oh. Hello, Jesse." My mom gives him an amused once-over and says, "I see you've added more tattoos to the collection."

My mom likes Jesse just fine, but likes him a lot more now that we are very firmly exes. Jesse and I never got into the kind of shenanigans that drove my mom up the wall the way Tom and I did growing up, but dating him right on the heels of Tom leaving probably didn't help matters. Jesse's love of tattoos and guitars reminds her a bit too much of her alleged "wild youth" in New York she has been afraid I'll make a sequel out of probably since the moment I was born. No offense to my mom, who was likely a badass in her day, but staying out all night clubbing to early 2000s hits in low-rise jeans while sneaking sips of Fireball from a glittery hip flask isn't exactly her nerdy daughter's scene.

(To be clear, I only have this hilarious mental image thanks to my aunts' retellings; my mom glosses over the details as if she's worried I'm going to take notes.)

"Yeah," says Jesse enthusiastically, pulling up the billowing sleeve of his graduation gown. "Look. This one's a guitar, but its strings are crying."

"Inspired," says my mom wryly.

I pull her away before she can ask if the tat was Taylor Swift–related, which it absolutely was—his band's punk-rock cover of "Cardigan" was voted as our school anthem as a write-in, which I may or may not have helped orchestrate (the school board was awfully upset for a group of adults who let the whole "earthworm" thing slide)—but we don't have enough time in the world for Jesse to go down one of his glorious Swiftie rabbit holes. I want that McFlurry *yesterday*.

"Wait," I realize. "My cap."

I was so eager to toss it that I forgot about the retrieving part. Wow. Fully graduated now and even Labradors have more common sense.

My mom lets out a *pfft* noise. "Don't you think we can live without that particular relic?"

"No, no, it's important," I say, panic seizing me. "I—"

Cut myself off abruptly, because my mom doesn't actually know about the Getaway List. Most of the conflicts on my end were because of her schedule, which is mostly devoted to any hours she can get at the coffee shop she comanages between classes to support us—the last thing I want her to think is that I'm ungrateful for any of it.

"Well, I'm sure it's around here somewhere," says my mom, starting to sift through the abandoned caps on the floor. I don't miss her quick glance at the clock on her phone. She moved her shift to be here. If we're going to maintain our sacred Mc-Flurry tradition, we're already cutting it close.

My throat tightens. Maybe this is just it. The sendoff the Getaway List deserves. It really is over then; we're moving onto the next chapter of our lives. There's no *TomandRiley, RileyandTom* anymore, the way everyone in the neighborhood used to say our names when we were a whole lot of things, but chief among them a package deal. We're just Tom and Riley now. Friends for life, but leading very different ones.

"My parents are over there," says Jesse. I give him a quick one-armed hug and when he squeezes back he adds, "For real, hit me up if you're in the city. I feel like you're overdue for an adventure."

"I will," I say, but the words sound hollow even to my own ears.

He lets me go and I feel flimsy, like I'm going to cry. Like there's suddenly this part of me that wants that adventure more than anything, but I'm too untethered to know where to begin. For all the ruckus in the gym, it feels unbearably quiet in my head right now. Like without all the noise of classes and extracurriculars and college applications there's just this void staring back at me where my reflection should be.

The trouble is I wouldn't even know what to look for—I

haven't really felt like myself in ages. The self that pulled one over on teachers who were mean to our friends, like when Mr. Zaff called Jesse a "baby" once for crying over a movie we saw in class, so Tom and I put baby safety locks on every drawer and cabinet in his classroom the next day. The self who pranked classmates at liberty, like when Tom hacked the school loud-speaker so I could put on my best teacher voice and ask if Ava and Josh would come to the front office (collectively there are twenty-three Avas and twenty-five Joshes enrolled, so that Fri-day afternoon quickly devolved into schoolwide chaos). The self that played what Tom dubbed the "sneaky elf game," leav-ing random trinkets stuffed in friends' lockers, and ran all over every corner of this town and asked enough questions to break any reasonable adult's brain.

My mom wasn't so much of a helicopter parent when I was a kid, but by high school Tom and I were getting up to enough mischief that she was practically deafening me with the propel-lers. After the incident that got me suspended she pushed me into so many extracurriculars on top of my part-time jobs that there wasn't a split second I wasn't accounted for—or, inciden-tally, a split second I could have any coherent thoughts other than "How do I make this boring thing less boring?"

Which is to say, I've mostly spent the past two or so years not-so-covertly reading fantasy books and my abandoned fan-fics on my phone while all these boring things happened around me. This survival strategy was all well and good un-til this moment now, because it turns out I am not a royal burdened with ancient power or a knight infiltrating a distant realm with a dark secret, but just Riley. Powerless and ordinary and unsure of myself. Only now that I'm standing here on the other side of half living my own life do I realize just how unsure I really am.

Just when I'm blinking back the deeply inconvenient and

unwelcome sting of tears, my phone buzzes in my pocket again. It's a text from Tom. A photo of his own version of the Getaway List, written in his endearingly large handwriting. Only instead of the eight things we originally had on it, he's added a ninth: *Actually see each other in our corporeal forms.*

I laugh, both out of relief and from the reference; as kids Tom and I were obsessed with Tides of Time, a time-travel book series with main characters who either traveled in their own bodies or as projections of themselves. As a result, "corporeal" was one of the biggest words our eight-year-old selves knew; I typed the word enough in the fics I used to write for the series that the letters are worn out on my keyboard.

The smile on my face only widens from there. Sharpens, even, into the shape of a smirk I haven't worn in so long that it feels like I have to break it in.

Maybe this is the shake-up I need. The defibrillator to reset my psyche. The idea comes together so quickly that I'm practically blinking myself to New York before it can fully form—for the first time in literal years, I have the weekend free. I could take a bus up so easily. I could be squeezing the life out of Tom with one of our trademark ridiculous hugs by nightfall. We could even knock some things off the Getaway List. What better way to reconnect to my old self than by doing all the things she wanted to do, with someone who's known me almost as long as I've known myself?

Maybe reconnecting will inspire me to write again, since it was Tom who encouraged me to post my stuff in the first place. Maybe I'll wrestle out of Tom why he's been so quiet these past few months, so I'll have my partner in crime back. Maybe I'll stop feeling like this boring version of myself who doesn't clown around for my friends' sake like I used to, but because being the class jokester was the only way to pass the time when I was overscheduled to the max.

And then maybe I can start to figure out my *new* self, get a sense for what I actually want now that high school is finally in the rearview mirror.

My heart is thrumming under my ribs like an overly caffeinated bird.

I'm booking the afternoon bus to NYC, I text back.

Tom sends back a string of laughing emojis. I'm not entirely sure if I'm joking, and judging from Tom's response, he isn't either. That's its own kind of relief. That the old version of me still lives in Tom's head—the daring, intentional, *fun* me.

Maybe if I find my way back to Tom, I can find her, too.

I find my mom squinting under a row of folded-up chairs, along with Jesse's parents, who have joined in the search in their matching Walking JED shirts. I make a mental note to demand where I can buy one of my own when I touch my mom's shoulder, suddenly giddy. "It's okay," I tell them. I don't need my list if Tom has his. "It's fine. Someone will probably find it. Let's go."

Admittedly I have access to McFlurries near every day of my human existence, but McFlurries are sacred happenings. At least they are for me and my mom. My mom got me one every time I got a shot as a little kid, and I drag her to get them every time she finishes up another semester of community college, and at some point getting a McFlurry just came hand in hand with accomplishing anything that seemed scary or tough.

"Oreos or M&M's?" my mom asks when we pile into her deeply unreliable but ridiculously adorable old Honda, which we decorated with flower stickers all around the bumper a few years back.

"I'm flying as close to the sun as I can today. Both."

"Atta girl," says my mom as the car sputters reluctantly into drive.

By the time we're settled in the parking lot and taking our

concoctions to the McFace, I've found the bus schedule and done a mental checklist of things I need to pack and have "New York, New York" stuck in my head despite not being entirely certain of any of the words aside from those two.

I clear my throat. "So I was thinking—it's Friday."

"Astutely observed," says my mom, fishing out an Oreo chunk.

I hike my knees farther up on the dash. "And I'm not starting at the coffee shop until Monday. I might take the bus up this afternoon to finally see Tom in New York."

My mom blinks like a bug just tried to fly into her eye. "Wait, what?"

I laugh. "Seriously. You realize it's been almost three years since I've seen him?" I stare down at my phone. "And Tom seems kind of—well, I don't know."

I really don't, and I haven't for a while. I know about the broader things in his life, like that he's been traveling with his mom, and finally settled on a psychology major out of the myriad of topics he has nerdy expertise in. I know how he spends some of his time, like watching the *Tides of Time* television adaptation or continuing to do bike deliveries for the "Dear, Love" Dispatch app people can use to send anonymous gifts to everyone from friends to crushes to family all over the city. The specifics were things I always meant to find out when we were together.

My mom's hands tighten around the steering wheel. "I was hoping we could hang out this weekend, you and me. Celebrate a bit. It's been ages since we've had a whole day together."

The McFlurry sours in my mouth, and not because of the leftover gummy worms I jammed into it. My mom's right. But that feels like more her fault than mine—in an effort to keep me out of "trouble," she signed me up for pretty much every extracurricular under the sun. I'm talking everything from track to Science Olympiad to salsa to Model UN, all of which had one thing in common, which is that I have no particular talent for any of them.

My mom thinks I didn't get into any colleges because of the two-day suspension on my record. I'm pretty sure it's because I don't have any discernable hobbies or personality traits—since she kept signing me up for things and I kept trying to weasel out of them, I never stuck to any of the school clubs long enough to look even remotely committed to them. It didn't help that coffee-shop shifts got in the way of me doing any of the competitions on weekends, too. As a result my college application probably looks like it was written by an AI chatbot that just regurgitated every hobby and part-time job in our hometown, and my semi-decent grades and test scores weren't enough to sway them back into my court.

Whatever the case, we're here now, with more free days than I've had in years. I've wasted enough time doing things I don't like to pass up on a chance to do something I'll love.

"Well, we could celebrate next weekend then?" I ask. And then, even though I'm itching at the seams to click PURCHASE on that bus ticket, I add, "Or we could hang out this weekend and I could visit Tom the next one."

My mom's not quite looking at me, staring into her melting ice cream. "I don't think that's smart, going up there on your own."

The tone of the conversation has shifted into territory we've never been. I feel not unlike our neighbor's dog Ribbit when they put up that electric fence—like I'm suddenly testing the edges of a boundary I didn't know was there.

"It'd just be two days," I say carefully.

"Two days?" My mom tries for a teasing smile, but the words still come out tight. "I know you. You could get in trouble in a paper bag in ten seconds. You expect me to trust you in Manhattan for forty-eight hours?"

"Trouble" isn't exactly the right word and she knows it. More like "mischief." Harmless stuff that mostly involved pranks and the occasional interruption in class and, okay, a handful of times playing hooky on dweeby endeavors like Tides of Time meetups with other kids on our local fandom Discord. But it's not like we were ever doing anything all that dangerous, unless the few times Tom trusted me to read a map counts.

I let out a laugh, also trying to keep it light, and say, "Yeah, well, I'm eighteen."

I don't mean for the words to start a fight, because that's just something we don't do. Even if we wanted to, between both of us working and going to school there's just no time for it. But my mom flinches like I didn't just start a fight but swung both fists without warning.

"I have to get to work," she says suddenly, starting up the car and pointing us toward home.

I grip the McFlurry in my hand like it's a tether. "Okay, but really, when can I go up to the city? There's a bus that leaves from the Metro, I can take myself whenever I want."

I mean for the words to come out as an offer, not a threat, but my mom immediately snaps her head toward me and says, "So that's it? You're just going to run off and do whatever you want now?"

"No." I squirm uncomfortably. "I'm just saying—technically I don't have to ask."

My mom shakes her head. "You're not going to New York."

My mouth opens in surprise, and the only words I manage to string together are, "Why not?"

"Because that city is nothing but trouble, and the two of you together are a magnet for it. We got all through high school without anything going too wrong, can't we just let it be? I mean it's been years, why do you suddenly need to see Tom so badly?"

I set the McFlurry down, strangely light-headed. "Wait a minute. Wait a minute," I say, like my mouth can't catch up to the gears turning in my brain. "This whole time—were you not letting me go up there on purpose?"

My mom sidesteps the question entirely. "I just think you need to take a beat here. You've never even been to the city. And now the second after graduation you're going to hop on a bus with two minutes' notice?" She shakes her head, clearly not looking for an answer. "I know you were talking to Tom today. You only did that handshake because he must have been watching. But that's not a reason to drop everything to see him."

"I'm not dropping anything," I protest.

"But this sounds impulsive. And that's exactly what happens when you and Tom get together. You egg each other on, bring out the worst in each other."

If she was looking for the weakest spot she could hit in me, she just hit it dead on. This version of myself that I've been scrambling to get back to—it's not just that I lost her. It's that my mom was actively trying to shake her off. It nearly stuns the words right out of me. I never thought I'd feel rejection this deeply or immediately, and least of all from my own mom. Especially not after I spent the back half of high school doing my best to play by her rules.

"That's not the worst of me," I manage to say. "That *is* me."

"That's you at your most reckless," my mom says. "And I know how busy Vanessa is with work. Nobody is going to keep an eye on either of you. The last thing you need is to be at Tom's in a city full of places just begging you to get in trouble at every turn."

The understanding is hitting me in waves. Like I've been asleep for the longest time and I'm waking up too slow, all disjointed and confused. "Oh my god. You really did keep me from him."

The wild thing is even though she may not have seen it, Tom has always been the more responsible of the two of us. The one who actually checked the time when we were off on our misadventures and lined his pockets with snacks like a soccer mom. And even if he weren't, it's not like we got up to anything all *that* bad. My mom's talking like we both were just short of booking one-way tickets to juvie.

My mom's voice softens. "I just don't want you doing anything you regret."

"Too late," I say, my voice choked. "Because I regret every single minute I didn't realize you were keeping us apart."

It's bigger than that, but I don't even have the words to explain it to her. At least words that don't sound like they're coming out of some Netflix teenage soap opera. It's not just that I'm hurt. I feel betrayed. Maybe my mom and I haven't always seen eye to eye, but I thought we were always honest with each other. And yet all these missed chances I thought were beyond my control, all these years I ducked my head and just accepted the way things were—if I'd just pushed a little harder. Pressed against the glass. Challenged her even once, the way I would have when I was younger and braver and actually present in my own life, maybe I would have realized much sooner she was keeping this from me.

Maybe I would have realized a lot of things much sooner, and I wouldn't feel so lost like I do right now.

My mom is idling outside of our apartment building—she's late enough for her shift now that there's no point in parking to let me out.

"When you're older and things are more settled, you'll see.

This was for your own good," she says, more to the windshield than to me.

I surprise myself then. I'm not asking anymore. I'm telling. "There's a bus that leaves at four P.M."

My mom closes her eyes and expels a long breath. "Riley."

"I'm sorry," I say, because I can't help it. Because despite everything, I mean it. "But you owe me at least a weekend. You have to let me go."

She opens her eyes again, shaking her head sharply. "Don't do this."

I'm so angry I could scream into my empty McFlurry cup, that I could slam this car door behind me like the Hulk, but I mean it. I'm going. And I don't want to leave her on bad terms. It's occurring to me even as I make the choice that it's the first time I'm leaving her at all.

I linger in my seat. Despite everything I'm still waiting for her cue. "I'll text you when I get there," I finally say.

She doesn't answer. Just leans her head into me for a brief moment and lets out a heavy, unreadable breath. I ease out of the car slower than I ever have, hovering at the open door. She glances over at me, seeming to ask, *What are you waiting for?*, and I realize it's her permission. I may have skirted around it as a kid, even jumped rope with it occasionally, but I've never outright defied it before.

She isn't going to give it, though. Now I finally have to decide something all for myself. The rush of it is thrilling and terrifying, my heart lighter than air, my stomach dropping like a stone. Like there's so much chaos in me that it can only give way to an eerie calm. I take a breath, give myself a new permission all my own, and gently push the car door shut.

# Chapter Two

When I get off the bus and stand in New York City for the first time, it's just as chaotic and crowded and exciting as Tom said it would be. My eyes catch on just about everything, already bursting with curiosity about every hole-in-the-wall sandwich shop and harried dog walker and random cast-out piece of furniture on the streets, all the life-sized stories passing me by in a blink. I'm stunned. I'm overwhelmed. I want to chase it all down, touch every piece, make myself a part of it, too.

But I'm a girl on a mission, so I don't stop for any of it just yet. The sun is just starting to set when I haul my duffel bag into the service entrance of Tom's Upper West Side apartment building, ride the elevator up to the thirty-third floor, and knock on the door. Still, it doesn't feel fully real until I hear his footsteps—solid and rhythmic and distinctly Tom, so much so that I'm already grinning wide enough to break my own face.

And then there he is and my first coherent thought is, *What the fuck.* Because it's Tom, but it isn't. It's Tom with his light-brown eyes and those lips that always curl upward at the edges, Tom with that same little cowlick at the part of his brown hair, Tom with that inherent steadiness in his posture and warmth in his face. But it's also Tom with a good five inches on me and shoulders all broad and his jaw and cheeks defined like someone took a sketch of him and slightly sharpened all the angles.

I blink, caught off guard not just by the eighteen-year-old version of Tom live and in color but by whatever the hell just fluttered under my ribs. This would be a deeply inconvenient time for any of my organs to go on the fritz.

But then Tom's face splits into a smile, his eyes misting up, so unmistakably himself that all I can feel is a rush of warmth flood through me when he opens his mouth and says, "Riley."

He says it with complete awe and a touch of amusement, the kind that makes me feel known. His voice is deeper. I knew this from when we used to talk on the phone or FaceTime every night, but those calls were rare in the past few months, and that voice is something else entirely paired with the rest of him. I wonder if I seem as changed to him as he does to me; wonder if it even matters, when it's clear from the way we're beaming at each other right now that for all the changes in the world, the recognition is still just as deep and immediate as it was when we saw each other last.

"Hi." I have to adjust my neck up several notches to fully meet Tom's gaze. Jesus. Last time I saw him I'm pretty sure *I* was the taller one. "I was in the neighborhood, so."

Tom peers down at me, tilting his head. His eyes are clearer now, his smile still threatening to burst even as he tries to commit to whatever bit I just decided we're playing. "You got shorter," he tells me.

I glance at his well-fitted jeans and white sneakers, at the mug of coffee on the small entryway table beside him. "You got New Yorkier."

And Tom evidently decides we're done with my bit, his eyes watering again when he says, "Come here already," pulling me in for one of our bone-crushing hugs.

At first the relief of it is so overwhelming that I breathe in the flowery detergent his mom always uses and that earthy, innate Tom smell of him, and all I can think is, *We're back.* Like we've been wandering a long time and only just found our way home. Only once we sink into the hug, I don't just see the difference in Tom but feel it, too. I used to be able to wrap my arms around Tom's lanky frame like we were one and the same, but there's so much more of him than there is of me. I can't crush his bones the way we did when we were kids because he's simply uncrushable now, and I can tell he's going easy on me, that there's a quiet ripple of new strength he's not using.

"Jesus," I say, burying my head in his shoulder. "It's like trying to hug Mount Olympus."

I can practically feel Tom's smirk as he lifts me slightly until my feet are off the ground.

"And *that's* a new trick," I add.

He lets out a laugh that I feel in my own chest before setting me back on the ground, not quite letting me go. Our arms are still hooked around our middles, grinning at each other. I'm half-afraid to blink, like the earth might just swallow him up for another three years and the next time I try to hug him he'll be tall as a tree.

He pulls away from me then, only because we both know what's coming—over the years our secret handshake became less ritual and more law. We take a deliberate step back and then devolve immediately into a nonsense sequence of claps, spins, and gestures, laughing at each other for still knowing every step of it. Laughing too hard, maybe, because it's such a damn relief that we both do.

We finish it off with the usual thumb to our noses, breathless and giddy, so unsteady with it we nearly fall into each other.

"You're not even a little surprised to see me?" I ask.

Tom just shakes his head. "I learned to stop being surprised at you approximately a decade ago. This is a very Riley thing to do."

I flush under my grin, because it hasn't been lately, but it feels good to hear someone say so. Like settling into an old, broken-in denim jacket that still fits just right.

I bop my head on his shoulder. "Good. Also I hope you don't think I'm going to start being civil to you just because you got hotter," I say, shucking off my sneakers and making my way inside.

Tom blinks because evidently I can still surprise him. "Uh, wouldn't dream of it."

"Is your mom home?" I ask, and then: "Oh, fuck. You're *rich* rich, huh."

Because the exterior of the building was nice, sure, but having snuck up the way I did I bypassed the lobby completely. A lobby that might have hinted at what I'm seeing now, which is vaulting living-room ceilings and massive windows that look out to the street and Central Park and the rest of the city beyond, the sparks of building lights starting to pop against the blue of the darkening sky. I've watched enough NYC-apartment TikToks of people cramming Murphy beds into their walls and using their windowsills as makeshift kitchen tables to know this is next-level real estate.

Tom lets out a breath of a laugh and says, "My mom's in Aglorapond."

"Bless you."

"It's a fictional island in her next movie. She's actually in Hawaii for filming."

I tear my eyes off the absurdly cinematic view to frown at him. "And you're *here*?"

Tom tugs the small duffel bag off my shoulder. "Lucky for you, or you'd be sleeping in a pizza box tonight."

"There's a bunch of open spots at a hostel downtown," I say, because as impulsive as the whole "run away from home, except not really because I'm a legal adult" thing was, I didn't plan to fully inflict myself on Tom and Vanessa without asking.

Tom's brows furrow. "Riley," he says, the *don't be ridiculous* implied as he walks the duffel down the hall. "How long can you stay?"

There's a little thrill in the way he asks it—not how long am I staying, but how long I can. I know there's no world where Tom doesn't want to spend time with me, but he's been so distant lately that it's nice to hear it just the same.

"I was thinking for the weekend," I say.

Tom nods. "Not near enough time to fully indoctrinate you into the cult of New York's dessert scene, but I'll take it."

"You're not busy?"

"Nah," says Tom, as we pass the room that's clearly his—I'd recognize that faded blue bedspread anywhere. The pillowcases still have little white stars on them. I push the door farther open and he looks just bashful enough about it that there's no way I'm not letting myself in now.

"You're sure?" I ask, when I see the fully packed backpack on his bed.

"Oh." Tom pulls it off the bed and pushes it into the closet. "I just forgot to unpack that from earlier."

I glance around the room, my eyes snagging on all the old relics I remember. A Tides of Time paperweight I got him for his birthday one year that's shaped like the blue, orb-like

time stone the characters use to move through time and space.
A bunch of well-worn sci-fi and murder-mystery paperbacks
crammed on a bookshelf. Some old plastic trophies from
Tom's seasons on the track team in middle school. All these
pieces of Tom that seem almost stubbornly, precisely the same
in the midst of this otherwise *Succession*-worthy apartment,
pieces that summon a feeling of nostalgia so intense I almost
want to hug Tom again for the relief of it.

There are newer things, too. A sleek laptop plugged in
at the desk. Posters from movies I haven't seen. A cluster of
blue WE ARE HAPPY TO SERVE YOU coffee cups on the bedside
table that must have come from the cart outside the building,
one more quiet reminder of how much time has passed, because we were mostly drinking my mom's hot chocolate from
the café the last time we were face-to-face. But the glow-in-
the-dark stars taped to the walls seem to tie it all back into the
larger Tom whole.

"Glad you're still a nerd," I tell him.

Tom tweaks my elbow. "Glad you're still a snoop."

"Speaking of," I say, reaching for the piece of paper randomly lying on his otherwise neat desk. It's his version of the
Getaway List. Even just glancing at it is yet another measure
of the time that's passed—how the handwriting is a little bigger and sloppier at the top, when we were writing things we
wanted to do at fifteen, versus the neater, tidier scrawl toward
the end when we got older. I lean in to peer at it, the exact
copy of mine word for word.

### The Getaway List

1. Go on a road trip once we've got our licenses.
2. Take the Tides of Time interactive fiction writing
   class.

3. Go on the Tides of Time exploration walk in Central Park.
4. See the Walking JED live in concert.
5. Go to karaoke.
6. Go on a camping trip.
7. Be "Dear, Love" Dispatch coworkers.
8. Make custom brownies at Brownie Bonanza.
9. Actually see each other in our corporeal forms.

Tom leans over me, his shoulder brushing my back as he grabs a pen and puts a checkmark next to item number nine.

"There," he says. "One down, eight to go."

I laugh, glancing down at the list. I came in full steam ahead on trying to get through it, but now that I'm actually here—now that I've got Tom close enough to talk to and prod and hug again—I'm wondering if it's right to jump into this feetfirst. If maybe we're too far past it now. If maybe our time would be better put to use some other way that this older version of Tom would appreciate more.

It turns out some of the problem is solved for me. "Shit. Half of these are undoable now." I skim a finger over item number one, the class that kicked off the list when we were just barely finished with freshman year. "Maybe if we had a time stone of our own we could."

"Actually, the class is still running," says Tom. "They do it every Saturday morning."

I turn to face him so fast that I don't account for how close he is, our faces nearly colliding. I feel my cheeks go warm as he has to pull back, but brush past it, asking, "Seriously?"

Tom clears his throat. "Yeah. My mom teaches workshops at the writing school sometimes." Tom's cheeks flush, too, and then he says, "She's got free faculty credits. We could go. I mean—if you want to."

"Only if you want to," I say back.

There's a two-second stalemate where we're both trying to feel the other one out until I come back to myself and remember this is *Tom*. I don't have to hedge around him. I don't have to be embarrassed about anything at all.

"Would it be patently absurd to try to do stuff on the list after all this time?"

Tom's lip quirks like he was hoping I'd ask just that. "Absolutely," he says. "But it would be more absurd *not* to, so the absurdity cancels itself out."

The relief washes over me so powerfully that I almost want to sag into him with it. Like I didn't have any real way of measuring how much doing all this with Tom meant to me until I knew for sure it still meant something to him, too.

"Look at you, flashing your fancy private school math skills," I say instead, nudging him with my shoulder. He's so squarely built now that it's a bit like nudging a warm wall.

"My next equation—Riley plus long bus ride probably equals very hungry and tired."

I am, all of a sudden, but only in my body. My brain is still operating at a hundred miles an hour, trying to catch up to what feels like a lifetime I just crammed into one day. This morning I woke up in my bed in Virginia and now Tom is setting my duffel on his mom's bed in a city I've never been to before; now Tom and I are ordering pizza from down the street on his couch like it's a regular Friday night when we haven't seen each other in years; now I'm a person who tells their mom off and hops on an interstate bus.

Once we're settled in with the pizza I check my phone to see if she's texted me back—I let her know when I got in. I can see she's read the message, but she hasn't replied.

"All good?" Tom asks.

I nod, setting the phone down and ignoring the slight churn

in my stomach. This is our weekend. She's taken enough time from us, so at least for the next two days, I won't let her take any more.

I wipe my greasy pizza hands on a napkin, pull Tom's copy of the Getaway List off the table, and say, "All right. We need a game plan. Do we try to do these in order, or go into full chaos mode for as many as we can in one weekend?"

Tom doesn't bother looking at the list, staring at me with the beginnings of a smirk on his face. "Is that even a question?"

"Unmitigated chaos it is."

# Chapter Three

The truth is when I first met Tom I wanted absolutely nothing to do with him. Our moms had both dragged us to some Facebook meetup for single parents in the area, which led us to a patch of dead grass claiming to be a playground where really there were only two swings, a broken slide, and an enormous tree, under which sat Tom, his nose buried in a chapter book.

"Doesn't that kid go to your school?" said my mom. "Go say hi."

A simple enough directive, except in my pre-Tom era, I was ridiculously, bitterly shy. It's not that I didn't have anything to say. It was that anytime I tried to interact with someone I didn't know, I could feel words getting stuck in my throat like an invisible fist was pulling them back down into me. So I ignored Tom, partially because of the irrational terror and also because even at seven I knew a nerd when I saw one, and the last thing I wanted to do was talk about *books*.

I lurked behind my mom instead. Ostensibly my mom and

Tom's had the least in common of the group—my mom was a twenty-six-year-old raising a surprise kid and pulling doubles in a coffee shop while I bounced around my aunts and grandparents like a windup toy, and Vanessa was forty-three, had Tom with a sperm donor, and had recently left her corporate finance job to focus on writing. When we showed up my mom's high-waisted shorts and glittery crop top got her mistaken for my babysitter by everyone aside from Vanessa, who demanded to know where my mom had gotten her dandelion shoulder tattoo done because she was feeling quite liberated post–job quitting and wanted a dainty ankle tattoo of her own.

Already bored out of my skull, I turned to glance at book boy only to find he'd been swallowed by a cluster of kids. It was clear even from a distance that he was the heart of the little group—his smile was wide and easy, eyes lit up with a quiet mischief, and everyone was looking to him, clearly jostling for his attention despite his clear willingness to give it.

By then I was used to hovering on the fringes of things and slowly inserting myself into them, not unlike a tiny ghoul. Kids were just accepting of newcomers in that way, even the quiet ones. Except just then Tom turned around as if he'd been waiting to hear me approach and said, with an easygoing smile, "Hey, what's your name?"

Naturally, I froze. I instantly and unrepentantly hated him for it. Now all these kids were staring at me and the whole point of not talking was so that wouldn't happen in the first place.

Even at that age Tom was a master at brushing over awkwardness. He just went on to introduce himself and the others as if I hadn't turned into a Riley-shaped rock. I stayed with the group but didn't speak the whole afternoon, one wary eye on the other kids and one always, always on Tom, who seemed to be the axis everyone else was spinning around. By the end of the afternoon I couldn't tell if I hated him or wanted to be his friend or wanted to be him, but it was all too complex for my kid brain to handle, so instead it just short-circuited.

To my absolute horror, our moms kicked it off so instantly that I went from meeting Tom to seeing him pretty much every other day. That summer Vanessa would pop by the coffee shop where my mom worked to do her writing, leaving me and Tom to split a brownie. My mom would take me to the park so she and Vanessa could jog on the circular path on Saturday mornings. Once school picked up they even started to carpool, my mom dropping us off in the morning and Vanessa picking us up. They hung out without us occasionally, too, and we'd end up watching Netflix with Tom's babysitter or one of my aunts as they went to a wine bar or a pottery class or to get Vanessa's first tattoo.

Tom still tried to talk to me, and sometimes I could even warm up to him enough to talk back—a massive relief to my mom, who watched me talk a mile a minute with my aunts and cousins but go frosty around just about anyone else. Most of the time we just sat quietly. Some of the time I'd even sneak-read over his shoulder, but apparently with the subtlety of a cowbell—he was always much slower turning the pages when I was hovering like that.

It might have just gone on like that forever, except one day Tom unceremoniously handed me a book and said, "If you're going to read parts of it, you should start from the beginning."

I'd only recently graduated to short sentences with Tom. "I don't like reading."

Somewhere there's a parallel universe where Tom shrugged and took the book back and Tides of Time didn't become my largest, loudest, and most enduring personality trait. But we exist in the universe where Tom pressed the book farther into my hands and said, "I want to know what you think."

Maybe it was just the shock of it that made me open the first book. That Tom spent plenty of time around people itching to give him their opinions but for some reason he wanted mine.

He ended up getting a whole lot more opinion than he bargained for. That night I did something I'd never done and read an entire chapter book in one night. We were picking him up the next morning for car pool and before he could slide into the back seat I demanded, "Do you have the second one?"

It was the first time I ever saw the full wattage of a Tom grin aimed at me—not the practiced one he seemed to wear to put everyone at ease, but a genuine, bright-eyed one that lit up his face like a firecracker.

After that Tom probably couldn't have gotten me to shut up if our lives depended on it. I tore through the entire Tides of Time series so fast that teachers were prying it from my tiny fingers during lessons, and I'd nearly take his mom's car door off its hinges rushing to talk to Tom about it after school. I was obsessed with the main character, eleven-year-old Claire, a student who went to a school separate from space and time so she and her friends could learn to move through the continuum and keep the universe in working order. She was like me— rough around the edges, impulsive, slow to warm up to new friends but always ready for adventure. And Tom loved her, too. For some reason that made it easier to believe he actually wanted to be friends.

It wasn't long before Tom and I started taking adventures of our own—some our moms approved of, some they didn't, and some they never found out about. We couldn't go to ancient Greece or 1950s New York or 3033 Mars, but we could sneak into the woods at the edge of the playground during recess and carve things into the dirt. We could use Vanessa's phone while she was locked in her office in a "writing sprint" to map out the walk to the ice-cream shop in town and sneak out. We could go on tangents about what we would have done differently, or what we hoped would happen in whatever book came next, like writing fanfiction before I even knew what it was.

Somewhere along the way it wasn't just Tom I was my loud, mouthy self with, but everyone else, too. Like being friends with Tom was the catalyst I needed to go ahead and spill my very opinionated guts out to the rest of the world. We were always *RileyandTom* or *TomandRiley* at the heart, but like Claire and her growing cluster of friends in the series, we both pulled kids into our orbit along the way. If Tom was steady like the sun, I figured I was like Mercury—the planet rotating closest to him, the one who got him in all of his shades, the one who showed the other planets how easy it was to be in his pull.

And then Tom left, and for a while it was like the sun went out. Like the Getaway List was an ember of it that was still keeping me in motion. I had to find new ways to navigate the universe without him, and even though it wasn't as scary or lonely as I thought it would be, it never once dulled the ache of him being so far away.

Only now that I'm waking up in the same place as him again do I understand how deep it went; only now that we're spending our morning packing our backpacks for the day and standing in line for breakfast, doing things that should be too mundane to feel so precious, do I understand the larger whole of all the little things we've missed.

We take the R train down to the East Village and I do my best not to gawk like the tourist I am, but I can't help it. "The subway is so fucking weird. You go into a pit of darkness and it spits you out into a whole different world."

"It's all interconnected, too," says Tom. "You can swipe into any station with the same fare and if you figure out the transfers you can just go anywhere in the city you want."

I have no idea how a person would figure that out when the message announcing one of the trains was going express sounded roughly like "akdfjgkljga" to my untrained ear, but I latch onto the thrill of it just the same. The idea that a few bucks could open up infinite new worlds like this one, which upon first glance seems to be filled with clusters of very sleepy-looking hipsters walking their dogs and hungover NYU students blinking themselves back to their dorms. Like the subway system is its own time stone and every day you could just close your eyes and pick a new place to go.

Tom unfolds a map he printed out this morning showing the route for the interactive writing class, which starts and ends at Tompkins Square Park. I make a show of stepping to the edge of the sidewalk.

"I have to give you a wide berth," I explain off his curious look. "That map is ruining our street cred."

"Oh, I'm sorry, did you not want anyone knowing you're a TOURIST?" Tom says loudly, tilting his face toward a group of coeds. "That's right, folks, she's sightseeing! The bacon-egg-and-cheese in her hand is a prop!"

I shove at him, an act of absolute futility because it does not so much as interrupt his stride. Instead he hooks an arm around me, merrily waving at the group giving us curious looks.

I wriggle out from under him and say, "So what the hell? You've had access to free writing classes for four years and this is the first time you've ever taken one?"

Tom folds the map back up. "I thought about it. But with my mom, it's kind of—well." He purses his lips. "'Whitz' is a very distinctive last name."

"Ah, I get it. Performance pressure."

Tom shakes his head. "More that I never get to just be like, *Hey, I'm Tom the person.* It's always an immediate, *Hey, I'm the son of the woman who wrote that movie you want to do your dissertation/write your fanfiction/make your latest Halloween costume for.* And then that's all they want to talk about."

I keep forgetting that by all accounts Vanessa is famous now, at least in Hollywood and writerly circles. She's only had two major hits so far, but her style is incredibly distinct, and her method even more so. She writes loose outlines of scripts based on an initial plot, but most of the writing happens literally in the moment during filming—she'll know the point A and point B of a scene, but refuses to try and shape it until she's with the actors on set, at which point it'll just pour out of her. It's all very visceral and raw and emotional and a bunch of other buzzwords I've seen in reviews, heralding her as everything from a genius to a flop to the next great movement in cinema. For better or worse, her name is more tied to her work than most.

Hence why she's in Hawaii right now, and constantly on location for filming for upcoming projects, often taking Tom along for the ride. As sympathetic as I want to feel about the whole secondhand-fame situation right now, that sympathy is chafing a bit against the wild jealousy that Tom's now eaten Parisian cheese and walked the Great Wall and seen Chris Evans with his own human eyes and I've never even been on a plane.

"Do people really write fanfiction for your mom's movies? I thought most of her characters bit it."

"Hence the fanfiction," says Tom sagely. "The 'fix-it' tag on Archive of Our Own for her stuff is like a hundred pages deep."

"Well, if that's not incentive to kill all our characters off today, I don't know what is."

We arrive at the park then, where there's a cluster of people by a bench with a sign that says IMMERSIVE WRITERS WORKSHOP on it. I fall back a step only because I'm used to the natural rhythm of us—Tom goes, and I follow—except Tom falters. I glance back at him, expecting to see him sliding into that ease with strangers he's had since we were kids, but he's got this look on his face I don't know if I've ever seen before. He seems almost nervous.

I tilt my head at him. The ease I was expecting slides back onto his face, and he says, "Last one to murder their character off today buys the other lunch."

"Your mom would be proud."

We get absorbed into the group, Tom still half a step behind me. We're the youngest ones there by far, or at least I think we are until the boy who's crossing his name off the sign-in sheet turns and says, "Oh, where are you on the list? I'll check yours off."

"We're the ones under Whitz," I say without thinking.

The boy goes so still that I'm a little worried his bones stopped working. "Wait a minute. Whitz? Are you . . . I mean, you're not . . ." He lowers his voice, or at least tries to. The question ends up coming out in a squeak. "Like related to *Vanessa Whitz*?"

I don't have to turn around to feel Tom stiffen behind me. I offer my hand to the boy, who is all big, earnest eyes and unruly auburn hair, and say easily, "That's right. I'm Tom Whitz. Vanessa's my mom."

The boy takes my hand so enthusiastically I might have just introduced myself as one of the Beatles, a smile splitting across his freckly face. "Vanessa Whitz is your *mom*?"

"Yeah," I say. "But I'm just Tom the person."

Tom lets out an amused breath behind me.

"I'm gonna pass out," the boy says, and then blinks hard, only just remembering to let go of my hand, which he's been shaking hard enough to rattle it off my wrist. "What I meant to say is I'm Luca. Luca Bales. And the passing-out thing was an exaggeration. I think. Oh my god. Your *mom* is *Vanessa Whitz*."

This causes several curious heads to turn around. A few of the gazes linger just long enough that it's clear Tom wasn't exaggerating about his mom's fan base. Before any of them can approach I turn my back and gesture to Tom, saying, "And this is my friend Riley."

The instructor, who seems to actually know Tom, quirks an eyebrow at us but doesn't correct me. Neither does Tom, who is biting down a smile and shaking his head.

"I can't believe it," says Luca in a rush. "I've been saving up to take this class for ages because I want to be her *so bad*— well, not be her, I just mean I want to have my own style like hers—and you're here! Holy crap! Okay, okay, I'll be cool, I swear. But also you have to tell me everything."

Mercifully, the instructor calls us to order then, explaining the concept of the class. It's still the same as it was four years ago when we desperately wanted to take it the summer after freshman year: a hybrid writing and walking tour, where you come up with story ideas based on prompts from your surroundings as you go. Each of us will randomly choose from a hat to get a character's age, one of their hobbies, and a weakness, and that's all we get to go off to imagine them in any of the places we'll see—all of them landmarks that have been in New York for at least a few decades, so we're free to imagine our characters in any era they might have been there.

The time-and-space concept for the class was initially inspired by Tides of Time, since that was when the television-series adaptation made the already brimming fandom erupt like a dweeby volcano. But the spur-of-the-moment writing was also so reminiscent of Vanessa's style that she taught a few specialized rounds of the workshop for a young writers outreach program when the initial instructors moved on, which would explain why Luca looks one light breeze away from passing out at the idea of her progeny being here.

Tom pulls out his random character first and says, "I'm nine, enjoy pranks, and my weakness is I'm loud."

I squint at mine. "I'm seventy-four, enjoy astronomy, and my weakness is 'being too nice to people.'" I look up at Tom. "Wait, so you got baby me and I got old you?"

Tom furrows his brow. "I'm not too nice."

"A lady bumped right into you on the subway earlier and you said 'thank you,'" I remind him.

"I was flustered!"

"*Nicely* flustered."

"And you're not loud," says Tom.

I press my shoulder into his, playfully sagging half my weight into him knowing full well he won't budge. "Sounds like a lie a too-nice person would tell," I say, prompting Tom to laugh and tap the top of my head with his chin.

Luca is standing off to the side, laughing nervously like he's not sure whether to insert himself in the conversation. I turn to him expectantly and he meets my eye with clear relief and says, "I'm fifty-eight, enjoy making my own cheese, and my greatest weakness just says . . . 'bees.'"

I nod. "High-stakes charcuterie boards, then."

We start walking as a group toward the first spot, not making it more than ten steps before Luca blurts, "What's it like having Vanessa Whitz as a mom?"

Luca looks so much like a puppy that I feel mildly bad about the prank then, but figure I'm never going to see him again. I commit to the bit but keep it brief. "Oh, you know. Lots of traveling," I say.

"I bet. What's it like watching her work?"

I turn to Tom. "Hard to say. What do you think, Riley?"

Tom's lips press into a bemused smile. "I don't know, Tom. She's in her own world for most of it. Sort of like she forgets anyone else is there."

Tom's eyes hit the pavement fast, almost like he's surprised at what just came out of him. Before I can follow the thought down, Luca says, "That makes sense. I feel like I'm stuck coming up with ideas—or I have a bunch but I just haven't found the *perfect* story to write yet, you know? One that's deep but still kind of flashy but real but personal but also, like, universal? Anyway, your mom just nails it every time. I saw some behind-the-scenes video of her once. She's so *in* it. So immersed."

I look at Tom conspiratorially, wondering if one of us is going to confess to the bit, but Tom's gone quiet. When he meets my eye it's as if corners of his lips are tugging it up to keep the smile there.

We settle at the first spot, a striking Victorian-style building that the instructor tells us was built in the 1850s as a newsboys' lodging house, then became a Jewish educational center in the 1920s before eventually converting to apartments in the 1970s. She gives us a brief background of what it would be like for tenants and students of the building in each of those times, then tells us we have ten minutes to talk among ourselves about where our characters might fit into some point in time.

Tom's still quiet, or at least I think he is until I realize he's stepping in between me and an older guy in the class who was clearly about to approach me to ask something, a slightly rabid look in his eyes. One of the fans of his mom, I realize. Good grief.

"Oh god. I don't know," says Luca, looking suddenly skittish. "Is it writer's block if your whole brain stops moving, or is that just human block? I can't think of anything except bees."

I clear my throat because this right here is my wheelhouse. Out of sheer boredom I've been making up harebrained stories in my head for years. "Maybe in the 1980s an eccentric rich neighbor set up a honey farm on the top-floor fire escape, then lured your cheese-making character into collaborating on a charcuterie board so he could sic his bees on you and get away with the perfect murder."

Luca's eyes light up with equal parts excitement and relief. "Oh, but then he has to have a good reason to murder me. Maybe I didn't invite him to my fifty-eighth birthday party."

"An audacious and unforgivable snub," I agree. "You only live because there was an eclipse that night and my character was climbing the fire escape to get a look at it. Used their telescope to knock your attacker out of the way before they released the bees."

Luca leans in closer, the words spilling out of him like his mouth can't keep up with his head: "And then the attacker stares directly at the eclipse, and the shock of it is so overwhelming he stumbles into his own bee cage and locks himself inside—I don't know how bee cages work, but he makes the queen mad and gets stung a bajillion times—"

"He's my character's grandfather," says Tom, "and I inherit his vast fortune and his killer bees."

Luca and I let out sharp, unexpected laughs and when I turn back around, Tom is Tom again—at least, the easygoing, relaxed version of himself he usually is in a crowd. We spend the next few minutes riffing other ideas. Apparently the boys who lived there when it was a newsboy lodging house weren't allowed to swear, so we decided Luca's character lived there as a boy and just yelled "BEES!" as a curse word well into adulthood. Tom comes up with an elaborate idea that Luca and I gently have to tell him is already the full plot of Newsies. We expand even further on our first plot, Luca and I piling on each other's ideas so fast that we almost don't notice when the rest of the group starts moving on.

"Sheesh," says Luca, shaking his head at me as we move on to the next spot. "I guess talent really is genetic."

The praise is so unexpected that I nearly trip on my own heel. I'm not used to it, is all—at least not lately. I had a decent following on the Archive back when I was still writing fic, but it's been ages since I've had the time or inspiration to write. I've been too distracted doing things I'm mediocre at, where my only actual talents were amusing fellow bored students with my antics or speed-reading my way through the Kindle account I share with my mom and aunts.

Tom nudges me with this proud curl to his smile, but even then I can't think of what to say. "You seem disappointed," Tom says to Luca, easily picking up the conversation I let drop.

"Well, yeah," says Luca glumly. "My parents are the most boring people on earth."

Tom claps a hand on his shoulder. "Don't worry. I read somewhere that boringness skips generations."

I catch his eye and mouth the words "too nice" at him and he shakes his head at me affectionately.

We spend the rest of the morning trekking through the East Village, stopping at an old punk-rock venue, at the second oldest church in the city, and at the block that makes up Little Tokyo, coming up with new backstories and wild happenings for our characters along the way. The instructor has a different person share their ideas each time, but as the youngest of the lot, we're spared from the public reckoning. That is, until we reach Veselka, a famous Ukrainian restaurant that has been in a bunch of classic New York–set films, and the instructor says to us, "I'd love to hear your groups' thoughts."

Luca takes a step back, clamming up immediately. Tom nudges me forward. The quick pulse of fear feels like lightning just crackled through my veins, but if I'm the lightning, then Tom standing behind me is the solid place for it to land.

I take in a breath.

"All right, well. My character is a disgraced former

astronomer since he misidentified a comet that wasn't actually hurtling toward Earth like he said it was, so now he's scraping up money with freelance gigs as a background actor," I say. "He scores one in the back of a rom-com movie scene set here. Except he wants to save money so he eats as much prop food as he possibly can and sneaks pierogies into his pockets. But because his fatal flaw is that he's too nice, he shares all his pierogies with his ridiculous best friend, even though that very same day she got into a fight with him because she hadn't booked the gig as an extra. They heal through the power of potatoes and friendship."

Tom's laughing behind me because this is a rough approximation of real-life events. In third grade he'd scored so high on our school's enrichment tests that he'd been invited to some kind of lunch thing that the other kids weren't. Baby Tom's version of "fuck the system" was to shove a bunch of brownies into his pocket like a tiny Robin Hood and deposit them on my desk, as I'd been wildly jealous at the time. (Of the free dessert, to be clear.)

People are starting to murmur around us in tones that sound amused and approving, and some part of me chafes at it because for all my loudness, there's still that little-kid part of me that doesn't like being seen. At least not too far down deep. I'm about to take a step back into Tom, only then I blink, remembering our bet.

"Oh!" I add. "But it turns out he hadn't been wrong about the comet, and an hour or so later it squashed them on the spot."

There's a cluster of laughs and the instructor gives me a quick thumbs-up that sends a ridiculous and unfamiliar thrill through me. It's rare that I've ever cared what a teacher thinks. I don't fully understand why it feels so different until the instructor slides in next to me just before the class releases.

"Hey, 'Tom,'" says the instructor. "I just wanted to make sure you knew we have regular classes that meet up once a week, some of them specifically for newer emerging voices. The next round of courses starts in the fall. I think you've really got the heart for this, if you wanted to join us."

There's absolutely no reality in which that can happen for me, but for a moment I'm too bowled over to care. It's just that it's been so long since I've felt like I'm in my element that I was starting to doubt I even *had* one. Like maybe I'd just lost the ability to be present and happy in something other than sneak-reading in extracurriculars or talking to my friends between classes. It's such a relief that all I can think is that I can't wait to tell my mom, only to remember that she still hasn't texted me back since I got here.

"So how long have you and Riley been together?" Luca asks me, stirring me out of my thoughts.

I have to do some quick mental gymnastics to catch up with that sentence, and once I stick the landing I feel my face flush. "Oh. We're not—he and I are best friends," I say.

Luca's eyebrows lift in surprise. "Really? I was sure you two were a thing."

I want to ask what he means by that, but I'm too self-conscious and apparently so is Tom, who's gone very still next to me like he's bracing for my response every bit as much as I'm bracing for his. This is decidedly uncharted territory in our friendship. Nobody would have asked us this kind of thing growing up—we were too young then, and even in the brief time we weren't, it was almost like Tom and I were *too* close to date.

In the end I shoot Tom a wry look and say to Luca, "Really? I always thought dating Riley would feel a little bit too much like dating myself."

This earns me a smirk from Tom. Luca nods like he

understands, then turns on his heel, then abruptly turns back and blurts, "Do you maybe want to swap numbers?"

"Oh." Cue the guilt. We got so swept away in the workshop that I never copped to my little prank. Also I'm leaving the city in approximately twenty-four hours. "Uh . . ."

Luca mistakes my hesitation and says quickly, "Not to—I mean, not because of your mom. It's just I don't have any writer friends, and I like your brain." Two flaming red spots form on his cheeks and he says, "What I mean is, your brain's good. Nope, that's worse. I mean—it's okay if you don't want to. But if you do—"

"Give me your phone," I laugh.

He does, the rest of his face as red as his cheeks. I put my number in and hand it back to him.

Luca tilts his head at it. "How come you put 'Tom' in quotation marks?"

"I'll tell you later. Nice to meet you, Luca."

He waves merrily as he heads down into the subway station. "See you guys around!"

I start heading in what is apparently the wrong direction, because Tom puts a hand to my elbow and guides me in the other one. "Respectfully, can I have my identity back now?"

"Ugh. I was really enjoying being hot and nerdy and six foot holy shit," I say, mostly to get a rise out of him. Trying to fluster Tom over the phone isn't half as much fun as doing it in person. "Can't you just let me have this?"

Except Tom answers smoothly, "You can just be hot and cool and five foot nine."

I blink because historically I am the one who teases Tom and not the other way around. Particularly not about hotness. Before I can overthink the way my entire body just started to tingle, Tom bops me on the head and says, "And I'm not buying you lunch, by the way."

"Excuse you?" I say, somehow both disappointed and relieved by the abrupt change in topic. "I won the bet fair and square."

"You killed me with a world-ending *comet*. It's a cop-out if you literally destroy the known universe."

"Fine. I'll rewrite it. The comet bypasses earth, but you die valiantly saving orphaned kittens from a fire."

"Slightly better."

"Thing is, you got all the kittens out but then as soon as you hit the sidewalk you slipped on a banana peel, right back into the flames—"

"All right, all right. Save it for your first novel," says Tom.

It's a joke but something in my chest goes warm at the idea of it anyway. I haven't thought of myself as a writer in ages—I've felt so crammed into the present of my life that there hasn't been any room left to think about the future. Even just in the past few hours it feels like that future is expanding to new possibilities, or maybe that I'm starting to open myself up to them.

"You know, it's funny," I say. "We only wanted to take that class because of Tides of Time, but I think it might just be the first class I've actually liked in like—possibly ever?"

"See?" says Tom, ribbing me. "I knew the nerds would get you eventually. Learning can be fun."

I use the ribbing as an excuse to lean into him as we stop outside of the deli he was leading us to. Tom's always had a way of drawing people in like this. A quiet magnetism. One that anyone else might use for their own sake, but Tom's only ever used for the sake of others.

But that ease repelled me so much at the start that I have to think it was the so-called nerdiness that got me in the end. The way he earnestly, unabashedly loves to learn—about everything from what makes people tick to how the universe works. He throws himself so wholeheartedly into books and research that

I could never help but want to feel the fringes of that passion, to go on adventures with him because half the fun was watching him thrill at learning something new.

Which is why something that's been tugging at the edge of my thoughts for a while finally gives itself a voice.

"Hey," I say quietly. "You never told me why you're taking a gap year."

Tom stares at our sneakers for a moment. "I guess because I feel the same as you? Like it's been four years and I just want to try something new."

This answer is satisfyingly Tom-esque enough that it eases some of the worry.

"So what are you planning to do with it?" I ask.

"Plan?" says Tom, scrunching his nose in distaste. "I'll just do it the Riley way. Unmitigated chaos."

His voice is teasing, drawing a warmth in me that's almost immediately tainted with something else. *That's not you, Riley. The fact is you and Tom bring out the worst in each other. Always have and always will.*

Tom's gone quiet next to me, too, like we're both somewhere deep in our own heads right now even though I'm still pressed against his side. We're creating a small traffic jam on the sidewalk, one that I'm too selfish to correct, because for a moment I can't pull myself away. Like if we just stay here in this little island of ourselves, maybe we can pretend the forces about to pull us apart again don't exist.

Naturally both of our phones buzz with texts at the same time. Mine is a text from Jesse, who must have seen my Instagram story.

You're in NYC???????? You gotta
come to our show tonight! 8pm at the
milkshake club! Make tom come too!!!

"Oh shit. The Walking JED is playing in the city tonight."

It's got to be kismet or destiny or some other grand universal happening, because the one other thing I was certain we wouldn't be able to do on the list—at least not in this weekend, anyway—was see a Walking JED show. The first time around Tom was going to come down from New York, but at the last minute Vanessa's filming schedule changed and Tom had to go with her. We'll never be able to see the specific one that Tom was supposed to see with our friends back in Falls Creek, their first big gig opening for a touring band the winter break of sophomore year, but I have to figure their big-city debut still counts for our purposes.

Tom winces and it feels like a needle popping my figurative balloon before I even know what the wince is for. I've been here long enough to know that Tom and I are not quite the people we were when we left each other last—that he's more reserved than I ever remember him being, and I'm probably a whole lot more existentially confused—but we've been side-stepping it easily enough that it was probably only a matter of time before we tripped on it.

"But we don't have to go," I say quickly, not wanting to dampen the mood. "I mean—there are a whole bunch of other things we can do on the Getaway List."

"No, no, it's not that, it's—" Tom sheepishly rubs the back of his neck. "Jesse texted a few times to say he was moving up here and I'm just realizing I didn't text him back."

"Why not?"

"I just—I feel bad. I forgot is all," says Tom. "He's probably pissed."

"Not at all," I say, showing him Jesse's text. "But seriously. We don't have to. We checked one thing off the list already and that's a damn miracle."

Tom looks so visibly relieved that I can't help the itch to

dig in a little deeper. Over the last few months Tom's texts got so sparse you'd think they were intercontinental letters, but I never thought too much about it because he's always right there if I ever really need him. It didn't occur to me that he might be so bad at keeping in touch that he'd dismiss texts about Jesse's entire human form moving to Manhattan.

But I can tell from Tom's tone he doesn't want me to dig, and selfishly, I'm not sure if I want to—it's been so long since I've seen him, and who even knows how long until I see him again. The uncomfortable questions can wait.

"No, let's go. We'll out-miracle the miracle," says Tom. "Cross three things off the list in one day."

"Two," I say, wondering when and how I suddenly got better at math than him.

"Three." He shows me his phone screen. "That is, if you're up for it."

It's a bright turquoise notification from what can only be the backend of the "Dear, Love" Dispatch app where the deliveries are assigned. The text reads, "A dispatch has been accepted!" with details indicating that the anonymous sender would like to gift the recipient with a mix of different chocolate bars. Just under it the text reads, "Accept this mission?" with options to offer the delivery to another dispatcher or accept.

I grab the phone from him, so excited I nearly barrel into a blond girl taking out the deli's trash. "I can finally be a dispatcher?"

Tom laughs at my eagerness, which, fair. Not many people would thrill at the idea of dodging taxis and people attempting to film TikToks on an eighty-five-degree day in New York. But the "Dear, Love" Dispatch has always had a special place in my heart because it reminded me of the old "sneaky elf game" Tom and I played for years.

It started in the same dweeby way most of our traditions

do: one of the characters in Tides of Time used to leave little trinkets in pockets of space and time for the others to find if they needed a pick-me-up or a tool, prompting the main villain to call him a "sneaky elf." (I imagine he would have had a more choice insult if it weren't a kids' series.) At some point I got it in my head that Tom and I should do a version of that, too. So when our friends were feeling down about something, we would sneak little things into their lockers anonymously— like when Dai didn't make the track team and we snuck in a guitar pick we'd hot-glued a picture of his dog onto, or when one of the Avas couldn't make it to homecoming so we got her friends to choose songs for a playlist we printed out a Spotify QR code for.

I don't think anyone figured out it was us, but everyone was always so happy to be visited by the school elf that I felt determined to keep it up even after Tom left. It's why I never felt totally disconnected from my classmates even when I was scheduled to the max, and it's why I loved the idea of the "Dear, Love" Dispatch so much from the moment Tom said he'd gotten a bike-messenger job with them. It seemed like the real-world version of our little game, one that could spread not just over the school but a whole city. Spreading little tokens of love without expecting anything in return. Making sure people felt seen even when they didn't think they were.

Tom was that person for me once. Getting to be the school "elf" and the helping with the "Dear, Love" Dispatch felt like opportunities to be that person for someone else, too. And now after all this time I'm finally getting my chance.

"I'll let you do the honors," says Tom, nodding at the phone screen.

I tap the ACCEPT button, and it gives us the cross streets of where to meet the recipient along with a time an hour from now.

Tom beams as I hand him back the phone. "Welcome to the team."

For a moment I'm so happy that I have to look away from him because I'm brimming with it, like it's filling me up so fast it's going to spill out as tears. "Literally fuck all other days," I say, "because this is the best one of my life."

# Chapter Four

We have some time to kill, so after we split two different flavors of grilled cheese so delicious that I practically see the multiverse when I bite into them, Tom and I head to a bodega to pick out enough candy bars to fill the ten-dollar budget the anonymous sender gave us. I opt for simple Hershey's and Crunch bars, while Tom, who notoriously loves desserts that have as much stuffed into them as possible, goes for the Snickers and Take 5 bars. We arrange them neatly in a little white paper bag and then head to the West Village to meet the recipient, who shared their public location with the app when they accepted the delivery.

"Wait," says Tom, pulling open his backpack. "So they know who you are."

He retrieves a turquoise cap with a white embroidered DEAR, LOVE on the front. He settles the cap on the top of my head and then steps back to assess me, satisfied.

"Perfect," he says, his eyes warm and fixed on mine.

I'm really going to have to reassess my biological responses, because for some reason that causes another weird ripple just under my ribs, one that I have no success in squashing even as I cross the street. Tom's letting me do this one on my own so I get the full experience of dispatching. Still, I glance back at Tom and stick out my tongue, and he gives me a thumbs-up like a pageant parent whose kid is about to walk onstage.

"Oh shit. Tell me it's not chocolate bars *again*."

Two feet in front of me is a strikingly beautiful human— bright-eyed, full-cheeked, with curls so dark and shining they're practically reflecting every color of the sun hitting us.

"If I did it'd make me a liar," I tell her.

She looks me up and down like she's trying to place me. She comes up short, but her smile is still genuine when she says, "You like chocolate?"

I blink, because Tom gave me some loose scripts for how these transactions usually go—namely that I'd hand over the gift, they'd swipe the ACCEPTED button on their app, and we'd all go on our merry way—and not one of them covered this. Also because on top of her striking beauty she's somehow mastered the perfect cat's-eye and matte red lipstick, two things I've only ever dared to do if my mom or one of our friends at school did it for me, and is rocking a patchwork crop top with wildly mismatched patterns that make all the other outfits on the block look like a yawn.

"Yes?" I answer.

"Perfect." She plucks the bag out of my hand, and then abruptly pushes it back toward me. "A gift from me to you."

"I don't think that's how this works," I manage.

She shrugs. "Whoever sent it clearly doesn't know me well enough to know I have a mild peanut allergy, so really, it's your civic responsibility to eat these so they don't go to waste."

I take the bag from her. "Well, if you put it like that," I say, as if I am not currently full of grilled cheese and a massive hybrid cookie-brownie thing I shared with Tom just an hour ago. I turn to look for him for some kind of guidance, only he's not across the street anymore, but right next to me.

"Hey, Mariella," he says.

Mariella's smile of recognition is so captivatingly wide and warm that I'm worried it's going to cause a traffic accident.

"Well, if it isn't Tommy boy!" she says, leaning in to hug Tom and somehow managing it despite the foot of difference between their heights. She keeps her eyes on me throughout, adding, "I was gonna say, I don't think I've seen this dispatcher before."

I wonder how often she gets sent stuff from admirers if she's familiar with the full roster of dispatchers, but after thirty seconds of her blunt charm I have no trouble guessing that the answer is "a whole lot."

Tom steps back after she releases him and says, "We saw the message come in and it was close, so we just grabbed it. I didn't realize it was you, though."

"Wait," says Mariella. She takes my hand and lifts up my arm as if to examine and make sure I'm not a puppet or a robot. I'm too amused by this turn of events to protest. She sets my arm back down and says to Tom, still examining me, "Tom Whitz, with a real live friend?"

I laugh because Tom's got those in spades, but it tapers off because Tom's cheeks flush so fast that I'm not entirely sure if it's a joke. Tom recovers, letting out a wry "Very funny," then turns toward me and says, "This is Riley."

"Get the fuck out! I didn't think I'd get to meet *the* Riley," Mariella says, one side of her mouth curling. "Nice to meet you. I'm *the* Mariella."

"Oh. Hi," I say.

Off my blank look she swats at Tom and says, "Really? Your girlfriend has no idea who I am?"

Tom lets out an undignified noise of protest and says, "I never said she was—I mean, Riley and I aren't—we're best friends."

Mariella's smirk deepens. "All right, all right, don't get your backpack straps in a twist." She turns to me and says, "Mariella Vasquez. Former classmate of Tom's, present menace to society, future world-renowned photographer." Then she adds in a faux whisper, "He mentions you a lot."

"Bad things only, I hope," I say back.

She cackles. "We're going to have fun. I didn't realize you were moving here."

"Oh, I'm just here for the weekend," I admit, with a reluctance that only seems to be getting stronger by the hour.

She throws an arm around my shoulder, squeezing as if she is the city itself claiming me. "We'll fix that. And when we do you have to let me take your picture." She pats her messenger bag, which is every bit as colorful as her top, and covered in enamel pins—one of a cat in a bandana and a cowboy hat, a heart-shaped one with the Puerto Rican flag, one with a logo of a brownie that is oddly familiar. Poking out of the top is a camera bag that looks brand-new in comparison. "I like your vibe."

I have no earthly idea what kind of vibe that might be, but rather than question it I turn to Tom. "I regret to inform you that you're not my best friend anymore. Mariella is replacing you."

Tom shakes his head. "Unfortunate, but inevitable. Also, since when are you into photography?" he asks Mariella.

"Since a month and none of your business ago, Tommy boy," says Mariella. She turns back to me. "I needed some better hobbies. Anyway, Tom's got my number. Hit me up. Unlike Tom I actually know how to have fun."

I tilt my head at Tom curiously, but he brushes past that comment as deliberately as the "real live friend" one. "Joke's on you," he says. "We're going clubbing tonight."

Mariella's smile flickers, her arm going loose on my shoulder. Tom quickly clarifies, "We're seeing a show at the Milkshake Club."

She brightens so quickly that I might have imagined the flicker altogether. "Excellent idea. I'm in."

She releases me then and heads off down the street, only looking back to blow a sloppy kiss in our direction. "See you two tonight!"

I blow a kiss back and Tom lets out an exasperated laugh like he's already looking a few hours into the future and knowing full well he's about to become a dance-floor third wheel.

"You're okay with that?" Tom asks just the same.

"The more the merrier," I say, genuinely meaning it. What I don't say is that it's a relief to see Tom has a friend in New York at all. It's occurring to me that Tom never really talked much about friends here—we talked so rarely these past few years that we mostly caught up on each other's lives and moms and not much else.

But I'm probably worrying for nothing. Tom is Tom. He makes friends by breathing.

"Hey," I say anyway, not sure what I'm going to ask first. Maybe why Mariella implied Tom doesn't seem to get out much, or why he seemed off this morning, or why he didn't seem to have any plans this weekend at all when I crash-landed onto his new planet.

But just then Tom's phone buzzes again. "What do you say?" he says, holding up the notification to another delivery. "You want to go a few more rounds? Could be a fun way to get in some sightseeing."

Is it a little on the nose to avoid a problem by literally

running away from them all over the city? Maybe. But Tom's eyes are gleaming again like they did back when we were full-time partners in crime, and the pull of it is too strong to resist.

So strong, in fact, that I can't help letting out a slightly hysterical whoop of laughter once we've collected bike helmets from Tom's place and are flying down the bike path in Central Park on rented Citi Bikes.

"All good up there, Tarzan?" Tom calls, pulling his bike up to match pace with me.

I turn to him and say breathlessly, "I can't believe we can just go wherever we want. Like this whole day! I don't even know what to do with all this free will. It's lawless. I fucking love it."

That is, naturally, the precise moment the universe decides to humble me by way of the squirrel that darts into the bike path. I have enough of my wits about me not to barrel my bike into Tom's, but apparently not enough to keep my balance, because the next thing I know I'm cutting across the pavement, jumping the curb, and toppling into the grass.

Tom's brakes screech to a halt and I shut my eyes for a split second because I'm fine, save for my irritation that I can't summon a hole in the ground to swallow me up and save me from what might be the most embarrassing public spectacle of my life.

"Riley? Shit, Riley, are you okay?"

"All good!" I say loudly, aware even from the ground that I have already amassed a small crowd of concerned onlookers. "Just mortally humiliated!"

Tom pulls the bike off me and hovers over me so close that I can't get up without knocking his head into mine. His hands ghost over my head and my shoulders, his eyes moving so fast over me that I can practically feel the waves of his panic like they're something solid in the air.

"You're sure?" he says.

"Very sure. And also fuck that squirrel," I say, hoping to make him laugh.

Tom's frown only deepens. "Your knee is bleeding."

"It's okay," I say, sitting up. "I've got another one."

Tom's already riffling through his backpack and I unsuccessfully stifle a laugh, because his Dora the Explorer–esque tendency to pack random things for adventures when we were kids has apparently evolved into full-blown mom-friend mode. He's got Band-Aids and antiseptic pads out in five seconds flat.

"Dibs on having you on my team for the apocalypse," I tell him.

Tom finally loosens up at that. "Like there's anyone else I'd bother with at the end of the world."

He uses one of the pads to clean out my knee and I manage not to hiss at the sting, but not quite hold in a wince. Tom gives me a sympathetic wince of his own and then says, "You were saying about free will?"

He asks the question lightly, but the look in his eyes is heavy. Expectant, even. Like he's been waiting for me to talk about this since I showed up on his doorstep semi-unannounced.

"Oh. Yeah. You know how my mom's been."

I swallow hard at the reminder that she hasn't texted me back. For some reason the skinned knee makes the pang of it feel deeper, like I've reverted into some little-kid-playground version of myself.

"Yeah. It seems like she was keeping you pretty busy," says Tom. "Every time you tried to come up here something got in the way."

I don't want to mention the part where my mom was actively keeping us apart because then Tom will know she didn't want me here in the first place, and that would mean opening a whole can of worms I don't want to dissect right now.

"I guess I can't blame her entirely. She got worse after the suspension," I say instead.

Tom shakes his head. "It was ridiculous that you got suspended in the first place."

Tom's allowed to make this assessment because he's one of the few people who knows the full details of said suspension. How at some point my mom had signed me up for so many things that it was abundantly clear that she was just trying to keep me out of trouble—or at least, her idea of it—so I devised a little scheme. Our after-school detentions took place in the hour between the end of school and the start of extracurriculars, an hour I usually spent in limbo just doing homework or reading books. One day Eddie was itching to get to rehearsal when he saw me sitting in the hallway with my aunt's old Kindle and offered me twenty bucks to sit in for him in detention instead.

I believe my response was something along the lines of "hell fucking yes," and why wouldn't it be? It was the perfect crime. All I had to do was say "present" when our alarmingly disassociated gym teacher called roll, then spend the next hour sitting pretty, doing my homework, and scamming twenty bucks to boot.

It wasn't long before word of my "services" got around, and I had more reasons to lean into it than not. I didn't even bother charging if I knew it was a kid who couldn't afford it. What did I have to lose? At least sitting in a detention chair was more comfortable than the hallway floor.

Of course, I did get found out in the end, and my whole detention empire came crumbling down. I was suspended for two days, which was put on my permanent record. I never had to give back any of the money, which my mom put into my bank account herself—"I'm very disappointed in you but you technically earned this from those idiots" were her approximate words—but that was the beginning and end of the perks. After that it was basically a life sentence of never having a free moment to myself again. I'd already proven I couldn't be trusted with a single free hour each day; it only made sense to squash out as many free hours as could possibly be squashed.

Tom finishes carefully setting the bandage on my knee, and the tenderness of it makes me say more than I mean to: "My mom thinks it wrecked all my college prospects, but honestly I don't even care if it did. I was kind of relieved not to get in anywhere."

It's the first time I've admitted it out loud. It's not that I expect Tom to fully understand where I'm coming from, the way I know a lot of my friends would have—it's just that of everyone in my life, Tom tries his best to understand. Not for his own sake, but for mine.

Sure enough, instead of trying to push me on it, he just says, "Yeah?"

I reach out and pinch his nose briefly between two of my fingers. "I'm not like you. I've got no idea what I want to do yet. And trying to keep up with all the stuff my mom pushed me into probably didn't help."

Tom stares down at my knee. "Probably not." He looks up at me then with a sudden sincerity and says, "But I'm not worried. I know you'll figure it out."

I'm not so sure about that, but it means a lot coming from Tom just the same. "Well, if the future psych major says so, who am I to doubt it?" I quip.

Tom clearly recognizes the deflection and mostly lets me get away with it. Which is to say, he doesn't press any further, but says, "Hey, I just—things must have been nuts for you and I'm—just really glad that even through all that you always made sure we stayed in touch."

It's sweet that he thinks he has to say this to me. As if there were ever a moment that I might have doubted the depth of our friendship, even in the times he's been distant in it. That's the thing about us—we didn't just decide on each other all those years ago. We decided on each other forever. It's the only decision I've never once doubted and never will.

"Thomas Whitz, you beautiful doofus," I tell him. "There's no universe that could keep you from me."

The corners of Tom's lips quirk, his eyes watering just enough to bring out the hazel in them. "Not even with a time stone and access to infinite realities?"

This much I know for a fact: "We'd still be best friends in every damn one."

Tom's eyes dart down to the grass for a moment, one that makes my stomach lurch, afraid I've said the wrong thing. But then he hoists himself up to his feet and offers me his hand and says, "Damn right."

I take his hand and feel it in its full force again: *TomandRiley, RileyandTom.* Two parts built to make one whole. Even if we don't fit the same way we did before, I can feel the easy way we're shifting to make a new one. I only wish I was staying long enough to know what it might look like before it has to change shape again.

# Chapter Five

Being in the Milkshake Club is kind of like being in the passenger seat of Barbie's bright pink convertible going a hundred miles an hour—everything is glittering and pink and loud and, true to its namesake, full of ice cream. The place isn't fully packed yet since the Walking JED is only opening, but when Tom and I arrive all scrubbed up and showered from the afternoon of deliveries, the stage is mostly set up for the night, save for the instruments that probably should be sound-checked by now.

There's a *click-flash* that makes both of us blink in surprise. Mariella lifts a squinted eye from the very fancy-looking camera she has looped around her neck.

"Ugh. I'm not great with indoor lighting yet. Also you two are so fucking tall I probably need to stand on one of those stools to get your faces. Also hi," she says, leaning in and attempting to hug me with one arm and Tom with the other, which can't be easy on her calves.

"Hey," I say, and I'm about to ask where she got her very cute glittery crop top when I am sneak-attack hugged from the side by what appears to be a very breathless, sweaty Jesse.

"Hi, shit, this is a small city but it's also huge? I just got so lost."

Mariella takes a step back, taking in Jesse with his floppy "you already know I can play guitar" hair and his ripped T-shirt collar and various tattoos. "This city's on a grid, my friend."

Jesse nods in agreement, but says, "But east looks the same as west and sometimes trains can just become *different* trains? I mean good for them, I support their choice, but a little warning might've been nice. Tom!" Jesse abruptly throws an arm around Tom, then pulls back to jostle him at the shoulders. "He lives!"

Jesse's aggressive brand of enthusiasm stuns a laugh out of Tom, and I watch him slide so easily into his old, composed self that it feels uncannily like I'm two Rileys at once—the one just before Tom left, when being around him and Jesse and our other friends was just a regular Saturday night, and the one I am right now, mystified that it's happening at all.

"Hold up," says Mariella, putting the lens back on her camera. "Tom has not one but *two* cool friends? You've been holding out on me. Mariella, by the way."

"I'm Jesse. And I'm also very, *very* late." He leans in and grabs my face between his hands, planting a sloppy, exaggerated kiss on my cheek, and says, "Fuck, am I happy to see you guys. Save me some ice cream if the rest of the Walking JED doesn't kill me—I was supposed to help set up the drum kit and that stage sure is looking empty of it."

Tom glances between my cheek and Jesse's mouth for a split second before snapping into gear, following to help Jesse and catch up with Eddie and Dai. Before they're even fully out of earshot Mariella turns to me and says, "Who is that gangly person and how many Taylor Swift tattoos did I just count on him?"

"That's between Jesse and his small closet's worth of Swiftie merch. And he's an old friend of ours from school. Well, technically my ex, too," I add, not entirely sure why. My cheeks are still warm from where Jesse pressed his hands into them, stirring up an old feeling.

"You dated that smoke show of a human?"

"When we were, like, babies," I say, stepping into the line for the milkshake bar. I already know Tom's order: vanilla ice cream with every single topping they have. "We mostly just held hands."

In fact, I'm not sure if it counts as "dating" at all. Dating with training wheels, maybe. By the time I met Jesse in fifth grade I was well out of my Not Talking to Anyone Ever era, having absorbed some of Tom's confidence by friendship osmosis. So Jesse and I were pretty tight by that murky summer before high school when Tom moved away. We started hanging out more often mostly because there was a giant Tom-shaped hole in our days that needed filling, but by September it became more than that. We were seeing some Marvel movie and he reached over and grabbed my hand and I squeezed his back, and we grinned at each other like it was a joke. Except we didn't let go even as we were walking out of the mall, like we were doing some kind of bit, half joking and half not. The half joke went on until we started doing it more often—in the halls at school, on the way to the skate park—until everyone else just started saying we were dating, and so somehow, gradually, we were.

We were fifteen, so our "dates" mostly consisted of Taco Bell runs and Netflix marathons and doing homework after school. We kissed a few times, shyly, sitting on the rickety swing set in his backyard and after the homecoming dance.

The end of the relationship was as accidental and unremark-able as the beginning—my mom started overscheduling me, Jesse's band started booking real gigs, and we went back to our old easy friendship without ever discussing it. Or at least, went back to it the best we could with schedules as laughably crammed as ours.

"What's in the water in that town of yours?" Mariella asks, glancing appreciatively at Tom and the members of the Walking JED setting up the stage and back at me. "Because considering the quality of all the imports we're getting from them this week-end I might need to try it."

We step up to order our milkshakes then, Mariella opting for an impressive combo of just about every fruity, gummy thing under the sun and me opting for a chocolate malt with chocolate whip.

I scoop up mine and Tom's, trying both of ours for good measure, and ask, "So how do you know Tom?"

"We were in the same comp-sci class. Tom needed help with a project or else he may never have deigned to speak with me."

"Is New York Tom, like—shy?" I ask, for lack of a better way to phrase it.

Mariella raises her eyebrows. "Is there some version of him that wasn't?"

Tom's milkshake is abruptly plucked out of my hand and the reach of my mouth by none other than Tom himself, who's smirking down at me. "I see you've been sampling."

"I'm like one of those court jesters that checks for poison, is all."

"It'd only be right to return the favor," says Tom, leaning down abruptly to take a sip of my milkshake still hovering in front of my face. His eyes are close, flickering with his familiar mischief again, the kind that's somehow only more endearing knowing that most people at his ridiculous height have long outgrown it.

We nurse our milkshakes until the band starts to play, kicking it off with—surprise, surprise—a cover of Taylor Swift's "Welcome to New York." Jesse winks in my direction at the opening chords and Mariella squeals, pulls my milkshake out of my hand to give to Tom, and pulls me onto the dance floor. We're in the dead center and the first ones out, leading the charge. There isn't even a moment to be self-conscious about it before people on the fringes are spilling out to join us, the Milkshake Club coming to life.

Even in those first few minutes it feels like the bright pink lights and the pulsing music are shedding some part of myself away, polishing me into something new. I've been waiting so long for a chance to be right smack-dab in the center of my own life instead of waiting on the sidelines. I feel like I'm brimming with potential energy, like even in this moment there are a thousand different things I could do—dance with a stranger, scream the lyrics at the top of my lungs, start a damn conga line—and every single one of them would lead to a different story of the night, and finally, *finally*, the story would be all mine.

The band transitions into one of their own songs, and I'm surprised it's one I've never heard before. "Wildflower," Jesse calls it, and it's pulsing, demanding, the rhythm changing from the verse into the chorus in this catchy, unexpected way that makes your brain instantly crave hearing it again. The first time the pause just before the chorus hits Jesse meets my eye and grins broadly, the stage lights illuminating the absolute joy on his face, the exhilaration in every breath.

"These punks better be on Spotify or I'm suing them for emotional damage. This song is the shit," says Mariella. She pulls out her camera. "I'm gonna go try and take some pics close to the stage."

"I'm gonna go mortally embarrass Tom," I say back.

I've let him hover with the milkshakes because he's never been one for dancing. Not because he's a spoilsport or anything, but when he enjoys music it's almost like he gets so into it that he forgets to move altogether. Sure enough I find him staring rapt at the stage, milkshakes essentially melted into goop behind him.

Tom's eyes brighten when he sees me approach, but he says, "Absolutely not."

"Life is short, Tom. That meteor from this morning could come down at any moment."

"You make a compelling point," says Tom, who I know won't actually take much convincing. "And yet."

I lean in close. "The good people of the Milkshake Club deserve to see all three of your dance moves. The 'checking the fiber content on this cereal' one in particular."

Tom laughs, starting to shake his head, and I reach out and seize his hand. I have every intention of using it to yank him the way Mariella yanked me, but seamlessly and instantly our fingers weave together in a way they never have before, locking tight. His eyes meet mine and for a moment we're both very still.

Tom snaps back first, squeezing my hand and saying, "Fine. But you have to promise not to be intimidated by my skills. I'm still just a mortal man."

Tom then proceeds to send me and a cluster of other dancers into a fit of giggles by solemnly pretending to steer a grocery cart along while bopping along to an Ariana Grande cover. Every few beats he reaches up to an imaginary shelf, squints at invisible nutrition labels and prices, and either shakes his head or chucks them into his imaginary cart.

"Don't worry," he tells me when the song ends, leaning in close. "I picked you up some invisible Pop-Tarts for later."

A few dancers around us look put out by our closeness, in what I realize with a start might be the third time today people have mistaken Tom for my boyfriend. I laugh at the idea loud enough to mildly alarm Tom, who, of course, is oblivious to all the eyes on him, and say, "My favorite flavor!"

Mariella joins us on the dance floor not long after that, and the Walking JED close the opening act to riotous applause. Jesse wastes no time after the band clears the stage to barrel into us on the dance floor, leaving only briefly to get a well-earned milkshake with the rest of the Walking JED before joining us in our newest dance strategy, which seems to just be jumping up and down in the throng of humans in milkshake-induced sugar highs and attempting not to step on each other's shoes.

At some point we form a semiprotective bubble of me, Jesse, Tom, and Mariella, when Jesse uses his lanky arms to gather us all in and says, "Shit. I'm sure you guys had plans tonight but I'm so glad you made it."

I lean into our sweaty circle, grinning cheekily. "We used you," I admit. "Now that we've enjoyed the vocal stylings of the Walking JED we can cross a pivotal item off of the Getaway List."

"Wait." Jesse beams between me and Tom with the pride of someone who's just been told they were nominated for an Oscar. "The Walking JED was on the Getaway List?"

Mariella nudges her petite frame deeper into the circle and says, "There's a Getaway List?"

Tom's backpack is hung up on a hook under the milkshake bar, so he leans down to open it as I explain the list to Mariella.

"I think it's only fair we let Jesse do the honors of crossing this one off," says Tom.

I nod in agreement. "And Mariella can cross off the 'Dear,

Love' Dispatch." I make a spinning gesture with my hand and add, "Now do the Hokey Pokey and turn your tall self around."

I press the Getaway List against Tom's back as Mariella grabs a pen off the milkshake-bar counter. Jesse crows in delight at the band's spot on the list as Mariella lifts herself to the tips of her toes, scrutinizing the rest of it.

"You're not even halfway through this," says Mariella, her tone disapproving even as her eyes light up with excitement at getting to check one of the items off.

"Well, they've got the whole summer," says Jesse. He's also combing the rest of the list now, jamming a finger at one of the items. "Oh shit, I forgot you two missed that camping trip sophomore year. You're doing that one, too? Listen, if you want company I've got a s'mores hack that's basically unholy."

I wince. "I'm actually leaving tomorrow."

"What the fuck!" Jesse exclaims.

"What the fuck," Mariella agrees.

Tom finishes his business as a sentient clipboard and turns around with a sad but resigned smile.

"Well, you have to come back to finish it, right?" says Jesse hopefully.

Tom and I meet each other's eyes in a brief moment of uncertainty, the kind that's tinged with something else that it's too loud and bright in here to fully feel.

Before the tension can thicken, Mariella takes the list and carefully folds it on the crease, handing it back to Tom. "She'd better, because I want in, too. Hell, we all have a stake in this now. I want to take photos of these ridiculous adventures and Jesse here obviously can't read a map to save his life, so he can't be left to his own devices." She turns to me and Tom sharply, pointing a finger at us both. "This isn't a list anymore, kids. It's a goddamn humanitarian project."

Soon after that the main band kicks it into high gear with a punk-rock Disney medley that nearly threatens the structural integrity of the Milkshake Club with our enthusiasm, and the night slides out from under us in a stream of glitter and bright lights and happy shouts until suddenly, abruptly, it's all wrapping up, and everyone's getting to-go milkshakes for the subway ride home.

We all collect our belongings and Mariella hugs me hard, saying, "You understand New York is the only place that matters, right?" She emphasizes it with an extra squeeze. "You're out of your mind for leaving after two days."

She turns around then to say something to Tom over at the milkshake bar. It's just me and Jesse when he leans in to hug me next, smelling like salty sweat and vanilla, warm and familiar. "What she said." He laughs, and I think he's going to let me go then, but he holds me for an extra beat. Long enough that I feel the slightest shift between us, tipping an old familiarity we had when we were dating into the newness of these taller, older selves.

He pulls in a deep breath I can feel against my own ribs and lets me go, keeping a hand on my shoulder. "I mean it," he says. "It'd be nice to have another familiar face around here."

I lean in, playfully pressing my weight into his palm. "You've got the band."

Jesse looks toward them, where they're polishing off their second milkshakes, his eyes lingering on Dai for a split second. "Things are a little — tense right now."

I don't want to pry but I also don't want to disregard whatever it was that just brewed in his eyes. "Is there boy-band drama?" I settle on asking, giving him room to play it off if he wants.

Jesse shakes his head, pushing me back into place before letting my shoulder go. "Nah. Just Jesse drama, probably."

I nod, letting it go, but not without wondering if it has anything to do with the rumor that Jesse and Dai were dating toward the end of senior year. It's not like it'd be the first time either of them dated another guy, but it would have been pretty surprising considering Jesse's maybe the only one at school whose mouth is bigger than mine. If they actually had gone out I'm assuming half the school would have known before they could so much as bat an eye at each other.

"Well, I'm just leaving the city, not the planet," I tell him. "Call me if you want to talk about it."

Jesse nods, blinking himself out of his trail of thought before his lips curl into a rueful smile. "Man, I thought this might be the summer we finally swapped skills! Remember how I was gonna teach you guitar and you were gonna teach me how to do a handstand?"

I do remember, even if my human body surely doesn't. I haven't successfully done a handstand since I was in braces — which is to say, a long (and embarrassing) time ago.

"I can't guarantee I can teach you that anymore without either one of us getting our brains rattled. But hey. Tom and I have more of the list to get through. I'll be back," I tell him, hoping that it's true even as the dread for tomorrow starts to trickle in under my skin.

Jesse opens his mouth to say something, but just then Eddie calls him over. He gives me another quick one-armed hug and says, "I'm holding you to it."

The lights in the Milkshake Club start to dim then, ushering everyone out, but it does nothing to dim this new flame that's igniting in me. I came to New York because I felt lost about the future, and the truth is, I don't feel any closer to figuring it out. But I feel a small kind of found just the same. In Luca's ridiculous stories. In the *click-flash* of Mariella's camera. In Jesse's wink from the front of the stage.

In Tom's warm shoulder pressed against mine the entire subway ride home.

# Chapter Six

Around one in the morning I give up on sleeping and instead open my text thread with my mom, scrolling through the unanswered blue bubbles: Went to a writing class this morning. My character bit it but Tom and I are still kicking! says one. You'd lose your shit over this grilled cheese—the sourdough bread is unparalleled, says another. One is a selfie of me and Mariella, both of us streaked with the glitter she had in her purse, captioned with Made a new friend. Not entirely certain she isn't my twin. Did you Parent Trap me, Genny Larson??

All of the texts have read receipts under them the literal minute they were sent, and nothing else. She's never not answered a text before. I'm too stunned to feel anything else about it, or maybe I just can't let myself while I'm still here.

I ease out of Vanessa's bed, my bare feet padding on the cold hardwood. I blearily head to the kitchen to get a glass of cold water—incidentally what my mom would always prescribe on nights I couldn't sleep as a kid—but the lights to the kitchen are already on, and Tom is on the couch to the connected living room, frowning at something on his laptop.

He closes it gently before he turns around to meet my gaze. "Hey, you," he says, his voice slightly hoarse from the not-sleep.

I tilt my head at him, all sweatpants-clad and messy-haired, and ask, "Why are you up?"

His eyebrows lift. "I could ask you the same thing." But off my look, he says, "I dunno. Probably just still thrown off from finals week."

I ease myself onto the couch, burrowing into him in a way I've done a thousand times before. Distantly I understand that this time is not quite like the other thousand, but my bones are so heavy that I don't have the wherewithal to examine why.

"That's all?" I ask.

Tom leans into me, resting his chin on top of my head. "Nah. I'm also going to miss you."

I'm glad he can't see my face, because my throat goes tight so fast that I can't even account for the rest of myself. "But I can come back, right?"

"Always," he says, but there's something in his tone that splinters in my heart: the understanding that he means it, even if he doesn't believe it's in the cards. Like even in this moment we're as close as we can be, he has to hold the idea of us at arm's length to protect himself.

I can't even blame him. I've done the same thing for years. I'm lucky not to have been hurt much in this life, but being apart from Tom has been the biggest one I've ever known.

We're quiet for a long time then, breathing in and out against each other until even our breaths seem to find a similar rhythm, until even the city seems to quiet in sync with us all those floors beneath us. My eyes are shut but I know Tom is still awake, too.

"I mean it," says Tom. "If you want to be here at all this summer."

I press my forehead into his side. "Tom," I say quietly. "How long is your mom gone for?"

The room is so still I can hear his slight swallow before he says, "Through August. Maybe longer. I don't know."

The words are light, but I can hear the hurt just underneath them. I want to press to know where it came from, but I'm realizing I already do. It's the same hurt I heard this morning, but couldn't quite place: *She's in her own world for most of it. Sort of like she forgets anyone else is there.*

"You'll just be here all by yourself?" I ask.

Tom shifts under me quickly then, and says, "Not really. I mean—I've got the 'Dear, Love' Dispatch. And Mariella, and Jesse and Eddie and Dai now, too."

My eyes well up and I'm glad Tom can't see my face all over again, because he might mistake the almost tears for something else when they actually boil down to a few miserable truths: the idea that Tom might be so lonely here that it seems like he's only got one new friend to his name. The way I've quietly resented all the fantastical adventures he's gotten to take with his mom these past few years, when, in fact, they might have stopped him from making this place a home. The idea that I'll be leaving in a few hours without any way to know how to help any of it get resolved.

"And you've always got me," I say, the words so thick on my tongue that I don't even realize how close I am to sleep until I say them.

"We've always got each other," says Tom easily, pulling me in close.

The next thing I know I'm waking up on the couch to the daylight streaming in through the absurdly large park-facing windows. Tom is behind me in the kitchen, the bag I packed the night before propped on the counter, some not-so-invisible Pop-Tarts popping out of the toaster.

Tom offers to walk me down to the bus stop, but I tell him I'm going to call my mom on the way to catch her up. It's the truth, but the larger truth is I absolutely hate goodbyes, and the entire twenty-block walk would just feel like an endless one. So instead we give each other another one of our trademark bone-crushing hugs, followed up seamlessly by our nonsensical handshake. He's smiling at me fondly when I go to close the door, and some voice in the back of my head is kicking up an unhelpful fuss—telling me not to leave, telling me to pick up the Getaway List and keep going, telling me to go beyond it to all the staggering, infinite things this city has to offer, chief among them time with my best friend again.

But this weekend was a borrowed one, and now I have to give it back.

I take a deep breath that feels swollen in my lungs until I hit the sidewalk, seamlessly entering the stream of people coming and going. It's comforting to let them swallow me up as I hit the call button on my phone and press it to my ear.

"Hey," says my mom.

Her tone is curt and wary, but then, so is mine.

"Oh good," I say. "I was starting to think you'd dropped your phone into the bottom of a well."

My mom cuts straight to the chase. "Are you coming home?"

"Are you really so mad at me you couldn't text back all weekend?" I ask right back.

There's a silence on her end that feels heavy enough to have its own gravity. "I didn't know what to say," she admits. "I feel like I've been holding my breath this entire weekend, just hoping something doesn't go wrong."

I come to a stop at the intersection closest to Tom's building. "Mom, you saw what we were doing."

"And I know full well what you could get into."

"What, matching Juicy sweat suits and Jell-O shots?" I try to joke, perhaps revealing more of the stories my aunts have told me about her time in New York than they'd have cared for me to share.

Turns out my efforts to lighten up the conversation are entirely in vain, because her next few words feel like they're aimed to wound. "It's not funny, Riley. You should be home trying to figure out your next steps and focusing on the future. The last thing I want is for you to end up like me."

The light changes. I have the walk signal but I can't move. "Like you how, Mom?" I ask, a challenge in my voice.

"You think I don't know Vanessa isn't home? That you and Tom just spent an entire weekend together completely unsupervised?" she demands. "I've been through all the motions of this before. How else do you think I ended up pregnant at eighteen?"

There it is. The implication I could hear between her words but didn't think she'd put as plainly as that. Especially not when the details of how it happened are vague to me even now. Most of what I know comes from my aunts, who told me my mom became friends with my dad just before she moved to New York. She's offered up bits and pieces about him whenever I've cared enough to ask—apparently he was in a band, and has my same loud sneeze, and moved out of the city for the West Coast when I was a kid—but the loudest fact of them was the one she never quite said, which is that whatever friendship she had with him must have ended with me.

So admittedly I don't know their full story, but I don't need to know much to know it's entirely different from mine. It's *Tom* we're talking about, a person I trust more than I trust my own self, and now that we're eighteen and "unsupervised" isn't a word she can throw around anymore. None of that matters compared to the hurt brewing in me like a storm.

"You and Tom are only going to get yourself into trouble, worse now that you're older and on your own," says my mom, digging in. "If you want freedom so badly then don't compromise it. You have so many options right now, more than you even realize, and it can all go away in the blink of an eye. I don't want you wrecking your life over this."

If the first part was a blow, then that was the knockout. Forget crossing the street—it feels like I can't even take one step. I know it's petty and I know it's only part of a much deeper issue I can't even see the bottom of right now, but I say, "Well, I'm sorry I wrecked your life, but this one's mine."

"Riley." My mom can't seem to settle on exasperation or horror. "That's not at all what I meant and you know it."

Even so, she's made a larger point beyond that. I *don't* want to end up like her. Which is to say, someone so scared of the past that she's not only ashamed of it but terrified of her kid repeating it.

But if I keep letting her fear hold me back, I'm never going to have a life of my own. Just one where the only joy I get is from reading other people's stories and making them up in my head. I want to make some of my own, and if I go back now, she's never going to let me. I don't want to live a life of *what if*.

"I'm staying for the summer," I tell her.

The decision isn't even fully made until it's out of my mouth. The relief is so instant that I know it was the right one to make, even if I can feel a sneaky wave of terror crawling just under it.

"You can't be serious."

My spine straightens, holding myself up like I'm bracing for a gust of wind to blow me over. "I am."

I'm expecting her to dismiss me again the way she did when I first brought up the trip, but she knows I mean it. I can tell from the way her voice flattens like she's talking through her teeth.

"I think that's a mistake."

I hold myself a little stiffer. "Well, if it is, it's mine to make."

She's quiet for another beat, then takes a breath and says, "All right, then. All right."

I'm momentarily relieved at the way it sounds like she's trying to come to terms with the situation. Then I quickly realize it's more like she's trying to *set* terms.

"You can stay a few more days. But only if you call or Face-Time every night. I mean it."

I scowl, pressing the phone harder against my cheek and turning inward, away from people walking by. "You froze me out this whole weekend," I accuse.

"And we sync ourselves up one of those location apps, so I know where you are at all times."

I ground my heels into the sidewalk. "Absolutely not."

My mom's answer is immediate, thrown like a whip. "That's the only way I'm going to be okay with this."

The anger has been threatening to tip over for so long that I'm not ready for the impact of it finally flooding through me, or the words that immediately chase it. "I don't need you to be okay with this," I bite out, loud enough that people's eyes flit toward me. "I need—I need to be away from you. You've decided my whole life for me for the past few years and I hated every damn minute of it. I can't wreck my life any more than you already did."

Even as the words come out of my mouth I know they're unfair. There is a whole lot more to it than that, and we've never actually talked about it. But I'm so hurt by what she said earlier—about "ending up like her"—that all I can think to do is hurt her back, as fast and effectively as I can.

"All right, then," my mom says again.

Her voice is hollow. It worked. I stand there almost numb with surprise at myself, with how awful I feel for doing it but how unwilling I am to take it back. It feels like I'm seeing sides of us I've never seen before, and it's scary to feel this unknowable to myself and to the person who knows me best.

The nerve starts to leak out of me then, so I hold on to what I can to stay firm. "I'll check in every week or so," I say quietly. "And I'll come back for the start of the semester. But I need some time to figure out what I want, and I think—I think I can find it here."

The compromise is the closest thing I can do to an apology, but she doesn't speak. It hurts the same way her silence did all weekend—like I only matter to her if I'm the Riley she needs me to be, and the mom I know doesn't exist beyond that.

"I love you," I say, not sure what else to do.

"I love you, too," says my mom meaningfully. "I wish you wouldn't do this."

The tears welling up in my eyes are part relief and part guilt, but they don't do anything to shake my resolve.

"I'll see you at the end of the summer," I tell her, and when she doesn't respond I realize she's already hung up on me. The tears start spilling in earnest then, blazing hot and dead silent, like my body is just leaking them. I turn around for lack of anything better to do and end up turning right into a person— right into *Tom*, whose arms are around me in an instant, pulling me in so firmly and easily that I'm crying into his shoulder before I can even fully register that he's there. He doesn't ask, just holds me there like we're a two-person island in the middle of the sidewalk, until I've gotten enough of a handle on myself that he pulls away and starts leading me back to the apartment.

In the elevator I see the Pop-Tarts I forgot wrapped in a paper towel in Tom's hands, the ones he must have run out to give me. My eyes blur with tears all over again, a memory unearthing itself—Vanessa never had sweets in the house when Tom was little because she didn't like them, and he lost his eight-year-old marbles eating his first Pop-Tart at our apartment. For years we were basically Tom's dessert dealers. Only in this moment it isn't just a memory—it's one more pivotal thing in our shared history that for some reason my mom doesn't want to turn into a future. A future she actively prevented us from having for *years*.

Tom settles us on the couch and hands me the Pop-Tarts. I munch on them through tears, explaining the whole of it—the real reason why we've been kept apart. The fight my mom and I had about it before I left. The way she didn't answer a single one of my texts, and the way she hung up on me just now.

I leave the bit about me ending up "like her" out of it, because it feels too close to me to touch right now, and it's not the crux of the issue. "I just don't even know who I am anymore," I say instead. "And even just being here for a *day* is the closest I've come to feeling enough like my old self that I can figure out a new one."

Tom is quiet a moment, staring thoughtfully at my hands. I know he's working out what to say but my problem is I've never been good with quiet, not even the kind I know I can trust.

"I know that probably sounds ridiculous," I admit.

Tom shakes his head. "No. That makes perfect sense. I think—I know exactly what you mean."

This time it's me who takes a moment to speak. Not because I need to think of what to say, but because I wonder if I'm right to ask it. "Is that also why you're taking the gap year?"

He nods slowly, just one bob of his head. Almost like he's not entirely certain of the answer he's giving. "These past few years—they didn't really go according to plan for us, huh?"

I choke out a laugh. "Not even a little."

"I heard you tell your mom you want to stay," says Tom, a question in the words even if he doesn't voice it.

I lean forward, newly hopped up on processed sugar and determination. "I can find a summer sublet. I have savings from all my part-time work. And if the 'Dear, Love' Dispatch is still willing to take me on, I'll still have plenty of income to help with—"

"Riley. Respectfully, shut up." Tom leans in, too, so he's close enough for me to see the sincerity in every inch of his expression. "You know there's literally no world where you're not welcome here for as long as you possibly want to stay."

"I just—don't want to presume is all," I say, even as the warmth of his words curls out of my chest and spreads all over the rest of me.

Tom nudges my knee with his socked foot. "By all means, presume. I only ever wanted to be presumed by you."

It feels settled then, in a way that isn't worth quibbling about. I push my knee back into him. "You'll be eating those words when I finish the rest of your beloved Pop-Tarts."

"Nah. We'll just cage fight each other for them, fair and square."

For some reason it's this and the playful gleam in Tom's eye that suddenly have me bursting into near-hysterical laughter. Like Tom's words have been just enough of a balm that I can finally make room not just for the hurt of what my mom said on the phone but the utter ridiculousness of it.

"Should I worry about being the punch line of whatever you're laughing about?" Tom asks.

I shake my head, still wheezing out a laugh when I say, "My mom—she's got this whole thing in her head—she's convinced we're holing ourselves up in some sex bungalow."

Tom lets out a choked laugh of his own then, his cheeks turning alarmingly pink the way they always do in the rare moments

I catch him off guard. "There's too much Crate & Barrel in the apartment for it to be any kind of bungalow," he says.

I couldn't stop laughing right now to save my own damn life, but I manage to say through it, "You might be underestimating the sexiness of a well-crafted faux-marble cheese plate."

Tom's laughing, too, but it tapers off faster than mine does. His eyes are steady on mine, his smile wavering when he says tentatively, "If you think it'd be weird being roommates, though—I totally get it."

Oh, shit. I only meant to bring it up as a joke, but Tom's always been less jokey than I am. Or rather, more likely to see whatever truths lie under a joke.

"I mean—would it be weird for *you*?" I ask.

"No, not at all," says Tom at once. A quick beat passes, and he adds, "Only if it'd be weird for you."

It's clear then that we're at risk of this becoming an endless feedback loop of "but only if it was weird for *you*," so I go ahead and say the thing that's awkward but probably needs to be said. "Okay. Worst-case scenario, our raging teenage hormones get the best of us and we make out and ruin everything and I have to go home."

"Worst case?" Tom asks, in a tone I can't quite decipher. Like it's teetering on some edge between amusement and hurt. Before I can answer, he adds wryly, "Seems like you've really thought this through."

I shake my head. "More like my mom has."

Tom hums thoughtfully. We're both quiet a moment, and either fortunately or unfortunately, that's where most of my schemes with Tom begin—in the easy shared silence between the two of us, the one that always felt like a blank canvas for whatever it was we were going to do that day. The one I'm conjuring right now, though, is decidedly different from the olden days of hopping on crosstown buses or trying to reenact scenes from Tides of Time.

"Okay, but here's the solution," I say, even though my brain hasn't quite yet caught up to my mouth.

Off whatever he's seeing in my expression, Tom asks, "Should I be worried?"

Maybe. Even as the idea is occurring to me I'm aware of how utterly far-fetched and possibly damning it is. But the words tumble out of me of their own accord: "You and me. We go outside right now—neutral territory—and we kiss."

Tom's cheeks aren't pink now but a full flaming red. Still, his voice is just calm enough that I know I haven't actually crossed a line when he says, "Just like that?"

"Yeah. Just to make sure there's no chemistry," I say, the words deceptively casual given the electricity that's crackling all over my body right now. It's close to the enticing, promising *tug* I used to get just before Tom and I went off on our adventures together when we were kids, but also not. Like it needs its own category entirely. I push past it and add, "If there is then obviously we can't spend the whole summer living together because that would be weird. And if not, boom, we're golden."

Tom considers me for a moment, his eyes searching my face with an intensity I've never seen before. The kind that makes me wonder if I should take it back—if in my effort to prove my mom wrong, I've inadvertently opened a door that's better off left untouched. A door that goes somewhere there's no coming back from.

But then Tom says, "Yeah. Okay." He stands abruptly, pressing his palms into his jeans. "Let's do it."

Only once we're down in the courtyard just outside his building do I realize how ridiculous I've been. It's not secluded by any means—we're still smack-dab in the middle of New York, with cars rushing past and the doormen gossiping and people headed to the park for their Sunday morning runs—but the space is just separated enough that it feels like we're apart from it all. We settle on the lone bench and I look over at Tom and immediately start laughing again. Not because it's funny, but because strangely, suddenly, there's a part of this that isn't funny at all.

"We don't have to do this," Tom says at once.

I shake my head, still laughing. "No, no, I'm just being ridiculous. I'm in if you are."

"Sure," he says, with a calm I apparently no longer possess. A calm I fully lose hold of a few moments later, when Tom slowly lifts his hand and settles it just under my jaw, the gesture gentle and warm, tilting my face up toward his.

Just like that the laughter ebbs out in my throat. Just like that I'm staring up at a Tom that every part of me recognizes except for my heart, which is thrumming like it's working overtime. Tom leans in and so do I. Tom holds my gaze and I hold his back. His thumb tightens slightly where it's resting just under my ear, sending an unexpected shiver through me, a quiet pulse of a question. He's waiting for me to lean in the rest of the way.

"For what it's worth," he says quietly, "nothing we do together could ever 'ruin' anything."

The words settle in me all at once, calm and heavy like a blanket. Tom is still watching me carefully, but my own eyes are sliding shut. I lean in, close enough to smell the mint of his toothpaste, to feel the heat of his breath, to feel a strange thrill tighten in my chest, and then—

"Tom?"

We both blink, going very still. We're so close that our noses are near touching, that I can't focus on any one part of his face. In a rush it all comes back—my too-loud heart, the even louder city, the crush of reality slamming back into our haze.

"Hey, Tom!"

Tom glances toward the sidewalk then, his hand sliding off my jaw. The loss of his eyes and his touch momentarily root me to the spot. Like I was briefly someone else in the moment I had them, and now I'm back in my usual body, trying to figure out how the bones fit.

"And Riley!" says the voice.

I blink again and there's Luca, his freckly face beaming at us from the sidewalk. He's got a backpack slung over his shoulder, the strings of a bright purple apron spilling out of it where the zipper is half-undone.

"Oh, thank god, it actually is you," Luca says to me, slumping into himself with relief. "I just yelled 'Tom' without thinking, and when you didn't look up I was like, oh shit, what if it's *not* Tom, but here you are, decidedly Tom. Hi. Good morning."

I bite my lower lip in a mostly successful attempt not to laugh. All things considered it's a miracle I'm in control of any of my physical form right now, given the aftermath of this almost-kiss, which is still tingling bizarrely all over my body.

"Luca," I manage, the guilt somehow pushing its way through the veritable storm of my human body right now. "Oh boy. Okay. Funny story. So it turns out—I'm not . . . *not* not Tom?"

Luca's brows furrow. I put a palm on my forehead because apparently I'm utterly useless right now.

"Is that a triple negative?" asks Luca after a moment.

Tom finds his wits before I do, and stands up from the bench. "So actually I'm Tom. And this well-intentioned troublemaker here is Riley."

"Oh?" Luca doesn't sound offended so much as deeply, profoundly confused.

I stand, too, wincing. "The thing is Tom gets a lot of people asking about his mom, so when you did I just sort of—took over 'Tom Whitz' duties for the morning," I admit. Luca's eyes widen like saucers, so I add quickly, "It was silly. I didn't even know I was staying in the city so I wasn't thinking. But the name thing was the only part of the bit, everything else was just us."

I'm bracing myself for a well-deserved telling off, but after a moment of processing Luca throws his head back, his laugh so easy and bright that it sounds like its own kind of sunshine.

"You're not mad?" I ask carefully.

"Why would I be?" he asks. "I totally deserved it. And besides, it makes for a good story, and I'm in *embarrassingly* short supply of those."

"You live in New York," says Tom. "That can't be true."

Luca slings his backpack forward, tugging at the apron string. "All I've ever done is go to school and work for my parents. There are doorknobs less boring than I am."

"Well, shit," I say. "That's bleak."

I mean for the words to come out funny and candid, but what they really do is fall flat. What they really do is remind me of what I can't quite say, only because it feels like there are simply too many emotions wrestling in me right now to go there. That I relate to that feeling more than Luca could possibly know.

Luca glances down at his sneakers, but Tom and I look back at each other. For a split second I'm all too aware of what we almost did all over again, but then something in his eyes goes soft, something I'm feeling in the precise same shade as he is. Tom nods and I nod back.

"Well," says Tom, speaking on both of our behalves. "Riley just decided to stay for the summer for various misadventures. So if you're looking for more story inspiration, you're welcome to join us on them."

Luca's grin splits wide enough to crack the foundation of this entire cramped island. "Yeah?" he says. "I mean—I don't want to intrude on anything—seriously, I'm sure you guys have plenty of friends—"

"A few," I say, Tom's calm easing off on me. "And I've got a feeling you'll like them as much as they'll like you."

Luca's face goes entirely red under his freckles. He stammers out a goodbye to us both because he's late for work, and when he starts jogging away from us I pull out my phone, opening a text thread that includes me, Tom, Luca, Mariella, and Jesse.

> Okay okay. New York wins. I'm staying for the summer. Any takers for the Getaway List?

I show it to Tom before I send it, just to make sure he's all right with the idea. As much as I enjoy the company of all our friends, mutual and semimutual, this isn't for my sake so much as it is for his. But I'll pretend it's for mine if it means that Tom gets closer with all of them this summer; if it means I'll be leaving him here with a large enough safety net of people who will feel just as much love for him as I do.

That part won't be hard. Tom is a person who is impossibly easy to love.

"Perfect," says Tom from over my shoulder.

"Yeah?" I ask, just to be sure.

Tom nods. I try not to notice that I'm breathing in that distinct floral, earthy *Tom* smell more strongly than I ever have. "We were going to do most of the things on this list as a group anyway. So now they'll really count."

I nod back vigorously, wishing I'd thought that up myself. Thing is, it's a miracle I'm thinking any logical thoughts right now because there's still a warm tingle in my lips where Tom's al-most were, still a strange current pulsing just under my skin. The one that's saying, *Hey dumbass. It turns out your mom was right and you're at least a little bit attracted to your best friend after all.*

Or maybe I already suspected. Maybe I was just hoping it wasn't true. But even if that's the case, the whole almost-kissing thing was strategic. Like how else would humans know fire was hot if they didn't get close to the flame first? And yes, maybe I can't depend on my caveman ancestors for a decent metaphor here because it turns out I might *like* Tom's particular burn, but the point still stands that knowledge is power. And now that I know there's some flickering potential between me and Tom, I can do my best to avoid it for the sake of what *really* matters: spending this summer going on the kinds of adventures that will settle us back into our old friendship, that will help us figure out what comes next in our lives.

Tom waves a hand in front of my face. When I blink out of the tailspin of my thoughts and meet his eyes, he loses the teasing look in his and says, "You all right?"

I clear my throat. I have to salvage this. A metaphorical fire extinguisher, if you will.

"So what's the opposite of shipping a couple?" I ask, taking a step back from him.

Tom's eyes flit across the cement, noting the distance. "Drowning them?" he supplies just the same.

I try to keep my tone light even though the words feel sticky in my mouth. "The universe really chucked the idea of us right into a river then. Seems like we're safe from Crate & Barrel's wiles."

My brain scrambles for a moment because it occurs to me that Tom might ask something to clarify. Like whether I mean it because Luca interrupted us, or because I didn't feel any-thing about the near kiss at all.

But Tom just lets out a long breath and nudges at a patch of grass in the courtyard. "Seems like it," he says.

Whatever just deflated in his chest almost feels like it's deflating in me, too. I should be relieved that he's agreeing. The last thing we need is *another* complication in this already prolifically complicated summer. But as that wisp of a potential complication floats off I can't help but wonder what might have been on the other side of it, if only for a moment.

Tom and I hover in an awkward silence and I'm not sure who's going to fill it, but in the end we're both spared. Both of our phones start buzzing in our pockets at once.

Oh good I can call off your kidnappers. Count me in, says the text from Mariella.

Jesse's texts just under it are an eloquent DFJGDLFGJDLFJ-DLFkdAF:LkaSFL:!!!!! And a SUCK IT, FALLS CREEK!!!!!!!!!! Followed by a (to be clear i am also extremely in).

Luca's response is just a GIF of Patrick from *SpongeBob* yelling "WHO ARE YOU PEOPLE?!" Tom and I must see it at the same time because we both throw our heads back with sharp laughs, our eyes snagging on each other's.

And just like that, all the complications seem to slide away. We're eighteen and we've got this entire city at our feet and an entire summer to tear through it. All of our *what if*s just turned into *what now*s—like finally the list isn't just to get away, but to get somewhere worth going. I've got no idea where it is or what it looks like yet, but as long as we've got each other, I know damn well we'll enjoy the ride.

# Chapter Seven

*An admirer would like to send you a gift from the*
*"Dear, Love" Dispatch! Log in to the app to accept*
*and meet up with your dispatcher.*

I blink at my phone screen, wondering if Tom set the app up wrong. After the dust from the "Riley has incited her mother's wrath, forsaken the whole state of Virginia, and upended her entire summer" storm settled this morning, he helped me set up a dispatcher profile of my own so I could make money doing deliveries, too. This feels like the opposite of the kind of notification I should be getting.

I tap into the app and see the options to choose an intersection to meet the dispatcher with this alleged "gift" and go ahead and tap the intersection closest to Tom's apartment, mostly because I'm assuming it's Tom himself. We spent the afternoon on separate missions: him taking a string of deliveries with the dispatch, and me scrambling to buy a ten-pack of underwear from the Old Navy downtown. Maybe he's finished his rounds and decided to be cheeky about it.

Only it's not Tom in the "Dear, Love" Dispatch hat holding a giant bouquet of mismatched, colorful flowers, but some other dispatcher.

"Wait, but who are these from?" I ask, accepting the bundle.

The dispatcher shrugs. "It's anonymous," he says, the "duh" implied.

People are openly staring at me as I walk back to the apartment like I'm some great woman of mystery. Even I have to admit that despite rocking unwashed jeans and one of Tom's giant white T-shirts after sweating through mine, the very loud and public flower delivery exudes some main-character energy.

I set them in one of Vanessa's nice vases when I get back, at which point Tom comes in with his arms full of so many groceries that he looks like he could tip over and cause a small earthquake. I book it across the hardwood to grab some of the bags out from under him.

"Are we opening a restaurant?" I ask under the weight of what appears to be an entire grocery-store aisle's worth of food.

Tom eases the rest of the bags to the counter. "I figured with two of us we'd need more supplies."

I don't bother mentioning to Tom that we are two humans, not prizewinning racehorses, because come to think of it the fridge was pretty bare when I got here. Besides, the larger issue I already see is that left to his own devices, Tom will quietly take care of everything there possibly is to take care of.

"All right, we need ground rules," I tell him abruptly.

Tom's eyebrows raise almost in alarm, but he nods vigorously. "Yeah. Anything."

Jesus, how this boy has survived for so long without getting pulled into a well-intentioned friend's pyramid scheme is beyond me. "For the sake of equal division of labor, I mean."

Tom nods again, slower this time, and then says, "All right. But if you've got other rules we should set them out now. Or add them as we go."

I wrinkle my nose because Tom is reaching for a literal legal pad on the kitchen counter, one of the few signs of Vanessa's presence in the apartment. She's always had one in every room in case an idea strikes her. Tom moves aside a page that just says "make them hornier??" and looks at me expectantly.

I think on it a moment and say, "Well, for one thing, we should probably text to let the other one know when we're leaving the apartment, just in case one of us gets kidnapped and/or murdered."

"Right," says Tom, diligently copying it down. "Also adding 'don't get kidnapped and/or murdered' to the list for good measure."

"Genius. But mostly we'll divvy up the chores. Including grocery shopping. I don't want you suffocating under a pile of extremely unreasonably priced cereal boxes."

"Not on Tony the Tiger's watch."

"What about guests?" I ask.

Tom's pen pauses in his hand. "What about them?"

I tap the pad for him to keep going. "Like if you want to have someone over."

"I assume they'd just be the same people you want over?" says Tom.

"Sure, but what about, like—a *guest*," I elaborate, and for some reason emphasize it by doing an absurd wiggle with my hips.

"Sorry, what kind of guest?" Tom asks with an amused smirk.

My face burns, wondering why I even brought it up. But of course I know why. Part of me is curious if that's something Tom's done before—if he's ever been serious enough about someone else to bring them here, or go to their place. It occurs to me that even when Jesse and I dated back in the day, Tom and I didn't talk about it much. For all I know, Tom's been breaking hearts all up and down Central Park West.

Because that almost-kiss downstairs? That was some suave shit. Like Tom knew what he was doing when he held my face in his hand—like he was poised and practiced and in control. Meaning Tom's probably kissed people before, which is strange because I've never imagined Tom kissing anyone before and now that I am, it is an irrationally displeasing thought. The thought equivalent of stepping on a LEGO. Which, thanks to Tom's brand of nerdery, I did plenty of times growing up.

Tom's trying and failing not to laugh at me when he says, "I don't foresee bringing any dancing inflatable tubes up here." He purses his lips briefly and then adds, "But if you ever want to—you know—"

"Nope," I say quickly. "All right, then. I'm adding 'no watching *Tides of Time* reruns without each other.'"

"Wouldn't dream of it," says Tom, dutifully adding it to the list.

That just about covers it, except for one last thing: "Also no being weird."

"That's an extremely broad condition," Tom points out.

I lean into his counter, sliding sideways against it and accidentally leaning closer to him in turn. He smells like sweat and sunshine and Tom.

"I mean about—you know. Personal stuff. Like if we're going to be roommates we're going to be witness to all of each other's bodily mishaps and nonsense quirks and, like, *feelings*. So no pretending things are fine when they're not, I guess."

There were probably more eloquent ways to put that, but I'm glad I didn't find them because Tom goes still for a moment, so still that I know he understands my meaning completely.

"No being weird," he echoes, adding it to the list. He sets the pen down and looks back up, his eyes settling on the flowers. "Oh. These are nice."

My eyes narrow at him suspiciously.

"Or not?" he says, confused.

"If you weren't my 'admirer' then we've got a regular Scooby-Doo mystery on our hands," I say.

"Someone sent you flowers on the app?" Tom asks, with enough surprise that I know for sure he isn't committing to some bit. I'm at odds with myself, trying to ignore both the pang of disappointment and the teensy self-important thrill.

"Yes. One of my many suitors," I quip.

Tom is examining the flowers intensely enough that it feels for a moment like he's trying not to meet my eye.

"Maybe your mom?" he asks.

I feel a quick lurch in my stomach. "Nah. We're locked in a super fun stalemate right now where neither of us is texting the other."

Tom's brow furrows. "Sounds healthy."

"I might try again when she cools off," I say, before he can go all "future psych major" on me. I don't want him worrying about this when he's clearly got his own issues with Vanessa to work out. "It's just if I text her now she's either going to keep ignoring me or guilt-trip me, and both of those options feel like a hard pass."

"You're sure you're okay with that?"

Not even a little. I may be the one who demanded space, but it's weird not texting her every other minute of the day. Even when we were at the height of overscheduled, we'd check in so often that it never felt like we were apart. The silence on her end is so loud it feels like a damn echo chamber.

"No," I say, with a stilted shrug, "but it'll be fine. It's just one summer."

"Riley," Tom starts, but I cut him off.

"Maybe it was Mariella," I say brightly, turning my attention back to the flowers. She and I have been texting back and forth all day about Broadway shows we want to join the ticket lottery for, and I've determined from her liberal use of caps lock that there is very little in her life she commits to halfway.

Tom searches my face carefully, like he's trying to decide whether to push the mom point. Finally he says, "Yeah, that seems like something Mariella might do."

Except it is very much not something she did, which we discover a few days later, when our little Getaway List group reconvenes to tackle item number four. Mariella comes by the apartment early for lunch because her dad "made enough sorullitos to fill the Lincoln Tunnel." When she explains they're sweet, cheese-filled cornmeal fritters, Tom and I supplement with our own culinary wiles (read: pulling soda out of the fridge).

After a hello hug that rival's Tom's trademark bone-crushing ones, Mariella grabs my hands and takes me in, eyes lingering on the oversized T-shirt with a Falls Creek Middle School track logo emblazoned on my chest.

"This is . . . a choice," she says.

I jut my chin toward Tom. "I'm cosplaying as this guy for the summer. All my clothes are back home."

It's actually come in handy for the past few days' worth of activities, which have included and are not limited to sweating, sweating, and—surprise—more sweating. I've loved every second of biking around the city shadowing Tom for random dispatches for delivery training, but summer in New York makes me feel jealous of fried eggs, because at least at some point they get to get taken off the pan. This city just sizzles until nightfall.

It's worth the copious amounts of sunscreen and chugged Gatorades, though, getting to see the city at full throttle. In the past few days alone we've gone as far up as the Apollo theater in Harlem and so far down into FiDi I could see the Statue of Liberty from Battery Park. We had one flower delivery where we got stuck between a couple loudly and colorfully breaking and then making up in the West Village; we bequeathed an absurd number of Spider-Man toys to a confused but pleased woman on the Upper East Side; we even swung by a Broadway stage door to deliver cookies to an understudy who was debuting that night.

I've also made an enemy out of every stubborn pigeon in this entire city, but have already lost enough battles to know I won't win the war.

"Oh, absolutely not. No offense, Tom." Mariella lets my hands go, reconsidering. "Actually, full offense, Tom. How can you live here and get away with having no sense of style?"

"Because he's good-looking," I say, before he can answer.

Tom sputters on soda, but Mariella nods sagely. "So are you, but fuck this. You're a New Yorker now. Your clothes should be *your* style. We'll go thrift shopping. Find you some Riley fits that don't have holes in the armpits."

I'm even more grateful for Tom's questionable hand-me-downs then, because I was looking for an excuse to hang out with Mariella one-on-one anyway. Not that I'm in any way dreading today's group excursion, which is equal parts tourist trap, workout, and unrepentant nerdery—we'll be walking the entire six-mile loop of Central Park with *Tides of Time* guides in hand, mapping out all the places the characters have been on the show.

Satisfied with solving my fashion conundrum, Mariella glances at the vase on the counter and says, "At least Tom has good taste in flowers, if not clothes." At which point we have to confess we have no idea who sent them to me, which delights Mariella so much that it's clear it wasn't her doing, either.

"Oh, to be young and in New York and living out a rom-com trope," says Mariella, leaning dramatically into the counter.

"Speaking of, did you ever figure out who sent you those chocolate bars?" I ask.

Mariella makes a *pfft* noise and says, "Why bother? Who-ever it was clearly didn't know jack shit about me. Not like whoever sent you these." She fluffs the colorful, chaotic bundle of flowers with the top of her hand. "They captured your whole essence."

She looks to Tom as if she's looking for his agreement, but he's picked up his phone and is suddenly very busy skimming the group chat again.

"We'd better head out," he says, picking up a backpack so full that if he dropped it I'm not entirely certain it wouldn't crash through the floor all the way to the lobby.

"Please let me carry literally anything," I tell him.

Tom obligingly hands me the map.

"Anything but that."

# Chapter Eight

Central Park is so ridiculously beautiful that even though I've been in it a dozen times already, I fall out of step with Mariella and Tom taking it in. Crossing the street into the park is such an abrupt shift that it feels like I have my feet in separate worlds— one of them this humming, electric city full of stakes that feel even higher than the buildings in it, and the other so green and bright and lush that I can't quite convince my brain that it's real.

Luca is already waiting for us when we arrive at the designated meeting spot on Central Park West, clad in a pair of running sneakers, track shorts, and an honest-to-god neon green sweatband around his head. He sees us and shoots his arm up to wave so enthusiastically that his body does an unintentional little jump with it.

"Oh, he's adorable," Mariella says at once. "I'm going to kidnap him."

"You'd be doing him a favor. He's desperate to cure his writer's block and needs a good story," I tell her.

"I don't know how much writing he'll get done from my front pocket, but maybe he'll manage."

Luca bounds over to me and gives me a quick hug, saying, "So my mom bought me some books on scriptwriting and plotting the other day and I'm still marking them up but you *have* to borrow them when I'm done," then moving on to hug Tom and saying, "Oh, *jeez*, you're tall, not-Riley," which causes Mariella's brows to quirk in confusion just as Luca turns to her and then suddenly, abruptly freezes.

"Hi," says Luca. I didn't think he was capable of being monosyllabic, but nothing else comes out of him.

Mariella extends out her hand, flashing a warm smile. "Hey. I'm Mariella."

Luca's eyes flit from her hand to her face, and inexplicably his expression seems to flatten. Like even his freckles have gotten less stark.

"Luca," he says, taking her hand just the same.

Mariella lifts her other hand to press both of hers on either side of his, still beaming with a full-wattage smile that Luca is apparently immune to. If anything he seems to have gone slightly catatonic. I look over to Tom, whose eyes are already on mine with the same confusion in them, when our phones all start buzzing with texts from Jesse.

Apparently the C train goes
to BROOKLYN??
Anyway some hipsters pointed me
back should be there in ten
Don't do anything dweeby without me

"Well, if we're going to be sitting here for a few minutes, I guess maybe I should . . . accept this?" says Tom, showing us his phone screen. It's the same message I got from the "Dear, Love" Dispatch a few days before, saying an admirer wants to send him something.

I feel a pinch just under my ribs, something that comes and goes too fast to fully identify. It's not that I'm jealous. It's just unexpected, is all, to have this interruption to our planned day. If anything I should be relieved at the evidence of another friend of Tom's, because even in my past few days here he hasn't mentioned any of note.

Mariella leans in and taps the ACCEPT button for him, and the four of us walk back into the melee of the 79th Street entrance to meet the dispatcher. It's the same guy who delivered my flowers, who evidently knows both Mariella and Tom — Mariella because it's clear she's had more than a few admirers, and Tom because he's a coworker.

"Don't go too wild with this one, man," says the dispatcher, offering Tom a bright yellow bottle.

"Is that a tub of sunscreen?" says Luca.

Mariella takes it from the dispatcher, shaking it experimentally. "SPF 100. The sun is going to cry."

Tom is also baffled, but genuinely pleased. "Well, you can never have enough of it," he says, unzipping the front pocket of his backpack to reveal two *other* bottles of sunscreen.

"Who would send you that?" Luca wonders out loud as Tom redirects us to a shadier spot.

I nudge him with my shoulder. "Seems like a good mystery for a story prompt."

Luca's eyes light up. "You're right."

"So you're a writer," says Mariella to Luca.

Luca blinks, his eyes skimming his shoes. "Yeah," he says. "Or — well — trying to be."

Undeterred by Luca's sudden shyness, Mariella pulls her

camera out of her bag and says, "Same. I mean—with photography. I don't have any patience for writing, but photos—I'm not any good yet, but I'm trying."

Luca relaxes marginally, just enough that I can sense Tom relaxing a bit beside me, too. I'm so used to him easing the tension between people in and out of our friend groups I'm starting to realize that I took it for granted, assuming it was second nature to him. That he's probably always on the lookout for little moments like this to smooth over.

"Okay, if you've got some torrid skin-care affair going on with someone, now's the time to spill," I say to him, hoping for a laugh.

It earns me a sheepish one, and in his distraction I take the other two sunscreen bottles and slide them into my own backpack before his starts splitting at the seams or crushes his lungs.

"Who knows? Maybe one just started." He taps his elbow into my arm. "Still not as romantic as flowers, though."

Or *more* romantic, given that it's Tom, who probably came out of the other side of puberty with overpreparedness as his one and only turn-on. I'm trying to talk myself out of overthinking it and peppering Tom with more questions about his mysterious admirer when I'm spared the trouble by Jesse's arrival.

"Oh, thank god," says Jesse, putting one hand on my shoulder and the other on Tom's like he just found home base. "Someone back there just catcalled my beautiful kidneys."

"If you've got 'em, flaunt 'em," says Mariella.

"Or maybe don't," says Luca in mild alarm. "I feel like you need at least one?"

"My thoughts exactly, buddy," Jesse says to him.

We do quick introductions over the small ocean of sunscreen we swap back and forth between us, where we learn that Luca, same as Mariella, is a native New Yorker, and that

Jesse and the band just came from doing a photo shoot, which is why Jesse's jeans and gray tie-dye shirt are looking even more ripped than usual.

"So I said yes to this because Tom and Riley have never once led me astray, but also someone please explain what we're doing?" says Jesse, once we take off in the direction of our first stop.

"Happy to," I say. "So Lily Thorn had a charity walk around the loop of the park that I was supposed to take the bus up to do with Tom—what was it, winter break of freshman year?"

"Oh, right. You were more devastated by that than our breakup, if I recall," says Jesse wryly.

I reach up and tug lightly on his ear. "Says the guy who never bothered breaking up with me in the first place," I tease right back.

Jesse laughs, opening his mouth as if in protest, but just then Luca asks, "Who's Lily Thorn?"

"Lily Thorn!" says Mariella. "Animal-rights activist! Beauty guru! TikTok air-fryer queen!"

If Luca was startled at her enthusiasm at first, it seems to be catching on now, because it wrestles a grin out of him.

"She's also the star of the *Tides of Time* TV show," says Tom, when Luca turns to us for clarification.

"That book series Riley almost got that tattoo of on her arm," says Jesse.

Luca's eyes widen on mine. "You almost got a tattoo?"

Tom turns to me and says, "Wait, of what?"

"More importantly, *where*?" Mariella asks.

"Thought about it, time-stone mantra, left ass cheek," I say, answering all three questions in turn. Off Tom's disbelieving look and Luca's mildly astonished one, I add, "All right, more like my forearm. Point being, Tom and I are very obsessed with this series and were very, very bummed not to be a part of this walk when it happened, because it was, in fact, Tides of Time themed—all the stops were places they used the time stone to travel to in the series."

"Bummed" being the understatement of the year. I was fifteen and in the prime of my "nobody understands me" phase. Doors were slammed. Guilt was felt. Now that I highly suspect this was just the first among many Tom-and-Riley get-togethers my mom intentionally prevented, I wish I could retroactively un-guilt myself for it.

But I guess if we'd gotten our way four years ago we wouldn't be with this ragtag little group—Luca with an honest-to-god legal pad poking out of his bag ("I read somewhere that's what your mom uses for ideas!" he told Tom excitedly), Mariella wrestling with several lenses to capture the goings-on in the park, Jesse unironically holding the map he took from me upside down and looking more hopelessly confused than he's ever been.

Tom meets my eye with a close-lipped, conspiratorial smile. The same one we used to give each other over the heads of all our friends when we were younger, and even then we were easily the tallest of the bunch. Sure, back then it didn't make my breath stutter in my lungs for a hot second, but it's a comfortably familiar feeling just the same.

Our first stop is Belvedere Castle, an honest-to-god miniature castle just chilling smack in the middle of the park. Instead of climbing up the back of it first like all the other tourists are, Tom makes us go around to look at the front of it.

"Holy shit," I say. "The cutaway shots in the series didn't do this justice."

The castle is tiny but raised on an unexpectedly high cliff that juts out of the otherwise flat park, looking over a little pond that's so still today we can see the reflection of all the greenery around it like it's a mirror. It looks like it was pulled right out of a fairy tale. I half expect any number of Disney princesses to be in some kind of cursed sleep once we reach the top.

"Well, they *were* preoccupied running from time worms at the time, and in 1930s floor-length gowns no less," Tom points out. "Hard to enjoy the view."

"I have an embarrassing confession," Luca says gravely. "I never read Tides of Time as a kid."

"You should be embarrassed. My god," I say, turning to Tom. "I can't believe we're being seen with him in public."

Tom laughs and tells Luca, "I know it's technically for the younger set, but I bet it'd still be up your alley. The characters grow up in it. It starts when they're eleven and ends when they're eighteen."

I try not to smirk at eighteen-year-old Tom luring a convert into the Tides of Time cult as earnestly as he did at eight and add, "It would definitely make for good story inspiration. The plots are absolutely wild but somehow all come together to make perfect sense."

Luca nods, pulling out his legal pad and writing *TIDES OF TIME—READ!!* in very aggressive scrawl. "And it's like— time travel? Fantasy? I mean, what is it you liked about it?"

"I don't *like* it, I *am* it," I tell him. "And yeah. It's kind of a mix of fantasy and sci-fi and even some good old-fashioned rom-com, toward the end. They really leaned in to the whole will-they-won't-they thing."

Luca nods and says, "Sort of like you and Tom when you almost kissed the other day?"

I let out a choked laugh, but Luca's cheeks flush so immediately that it's clear he was going to be waiting for an opening to ask this all day. Mariella's jaw drops from behind him, eyes lighting up with mischief and a clear *you'd better spill your guts right now or we're going to discuss this later.* I don't bother coming up with an excuse at first, fully expecting Jesse to tease either one of us, but he's looking into his phone.

"Oh, that was—not what it looked like," I manage.

Luca's suddenly biting down a smile. "It wasn't?"

Tom nods and says very seriously, "I was getting Riley's opinions on well-crafted faux-marble cheese plates and needed to lean in to hear her better. It's not a subject to be taken lightly."

Everyone lets out a laugh at that and Tom points us toward the castle so we can walk around and climb up the stairs in the back. Jesse's head pops up from his phone, brows furrowed for a split second before he meets my eye and smiles so easily I might have imagined it.

"All cool?" I ask.

"As a cucumber," he says easily, falling back into step with us.

At the top of the castle there's a sweeping view of the pond just below us, of the bright green lawn beyond it and the massive trees that frame it, of the city buildings beyond them. It's water and green and concrete and sky all at once. Luca leans against the edge of the castle beside me and for a moment we just stand there and try to take it in from all sides.

"To answer your question from before," I say, not even sure I'm going to say it until it's spilling out of me. "What I really love about the series was the characters could just go and do whatever they wanted. Claire—the main character—nobody ever tells her what to do or where to be, or if they tried she just trusted her own gut. She got to be a bit of everything all at once and learn from her own mistakes."

Luca nods, uncharacteristically quiet as he considers this. "So it wasn't even the plot so much. Just the feeling of it?"

My throat gets tight, because shit. He just hit an unexpected nail on the head.

"Yeah," I say. And I could tell him more about that feeling. How sometimes it's felt less like a story and more like home.

Almost like the series was written so it could bring me all the best things in my life—a love for reading. Inspiration to write. Ideas for adventures of my own. Tom.

"Maybe that'll be the ticket, then," says Luca, his eyes shifting between me and the view. "A feeling worth writing about."

I clear my throat. "Maybe," I say.

I turn to look at Tom but just then Jesse has distracted him by pointing out a cluster of turtles in the pond below. It's Mariella behind us instead, her camera poised halfway to her eye, watching Luca carefully like he's the viewfinder. She senses my eyes on her and gives me a quick smile, lifting the camera and saying, "Say 'cheese.'"

Luca beams, throwing an arm around me, and I stick my tongue out, putting bunny ears behind his head. She gets Jesse and Tom next, the two of them immediately shifting to stand back-to-back like secret agents, the way they did when we were clowning around in junior high. Then I take the camera from her and pull her in for a selfie. She's so surprised she almost forgets to smile, then squeezes me into a hug so effusive that I can't hold the camera straight, prompting Tom to take pity on us and come over to take the picture himself.

"Very cute," he says. "Particularly since none of us are suffering from the oozing sores left from poisonous time-worm bites."

"We look after our own," I say.

Our next stop is the Bethesda Fountain. Mariella leads the way because she's already been plenty of times—"They filmed scenes from that *Gossip Girl* reboot out here," she tells us by way of explanation—while the boys hang back, Jesse regaling Tom and Luca with some kind of shenanigans he and the band got into where they got locked out of their apartment and rented a karaoke room so they could power nap until their super let them in.

It's a Saturday so the entire space is crawling with tourists, not just by the towering fountain with its imposing angel statue staring down like it has eyes on every one of us, but in rowboats in the lake just beyond it and the little tunnel that leads to it, with the interiors all done up in elaborate, ornate art that makes it feel like we've stepped into a mini cathedral.

For a moment I'm so stunned by the beauty of seeing it all up close—the tunnel so strangely holy-seeming and out of place in this bustling city, so much so that everyone in it seems to be talking in hushed whispers despite a man performing with a giant bubble-blowing rope just outside of it—that I forget to speak. Mariella doesn't seem to mind, though, raking over the space like she's trying to see it again with fresh eyes before she looks at it through her lens.

I open my mouth to blurt out that this was the spot where Claire and her friends used leftover energy from the time stone to bring the angel statue to life to prevent a doomsday flood brought on by misplaced space matter slowly leaking into New York throughout the 1890s, but Mariella pulls back from her camera lens before I can deeply alarm both her and myself with the amount of fake history I know about this city.

"I'm glad we did this. I feel marginally less dweeby out here with my camera when I'm not alone."

"Excuse you?" I counter. "Tides of Time is dweeby. Whatever rabid animal Jesse just mimed at the boys back there is dweeby. I'm pretty sure chic girls with cameras don't apply."

Mariella jokingly flips her hair back, but can't quite commit to the gesture, like she's out of sync. She sighs and says, "I don't know. I'm new at this. I'm running off a few YouTube tutorials and I feel like every legitimate photographer in the city can take one look at me and know I'm a shiny little fraud."

"Well, everyone has to start somewhere," I remind her. "Those shiny little non-frauds all probably sucked at first."

Mariella cackles. "So you admit that I suck."

"Nah. I don't have an eye for it anyway." I tilt my head at her, taking in her fancy camera bag and the zipped-up pockets for lenses. Her inexperience is maybe more apparent in the overly cautious way she's handling the equipment she still doesn't know how to use, but clearly carefully chose. "Why photography, though? You said you needed new hobbies. Did you just sort of spin a wheel and decide on this one?"

To my surprise Mariella tilts her head back at me and says, "It's okay, Riley. I'm sure Tom's told you by now."

"Told me what?"

Mariella half rolls her eyes, like she's trying to hold on to her usual edge but can't quite. "About my whole *thing* in high school."

"Tom hasn't said anything," I tell her. "Just that you're a whiz with computers."

If I'm not mistaken Mariella's expression wobbles a bit before she says, "Ugh. Of course he hasn't. He's just an insufferably good person, isn't he?"

"From the start," I agree.

Mariella looks over her shoulder to where Tom is no doubt animatedly giving Luca and Jesse the same pseudo-tour-guide lecture about the history of the fountain that he gave me over dinner last night.

"Well. The long and short of it is I was hanging out with a different crowd back then. And they got into things I felt like I had to get into, too. And then when I decided not to anymore, they just kind of—" Mariella makes a "poof" gesture with her hands, then gives another wry eye roll to play it off. "Anyway. I felt like I needed something that was just mine. Except doing something that's just mine is kind of lonely business, it turns out."

There's no way for me to fully understand where she's

coming from—not without knowing the details and how she feels about the whole thing in the aftermath, at least. But I recognize the feeling just the same. That untethered, scary feeling when time slides out from under you so fast that you're not expecting to look up from the rush of people passing through it and realize you're on your own.

"Well, I'll be here the whole summer," I tell her. "If you ever need an emotional-support bystander for your photography adventures, I'm on board."

Mariella smiles at me then, and it's not the broad, sweeping grin she usually has. It's something quieter. Something just as grounded in her heart as her head.

I'm about to tell her if she wants to talk about the rest of it, I'm here for that, too. But just then the boys catch up to us, in a lively debate about what to do with the penny they just found on the ground (with Tom dutifully explaining that they can't use it to make a wish in the fountain, pointing out the signs saying it's to help preserve it).

Jesse tosses a few coins in the bubble man's tip jar and says, "I like this better anyway. I trust the magic of these giant bubbles to make my dreams come true."

"What dreams might those be?" I ask. "You're already here, after all."

Jesse grins broadly. "Too true," he says, throwing a loose arm around me and pulling me in. "And I snagged a stowaway to boot!"

We walk down the Central Park Mall and back up alongside the running path to get to the next stops—the Balto statue and the carousel—then work our way back west to where we started, this time through the patch of woods called the Ramble where we dodge clusters of bird-watchers. We fall into an easy rhythm as Tom and I nerdily explain the Tides of Time plot points associated with them, Luca riffs off some of them with me like we were back in our writing class, Mariella snaps pictures, and Jesse sprinkles in funny commentary to keep us all amused the way he always does, while collecting little scraps and tokens along the way—someone's lost grocery list, a fortune from someone handing them out, a lucky penny. But I know Jesse too well not to notice the tiny dent in his usual brand of enthusiasm, or miss the sneaky glances at his phone.

On the other side of the Ramble Tom leads us not to a Tides of Time spot, but a gazebo on the water that's tucked away off the main path. There's a big rock structure just beside it and from the top of it a view of a cluster of skyscrapers in Midtown, so perfectly framed by the trees that it feels like New York in a nutshell.

Tom shakes his backpack off his shoulders and says, "I brought snacks."

"Aw," says Mariella. "I should have realized you'd be the mom friend."

"The Tom friend, if you will," I say.

Tom proudly produces a bag of Goldfish, a box of Sour Patch Kids, a box of Pop-Tarts, and a bunch of water bottles, leaving the bag open for the rest of us to parse through its offerings. I take the opportunity to follow Jesse as he ducks over to the gazebo, still frowning into his phone.

"Okay, I'm going to ask you if everything's cool again and this time you're not gonna do that Jesse thing you do and say everything's fine," I say.

Jesse looks up with a sheepish if not appreciative smile, rubbing the back of his neck. "It is and it's not. But I probably should bounce soon. The band has rehearsal."

"You got a minute?" I ask, sitting down on one of the benches in the gazebo. This is an old trick in the Jesse handbook. Left to his own devices he has the tendency to *go go go* like a punk-rock wind-up toy, but once you get him to sit still he'll usually fess up to whatever's eating at him.

Jesse hesitates, half of him poised to go and the other coming to an uneasy stop, like his whole body is skipping a beat. After a moment he nods, settling down next to me.

"Was I a good boyfriend?"

It takes every fiber of my being not to laugh out loud at that, only because it's deeply unexpected and also a bit of a misnomer. As easily as we say that we used to date, it's not like it was ever serious as that. But Jesse is asking so earnestly that his whole body is shifted toward me in anticipation of my answer.

"What's making you ask a question like that?"

He rubs the back of his neck again. "I don't know. I mean—you're right. We never even really broke up. It was just over."

Oh boy. I didn't think he'd take that to heart. I can count the number of times Jesse and I have even brought up our teenybopper relationship on one hand. But then again, Jesse's a lot more sensitive than his sunny disposition would suggest.

I put a hand on Jesse's shoulder and say in mock solemnity, "Fourteen-year-old Jesse was a very good boyfriend. He always let me hog the movie-theater popcorn. We just spun out doing our own things, is all."

Jesse nods, teeth grazing his lower lip like there's another question at the edge of them.

"Well, I'm glad we're spinning back into each other. I missed this," he says instead. "Being part of the Riley-and-Tom crew."

I squeeze his shoulder and he perks up.

"Also the band was wondering if you'd come up with more fun ideas for posters we can put up for our gigs. Like the ones you did back at school. Maybe we could work on it when you come over to learn guitar?"

"Done and done," I say.

And Jesse seems just at ease enough after that for me to decide to let it go when his phone starts to ring and he says, "Okay, I really gotta jet." If there's something bugging him I'm sure it will come out soon enough.

After Jesse takes some snacks for the road I join Tom where he's sitting at the top of the rock formation, watching Mariella take pictures of the city as Luca gets roped into a game of tag with a group of little kids. He smiles, shifting to make room for me on the flat part of the rock, and breaks me off a piece of his Pop-Tart.

For a minute or so we just sit in silence, eating and taking in the view of the city. It's beautiful. Cinematic, even. But I don't think it would matter half as much to me if it weren't for the beauty of who I'm finally getting to share it with.

"No wonder there were so many *Tides of Times* scenes in Manhattan," says Tom. "From here it feels like it goes forever."

"'Take me to the realms of possibility,'" I say, teasing. It's the mantra the characters would say to awaken the time stone before it took them off to another adventure—half the time where they wanted to go, and half the time where the stone decided they needed to be instead.

"'Take me back to the home where I'm known,'" says Tom, echoing the phrase they'd use to return.

He nudges his knee into mine, only he doesn't move it away. I feel the gentle pressure of it spread like warmth all over my body. Then he leans in so close that his voice is right next to my ear when he says, "You know, I always thought you'd be a *right* ass cheek tattoo kind of girl."

I let out a sharp and happy laugh. When I turn toward him his eyes are gleaming with that familiar Tom mischief, the kind that sneaks up on me when I'm not expecting it.

"Even after all these years of quiet you still know me best of all, huh?" I say affectionately.

Only Tom's expression wavers at that, his eyes dropping to our laps before rising to meet mine again. There's an apology in them. One he's already given and one I don't need.

I reach out a hand with every intention of putting it on top of his when we're interrupted by the group of kids shrieking happily and running from Luca, who is apparently "it." He comes bounding up just behind them, wheezing slightly, and says, "This is fun! Almost like being good at sports!"

Mariella strides up the rock to meet us then, calling out to Luca, "Didn't you say you had work at four?"

"I'll just have to tell my family I'm very busy being a jock now!" he calls back.

"Hold up a sec," says Mariella.

Luca blinks like he thinks she meant to call for someone else, but abruptly halts when she gets close.

"I can't stop long," he says. "I'm 'it.'"

Mariella bites her lip like she's biting down a smile. "You are, aren't you?" she says, and then reaches up to adjust the sweatband on his head so it's sitting against his curls just so. Luca's face flushes all the way up to the edge of those curls and Mariella really does smirk then, seemingly satisfied with her handiwork.

"Go get 'em, ace."

Eventually we dislodge Luca from his new group of tiny friends and start making our way back to the entrance of the park, Mariella showing us a few highlights from her camera roll on the way. We're all of us sweaty and worn out and pleased with ourselves when we part ways by the subway station, marking the goodbye with a sloppy group hug. In that instant I'm overwhelmed by the hope of it all, by the way it feels like this summer is stretching out in front of me as far as that skyline. Like I'm standing on the edge of the best part of my life, and won't have to be alone enjoying the view.

The trouble is that view only stretches as far as August. A week ago I wanted nothing more than for time to pass faster, and now all I want is for it to stand still. I squeeze my new friends a little tighter as if to hold them there, making an enemy of time all over again, now that it's something I want to keep.

# Chapter Nine

Once we're showered and scrubbed up for the night, Tom and I do the only thing two people can logically do after taking a three-years-belated Tides of Time walking tour, which is binge-watch half the first season of the show together in our pajamas. Tom swaps out his contacts for his glasses while I do a full-on face mask that I got from the drugstore downstairs, amusing myself by wondering what sort of hell my mom thinks we're raising right now when we are, in fact, giving the oldest married couples in New York a run for their money.

We pause at the sixth episode for a snack break. I come back from the kitchen with a dip concoction of salsa, guaca-mole, shredded cheese, and sour cream, because the same way Tom likes to stuff as many things into desserts as possible, he does that with savory food, too.

"You're a culinary genius," he praises me.

"I'm a girl who knows how to open a jar and tip it over," I correct him.

I settle next to him on the couch and there's something about being wiped out and squeaky clean and still brimming from the joy of the day that I can't help myself from blurting, "I think a lot sometimes about how lucky I am that you made me read that book. So many good things in my life came from it."

Tom is suddenly looking far too emotional for someone who has a precariously loaded chip several inches from his mouth. "I'm the one who's lucky you read it," he says.

"What made you read it in the first place?" I ask. Back when he was first indoctrinating me into his nerdery, the series wasn't remotely as popular as it is now.

Tom shrugs, but he sets the chip down on the edge of the dip bowl, considering. "There were so many people on the cover. I always liked that," he says. "Every adventure they ever went on, they stuck together. And even when things got rough they found their way back to each other. I loved all the time travel and space bending, but I think a lot of it was just—I loved that they were all friends first, explorers second."

*Friends.* It used to be a simple word, but time sure has a way of complicating it. Because there's some warm cavern in my heart where that word has always lived, but it's almost like there's too much room in it now. Enough for it to ache like it wants more. Like it wants more of Tom, specifically.

I press it back down into myself, because right now the feeling overwhelming me is gratitude. Both that I was able to grow up with a group of friends like that, and that we're building another one now.

I press my socked foot into his calf. "That makes sense. That's always been your whole thing, bringing people together."

Tom lets out a breathy laugh, eyes skimming the television screen. "I don't know about that."

"I do," I insist. "I had front-row seats. And boy, did they

come with perks. I'd probably still be hiding under the bleachers somewhere if you hadn't taken me under your wing."

Tom shakes his head, turning to me again with a fond kind of sternness. "You were shy, is all. But you were always you. And you would have found your voice just fine without me."

This makes my eyes sting because only someone like Tom would have noticed that—the person I was under the very crusty, silent surface. Even when we were way too young for that kind of patience and understanding. Tom's always been an old soul.

"Sure, maybe," I concede. "But it would have taken an excruciatingly painful long time, and I would have had to write a whole soppy memoir about it to cope. And title it *I Would Have Been Less Pathetic If I'd Just Had a Tom Whitz in My Life, Dammit.*"

Tom smiles, lightly bopping my foot with his fist. "I think you've got the wrong idea about me. A flattering one, but the wrong one."

"Oh, bullshit," I say candidly. "Like I said before. We'll always know each other best."

Tom's eyes dip away from mine again. I stare at him like I can bring them back, but he's lost in a thought. His fist stays on the top of my foot and I go very still, hoping he keeps it there. Hoping he can feel the way I want to pry out what it is he's been holding inside without cracking him open in the process.

"Earlier you said—after all the quiet," says Tom.

"I didn't mean anything by that. Really, I didn't," I say.

"I know," says Tom quietly, staring at his hand. At the fist slowly uncurling itself as he grips the top of my foot, almost like he's trying to press some kind of understanding into it. "I just—I wanted to explain. Or at least have it out in the open. It never, ever had anything to do with you. You're my favorite person and always will be."

This isn't news to me, because I've felt the same way about Tom since we were eight. But the way he's saying it still scares me a little. Maybe even the fact that he feels like I need to hear it at all.

"You're mine," I say back, in case he really does need to hear it.

The edges of his lips quirk, but his eyes stay cloudy, still not meeting mine. "I guess you could probably tell by now that I, uh—I'm not like I was back home. Coming to New York was like getting dropped onto another planet. It wasn't even that everyone knew each other or that people weren't nice, because they were. I just—felt like I was separate from everything. Like I'd spent my whole life so grounded in who I was and who I loved and here, it's just—everything is constantly moving. All the time. I couldn't keep up, and at some point I just—got overwhelmed. I just stopped trying."

It feels like the wind has been knocked out of me. Like I'm feeling some shade of his hurt slowly absorb into me, but not near enough of it, and not fast enough. I want to reach out and take it from him. I want to push it out the window of this very high-up movie-set apartment.

"I wish you'd told me," I say instead, trying very hard to keep my voice steady.

Tom squeezes my foot lightly. "I didn't want to. And I think that's why it was easier to just fall off the map sometimes. In some ways it was like—if I could stay the Tom I was in your head, it wasn't so bad."

I know what he means to an extent, even if it aches to hear it. I've felt the same way these past few years, slowly losing my sense of self. Like there was still some substantial part of it that didn't matter as long as I had Tom, who knew me no matter what.

But I guess I don't fully know what he means, and never

can. Tom built us a group of friends a mile wide, and I got to keep every one of them. Tom came here on his own without any soft places to land.

"Well, respectfully, that's ridiculous," I tell him. "There is no version of Tom that could ever live badly in my head. I love all of them. Even the ones that are bad at texting back in a timely manner."

Tom swallows hard, his eyes finally meeting mine, red-rimmed and a little misty. I'm remembering suddenly the moment he met me at the door a few days ago. How he was happy and how quick he was to meet my energy, but how neither of those feelings were half as pronounced as his relief.

"But mostly I just wish you'd told me so I could have helped," I say, my voice low.

"You did," says Tom, quickly and effusively. "You don't even know how much. I was so shit at being in touch, but you always were anyway. Every time you texted me it was the closest I'd come to feeling like myself again. And this sounds weird, maybe, but sometimes I had—" Tom pauses like he needs a moment to phrase it. "Imaginary conversations with you, almost. Like what you'd say if I did tell you."

I lean in closer, settling my head on his shoulder. The electricity I've felt being near to him is still there, but it's a distant hum. There's only an ache in this, and a need to heal it.

"I hope imaginary me was wise," I say.

"She was. And even if she wasn't—there is no version of Riley that could ever live badly in my head," says Tom, with a smile I can hear in his voice even if I can't see it in his face.

I smile, too, even if my face feels strangely heavy with the effort. "Touché."

We stay like that a little while, my head on Tom's shoulder, his hand on my foot. I stay quiet in case he has more he wants to say, but it feels like whatever we need it's already right here, in the way we're carrying each other's hurts—the old ones and the new, the ones we saw coming and the ones we couldn't have. We stay still for so long that I wonder if maybe we're just going to fall asleep like this, and my eyelids start to drift. But at some point my phone buzzes in my pocket.

I don't want to look, but Tom says quietly, "It could be your mom."

It's not. It's another notification from the "Dear, Love" Dispatch, asking if I want to accept another delivery. I set the phone down, biting down my disappointment as I raise a finger to hit the NO button, when Tom takes his hand off my foot and sets it on my wrist.

"Go ahead," he says. "You can just have them deliver to the lobby."

"I don't wanna move," I grumble, burrowing my head farther into him.

Tom laughs softly, his shoulder lifting against my cheek.

"Maybe you'll unravel the flower mystery," he says. He holds his finger over the ACCEPT button, waiting for my permission. I let out a sigh that he knows is a yes, and he taps it for me.

There's another disappointment then, one that's fainter and harder to define.

"You have to come down with me, though, so I look like less of a gremlin on my own," I tell him.

He does, and ten minutes later we are the proud owners of a hunk of aged gouda cheese.

"Do I even want to know what's going on in your life, man?" asks our dispatcher, who delivered both my wildflowers the other day and Tom's tub of sunscreen this morning.

Tom examines the gouda and says, "Well, if we figure it out we'll let you know."

Naturally we break into the gouda the moment we get back

upstairs, despite the very large and looming question of "Who the heck would send us these things, if not each other?" And it's then that I fully cop to the strange disappointment—that it doesn't matter, really, who sent the flowers or the cheese. There's some not-small and decidedly silly part of me that wishes they came from Tom.

Halfway into the next episode of *Tides of Time* and three quarters of the way through the hunk of cheese and I'm worried that Tom's in the same funk I am. We usually would've both pointed out inconsistencies from the books ten times over by now. Tom must be wondering the same thing, because he nudges me with his arm, his eyes clearly asking, *Everything okay?*

I bop my forehead into his shoulder. "Thanks for telling me about the texting thing," I say.

Tom pulls in a quick breath, like he's about to thank me right back, but I don't want that.

"And I just want to reiterate," I say, pressing my forehead deeper into him. "You can tell me anything. I'd always rather know than not."

Tom rests his chin on top of my head. "Same to you," he says after a moment.

I know he means it, but it still feels like a deflection. Like there's something there in that beat he hesitated, if I'm willing to risk chipping away at it. But right now I'm somewhere I haven't been in years—unscheduled and unhurried, with my best friend at my side. I close my eyes and breathe the calm of it into my lungs, letting it settle over me like a heavy blanket until we fall asleep pressed into each other, the city and every bend and break that brought us here nothing but a distant hum far below.

## Chapter Ten

True to her word, Mariella takes the train up to the Upper West Side the next day to meet me to solve my "fashion emergency," which is admittedly getting more dire by the minute. By the time I finish dispatch deliveries for the day, Tom's borrowed clothes are turning into giant sweaty tents on my human form. The audacity of him to have those newly broad shoulders.

Once we've met up and secured coffee from a cute little French bakery Mariella loves, she turns to me and says, "Okay. Give me a sense of your style."

"Comfy. But not this comfy," I say, lifting my arms, which are half-swallowed by Tom's ginormous NASA T-shirt. "More like—sporty. But sometimes edgy? Like if Jesse's sense of style and a very cozy beanbag chair had a baby."

Mariella nods and says in the tone of doctor giving a diagnosis, "Punk-adjacent athleisure. Got it. We'll start at Housing Works and work our way up to the bazaar."

She leads me to a thrift shop on Seventy-Fourth Street

crammed to the gills with clothes, old records, and all kinds of trinkets, and immediately dives into the racks with the authority of someone who is quite familiar with the art of style hunting. It makes sense, given how unique Mariella's own style is—today she's rocking a pair of pastel green high-waisted shorts, a white crop top with a fringe trimming, and a pair of bright blue boots. It's not unlike she stepped out of an ABBA music video.

"All right, these are some good bets," she says within five minutes, handing me a pile of clothes. "You go try those on while I go look at these shiny things."

Unsurprisingly, she captured my usual style to a T—well, an improved version of it, at least. Everything she picked out is very *me*, but with the volume dialed up just a bit. The vintage black jeans she found have tears in the knees; the sporty crop top she found has an unexpected strappy racer back to it; the black bike shorts have electric blue seams.

"You're a fashion savant," I declare on my way out of the dressing room.

Mariella is pouting at her phone. "Ugh. But a flirting disaster."

"Oh, is that why you're constantly getting sent stuff from the dispatch?" I ask innocently.

She smirks but says, "It's Luca. I have this weird and kind of ridiculous crush on him?"

I pause like my brain is recalibrating. "You do?"

The initial surprise fades fast, though, especially when Mariella doesn't so much as blink. Maybe it even makes sense. On our walk the other day the two of them had a few quick but animated conversations only actual New Yorkers could keep up with (including lore about "pizza rat" and a "hot duck" I'm still mildly confused by), and were laughing loud enough at each other's jokes that they nearly fell behind a few times.

Huh. I'm not sure who I would have imagined either of

them with, but now I don't have to, because I'm already picturing it. They'd be very cute together. Mariella with her blunt cool-girl edge and Luca with his unabashed dweeby sunshine. I'm a sucker for an opposites-attract trope.

"I think I'm barking up the wrong tree, though," says Mariella. "He clearly likes you."

I shake my head. "Nah. He's just so deprived of 'writer friends' that he decided I am one."

Or maybe just turned me into one by sheer force of will. His enthusiasm is contagious. Tom and I have gotten into a routine where we sit on opposite sides of the couch and drink decaf coffee with our laptops every night, and more than once I've found myself opening a blank Google doc on my computer, some undeniable tug pulling me out of the present moment and into imaginary worlds.

I haven't gotten as far as actually *writing* anything yet, but not for lack of inspiration. It's almost like there's years of completely repressed inspiration that if I let loose is probably all going to explode out of me like a geyser. All the scenarios and spinoffs I imagined for all the books I have downloaded on my phone, all the loose ends of stories and daydreams I used to dissociate from whatever the "keep Riley out of trouble" flavor of the week was.

Mariella pats me on the head, which is no small feat considering the difference in our heights. "Riley, that boy was looking at you with heart-emoji eyes."

"Writer-emoji eyes," I correct her.

"Ugh," she says, riffling through another rack of clothes. "Why can't I do the responsible thing and have a crush on Jesse?"

I laugh, and before I can answer Mariella's shoulders go loose and she says, "Luca's just so—earnest. And people I've been around were mostly, like, trying so hard to be all unaffected by everything." She pauses for a moment, like she didn't expect to say something so bare. "Also he's only a few inches taller than I am as opposed to all the other guys I've dated, which, like? *Ow.* My ankles, my neck, my lower back. It's hard out here when you're fun-sized."

"Well, have you thought about maybe asking him to hang out one-on-one?" I ask.

Mariella's lips purse sheepishly. "I tried just now," she says, holding up her phone. "He said yes, but then asked what time I thought would work best for the whole group."

I wince and she raises her eyebrows as if to say, *See?*

"Anyway, at least one mystery is solved. I'm guessing it was Luca who sent you the flowers," says Mariella, pulling a glitzy denim skirt off the rack and holding it experimentally to her waist.

"Actually, the mystery has only gotten deeper. Someone also sent me a hunk of cheese."

Mariella looks suitably impressed. "Now that's what I'm talking about. Something a girl can actually *use.* Although bold of them, considering you and Tom are attached at the hip."

I'm still chafing at the disappointment that it probably wasn't Tom, so it takes me a beat to reflexively say, "Tom and I aren't like that. We're best friends."

Mariella squints at me disbelievingly. "You have actually looked at Tom, right? And also in a mirror? You're both too hot to just be friends. I don't make the rules, but I do enforce them."

"You're a hot person who's friends with him!" I protest. "Actually, wait. Why haven't you ever had a crush on Tom?" I ask, more out of curiosity than anything.

Mariella considers for a moment, pressing her tongue to the inside of her cheek. "I don't know. He was closed off for so long I just never thought about it. Then by the time we

were talking junior year, it was sort of like—" She sets the skirt
back down on the rack but keeps her hands there, almost as
if to steady herself. "We were mostly spending time together
for comp-sci stuff. But I guess Tom was lonely and I was in
the process of extricating myself from the assholes I used to
hang out with, so the friendship part was sort of an accident?
We would hang out by default. Almost more like we were life
preservers more than friends. And life preservers aren't very
sexy things to be."

"That makes sense," I say, only because I'm scrambling to
say what I really want to, which is *Thank fuck he had you*.
Because based on this and what Tom has already told me, it
seems like he needed someone to half bully, half wait him out
to be friends, and Mariella is the perfect person for that. It's
not lost on me that Mariella did to Tom what Tom once did to
me, and I feel such a sudden wave of gratitude for her that it
takes everything in me not to hug her right now and possibly
make a scene.

"Also I was so certain you two were dating that I was half
expecting him to ask my opinion on engagement rings," Mariella says casually, redirecting us to the register.

"Ha-ha," I deadpan.

"'Riley this, Riley that,'" she says, making a chatterbox gesture with one of her hands. "Years of silence from Tom Whitz
and it turns out when you crack him open all he wants to
talk about is time travel and space and his long-lost girlfriend.
Thank god you're actually real, I was this close to staging an
intervention."

We pay for our clothes and head back out into the sunshine, walking up to the open-air bazaar where Mariella as-
sures me there will be plenty of vendor tents with snacks and
secondhand clothes. Most things are out of our price range,
but we find some wacky vintage Disneyland shirts and cheap

matching rainbow bracelets, then get in line for kimbap and lemonade and a giant chocolate-chip cookie.

Once we're settled on a bench in the little garden by the natural history museum with our lunch spread, my brain is unscrambled enough to say, "I'm glad you and Tom could be each other's flotation devices."

She smiles the same quiet smile from the tunnel yesterday. "Yeah, me, too. It sucked that he was on his own so much, but at least he missed most of my very embarrassing fall from social grace." Then she pulls in a hesitant breath, like she can't decide if she's going to say more.

"You don't have to talk about it if you don't want to," I tell her.

She shakes her head. "It's fine. Thing is I'm not just good with computers, I'm fucked-up good with them? I was practically coding before I could tie my shoes. My parents were over the moon because they were like, 'She's set for life!,' you know? Not like my older cousins who were all into art and dancing and still living at home with barista jobs, heaven forbid," she says, with an exaggerated eye roll.

"Do you not like coding?" I ask, surprised.

"Oh, no, I love it. I have a bit of a god complex when it comes to design, you might have noticed," she says, tilting her head at our shopping bags. "And coding is the ultimate in that. You get to bring shit to life out of literal thin air and make it exactly the way you want it. No materials, no waiting around on anyone, no stopgaps. You just decide you want it to be a certain way, and it is."

"I get that," I say. "Wanting something just for yourself that you can control, I mean. I couldn't code my way out of a paper bag."

Mariella nods. "Yeah, that's really what it was for me. Something all mine. Except my parents were so happy to have birthed a surprise nerd that they spent a ton of their savings putting me in the fancy private school Tom and I went to—like, money I didn't even know they had. So they were super adamant that I *only* study academic stuff. Like they were afraid the creative arts were contagious and I'd catch them if I took classes in anything else. So then I got restless and did the kind of shit restless teens do."

"Oh boy. I have a feeling you and I are about to swap some detention horror stories," I say. "What did you do?"

Mariella's lip curls the slightest bit, undeniably proud of her skill set even if she's not pleased with how she used it. "At first it was little stuff. Hacking into the school's database to tweak grades or change attendance records. I always had friends, don't get me wrong, but suddenly *everyone* wanted to be my friend. And in a school like ours where most of the kids have that vague untouchable New York eliteness to them, it's hard not to get swept up in it." The smile uncurls itself from her lips when she says, "I don't have any detention stories, though. I was too good to get caught. And I don't mean that in a braggy way. I kind of wish I had been."

I wonder if it's worth warning her off that wish, considering my permanent record is one of the reasons why there's a graduation cap in a landfill right now full of letters from schools sending their "sincerest regrets." But her expression is unsettled and unfocused, like she's trying to turn a bad memory into words she hasn't actually said out loud yet.

"Because it was worse stuff, too," she explains. "Like, some of the kids were doing ridiculous betting circles or selling weed to each other. Big fucking private-school clichés, you know? And they wanted a safe way to send money back and forth without getting caught. And I knew it was a bad idea but damn, did I love the challenge of building an app for it." She meets my gaze then, the regret so plain in her face that it's dimming all the usual brightness in her eyes. "Except by the time I finished it I'd seen enough of what they got up to that the whole thing just kind of made me sick. I mean shit, I was sick of myself. I was drinking with them a lot. My grades were slipping. I just didn't feel like myself anymore. So I destroyed the app before I was supposed to launch it. All the kids involved basically shunned me, and anyone in their right mind followed suit."

I blink, trying to digest this all at once. It's so far removed from the hijinks my classmates would get up to in our small town that I feel like I was on the bunny-hill version of high school, with no idea how steep the stakes could get.

I finally settle on "What the fuck? After all that, they turned on you over a stupid app?"

Mariella shrugs, but more out of indifference than confusion. "I guess they were afraid I was going to rat them out or something. I wasn't, but it's a power thing. They punished me by shutting me out, but that was just their warning shot. You know—the 'we could do worse.' They made sure I knew how well-connected their parents were. It was especially fucked up because, like—even if I wanted to bring them down, it's not like that even mattered. Who are they going to blame for that kind of thing in the end? Not the pack of rich white boys, that's for damn sure." She picks at her kimbap like she's only just remembered it's there. "But the real reason I wish I'd been caught is I just got carried away with their shit. The drinking. The lying to our parents. I even liked it at first. It felt like I was getting back at them for choosing everything for me."

I feel the weight of those words so instantly and so viscerally that for a moment I'm not on the bench with her but too many places at once. All the tired conversations I had with my mom about the next shift she wanted me to cover or group she wanted me to join. All the moments I sat around wasting time and thinking I didn't have any other choice. I don't realize

I'm tearing up until Mariella meets my eye and says candidly, "Oh, shit."

"Sorry," I say, rubbing at my eyes with the heel of my hand. "It's just—fuck. I know exactly what you mean. It's like when all your decisions get made for you like that, you're just sort of—set up to fail, trying to get out from under it. Like you're either going to disappoint them or yourself."

To the surprise of approximately none of me, it's my mom I'm thinking of then. How it's been more than a week since I got here and despite her demanding we stay in touch, she hasn't called or texted or even emailed. How I've been so busy *go go go*-ing to keep up with the pace of this city and the temporary life I'm making in it that I haven't felt the impact of it just yet—of the way this constant stream of back-and-forth between us has been cut off all at once, and I feel untethered without it in a way I've never been.

But I manage to get ahold of myself even as Mariella nods, clearly sympathetic. "It's ridiculous because I can't do anything to change what I did, but I'm still disappointed in myself."

I laugh wetly. "Even after you basically said *fuck you* to richest kids in this city? That takes guts," I tell her. "I think that's automatic badass territory."

"For me it was automatic loser territory," Mariella groans, taking a bite of kimbap.

"Badass," I say firmly, before echoing her: "I don't make the rules. I just enforce them."

She smiles then, and for the moment the conversation comes to an easy quiet. A shared understanding that's made not just of the words, but the absence of them.

"Well," Mariella says once we move on to the giant cookie, "now you know my deep, dark secret."

"Yeah. And to watch my back if I ever commit fraud, since you're inevitably going to get scooped up by the FBI."

Mariella makes a *pfft* noise, straightening her shoulders again. "Those squares *wish*." She gestures out vaguely enough that she's either encompassing this little park or the entire city, then says, "Anyway, that's what this photography thing is about. Something that doesn't have anything to do with that old crowd or my parents or even anything to do with my future. Something that's just mine."

"You don't think coding can be again, too?" I ask through a mouthful of cookie.

She takes another chunk of it herself. "Close to it, maybe. I think it will never be just *mine* again because I want to put my stuff out in the world, and once you do that it's not just yours anymore. But I guess it's more mine than it has been in a while. I had a long talk with my parents about not going to college yet. I want to see where the next few months take me with it. I've got some ideas, and friends with ideas, too."

She goes quiet then with the suddenness of a car braking without warning. I tilt my head at her in curiosity, but she blinks like it didn't happen, settling her focus back on the cookie.

"Well, shit," I say after a moment. "I wish I could be that brave. I don't even know what I want to do with my life, let alone how to talk to my mom about it."

Mariella swats me on the shoulder. "Sorry, did you fall on your head and forget that you just up and moved to New York City? That's brave as hell."

"Up and temporarily moved to Tom's for the summer," I correct her.

"Technicality, because we'll get you in the end," she says, waving me off. "The way I see it we're both leaving all our shit from high school in the rearview mirror. This is our new start. One we make on our own terms. In clothes that weren't previously owned by a perilously tall space-obsessed dweeb."

I let out a sharp laugh, but feel the comfort of those words settling over me like a weighted blanket. A grounding reminder that I might be on my own for the first time, but I'm not alone in it. That we're all playing jump rope with that murky line of what our parents think is best and what we want for ourselves, knowing we'll trip along the way and hoping we'll be able to pick ourselves back up again.

But knowing Mariella talked it out with her family makes me feel a little less daunted about talking it over with my mom—whatever it is I decide to do with my life, and however I decide to do it. Now all I have to do is somehow figure those impossibly large, decidedly life-altering, ridiculously high-pressure things out.

"C'mon," says Mariella, leaping up from the bench so fast that the crumbs from our cookie spill to the concrete. "There's a dog that knows how to skateboard in the park. We should go see if he's out today."

I follow, happy for a reason for the day not to end just yet, and happier still that at least for now, it gets to be whatever we make of it.

# Chapter Eleven

"Lunner," says Mariella slowly. "As in—lunch and dinner. Combined."

I hold my phone to my ear, narrowing my eyes. "I'm ninety-nine percent certain that's not a thing."

"I'm the New Yorker here. You dare question my authority?"

In the brief time I've spent in this city I've kept an open mind. It's a requirement of the job, when you're anonymously delivering everything from a tub of faux-bacon bits (the recipient was positively thrilled) to several pints of Ben & Jerry's (the guy nearly started bawling in gratitude at the sight of them) to a bouquet with a note that read "Sorry about the unholy things I did to your wedding cake" (I did not stick around long enough to find out). But I draw the line at "lunner."

"Best tater tots in the city," Mariella adds.

Incidentally I may be redrawing some lines. "What time?"

At four o'clock I meet Mariella, Luca, and Jesse on the

curb outside of a kitschy, retro restaurant with the walls all plastered with magazines and ad prints from the 1950s, Christmas lights in various degrees of broken and functional, and a jukebox with a BROKEN sign on it that looks like it's been there possibly since the day I was born.

"This is the sickest dive I've ever seen," says Jesse, which is a bold statement from someone who grew up in a Virginia town where the closest thing we have to a dive is Shake Shack.

He fits right in, though, with his acid-wash denim vest and purple shirt, the same combination of worn out and overtly colorful as the surroundings. He immediately plants himself on one of the shiny padded stools and gives it a whirl.

"Where's your other half?" asks Jesse.

"Tom took on some scheduled afternoon deliveries, but he'll catch up with us later," I explain.

"You were right, Mariella," says Luca. His eyes are skimming the walls up and down, wide with glee. "Tons of cool story inspiration."

"What can I say, ace?" Mariella leans back on one of the dinged-up neon tables. "Stick with me and you'll never get bored."

Luca's eyes settle on Mariella with the full magnitude of his broad grin, and for once I catch *her* blushing. "Well, I'm pretty sure I knew that the minute we met," says Luca.

Mariella unsuccessfully tries to bite down a broad smile of her own and that's all the confirmation I need to know that this was probably where Mariella invited Luca before he suggested opening it up to the group. It's a good find, too—Luca hasn't stumbled on his big-ticket idea yet, so he's started collecting writing prompts to "keep himself in the headspace," as he told the group chat. He's been sending me quirky short stories all week, and judging from the number of newspaper clippings from old celebrity dramas and vintage advertisements plastered to the walls of this place, he'll have more than enough to draw from for more.

"That reminds me," says Luca, unceremoniously dumping two large books on scriptwriting and novel plotting in my lap. "I'm finished with these for now, if you want to borrow them."

I don't have the heart to tell Luca that as far as writing goes, I'm still staring into the abyss of a blank Google doc. Some of it is the same issue as before—I feel like a zookeeper just uncaged all these ideas I've had locked up in my head, and they're all running in different directions. Old fanfic ideas and new original ones. Time travel. Fantasy worlds. This new world of the city constantly shifting in front of me.

But a small but not dismissible part of it is another issue entirely. A thought that is running in a very deliberate and singular direction, one that always, always leads to Tom.

Because the thing about living with Tom is finding out the edges of him that I either didn't know when we were kids, or have developed since. Little tics, like how for some reason he always yawns loud enough to wake the dead ten seconds after getting into the shower, or how he'll absentmindedly tap the G key on his laptop keyboard when he's lost in thought. New habits, like making handmade pasta with some gadget his mom bought and forgot about, or staying up late into the night with his reading glasses on, poring over fantasy novels at his desk.

And knowing those things about him comes with even more surprise knowledge. Like that ten seconds *after* Tom steps out of the shower, his very well-toned stomach and broad shoulders are on full and dripping display in the apartment hallway. Or how he'll tap the G key long enough that the rest of him will get restless and he'll give his exaggeratedly long catlike stretch on the couch, his warm limbs grazing mine.

Like how he'll bite into that pasta and make that content "this thing I am eating is delicious" noise he's always made lower in his throat, a rumble that feels like it's stirring me from across the room.

Like how the other night I had a very, *very* vivid dream about walking into Tom's room, swiveling his desk chair toward me until he was blinking at me from behind those ridiculously endearing glasses, then kissing him so resolutely that I woke up with a sharp gasp and an embarrassing amount of sweat.

So yes. Sometimes it's hard to focus on writing. But that is surely a temporary technical difficulty, one that Luca's books will distract me from until it's fixed.

It's less likely to distract me from the absence of Vanessa, who seems to be as out of touch as my own mom. I just assumed that Tom was catching up with her while we were apart during the day—at least I did until the landline in Tom's apartment rang last night. I was certain it would be Vanessa checking in on us, and was already coming up with a way to extricate myself so they could have a moment alone, but Tom laughed and told me his mom never calls when she's on set. Sure enough, it was a fruit-basket delivery from one of the producers of Vanessa's latest released film, which apparently was up for some kind of scriptwriting award.

We were halfway into eating a giant pineapple shaped like a butterfly when I asked Tom point-blank, "Does your mom even know I'm here?"

"I hope so," said Tom, and I thought he was kidding until he added, "I texted her and left a voice mail. I've debated carrier pigeon just to be extra sure. So she probably knows, but maybe doesn't?"

I blinked at his tone, at the alarming ease in it.

"Does she just not pick up the phone?"

Tom shrugged. "If I really need to get in touch with her I

can call her assistant. But I'd only do that if there was an actual emergency."

I've known since I got to the city that Vanessa wasn't exactly gunning for Mom of the Year, but until then I didn't realize just how disconnected she was. For all my mom's grandstanding, I knew if I called her right now she'd pick up on the first ring.

"So when do you, like—talk to her?" I asked.

"Oh, you'll see when she gets back," said Tom, helping himself to another vaguely wildlife-shaped fruit. "She does parenthood like it's an Olympic sport and tries to cram a month's worth of it into a day. It's actually pretty funny. And definitely means we'll get taken to some kind of fancy lunch spot for steak."

It didn't sound funny at all, but we'd had such a fun day teaming up on a few of our nonoverlapping deliveries and planning how to go about our remaining Getaway List items that I didn't want to poke too many holes in him and ruin it.

"I shouldn't intrude on your guilt steak," I said instead.

"I am humbly begging you to intrude," said Tom. "That steak comes with a side of a hundred rapid-fire questions about what I've been 'up to,' and you're the only one I know who has half a chance of keeping up."

All this to say, my mom wasn't exactly wrong in emphasizing just how "unsupervised" we'd be when we last spoke. Our lives feel a little bit like one of those dystopian novels where all the adults disappear and the kids are left to run the show. And apparently, left to our own devices, Tom and I will do any number of reckless things like binge-watch reruns, take turns grocery shopping from the list we put up on the fridge, and commiserate over the unideal states of our relationships with our moms.

Not to be outdone by the recklessness of "lunner," during

which we order a literal tower of tater tots, chicken wings, potato skins, and french fries, and put ourselves into a food coma before most of New York is freed from their nine-to-fives.

"I am more potato than man now," Jesse declares, leaning back into the shiny blue booth we settled in earlier.

I take it upon myself to eat the last of the wings, since everyone else is out for the count. "That can be the band's new schtick. The first-ever potato front man."

"The first ever front man to fall asleep during their own show," says Jesse, referring to the band's gig tonight at a hotel rooftop lounge.

Mariella snaps in Jesse's face. "You are disrespecting the institution of lunner. We did this so we could go adventuring while the rest of the city is eating dinner, and also to sustain our organs until dinnert."

Luca blinks, then says, "Dinner dessert?" Which is encouraging if only because it means one of us still has a brain cell left. I'm pretty sure I dipped my last one in the ketchup twenty fries ago.

"Precisely," says Mariella. "I'm giving you all five minutes to digest and then we're up and at 'em."

Jesse has to duck out to prep for the show, but Mariella leads me and Luca down and across a few blocks to Chelsea Market. The area is teeming with groups of friends and families and dates walking up and down the stairs to the narrow, raised walkway of the High Line above us, but Mariella sweeps past them all and says, "We're going to Little Island."

"We're already on one, last I checked," I say in mild alarm.

But Luca perks up instantly and says, "I haven't been yet! I heard it's— *Whoa.*"

We cross the street and there, just off the Hudson River, is an island built with narrow pillars that bloom upward to create an insulated little world with all these different levels of compact, winding paths, bright flowers, and play structures. It looks deceptively tiny but once we cross the pedestrian bridge to get in, it feels like there are too many paths to decide on just one. Luca and Mariella are similarly overwhelmed, Mariella with her camera lenses and Luca with his notebook, which he's stopped dead in the middle of everything to start scrawling in.

"It's been two seconds and you're already spitting out a whole novel about this place?" Mariella teases, looking over his shoulder.

Luca beams and says, "I hope you get some good shots to send later. Otherwise I might just have to move here to keep soaking it in."

"Well, my shots aren't going to be half as good without your cute face in them. Stand there," Mariella demands, pointing at a cluster of bright flowers.

Aforementioned cute face instantly reddens like a five-alarm fire. "Oh, I don't want to—I mean, I'm not like—your shots will come out better without me in them, trust me."

Mariella puts an arm around Luca's shoulders and physically moves him over to the spot where she wants him to pose. "Aw, don't tell me you're camera shy, ace."

"I'm most objects shy," Luca bleats out.

Mariella stops him in place and puts a hand under his chin as if to pose him for an oil painting instead of a quick shot. Luca just watches her, transfixed, and lets her nudge him this way and that until she's satisfied.

"We'll work on that," she tells him with a smirk, lifting the camera up to her face. It's clear from the direction of the lens that there's not much other than Luca in the shot.

Luca blinks like he's forgotten not just the conversation that's happening but quite possibly his own first name. "Work on what?"

Taking this adorable exchange as a promising sign in Mariella and Luca's potential courtship, I wander off on my own, higher and higher up the little peak of the island until I can see the sweeping view of downtown Manhattan. It's a balmy night, the early-evening shade starting to cool off the heat of the sun, with a strange golden kind of magic seeping in between. I can't stare too long before I'm jostled by other people trying to get pictures, but there's this moment when I'm not just staring at the city but it feels like it's staring back at me. Like even stepping off it as far as this man-made island is far enough for me to understand the future ache of leaving it behind. Like I'm not just pushing myself into this place, but it's got ahold of me, and it's pulling me back.

Eventually we wander back up to the hotel rooftop where the Walking JED is performing. By then night's starting to fall and a cool breeze has settled in. I'm uncharacteristically quiet as we stand at the edge of the roof with our sodas — partially because Luca and Mariella are swapping stories about growing up on the Upper West Side versus in the East Village that have all three of us in stitches, but also because it feels like the words are stunned out of me. Like I'm coming up on some kind of understanding about this place and the person I am in it. Or rather, the person I'm *not*. Like somehow being here has done nothing to clarify what I want to do or who I want to be, but has opened so many doors to possibilities that I feel like I can safely shut the ones that made me unhappy for good. Like New York isn't a place where I have to make myself fit, but a place so constantly shifting that I'll fit in anywhere, if I'm willing to leave the old possibilities behind.

It's not just the city, though, but the people in it. It's Mariella with her tongue sticking out in concentration as she tries to get good angles for shots of the band. It's Luca with his legal pad stuffed to the brim with words poking out of his bag as he bops along to the music. It's Jesse and Eddie and Dai sweat-soaked and grinning into each other's faces, giving every inch of themselves to the crowd like they're playing Madison Square Garden instead of a rooftop with a cluster of tourists who seem surprised but pleased to have stumbled on it.

It's the way none of us really know what we're doing yet, but the city is such a wide, forgiving canvas that it doesn't matter. There's magic here. Too much of it to walk away from so soon.

"Hey, you."

Tom settles an arm around my waist instead of his usual hug and pulls me in, and I'm so deep in my thoughts that there's this fleeting moment it all feels so natural—Tom being at my side, me leaning into him after a long day of missing him—that when I tilt my head up to meet his eye, I almost kiss him. It's reflexive. Easy, even. Like I'm the Riley I was in that dream, and Tom is mine to kiss without thinking.

Tom pulls in a quick breath and I come back to myself in a searing instant. I look away fast before he can see the embarrassment in my face, before either of us have to cop to what I almost did. His hand stays on my waist, steadying me. There's this quick little pulse of his fingers just above my hip that feels almost like a quiet forgiveness, or maybe something else.

I let myself lean into him, almost to prove a point to myself. That it won't have any effect on me, and the almost-kiss was just a fluke. Except my body fits so easily into Tom's, like the seams of me were perfectly formed to fit into his, that it feels like I'm the universe's favorite new joke.

I'm expecting either one of us to say something, but we just stay standing in our own little bubble, not quite on the edge of the pandemonium. We stay long enough that I don't just feel the electricity of it, I feel the warmth grounded under it. The understanding that these past four years have been rocky in a lot of ways, but that the worst of it is behind us. No matter what we are to each other, we'll never be apart like that again.

Tom pulls me in lightly, just enough that I almost forget to breathe, and says, "What's on your mind?"

I could tell him any number of things. *I missed you today*, because even though I should have had my fill of him by now, it's true. *I have no idea what's next, and it's the happiest I've ever been*, because the thrill of it doesn't know how to settle in me, and maybe never will.

I could even tell him the loudest truth of all, the one that was only a seed when I got on the bus up here and is quickly outgrowing the girl I was, starting a life of its own: I want to stay here. Not for a weekend, not for a summer, but as long as New York will have me. Maybe I don't know what for yet, but I'd rather be running toward the unknown here than standing still anywhere else.

It's too soon to say any of that yet. I don't want to go into it thoughtlessly, the way I have with too many things these past few years of drifting through my life. This decision almost feels like the way we made the Getaway List and held on to it for so long, making the intentions behind it all so much more special—for the first time in a while, I care enough about something to let it settle, to make a plan.

So instead of telling him any of that, I tilt my head up to look at him with a close-lipped smile. He smiles one back, so conspiratorial that it's as if he heard every thought I had out loud just the same.

"Everything," I tell him happily.

Tom smiles back and I feel the beginnings of that plan starting to snap into place. A room in an apartment of my own, enough gigs to support myself with, an independence that's so thrilling and terrifying that it feels like something electric I can reach out and touch.

But I tuck that something away for the night, if only to keep up with our usual brand of unmitigated chaos. It's all of us cat-calling and wolf-whistling Jesse and the rest of the band when they meet us on the street later, acting like paparazzi until they're blushing so hard that Dai shoves his head into Jesse's back to avoid looking at any of us and Jesse playfully wrestles him back into our spotlight with a lanky arm around his shoulders. It's Luca and Mariella debating the best late-night spots for "dinnert," which results in ice-cream sundaes on a bench at midnight, watching people head in for the night as another crowd starts to head out for the start of it. It's Tom sharing some of his weirdest dispatch stories and keeping all of us in stitches with his wry delivery.

I'm in a happy daze, my knees hiked up on a bench outside the ice-cream shop with my back pressed into Tom's shoulder, the rest of us similarly tangled and splayed out with our empty cups, when Mariella nudges me with her foot. "You're quiet."

"Nah," says Tom. "She's everything."

I nod sagely, spreading my arms wide just as a cool summer breeze hits us. "That I am."

"Damn, what'd they put in your sundae?" Dai asks from the other side of Jesse. Out of the corner of my eye I can see they've migrated closer to each other, with Dai's hand not quite resting on Jesse's knee. "Because I want some."

"Realms of possibility," I say with a grin.

I feel the faint twitch of Tom's shoulder laughing from under me. My grin widens but my eyes close and I breathe it all in—the buzz of everyone talking, the sweet smell of vanilla in the air, the warmth of our cocoon of friendship—hoping that no matter how long I stay in this city, I never take moments like this for granted. Ones where I have nowhere to be, so I finally have the chance to be exactly where I'm meant to be instead.

As if on cue, my phone hums in my pocket. I know there's only one person it can be. My mom's text is short but cuts straight through the haze: Call me. We need to discuss when you're coming home.

# Chapter Twelve

There are a lot of things I should probably figure out before committing to moving to an entire city, including and not limited to finding a place to live and somehow telling my mom in a way that doesn't feel like I'm actively pouring gas on the "your daughter ran off to New York City" fire. What happens instead is the moment I get home after making the decision, I open my computer to the blank Google doc, and write.

And write. And write. And write and write and write, and then write some more.

The Google doc turns into a browser full of so many tabs that my laptop might as well be a clown car, for all the fictional characters it's holding. There's the short story I had an idea for two years ago when Tom and I were supposed to go camping with friends and we all vowed to have spooky ghost stories to tell. There's the idea I've been playing around with in my head for a Tides of Time fanfiction where Claire decides to transfer to their rival time school in another universe, and how it affects everything that happens in canon. There're a few of the prompts Luca filled in based on the vintage tabloid articles on the walls of the restaurant and Mariella's pictures of Little Island. There's nothing fully formed enough to do anything with, but I don't care. They're something more important than that. They're *mine*.

The next few days I feel less like a person and more like a supernova. Like I finally destroyed whatever was holding me back, and now there are all these new universes sprouting up in its place and I really am Claire, hopping from realm to realm not with a time stone but the flick of a browser tab. I never know what I'll be in the mood to write when I sit down, but I'm never not in the mood to write *something*. It feels like an adventure inside an adventure—I spend all day biking around New York where every few blocks shifts into a different world, then all night living in the different worlds inside my own head.

Incidentally, I'm busier than I've ever been. Between delivery shifts and writing and quietly piecing together a plan for what I'd do to support myself living here long-term, there's barely a free moment of the day. But it isn't draining like it was in high school. It's electric and energizing, like I'm taking a bite out of the world and now that I know how good it tastes I just want to gobble up even more.

As firm as I am in my resolve to stay, I find myself stopping just short of every step. I'll start an email to someone looking for a subletter beginning in mid-August, but won't hit SEND. I'll look at the round-trip bus tickets to and from Virginia I'll need to buy to go back and get my stuff, but don't add them to the cart. I almost tell Tom a dozen times, but the words dissolve on my tongue. Eventually it becomes clear that I'm waiting on something that I can't put in an Excel sheet or hear from my friends. I can't ignore her text any longer. I need to call my mom.

It's not that I need her permission to do this. I'm past that now, whether I want to be or not. But I want her blessing, or if not that, then at least her understanding. I may want a life different from hers, but she's my mom. I can't help that her opinion still feels like the one that matters most.

I decide to wait until Friday afternoon when Tom is out for a delivery shift to take a walk and make the call. Right as I'm about to head outside, I get another ping to accept a delivery from the "Dear, Love" Dispatch. Hesitating, I tap the ACCEPT button, agreeing on a meetup time in front of the building in a half hour. I figure either the call will be disastrously short and I'll make it in time, or maybe my mom and I will actually catch up, and I can use the interruption as an excuse to tell her all about my mysterious deliveries.

I hit the CALL button and when she picks up on the first ring, the way I knew she would, all the words I had planned to say rattle out of my head onto the sidewalk. I can barely open my mouth, my throat stupidly clogged just from the relief of hearing her voice.

"Riley?"

It takes me a second, only because the last thing I want to do is sound choked up and set off every parental alarm bell in her head.

"Hey," I say. And then because I apparently have the social skills of an eighties radio DJ reject, I add, "How's tricks?"

My mom's quiet for a moment, too. Then she says in a too-bright version of her usual voice, "Well—you know. Shop's busy in the summer."

"Right," I say, my voice also up half an octave.

Another beat. Shit. I'm not sure whose turn it is to talk next, like it's a play and we've both forgotten our lines.

"I've missed you," says my mom.

"Yeah," I say, feeling relief flood through me so fast that

my hand flies to the back of my neck like I have to contain it. "Missed you, too."

The silence that follows is a short one, but no less excruciating for it. It's my mom. I've never not known what to say to her before. It's unnerving how so little time can pass but so much can shift in it that we almost feel like strangers.

"How are your . . . tricks?" my mom asks.

Her voice is just wry enough for me to relax a notch. "Good," I say. "I'm, uh—really getting into the swing of things. You know that delivery service I was going to do with Tom that summer? They took me on. Yesterday I biked forty whole miles."

"That's—" My mom pauses. "During the daytime, right? And with a helmet?"

"Yeah," I say, so effusively I'm nodding into the phone. "Tom taught me the ropes."

"Did he?" my mom asks, her voice tight.

All right, hard pivot on the Tom talk, then. "And I, uh—I took a writing class," I try instead. "And made a few friends here. We've been going to Jesse's shows and thrift shopping and hanging out in the park a lot."

"Well, that sounds nice," says my mom.

I wait for a moment, but there aren't any follow-up questions. I clear my throat. "So I know you weren't here for long, but—I was wondering if, uh—if you had any good picnic spots? Or thrift shops that might still be around? My friend lives in the East Village like you did. I bet there are a ton of places you liked that are still down there."

"When are you coming home?"

My stomach drops. Hard pivot on the "try to make her reminisce" talk, too, then. There's really nothing I can say here except the thing I called to say in the first place, which is so simple that I didn't bother rehearsing it in my head. A decision

I am sorely regretting when I open my mouth and all that comes out is, "Um, so."

"So?" my mom echoes.

My mouth is still open, but all the bravado has leaked out of me. I feel like I'm ten again. Worse—I feel like I did all through high school, when my mom took the reins and I didn't question it because it was easier not to push back. I used to think we never fought because we were so close. Now that we're on the brink of another fight, I realize it's just because I always rolled over before any could start.

"Riley," my mom says, with just enough warning in it that I know I better spit it out fast if I have a chance of saying it at all.

"I was thinking I might stay. Like—past the summer, I mean."

My mom answers so fast that I realize she must have expected the call to take this turn long before I decided to make it. "Is that what Tom's trying to get you to do?"

"What?" I stammer, nearly stopping dead on the sidewalk. I glance back reflexively at the apartment building. "No. I haven't—he doesn't even know I'm thinking of staying."

"So that has nothing to do with him," says my mom.

I'm almost too stunned to be mad, but I get there in the end. "It doesn't," I say, the words steely. "Why is it that you think every decision I make this summer comes right back to Tom?"

"Well, who else would it come down to?"

"*Me*," I blurt, with so much anger in my voice that a group of pigeons, the most unflappable animal on earth, gust away in shock. I pull off to the edge of the sidewalk, pressing the phone to my cheek and saying into it, "And you, too. You spent all these years trying to keep me out of trouble but you kept me out of the whole *world*. And I have it now, and these are my choices. This is what I want when I get to choose. I want the same things you did. How can you be mad at me for that?"

"This whole thing feels like an overreaction," says my mom. "You're upset with me. I hear you. But instead of talking about it you just up and left, and you're not ready for this like you think you are."

My eyes sting, because I know there's some truth to that and I don't want to hear it right now. Especially when there doesn't feel like much point in talking about it, seeing as I can't change the past. I can only change the future, and she doesn't like my version of that, either.

"And you were?" I say instead. "You think the aunts didn't tell me everything? You didn't even bother going to your own graduation before you took off. You were fighting with your parents all the time—"

"Exactly. Because I wasn't ready. That's what I'm trying to tell you, and why I don't want us to have the exact same fight."

"This isn't me fighting you, this is me *telling* you. Me trying to get you to understand."

"All right, I'm listening," my mom challenges me. "Give me one good reason why you are staying in New York, of all places, where you have no family, no plan, and no experience with the real world to rely on yet. Go on."

I have so many reasons. Reasons that I was excited to share with her. I've spent the last few weeks firming up such a strong sense of myself in this place that it seemed impossible that she wouldn't be able to sense the change in me, that she wouldn't want to hear me out. That she wouldn't recognize some part of her own self at my age and try to understand.

But even if I had the confidence left to tell her, I can tell she doesn't have the patience to listen. I can practically feel her poking holes into words I haven't said yet, and I can't let that happen. My life finally feels like it's *mine*, and it's all still too fragile and new to let her pick it apart. Like it's taking shape but it hasn't taken root.

I thought maybe she could help me find those roots. My whole life my mom has felt like gravity to me. The one place I've always felt settled and known. But now I'm something she doesn't recognize, something that can't be grounded the same way, and the worst part is I think it's just as scary for her as it is for me and neither of us knows what to do about it.

"You lived here once," I say quietly. "You *know* why."

My mom lowers her own voice in turn. "And it's because of that I know you're making a mistake. About to make one, at least. It's not too late to change your mind about this. I'm here when you do."

"And if I don't?" I ask. "What then, you'll just be mad at me forever?"

"I'm not mad, Riley. I'm worried. I'm trying to give you space here so you can work this out for yourself, but you should be *home*. Getting ready to start classes and save your money and build a life. If you're so set on this then you can wait for it. The city will still be there when you're done."

I shake my head, glad that she can't see me, because it's more for myself than for her. A reminder that I've already wasted enough time waiting. I've seen what my life could look like cast in all these new colors, and I can't go back to the gray.

"Just think about it, okay?" my mom asks.

I backslide then only because I don't know what else to do. I don't want to end this call on the same terms we ended the last one. I don't want another few weeks to go by without us saying a word to each other. Tom may be my best friend, and I may have plenty of others to rely on, but there's nothing in the world that compares to the comfort of knowing and being known by my mom.

"All right," I say. "I'll think about it."

It works, because after that we talk. Like, *actually* talk. She tells me about drama between the coeds at the coffee shop and the summer courses she's taking before she finishes up her degree next semester. I tell her about some of the more romantic deliveries I've been a part of, like the old couple who keep sending each other fries from different delis every week, knowing that she'll appreciate those stories more than the wackier ones. We talk long enough that she has to leave because her lunch break is probably long since over. We both say "I love you," but there's a resigned weight in the way she says it. Like she's worried this call is the last of its kind.

I swallow thickly when we hang up and have to swipe at my eyes fast. Apparently my tear ducts were just waiting for the second the connection dropped, which, honestly, good for them. Maybe I only have half a backbone about my decisions, but at least I didn't get sabotaged by my own waterworks.

I sink into one of the benches in the closed-off courtyard outside Tom's place and let myself blink a few more tears out as the reality of the situation makes itself clear. I have a choice here. New York or my mom. It seems suddenly impossible to have them both. But every time I try to settle on a decision—stay here with this life I'm building for myself, or go home to the person who is the only life I've known—I start crying all over again for the part that gets lost along with whichever I choose.

My phone pings just before the same dispatcher who keeps getting saddled with all our deliveries arrives. "You again," he says, as I jolt up straight from the bench. He winces when he registers the tears, then says with his usual born-and-bred New Yorker candor, "Shit. I'm starting to feel like I'm an extra in you guys' soap opera."

I let out a wet laugh and take the paper bag from him. "Watch it, or I'll anonymously send someone a pile of bricks and make you take them all the way to Brooklyn."

"It would still be less weird than the single hunk of cheese."

Once he's off I take a moment to collect myself before looking down into the paper bag. Inside there's a bound notebook with a solid brown leather cover. I pull it out and see all the pages are delightfully blank—no lines, no structure in place. But as I flip to the first page I see there's something written in ink.

*For your realms of possibilities,* it reads.

This time when a tear falls, it's with a sweet kind of ache, one that starts in my chest and swells everywhere else. It's not the gravity I was hoping for, but it's enough. It's like someone sent me a piece of myself, and now that it's here in my hands it has the weight I need to keep myself steady, to keep my resolve. I may be new here, but I'm known.

I close the notebook carefully and set it back in the bag. For once I know I'm not going to tell anybody else about this delivery. I don't want to wonder about that mystery anymore. Not when this gift is so personal, so *me*, that it might break my heart a little if it didn't come from the one person I'm hoping it did.

The truth is it doesn't really matter. Because of all the things I didn't say to my mom just now, I got to say the most important of all: being here is my choice. And from here on out, so is everything else.

# Chapter Thirteen

"Okay, we have a moral responsibility to other New Yorkers to leave *some* candy in this store," I say to Jesse and Tom, who have a cart so full to the brim with it that we're going to need a magic carpet to carry it home.

Jesse bops me on the head with a bag of Twizzlers and says, "You need the extra sustenance. It's not every day a girl turns sixteen twice."

"I beg you to stop saying that. I've worked so hard to repress those memories. You're going to make them fester in my bones."

Tom looks mildly concerned as he also disobeys me by adding a box of Oreos to the cart. "You guys looked like you were having fun in all the karaoke photos from the party."

"Because it *was* fun," Jesse says, and then backtracks: "Well, as fun as it can be without the vocal stylings of Tom Whitz."

Tom nods and gives a gracious little bow, knowing full well that his vocal stylings are about on par with a dying cat's. It's the only part of the whole "re-create Riley's sixteenth birthday party" thing I'm looking forward to tonight. At some point we're going to get Tom amped enough to do a rendition of "Before He Cheats" so unholy that somewhere in the world Carrie Underwood will flinch without knowing why.

Actually, I'm hoping to get him to do another song, too. But I'm not sure if he'd even remember the gist of it, let alone the elaborate series of dance moves along with it, so I've mostly been focused on the snack heist.

"That reminds me," says Tom, skimming the aisles. "Better grab everyone some earplugs."

I lightly swat at him, then turn back to Jesse. "Maybe it was fun for *you*. I had just made the mistake of getting blunt bangs I had no idea how to style *and* wearing combat boots that gave me blisters the size of the moon *and* was—"

Crying a whole lot, if I'm being honest, because we only found out a few hours before the party that Tom wasn't going to be able to come. I forgot how worked up I'd gotten about the whole thing. How I didn't even care so much about the party itself as I cared about finally getting to see Tom, because at that point it had been just over a year. Back when the Getaway List was something we were adding to in earnest, never imagining we weren't even halfway into our separation.

That time it wasn't even my mom's fault. Vanessa was going to take a road trip to her next film set in Florida and drop Tom off in Virginia on the way down. Only that afternoon she found out they needed her immediately, so she took a flight down and took Tom with her. My mom had just let me open the combat boots early and done me up in a fresh face of glittery makeup for the party when I got his call from the taxi on the way to the airport, and even though I held it together while he told me, I was a mess of bright blue eyeshadow streaks and snot within a minute of hanging up.

I pulled it together for the party an hour later—about fifteen of us rented a karaoke room for the night and brought a bunch of snacks—but the whole time I was singing *High School Musical* throwbacks and sucking on Atomic FireBalls, I just sort of wished it was over. I didn't feel like celebrating anymore. I had one wish, really, something that shouldn't have even been a *wish* so much as a given, and it hadn't come true.

What happened instead was it got added to the Getaway List, same as all the other missed chances. We wrote it down as "go to karaoke." What we *didn't* write was "semitraumatize Riley by re-creating her sweet sixteen two years later, while also unearthing the pictures of the terrible bangs everyone tried to talk her out of but she was determined to get."

Alas, that is how Jesse and Tom interpreted it, and Mariella and Luca were more than happy to get on board.

"And was what?" Tom asks.

"Awkward as all fuck, I'm sure," I mumble, because Tom's got enough of a self-inflicted guilt complex to know I openly wept about missing him when Jesse got lawless enough to put the ten-minute version of "All Too Well" on that night.

"All right," says Jesse, surveying our cart. "I think that ought to do it. At least for now. You still on for getting the rest of the camp supplies tomorrow?"

I nod, grateful for the change in topic to the part of the weekend I'm actually excited for. Everyone took this weekend off work, so we're knocking two items off the Getaway List back-to-back—Friday is karaoke night, and then Saturday we're going to take the train upstate to a campground and pitch some tents to stay overnight to make up for the camping trip we were supposed to go on junior year. Our plan is haphazard at best, but between Luca's experience camping, Mariella's parents' camping gear, and Tom's mom-adjacent paranoia, I'm pretty sure we'll be fine.

Unless Jesse and I forget the s'mores supplies, which is probably grounds for leaving us out in the wild as bear food.

"Good," says Jesse. "I feel like we haven't had any time to catch up yet."

This is an unfortunate truth that is only getting truthier by the day, and not for lack of trying. Between Jesse's shows and my shifts we haven't had a chance to catch each other one-on-one yet. And the way Jesse's looking at me with a hint of that same uncertainty he had in the park a while back, I can tell it's less about the guitar playing and flyer making we were going to do, and more about something else.

Tom dips back into the candy aisle so I lean against the cart and say to Jesse, "Yeah. I've been meaning to ask, how's the band adjusting?"

He shifts his weight to his other foot and says, "Good, good, good. Busy. Going through a lot of peanut-butter jars. Also we all just gave up on keeping them separate and decided all socks are everyone's socks." He shows me one blue-striped-clad ankle and a wooly brown one, which I somehow missed with the rest of his mismatched-but-in-a-cool-way getup today.

"So everyone's getting along in cramped quarters?" I ask.

Jesse goes entirely pink before ducking down to a lower shelf with alarming speed to examine the laundry detergent at his feet. "Yeah," he says. "Peachy. Like you and Tom."

Now I'm turning pink because there's a slight edge in Jesse's voice and I'm wondering if the two of us just accidentally touched a nerve here. The unspoken "what's going on with Jesse and Dai" line rubbing right along the "what's going on with Tom and Riley" one, both of which we have diligently avoided, even if Mariella certainly has not. I think her precise words when the two of us got lunch yesterday were "There's enough sexual tension between the four of you to crack this island in half."

The imminent destruction of Manhattan aside, whatever these feelings for Tom are that I'm contending with, I'm squashing them down nice and tight for now. It's not just because of all my mom's cryptic opinions on the matter. It's that before I even examine those feelings, I want to be set in my plan to move to the city. Set enough that I can tell Tom about it before I tell him anything else.

And that's the plan—to tell him after we get back from karaoke tonight. I've already taken a good look at my savings and calculated how much money I'll make if I keep doing the delivery service and get a job as a barista up here, and done the math on how much I can afford to pay for rent with roommates and what neighborhoods I can start looking in. I'll stay at Tom's through early August like we initially planned, but after that I'll move into a place of my own. Start looking into classes I can take on my own terms. Make my own schedule. Live my own life.

If something else happens between me and Tom after everything gets squared away—well. I don't want to look that far ahead just yet. It feels like everything is too jumbled right now. I've been so absorbed in my stories and my planning that I haven't come up for air long enough to examine the strange new friction of loving Tom as a best friend and biologically responding to him as a something else entirely. I don't even know what I'm feeling, let alone any idea what he might.

So I dismiss that whole train of thought in favor of another, which is that Jesse and Dai are one moony-eyed look away from someone screaming "JUST KISS ALREADY!" during one of their shows, but have done everything just short of it. Everyone in the band is very publicly out and their families and friends have always been supportive, so all I can think is there's some unspoken punk-rock rule against band fraternizing I don't know about. Or maybe they *are* together, and Jesse somehow hasn't hired a plane to announce it in skywriting like he nearly has anytime he's dated someone.

Tom returns then with a slight frown.

"Oh no," I deadpan. "They didn't have a sixth flavor of Oreo?"

Tom shakes his head. "Just one other thing I was looking for," he says, "but maybe we can find some on the way."

He reaches forward then and suddenly, unexpectedly settles his hand on the crook of my neck. I lean into it without thinking as Tom's thumb grazes my collarbone, his eyes settled on a spot just above it.

I stop breathing and we both go very, very still until Tom clears his throat.

"You've got some . . ."

He eases his hand away to show me. There's a streak of bright green chalk on the pad of his thumb, and a warmth on my neck where his hand was that's spreading all around me, a slow inferno.

"Right," I manage. "I, uh—biked past a big chalk mural in Union Square. They were letting anyone grab a piece and join in."

Tom smiles and there's something so unmistakably fond in it that the heat in me is starting to simmer, like it's planning on sticking around.

"You always know where the action is, huh?" he says, before abruptly reaching up and rubbing the chalk from his finger on the tip of my nose.

"Hey!" I protest as his smile hooks into a smirk, and he makes off with the cart toward the register.

"Don't worry," he calls back, "it suits you."

It decidedly does not, but something pleases me about it so much that I don't make any move to smudge it off for the rest of the day.

# Chapter Fourteen

A few hours later Jesse, Tom, and I have ducked up the slim stairwell to the karaoke joint in the East Village that he and the band slept in the night they got locked out. It's deceptively larger on the inside, dim, blue-lit hallways thrumming to disjointed beats that swell and muffle every time someone opens or closes a door. We don't have to wait long until Mariella and Luca arrive together, which is not too surprising—she told me the two of them were going to check out some street art in Bushwick. What is surprising is that Mariella seems uncharacteristically subdued, her eyes grazing the floor, and Luca is looking around at all of us with mild "help me" eyes.

When I glance over at Tom, his eyes are already on me with the same unease brewing in them.

Mariella's managed to smile by the time we're looking back, though. "Is this a birthday party, or are we luring Hansel and Gretel to their deaths?" she asks, looking at the mountain of candy on the table with the binders full of songs.

"Neither of the above. This is, in fact, a ritualistic humiliation of Tom Whitz, who needs at least three Take 5 bars in his system before he'll let loose enough for Disney karaoke," I say, hoping to get a laugh out of her.

But Mariella's already distracted again, aiming a pointed look at Tom that I can't quite read. I take this as a sign I should leave Tom on Mariella detail, seeing as she's still technically more his friend than mine.

"Hey, I think I'm gonna grab some soda from the bar. Anybody want some?" I ask, and then without waiting for anyone to answer, I say, "Luca?"

"Yes, yeah," he says, following me out.

I don't have to wait too long until we're out of earshot, considering a group is screaming Miley Cyrus's "The Climb" loud enough to wake the dead down the hall.

"So did I imagine the weird vibes when you and Mariella walked in?" I ask.

"No," says Luca, half-relieved and half-miserable to be asked. He fiddles with his watch, staring back at the door to our room. "I think she's mad at me? And I don't know why, which is bad because I say a lot of things, so I can't figure out which thing might be the one she got mad at? But whatever it was I think it was from some other day, because she was like that when we met up."

"Then it's probably got nothing to do with you," I say fast, because Luca looks like he's one thought spiral away from drilling a hole in the floor.

"Or maybe it does and I can't figure it out because I'm a monster."

I pat him comfortingly on the shoulder and say, "All right, that's a little dramatic, even for a writer."

Luca's spirits lift marginally at that. While we're waiting for the bartender to finish pouring an alarming number of lemon drop shots for a bachelor party to get to our sodas, I peel off to figure out where the bathrooms are and see just how deep the hallways in this place go. I don't make it very far before I hear familiar voices coming from a small lounge area at the end of the hall.

"I don't know why you checked in the first place."

Tom sounds not quite upset, but definitely exasperated, which gives me immediate pause.

"What, and you've never been curious?" Mariella asks back.

"Not enough to go looking at it," says Tom. "And I kind of wish you hadn't told me you did."

"Well, shit," says Mariella. And then: "Wait, that's an actual notification. You'd better get that."

A cluster of bachelor-party revelers erupts into laughter then, loud enough to make me hightail it out of the hallway before Tom or Mariella notice me lurking in the corner of it. I hadn't meant to eavesdrop—I'd never know anyone's gossip if I had my way—but now that I have I feel like the words are ricocheting through my head like a pinball machine.

It isn't just the question of what Mariella checked, or why Tom would be upset with her for it, but the sense that this is an extension of a conversation they've already been having. Something I've been kept in the dark about. And while I know I'm not entitled to anyone's business, I can't help the uneasy sense that whatever this business is, it's got something to do with me.

I manage to shake it off by the time I make my way back into the karaoke room, where Jesse's got the song binder splayed on his lap.

"Okay. Things are weirdly bleak out there," I report. "We need to liven things up."

"Well, there goes my plan to make us sing every song from

*Les Mis* in order," says Jesse. "But don't worry, I queued up 'Mr. Brightside' and 'Truth Hurts' and like half of *1989*, so we're good."

"Excellent. Also I need everyone to agree that when we throw Tom the mic during 'Let It Go,' nobody helps him."

"I'll be too busy recording it." Jesse sets down the remote for the song queue and glances at the door. "Actually, I had something to run past you."

"Yeah?"

Jesse nods, then takes a quick breath like he's steeling himself and says, "Ever since we broke up, I—"

I don't even have time to register the surprise of those words before Luca comes back with arms precariously full of soda and wide eyes and says, "Get this—a bunch of Mariella and Tom's classmates are in the room next to ours. One of them is about to leave for Harvard? They're, uh, very intimidating."

Shit. I forgot about the sodas. Also double shit, because if these are the classmates that made Mariella's life a living hell, her night is only about to get worse.

As soon as Luca's hands are free of the sodas Jesse gives him the other mic. "Not as intimidating as you're about to be duetting 'A Whole New World' with me."

I meet Jesse's eye as he nudges Luca closer to the screen and he shrugs at me like he didn't just leave a sentence hanging in the most cryptic way possible, but there's really not much to be done for it anyway, because another few seconds later Tom is walking back into the room frowning at a box in his hand. In the maelstrom of "what is going on with literally every person in our friend group right now," I almost don't notice that it's not just any box.

"Atomic FireBalls!" I blurt. "Where did you find these?"

"I didn't," says Tom. "Actually, these were what I was looking for earlier. But someone sent them anonymously just now."

"Why would someone send you Riley's birthday candy?" Jesse asks.

This was from a running joke that I'm surprised Jesse remembers, if only because we were so fixated on the singing (and for me, the not crying) that night to remember that there was, in fact, a "theme." I thought Sweet Sixteen sounded ridiculous so I decided it would be Spicy Sixteen, and we'd all dress in red and orange and eat spicy pepperoni pizza and Atomic FireBalls. It was both a delicious and aesthetically pleasing decision.

"Beats me," says Tom, handing me the box. "But extremely belated happy birthday."

As I take it from him I search his face for some remnant of the hallway conversation, but don't find any. "Where's Mariella?" I ask.

Right on cue the door swings open and Mariella says, "Well, Gunner and his pack of goons are getting wasted in the room next door. Someone better queue me up Olivia Rodrigo because I'm gonna blast them sky-high."

I walk over to her and say, "Hey, there are, like, ten bajillion karaoke spots downtown, right? We can always move."

Mariella grabs a Twizzler from the table and bites into it with her back molar. "Nah I guess everyone's all good with me now," she says with an eye roll. "One of them just tried to hug me. I might need you to check me for fleas."

Approximately none of this bodes well for the rest of the night, but when I look over at Tom he's frowning into his phone. I glance back at Mariella, who obtained her own soda, apparently, and is taking a large swig of it, and then back to Luca and Jesse, who are vibing so hard to their fake magic-carpet ride that they've each gotten on one knee as if to re-create it in all of its animated glory.

All right, then. The solution is clear. Less talking and more pumping karaoke songs through the speakers, and everyone will loosen up and be just fine.

Sure enough within a half hour we've all assumed our various karaoke roles. Jesse serves as the DJ, Tom as the hype man, Luca as the unabashed ham, and Mariella as the actual pipes—Jesse is so impressed that I wouldn't be entirely surprised if there wasn't some kind of Walking JED collab proposed by the end of the night. I'm a little bit of everything, joining in on the group numbers, jumping on the adrenaline of our favorite bops and an abundance of Atomic FireBalls, standing on the worn-out couch to get aerial footage of everyone losing their marbles during "Bohemian Rhapsody."

I flop back at the end of that one, sweaty and exhausted, and give a little "oof" as Tom rocks the couch by flopping directly next to me. We're both boneless and happy when he turns his head to mine and says, "You better have some energy left for the next number."

I'm about to declare my plans to burrow into this couch with the open box of Chips Ahoy! for the next five when I hear an electronic piano chime a distinctive few notes. My eyes widen so fast that Tom laughs at me, pulling himself up and wrapping his hands around my forearms to sweep me up to my feet as easily as a gust of wind.

"You can't be serious," I say.

Tom hasn't let me go, squeezing his grip on me, his eyes light with mischief. "Riley Larson. Will you do me the dishonor of this truly horrifying dance?"

In the periphery I can sense the confused amusement of the rest of the group, which is fair. This song is so niche that I'm surprised the place even had it in the karaoke binder. See, proving that there is no brand of nerd quite as aggressive as the Tides of Time fandom, we kind of accidentally collectively wrote a song.

It started with a scene in the sixth book. The characters traveled to the distant future where they went to a "Museum of the Past" that was really just our present, and every artifact and exhibit they stumbled upon hilariously garbled its "history." There was a "typical American dinner," which was a turkey stuffed to the brim with mac and cheese and potatoes and cranberry sauce. There were a bunch of mannequins in a chaotic mash-up of fashion through the decades that only Jesse would be able to believably pull off. Most notably there was what the heroine, Claire, and her friends dubbed "The Worst Song Ever Written"—a combination of country, techno, rap, pop, opera, and jazz, as if they shoved every musical genre into a jar, shook it, left it on the road to get run over by a truck, and shook it again for good measure.

Naturally fans took to the internet to create their own version, and enough people collaborated on it that one unholy definitive version stuck. A version that is currently about to blast through this entire room and spend the next two minutes and fifteen seconds scarring all of its occupants for life, because fans made a whole routine to it, too.

I squeeze Tom's arms back and say, "Yes. A thousand times yes. My whole life was just a buildup to this humiliating moment now."

Tom grins widely as he lets me go to walk to the space in front of the screen. I reach for a soda and Mariella says quickly, "No, wait, that one's mine," pulling it from my grasp fast enough that it spills over a bit.

"Oh, sorry." I find my own and take a long swig of it before settling in next to Tom. "All right, anyone who values their limbs is gonna need to give us an extremely wide berth."

Tom extends his hand to me just as the song kicks off and pulls me into him with a spin so satisfyingly sharp and steady that it suctions some of the air out of my lungs.

This is, of course, the first and last graceful dance move the song has to offer. The rest of it demands that we leapfrog over each other during a verse where the singer just goes, "Health insurance! Capitalism! Everything is bad" in a jazzy swoop underlaid with a country guitar plucking; that I jump on Tom's back while he extends his hands like a crosswalk safety guard and spins during a brief interlude that's just someone blowing the same note on a harmonica over and over again; and that we crab walk on the floor around each other during an operatic verse mashing up "Itsy Bitsy Spider" and "Twinkle, Twinkle Little Star" with no regard for rhythmic structures or the human ear.

Ostensibly we are supposed to be singing, too, but I doubt our lungs or our friends' brains could come back from that.

We end the song half stumbling, grinning into each other's faces, finishing off the long dissonant closing chords with our own grand finale: the very complicated series of nonsense gestures that was our secret handshake. We end with our thumbs pressed to our noses and hands splayed out as usual, but so enthusiastically that our chins nearly bump into each other, that there's a not-at-all subtle voice in the back of my head egging me on to get even closer, just to see what might happen if I did.

As it turns out we're so breathless with laughter by then that I can barely hold myself up. We end up colliding with each other, half-intentionally and half-not, until Tom turns it into an embrace by wrapping his arms around me and pulling me in so tight that my feet leave the floor. He spins me around for good measure and I hook my arms around him tight, breathing him in, trying somehow to pull him even closer to me even though we're as close as two sweaty, panting bodies can get.

I'm dizzy when he sets me down, but doesn't let me go. His hands are still on my waist, his fingers digging into the thin fabric of my shirt, and his face—

I realize in that moment why it's so easy to tease Tom for being beautiful. It's because anybody can see that about him. It's the first thing you notice about Tom; it's been true every single day of his life.

But very few people will ever see Tom like this—that beautiful face of his split wide open in a grin, hazel eyes brimming with happiness and crackling with mischief, cheeks flushed all the way to his hair. He spends so much of his life composed for other people's sake, but there's nothing like being one of few people who gets to see him completely undone.

Like being one of the people who has the satisfaction to undo him.

Tom takes his hands off me only to skim his fingertips just above my ears and through my hair, his eyes teasing. I realize as he smooths it down that my hair has all but evicted the scrunchie from my head. I roll my eyes even though my skin is tingling in every place his fingers roam, even though I'm leaning into his touch without even fully meaning to, like we're the only ones in the room.

"Worth the wait?" he asks me, so low I can barely hear it over the sound of the next song starting to play.

*No*, I want to tell him.

I've read so many stories about magic. Made up plenty of my own. But I don't think I understood the heart of it, really—that I couldn't until this moment now, standing on the other side of the most magical few minutes of my life.

It wasn't worth the wait, because there shouldn't have been any waiting at all. We've had these stolen few weeks, these past few minutes, when we deserved years. So much wasted time, but for once I'm not sad about it. Not angry or frustrated or stuck. It feels like a new understanding has shifted in me, and instead of being upset for the time we lost, I suddenly can't bear to think of taking any of the time we have for granted.

I suddenly can't imagine a world where I don't tell Tom that I love him, every way I've ever known him and every way I ever will.

Something in my face must give way, because Tom's own expression softens, his eyes settling on mine. I hold his gaze and know it has to be soon. Maybe not tonight, when I tell him I'm staying, but soon.

"Tommy boy, your phone's blowing up," Mariella announces.

Tom doesn't seem surprised by this, his eyes still trained on me. "I'll get to it," he says.

It's strange, but the idea of telling him doesn't scare me. It's Tom. Even if he doesn't want me the same way I want him, I know I'll never lose him. The worst of what could happen to us is already in the past. So maybe my heart will break a little bit, but at least I will always have Tom in my corner—at least I'll always have this person I trust above everyone else, who knows me better than anyone in the world.

"It's about the bug I fixed," says Mariella, stirring me out of my thoughts. "Well, it might be unfixed now. Shit. My bad. I could hop back in now, but I've never fixed an app bug drunk before."

Tom eases his hands off me and I feel strangely cold without them. So much that it takes me a moment to register what Mariella just said.

Luca beats me to it, lowering the mic he just picked up from the table. "You're drunk?"

"Bug for what?" says Jesse.

Mariella holds Tom's phone to him. "For the 'Dear, Love' Dispatch. It was bugging all morning before I fixed it."

"Mariella," says Tom. There's a warning in his voice, but a slight resignation, too. Like whatever's about to happen, he's already a few seconds ahead of it, anticipating the blow.

He's right to, because she doesn't hear him over the sound of me turning to her and saying, "Wait, since when do you work on the app?"

Mariella frowns. "Since Tom asked me to build it," she says, as if this is obvious.

The room goes very quiet. Scratch that—the room goes very quiet, save for the clunky karaoke-version of the opening chords to "Let It Go," and Mariella glancing at Tom and saying quietly, "Wait. Shit."

Luca sets the mic down, laughing nervously. "The way you said that almost sounds like you and Tom made the dispatch app."

And then I'm not looking at Luca and the mic, or Mariella and her boozy soda, or Jesse, who's gone very quiet in the corner. I'm looking at Tom, who is looking down at his feet and pulling in a long, slow breath.

"I'm sorry," says Mariella. I can already hear the tears clogging her throat. "Fuck. I'm sorry."

"It's okay," says Tom, even though it clearly isn't. Even though he won't meet my eye, which suddenly gives this whole scene an out-of-body quality, like I stepped into a weird dream. The tinny Elsa harmonies whining "I am one with the wind and sky" from the machine are doing nothing to help matters.

It's Luca, surprisingly, who breaks the silence again, just as Mariella presses her eyes into her palms, clearly trying not to cry.

"I think I should get Mariella home," he says.

He sits down on the couch and puts a tentative arm around her, and she shakes her head but leans into it.

"I better fix whatever this is," Tom mumbles, half-heartedly holding up his phone. "I'll be right outside."

Tom's eyes barely graze mine before he goes, too fast for me to read them. Luca leads Mariella just after, leaving me and

Jesse to start cleaning up the mountain of snacks left behind. We load up the bags without saying anything to each other, listening to the bass beats of other people's songs bouncing dully off the walls.

"We can take everyone back to our place if you want," says Jesse. "It's not far."

I shake my head. I open my mouth to say something but stop just short of it. It feels like all the words have been stunned out of me.

"I'm sure he had a good reason. It's Tom," says Jesse.

If anything this only makes the urge to cry even stronger, so much that I feel like I'm sixteen again, swallowing down tears over Tom in a karaoke room just like this.

Jesse puts a hand on my shoulder. "Offer still stands. The Walking JED always has a Riley-sized spot on the couch."

I manage to look up and smile in his direction, guilt mingling with my hurt. I've been so busy I haven't even seen the band's place yet. And Jesse clearly has issues of his own he wants to talk through.

"Thanks," I say, putting a hand on top of his and squeezing, too. "But do me a favor, will you? Don't ever let me turn sixteen again."

Jesse lets out a laugh. "Deal."

With that I swallow down just enough of the strange, misplaced hurt to pull myself together, grab the last of our stuff, and follow Tom and his secrets out into the night.

# *Chapter Fifteen*

Tom and I are quiet the entire subway ride back to his place, but not for lack of Tom trying. I can't talk to him yet, though. It feels like there are two different voices in my head, one a hum, the other a slither: *I love him, I love him, I love him,* says one. And then just under it: *He lied.*

I'm not angry, but I can't decide if it's because I shouldn't be or because I haven't fully wrapped my head around it yet. It's like there are two different Toms in my head—the one I trusted, and the one I'm not sure if I can—and I don't know which one is in front of me.

The moment we emerge up the station's stairs to the street, Tom slows his pace and says, "Riley." My name half plea, half apology in his mouth.

I shake my head even as I slow my pace, too. Tom drifts off to the benches by the museum and I follow him there but don't sit. I just hover there with no idea what to ask, no idea where to start. The hurt is too unsettled, brimming just under my skin like it doesn't know what shape to take yet.

"I'm so sorry," says Tom.

And he means it. I can hear the sincerity of it in his voice, feel the weight of it in his eyes. The thing is I don't think either of us quite knows what he's sorry for yet, because I still have no idea why he did it.

"If you started this it must have been—what, two years ago?" I finally ask.

My voice is surprisingly calm.

"Yeah," says Tom. "I didn't mean to keep it from you. It wasn't meant to be like that. It was just—I came up with the idea and Mariella took off with it, and it all happened quickly."

"Two years ago," I repeat.

Tom swallows hard. "I made the app when things were just—kind of at their worst. When I felt so separate from everything here and didn't feel like it would ever change. I just wasn't really talking to anyone at the time." He lowers his voice. "I felt like if I told you I made the service I'd have to tell you the rest. And I didn't want to."

I search his face, seeing the guilt that lines his features and wishing I weren't so upset with him. The last thing I want to do is make Tom feel any worse, but if we're going to get past this, I need to understand.

"I already knew something was wrong. And I could get over you not telling me that, because I get it. I felt the same way. I didn't want to be the Riley high school turned me into either," I remind him. "But shit. You *did* tell me about the app. Everything about it, just short of the most important thing, which is that it came from you."

I think of all the countless snippets of conversation between us, not just back and forth over text the past few years, but face-to-face these past few weeks. All the nights he spent sitting next to me on the couch on the laptop that he must have been using to work on the app. All the dispatches he took me on knowing full well he was the eyes and ears behind it, and I was totally in the dark.

Tom has made me feel so many things in my life—brave. Understood. Loved. But now that another thought is occurring to me, for the first time I wonder if he'll make me feel like a fool.

"Does this mean you know who sends things?" I ask. Maybe I've been gabbing all up and down the city about the mysterious admirer sending me things when it wasn't a mystery to Tom at all.

"No," says Tom quickly. "Mariella keeps the backend anonymous. I don't know who sent you anything, same as I don't know who's been sending me things."

This comes with yet another unexpected sting, because Tom not knowing who sent anything is a final blow to that tiny, ridiculous hope that it might have been him. I think of the notebook I have tucked away at the bottom of my bag right now, the one I haven't written in yet because I was too busy pulling everything together this week, and feel my stomach churn with an embarrassment so immediate that it makes me feel like a little kid. I'm glad at least that I never mentioned it to Tom.

"Were you just never going to tell me?"

Tom takes a small step back from me. "The thing was—I wasn't planning on saying anything this summer at all, because I didn't know we'd be together," he admits. "And then you were here and it all just kind of got away from me."

"That still doesn't explain why you wouldn't have told me now, Tom. I know about how things were for you these past few years. It's not like there's anything left to hide." I take a step back of my own, this one larger, with intention. "I mean, it's *me*," I say, my voice cracking.

Tom looks at me then with such regret that it feels like it splintered in him, too. "I know. I know," he says quietly, reassuringly. He lifts his arms up a fraction, like he's going to reach for me but thinks better of it. "It wasn't anything to do with you. The truth is I didn't want to say anything because it's not going to be mine anymore. I'm looking for someone else to run it."

I shake my head. "Why? Because of school?" I ask. But no—that can't be right. Tom's taking a gap year.

Tom worries on his lower lip. He's only quiet for a few beats, but I feel every inch of the tension in them just the same.

"Because I'm leaving New York."

The words feel like a cartoon piano falling from the sky. Like they're just as ridiculous and incomprehensible, but still hold an impossible, crushing weight.

"What?" I manage.

Tom's voice is so resigned that I get the sense he's been waiting to break this news to me for a while now. "After you head home, I'm taking a job with my aunt in North Carolina."

It's been so long since I've thought of Tom's aunt that it takes me a second to conjure a mental image. She runs a small winery way out in the middle of nowhere that's quite literally called Ornery Bitch Vines, and with good reason. She's about as kind as a cactus is to a bare foot.

"When did you decide this?" I ask numbly.

Tom lifts a hand to the back of his neck, tightly threading his fingers through his hair. "Actually, I was going to leave the day you got here. The backpack on my bed—it wasn't because I came back from a trip. I was packed to leave."

"And then I showed up," I say, strangely hollow.

I blink myself back to that day, to those full first few of

them. There were a lot of questions I thought to ask him, but apparently I should have asked him more. I'm suddenly just as frustrated at myself as I am with him—I knew something wasn't right. Something beyond Tom's new shyness or the mysterious gap year or his mom being so busy.

The truth is I don't know Tom as well as I think I do. Not just because I didn't see the signs well enough to dig for Tom's secrets, but because Tom had one this big in the first place.

"Leaving the city is kind of why I made the app in the first place. I was feeling so cut off from everything and so out of place here, and my mom—well, you've seen the apartment," he says, gesturing upward. He's kept himself together for most of this conversation, probably for my own sake, but I can see him unraveling now. There's something wobbling in his expression, an unsteadiness just underneath every word he speaks. "Everything's like that now. We went from living in the suburbs to living in this high-rise and going to fancy restaurants with famous people and traveling all over the world without a moment's notice, and I just—I don't recognize any part of my old life, and I've hated every second of it. I wanted something that was just mine."

The same pang of recognition aches in my chest. The one I felt when Mariella was talking about taking up photography on her own; the one I've felt for so many years that it feels like a separate organ in me, like another beating heart. This yearning to have a life that's just mine, with untouchable things in it.

"I figured if the app did well, then I'd have my own money to leave," says Tom. "It just felt important that I did it on my own."

Something cracks in my heart then, because I know Tom's lying about this, too. More to himself than to me. Tom could have done anything to make money to leave. Whatever reason he had for making the app, that wasn't it.

"You could have told me all of this," I say instead. I'm hurt, but not accusatory. Just genuinely confused. It's not like Tom had anything to be embarrassed about. None of this has ever been in his control.

Tom doesn't speak for a long moment, like he's trying to figure out how to say it. "I just—it was all so weird. I feel like an asshole about how much I've hated all this. So guilty I didn't think I had a right to feel that way at all. I didn't think you'd understand."

My eyes sting immediately, more out of frustration than anything. That Tom would think that about me, of all people. That I'd ever see him as anything but himself no matter the circumstances, and be able to understand because of that alone.

"Maybe I'm not—getting yanked onto planes and rubbing elbows with famous Chrises, but of course I'd understand," I tell him. "I mean, shit, Tom. I told you. I told you how controlling my mom was, how I didn't have anything that felt like my old life anymore. I know exactly what it means to want one that's just yours. That's why I'm *here*."

I take a deep breath, trying to ground myself again. I shouldn't have said that just then, maybe. It's not what Tom needs to hear or what I really need him to understand.

"And even if that wasn't true—I'm your best friend," I say. "It's my job to try to understand."

Tom leans in and says quietly, "I didn't know. You didn't tell me much about that stuff with your mom at the time."

"Well, when the hell was I supposed to?" I ask, the words unexpectedly sharp on the tip of my teeth. "It was hard enough to get you to answer a single text."

And there it is. The truth is I've been lying to myself, too. Telling myself that it didn't hurt, the past few months Tom spent shutting me out and how I had to pry myself back in. That it doesn't hurt now, realizing he was still shutting me out in a way I couldn't have seen coming. But it did, and it does, and it's going to take more than a few weeks of us being friends again to get over it. Especially now that it's somehow worse.

"I know. I know," says Tom again, his voice hoarse with feeling. It means more than an apology, hearing him say that, but it also hurts more, too. Like we're acknowledging out loud that we're at a level beyond apology, one that's deeper than we've ever been. "It's been a long day. Let's head up for the night and talk inside."

Tom shifts in the direction of home, but I stay rooted to the cement.

"I'm going to spend the night with the band."

I say the words as gently as I can, but Tom's eyes immediately water anyway. He swallows them down and nods.

"All right," he says. "Let me take you there at least."

I shake my head. "I just need to be away from you for a little bit, okay?"

He looks down at the ground fast, but not before I see the hurt flash across his face. Like I reached into his rib cage and wrung out his heart.

The thing is I already feel too much of that same hurt to account for his. Because it occurs to me as I reach up and throw an arm around him—the quickest, loosest excuse for a hug either of us has ever given—that I was wrong. Tom doesn't feel the same way I feel about him. He spent years hiding the biggest thing he has going on in his life. He made all these plans to leave without even telling me about them. He didn't consider me in any of his plans; he didn't even consider my thoughts on any of it important enough to clue me in.

It's not just that I was wrong. It's that my mom was right. It's that there's nobody else in the world I want to talk to more than her right now, and I know I can't. Not if I want to look like I'm in control of my life, like I know what I'm doing out here.

One call to her about Tom and I'm scared she'll see it as proof that the whole thing is falling apart.

I wonder for a moment if it is. My throat is so tight it feels like a bottle top on a shaken soda, like all the words I planned on saying to him tonight are trapped in my chest, threatening to spill out of me. I don't let them. It isn't the time to tell him about staying, and as for the rest—there's probably never a time now.

I release Tom fast and duck back down into the subway without looking back.

I let myself cry a few tears on the subway platform. A woman hands me a tissue without breaking her stride. It's all very New York, I think, this feeling of being lonelier and less known than ever but being in a city teeming with people who have all felt shades of the same thing. The subway train feels like a strange safe haven from my thoughts, lulling me into a calm with its newly familiar rocking and whining, with these strangers who shoot me sympathetic glances that all seem to say, *Been there, publicly cried about that.*

There's a deeper comfort in it all that I can't fully process until I've stepped back out of the subway and back into the crowded, warm city night, the current of people swallowing me up with the same ease as ever. That for all my hurt over Tom, for all the heartbreak I know is just on the horizon, I feel more certain than ever that this is where I belong.

I've mostly pulled myself together by the time Jesse's opening the door to me, revealing not just Eddie and Dai but a giant pepperoni pizza on the coffee table.

Jesse leans in and hugs me hard. "We saved you a slice."

"Thanks," I say, squeezing him back. "I'm just gonna go wash up."

I see it on my face just as the old lights in the bathroom flicker on—the faint green chalk still on the tip of my nose.

I skim my thumb over it, thinking of the fond look on Tom's face when he smudged it there, of the electricity in his eyes when he pulled me in to dance, of the heat radiating between us when he held me just after. Of the near-smug certainty I had in thinking I had nothing to worry about, telling Tom how I felt about him. How I still feel, despite everything.

I smudge the green off. All these feelings—my love for the city, for the life I'm building here, for Tom—are all so new and flashy and bright. I should have known that some of it wasn't built to last.

# Chapter Sixteen

When I wake up on the couch the window is cracked open, and I can see the back of Jesse sitting on the fire escape. I rub my swollen eyes to wake myself up, then make us both cups of instant coffee in mismatched mugs in the kitchen and join him out there.

He gives me a sleepy smile. He doesn't look very punk rock right now with his mop of bed head and his sleep shirt and a pair of sweatpants with our school's infamous earthworm screen-printed on the pocket. More like the little-kid version of himself he was back in elementary school, before he told his parents he would be dressing himself from now on, thank you very much, and promptly showed up to school the next day in a Snuggie. (At least his parents were amused, even if the principal was not.)

"How'd you sleep?" Jesse asks.

"Like a rock," I say honestly. It was like my bones were too tired to process being a human anymore. "You?"

"Also like a rock. If the rock was in a volcanic explosion, that is."

I wince as I settle down next to him, the fire escape creaking slightly and deeply uncomfortable against my butt, but otherwise sturdy enough to hold us. It's quiet down below, a sharp contrast to the lively bar scene we could hear outside their window all night when we were up eating pizza and watching Eddie and Dai attempt to demolish each other in some video game. Now it's just early-morning joggers and a slow-moving line outside the bagel shop below.

"You've had something on your mind, huh?" I say to Jesse.

He smiles wryly into his coffee mug. "Yeah. This feels like the incorrect time to pick your brain about it, though."

"Nonsense," I tell him. "My brain is extremely pickable right now."

I mean it. The last thing I want to do is think about the conversation I had with Tom last night, because I still have so many unfinished thoughts and unanswered questions about it that I can't risk following any of them too far down right now.

Jesse's still staring at his coffee, considering. "Well. First of all, I should come clean about something."

"If you're about to make me an accomplice in a murder can I at least finish my coffee first?"

Jesse loosens up a bit at that, leaning farther into the brick wall. "I was the one who sent you those wildflowers."

I blink. "Wait, really?"

"I thought maybe then you'd make the connection about the song? The, uh. The 'Wildflower' one we sang the first night we were all here," says Jesse, uncharacteristically self-conscious. "It was about you."

Before I can even process what he's said, a string of the catchy lyrics swims through my head: *You're every season, always*

*in bloom, you've got every color living in you / Forget where I'm
planted, I'll follow you, you're a wildflower, always in bloom.*

I feel my face start to flush—feel a lot of questions and
thoughts coming on—but none as relevant as this: "When you
introduced that song you said you wrote it two years ago."

Jesse clears his throat. "Yeah, well." He nudges someone's
abandoned cigarette butt with his slipper. "Two years ago I still
wasn't quite over you."

"But," I start, and then stop. Jesse doesn't need my help to
do the math on that. We stopped dating two years before that
song was written. Which might mean something I'm hoping
it doesn't.

Jesse's eyes are rueful when I lift mine to meet his.

"Jesse," I say, not sure what's hitting me harder, the confusion or the guilt.

He lifts a hand up. "Hey, I knew what I was getting into.
You're a heartbreaker, Riley Larson," he says with a quirk of a
smile, as if to play it off.

"I'm not." I set my mug down, pressing my palm to my forehead as if it can make me process this faster. "Oh, shit. Jesse.
I'm so sorry. I really didn't know."

"I know," says Jesse quickly. "It's not—I'm not upset with
you. The whole thing was more my fault than yours, really.
Looking back I get the sense that it was like—you weren't in it
the way I was. And why would you be? I never said anything.
If I had then you would've known."

I run a hand through the tangle of my hair, trying hard to
put myself in past me's shoes. It only makes the guilt in my
chest widen. That year feels like all the others in high school—
like a Band-Aid that got ripped off so fast that I didn't feel the
*ouch* of it until it was already over. So fast that in retrospect, I
was barely considering anybody else.

"I guess it's just been on my mind lately, now that we're

hanging out more again," says Jesse. "Enough that I felt like I had to pull that song out, and send those flowers anonymously. Like getting some closure by doing some of the stuff I probably should have done when we were actually together, you know?"

I'm about to protest, but the way Jesse's blinking with hesitation it's clear that he has more to say first. When he does his voice is so thin it feels like it's evaporating in the air between us.

"When we broke up, was it—something I did?" he asks. "Or was there some way it would have been different?"

"Oh, Jesse," I say, feeling like something in my chest is crumbling. I lean in so fast that the fire escape gives an unholy *creeeak* beneath us. "Fuck. No. You're one of my best friends. I love every second of hanging out with you. I really just—I had no idea you ever wondered that or I would have said that a hundred thousand times, directly into your ear. Announced it on the damn loudspeaker at school."

Jesse laughs and says, "All right, all right."

"I mean it," I say effusively. "And as for breaking up—I feel terrible. I really thought it was mutual. This is a shit excuse, but—on my end it felt almost like we hadn't really started dating in the first place. It didn't seem like there was an ending to it so much because we never really said anything when it began."

Jesse nods in agreement. "Yeah. I think it was just—I really, really liked you. More than I knew how to deal with or express at the time. So I just didn't. And then one day after Christmas break someone called me your boyfriend in the hallway and I heard you say that we'd been broken up for weeks, and I just— guess I hadn't really realized it was over, until then?"

My throat isn't just tight with guilt then, but something else—a sudden surge of gratitude that we managed to stay friends through this. I don't know if a lot of people would have, after such a mess.

"I'm sorry," I say. "I think I just took it all for granted. We were so close that I figured we'd always be around for each other no matter what we were, that I just sort of thought it didn't matter if we weren't 'dating' anymore. But clearly it did, and I'm a shit friend for not realizing that."

Jesse shakes his head. "It's not your fault," he reiterates.

"Fuck that," I say teasingly. "Let me have some blame, will you?"

His lips lift into a slight smile, but his eyes are staring through the grates of the fire escape and down the narrow street.

"Where is this coming from?" I ask. "I mean—the flowers were beautiful. The song—I don't even know what to say. But I think it's safe to say you don't have those kinds of feelings for me anymore."

Jesse sets his own mug down then, and goes quiet for long enough that we can hear the disjointed sounds of the city slowly, creakingly start to wake itself up. Sidewalk cellar doors opening and dogs barking and delivery trucks ambling down the street.

"I'm in love with Dai," he says.

I bite down a smile but can't stop it from reaching my eyes. When Jesse meets them he can't help a shy smile of his own.

"I, for one, am absolutely shocked," I deadpan.

"Shut up," he mumbles. But then after a moment, he says, "The thing is—Dai is my best friend. And you were my best friend when we started going out. So it made it hard to wrap my head around it when it just—ended, I guess. Because we knew each other better than almost anyone, and it didn't take anything for it to just be over."

I want so badly to reach out and hug him right now. And maybe build a time machine and rattle both of our baby selves by their lanky little shoulders. But Jesse's letting something out of his system right now, and it's clear it needs to be all the way out before we can try for any of that.

"I've seen other people since you and I dated, but—none I was especially close to beforehand. So this is scary to me. I guess I've just been afraid. Trying again with someone I'm that close to, and having someone who knows me—*really* knows me—reject me if I muck it all up again, like I did with us."

The worst part of this is the way Jesse can deflect almost anything he says with a joke, but can't even try for one now. I don't have to do that thing where I look past the joke to see what he really means. It's all there, bare and raw on his face, cast in golden pinks from the early-morning sunlight.

I make myself think carefully before I speak, because I want the words to land.

"You didn't muck anything up between us. We're still here together, aren't we? That's all because of you. You helped inspire me to do this and I'm so fucking grateful for it every day." I scoot my butt a little closer to him, lowering my voice. "And as for Dai—I don't think you have to worry. It's clear how much he likes you. Hell, Eddie stabbed his avatar like eighteen times because Dai couldn't stop staring at you after you took your damn shirt off last night. And Dai always laughs *way* too hard even at your worst jokes."

"Hey," Jesse mock-protests.

I kick him lightly in the shin. "I'm only allowed to say that because we were the two biggest clowns at Falls Creek High. Anyway, the most important thing is—things are different now. You're different now. I know you'll be able to make Dai understand what this means to you. I mean, you just told me what he means to you, didn't you? Tell him the same thing."

Jesse purses his lips like he's trying not to get overly emotional, but that's too bad. We're in for emotions now. So I add, "Don't let fourteen-year-old Riley being a total dope get in the way of eighteen-year-old Jesse dating his extremely hot best friend."

This seems to be the perfect compromise between keeping it light and letting Jesse feel the impact of it, because he lets out a wet, stuttering laugh, swiping his eyes with the heel of his hand.

"Yeah. Okay. You're right."

"Hell yeah, I am," I say, holding up my coffee mug. "Now let's cheers to you actually fessing up to Dai sometime in the immediate future, all right?"

Jesse holds his mug up, too, but hesitates.

"What if . . ." he starts.

I shake my head so abruptly that it stuns whatever Jesse was about to say right out of him. "Your worst-case scenario is a great scenario. You stay friends. Like you and me." I point a finger at him. "The only actual worst-case scenario is you never telling him how you feel and having to live in the abyss of *what if* for as long as you're alive."

Jesse clinks his mug with mine, and as we each take a long swig of our coffee, I try not to let the irony leave a bitter taste knowing that I'm not planning to say a word to Tom about my own feelings.

My hypocrisy feels justified, though. Tom is leaving. A fact is a fact, no matter how badly I want to un-fact it. If I tell him how I feel now, I'm worried it'll only come off as a ploy to make him stay. I could never do that to him. As upset as I am, it doesn't change that for him, leaving New York is my version of staying here—a chance to start fresh, and on our own terms. I could never deny him the same happiness I've already found.

"All right. Thank you," says Jesse sincerely. And then, with every bit as much sincerity: "Also, let's go the fuck back to sleep."

I shove the window to the apartment back open. "Count me in."

# Chapter Seventeen

By the time we all crawl back out of bed around eleven in the morning, it's clear that the camping trip isn't happening tonight. We all would have needed to be on the train with camping gear and supplies in hand within two hours, and the group chat might as well have crickets chirping in it, for all the effort we're making to set that in motion. The only text on my phone is from Mariella: Can we meet up? I can come to you.

I explain that I'm actually not far since I'm at Jesse's, to which she responds with three "yikes" emojis, which pretty much covers it. A half hour later I'm at Mariella's place, a cozy apartment that faces an inner courtyard, sparing it from the noise down below. I catch her parents on their way out the door, clad in running gear that includes belts full of enough of those energy-goop packets that I'm not uncertain they're leaving for an apocalypse.

Her mom's smile is as full-cheeked and broad as Mariella's when she instantly clocks me as "Tom's friend Riley" and pulls me in for a warm hug. I sink into it gratefully—at her tiny height it's nothing like a hug from my own mom, but it's the closest I've come in weeks and I don't know how much I need it until her mom is giving me an extra little squeeze like she knows it, too.

"Are you one of the kids our Mariella's been running ragged with deliveries?" her surprisingly tall dad asks. He must have clocked the "Dear, Love" Dispatch hat I am wearing to cover up some gravity-defying bed head.

"Sure am," I confirm.

I assume he means the deliveries from her secret admirers, only her mom adds, "The whole idea is just so sweet. And the coding so advanced!" Her mom taps a finger on top of Mariella's nose. "You should be putting that app on resumes."

I raise an eyebrow at Mariella. If her parents didn't already know about it, then I guess the cat of her being involved in the app isn't just out of the bag but fully wandering around the city now. She gives me a rueful smile back and then rushes her parents out "before you embarrass me any more thoroughly than your matching T-shirts," which do in fact both say VROOM VROOM, VASQUEZ on the back in what appears to be Comic Sans.

"They're training for a marathon together, it's gag-me cute," Mariella explains, letting me inside and leading me from the front entry into the small kitchen.

It's sun-dappled and cozy, with a yellow-tile backsplash and little flower accents on the teakettle, on the cups, on the little tea-bag rest. Along the walls are mismatched, framed family photos of Mariella's parents on either side of her in all her different iterations—little-kid Mariella in princess pajamas, middle-school Mariella in a glittery party dress, Mariella beaming with her diploma.

I linger on what must be a recent one of Mariella in a

bright purple bathing suit at the beach, surrounded by a cluster of kids of various ages all clinging to one another, some midlaugh, some midscowl, all in motion.

"My cousins. We go to Puerto Rico every year," she explains. "My parents met here, but grandparents on both sides are still over there, plus some of my aunts and uncles."

"What time of year do you go?"

"End of August. When you're leaving." She cuts a quick, knowing glance at me from the little kitchen. "Allegedly."

I bite down a smile even if I don't cop to it just yet. Mariella may be back to her ordinary sunny self, but I can see she's every bit as worn out as Jesse and I were during our fire-escape talk this morning. It's clear she wants to get last night off her chest.

Sure enough, when I look up from the photo, she turns to me and says abruptly, "So I fucked up hard."

Mariella says this while offering me a cupcake, which is a deeply unnecessary gesture, although an appreciated one. What the Walking JED have in talent they severely lack in their ability to stock a pantry, so I'm hungry enough to eat her kitchen table.

"I know you didn't mean anything by it," I say carefully.

Mariella sinks onto one of the stools by the little kitchen island, propping her elbows on the counter and planting her face in her palms. "Yeah, well. You have full license to be pissed. I'm sure Tom is, too."

I sidestep this because I'm not sure how Tom feels about it. "I'm not," I say, and I mean it. "It was going to come out eventually. I'm more worried about you. You were upset yesterday."

"A smidge," she says ruefully.

"Did something happen with Luca?"

She momentarily buries her face in her hands, embarrassed. When she pokes back out of them she says, "Well, something happened with everything? Not to excuse my idiocy, but to paint a picture for you, the whole day was a self-sabotage snowball. Yesterday morning my parents were planning this year's trip back, and everyone there is so proud of this whole 'computer nerd in the family' thing that they were suddenly getting on my case about wanting me to tell everyone I was still studying next semester so nobody would think I wasn't their nerdy little golden child anymore. And I was like, 'I'm an adult, mind your business,' blah blah, the works. So apparently that conversation wasn't put to bed after all, which, you know. Cute."

"Oh, shit," I say.

She lifts her hands in a "what can you do" type gesture, then says, "So I was already in a mood and figured, why not make it worse? So then I did something stupid and—" She winces. "Well, Tom's told you by now that I set up the backend of the app, right?"

"Among plenty of other things," I say. It occurs to me that if Tom was trying to find someone else to run the "Dear, Love" Dispatch that Mariella has likely known he's planning to leave, too. I'm not sure if that's another secret I can swallow after all this.

"All right, well, then he also told you it was supposed to be anonymous even to us, but I was already upset and feeling reckless so I looked up Luca's number in it before I met up with him yesterday. It turns out his phone number was connected to yours, which means he's sent you something through the dispatch, which of course I reacted to with all the maturity of a sleep-deprived toddler."

My eyebrows shoot up in surprise. I know Mariella put him as an early contender for the mysterious admirer sending things, but I dismissed the idea as soon as it came up. Luca certainly never said anything to indicate he might have, and

Luca seems about as incapable of keeping a secret as a Times Square billboard.

So which one was he, then? The random hunk of cheese or the notebook that I've been opening and skimming my fingers along the edges of, reading the inscription of over and over again, scoring into my heart? They came one after the other, after Jesse sent his—is it possible that he's both?

Before I can think to ask, Mariella adds miserably, "Which would have been bad on its own except—well—the kids from our school who were at the karaoke place last night were the same ones who were so shitty to me about that app. And they were all drunk and being buddy-buddy with me and I was a goddamn idiot and let them be? Like I guess even now it was such a relief to have them be *nice* to me that I just acted like it didn't matter that they threw me to the fucking wolves?"

"Shit," I say. In all the chaos it didn't occur to me that they might have gotten that far under her skin last night. But I guess given the history she had with them, it wouldn't have taken much.

"Yeah. Well. Just so I could make the backslide nice and thorough I let Gunner top off my Sprite. Hence why I was a drunk mess who was apparently determined to make a mess out of everyone else's night, too." She pulls in a deep breath. "None of which excuses me turning into a human wrecking ball, but you know. Context."

I put a hand on her elbow. "I'm sorry about your parents. And Luca. And the whole thing with your shitty ex-friends."

Mariella's eyes fill up with relief, like they were threatening to this entire time but she was holding it together for the apology. "Don't be sorry at me, I'm the one trying to be sorry at you," she complains, smiling at me.

I smile back, the last of the tension easing out of us both. I lean in and reach out for her and she nearly topples the chair over hugging me back with that surprisingly sharp squeeze for such a small person.

"I hated not telling you about the app," says Mariella into my ear, just before we let each other go. "Once I realized you didn't know I told Tom a zillion times how ridiculous he was being."

"Thank you for trying," I say. "It sucks he put you in that position in the first place."

Mariella waves a hand at this, clear that she was more worried for my sake than her own. "I'm sure he was going to tell you soon enough. What was he going to do, put a ski mask on if you ever wanted to meet your boss?"

I laugh out loud at the thought, simultaneously realizing Mariella must not know Tom is planning on leaving. I feel such a large rush of relief that I finally reach for the cupcake and take an inhumanly large bite, and fuck if every dessert isn't twice as good in this city than it is anywhere else.

"Well, at least he won't have to raid a sporting-goods store. We talked a bit last night. About why he kept it from me and all, and how it started," I say, nudging the cupcake toward her.

Mariella scoops some of the icing from the cupcake with the tip of her finger. "Yeah, well. Now you know why Tom and I were only kind of sort of friends when you got here. As gung ho as we both were about working on the app, I don't think a crowbar could have wrestled any personal information out of him aside from talking about you."

I feel another uneasy wave of confusion and guilt, the same kind that's been ebbing in and out of me like a tide all morning. It feels like it goes against everything in me, being upset with Tom when I know in my heart the last thing he ever wanted to do was hurt me. But knowing Tom could keep something like this from me also feels like it goes against the whole understanding of my world.

"Did he say anything about why he made the app in the first place?" I ask.

Mariella shrugs. "Honestly, I was more intrigued by the infamous school loner approaching me to ask too many questions. Felt like I was getting to ride out an eighties teen-movie cliché. And I was so burnt out and desperate for friends that Tom could have been a serial killer and I would have been like, you know what, at least I'll still have a buddy in comp sci for a few weeks before he harvests my organs."

"Always good to weigh the pros and cons," I agree.

She's smiling, but it softens a bit when she says, "Anyway. I'm sorry it came out the way it did. I'm sure he had a better way of telling you, but drunk me blew it sky-high."

I shake my head. "I'm not sure he did. So weirdly, I'm glad you spilled the beans. Better to know now than later."

I don't mention everything that hinges on that *later*—my being here, and Tom being about as far from here as he can get.

"Well, in that case, I'm glad something good came out of it," says Mariella wryly. She sinks a bit lower into her hands, her eyes flitting to the front door. "That and—well. It made me finally talk to my parents this morning about everything. Not just how serious I am about the app and coming up with other ideas on my own instead of going back to school, but some of the situation with Gunner's crowd. I just felt like maybe they'd be able to understand more where I was coming from on my plans for this year if they knew."

"Did it help?" I ask.

She nods carefully. "They were upset. But not for what I did. More just upset that it happened to me. And a little that I didn't tell them, so they couldn't help."

I think of my own mom then, of our last phone call. *Instead of talking about it you just up and left.* Maybe I can ignore all her warnings and rejections of my plans, but I can't dismiss that she's right about that. We never did talk about it.

"Ugh," I groan.

"What?" Mariella asks, half-amused, half-indignant.

I bury my face in my hands. "You're being all mature about talking to your parents about things and now I'm going to have to do that, too, huh?"

"Yeah. Shit. Evolving as a human is a bitch."

I know it's not just my mom I need to talk to, but Tom I need to hear out. There was more he wanted to say last night and I was too upset to listen. I don't regret leaving when I did, because it was too fresh to have a meaningful talk about it right on the heels of finding out. But I can't put it off, for both of our sakes.

It's strange—I got so used to Tom's silence over the past few years, but now even a day without speaking to him unsettles me. I hope no matter what happens on the other side of this that we don't fall into that pattern again. Yesterday I was so confident there was nothing that could happen to lose his friendship, and now it all feels just as fragile as it did before I came.

I reflexively look at my phone the way I did a thousand times over in high school, just hoping Tom might text me back. I don't have to hope though. There's already a message from him.

I know you know but I really am sorry. And also I miss you. I know you need some space but I just wanted you to know that, it reads.

"Tom?" Mariella asks.

"Yeah," I say thickly.

"I thought that might be why your face got all goopy."

I swipe the cupcake back from her, blushing reflexively. Blushing even though there's nothing to blush over anymore.

I type back, Miss you too. I have a delivery shift, but I'll see you tonight?

Tom types back, Sounds good. Stay safe. See you then.

"You know, goopy recognizes goopy. That face you make is the same way I feel about Luca."

I smile thinly. There's a moment when I consider asking Mariella something that I know is crossing a line but feel certain she'd do anyway—I consider asking her to hack into the app to find out for sure who sent what. Just to know for sure whether any of it was Tom or not.

But knowing won't change the fact of Tom leaving, or that I have feelings for him I don't think he'll ever return. Knowing can only make the hurt of all that worse.

"Tom and I are just friends," I say. I've spoken those words more times than I could possibly count, but it feels like the first time I've ever said them. I think it might be the first time I ever actually meant them—the first time I closed the door to any possibility of something more.

Mariella's smile is just as small as mine. "Yeah. I think Luca and I are the same. But last night when he was so nice and got me home and everything—I think I feel better about the idea of us not working out, because it reminded me that I'm lucky to have him as a friend in the first place. I mean, shit. All of us are lucky to have each other."

I feel myself getting a little choked up all over again, so I clear my throat and say, "At least until Tom harvests our organs."

Mariella sighs. "At least until then."

## Chapter Eighteen

When I get back to the apartment it's nearing eight o'clock and Tom is oddly nowhere in sight. I take a quick shower and wander over to the fridge, where I find the note scrawled in large letters on one of Vanessa's legal pads: *Meet me on the roof?*

I yank my wet hair back into a braid and shove on my flip-flops with my sweatpants and T-shirt. I haven't been on the roof before, but I've seen the door to the stairs at the end of the hall. Sure enough, it's one quick flight up before I'm pushing the door open to the balmy night air.

"Finally!" I hear Luca blurt out. "I thought she'd never get here!"

I blink and there, on the expanse of the roof, are Jesse, Mariella, and Luca standing around a giant, fully pitched neon-orange tent, a nest of sleeping bags, and a portable speaker that Jesse is clearly in command of, considering it is currently blasting a track from Taylor Swift's *evermore*. I take a surprised step forward and find Tom in front of a little heater, beside which sits a grocery bag full of marshmallows, graham crackers, and chocolate bars.

Tom spots me and the relief is so palpable in his face that for a moment I forget that his entire roof has been transformed into a teenybopper sleepaway camp. It takes everything in me not to cut past everyone directly to him, just to have him closer in my line of sight.

Well. So much for me being able to take this whole "having feelings for Tom" thing on the chin.

"What on earth is this?" I ask, a disbelieving grin curling on my face.

"We couldn't let a Getaway List item go unchecked," says Jesse. "We're all way too invested in this now."

"Also I came up with like, eight different ghost stories to try out on you guys," says Luca proudly. "I've rated them from 'mildly spooky' to 'potentially life-scarring,' depending on how grim we wanna get."

Mariella shrugs, eyes twinkling, and says, "I'm just here for the snacks."

I wander over to the middle of the roof where everything is set up, too impressed and overwhelmed to speak. Not a feeling I'm used to, with this mouth.

"Guys," I manage, looking at all of them in turn.

Jesse puts his hands up. "It was Tom's idea. He was the one who organized the whole thing."

"And obtained enough s'mores that I'm worried we created a city-wide shortage," says Mariella, holding up the bag as if to test the weight.

I smile at Tom and mouth the words "mom friend." He rolls his eyes but looks unmistakably pleased about it.

"Don't listen to them. They brought all the supplies," he says. "All I did was have a roof. I know it's not camping in the traditional sense, but—"

"It's perfect," I say firmly.

Tom holds my gaze for long enough that I see the same ache in it that I've felt all day. As grateful as I am for this camping Hail Mary, I can't help but wish we had a moment alone to talk. I'm worried if we spend the rest of the night pretending everything's fine we'll just start feeling like everything's fine, even when it's not. And if the past few years have taught me anything, it's that the issues we're glossing over only get wider the longer they're ignored.

Jesse abruptly clears his throat. "Anyway, now that you're here we're going to get the takeout."

"Oh. Do you need help?" I ask.

"Nope!" says Mariella firmly, following him to the door. "Luca and I are coming, too."

Luca looks surprised by this information but follows without question as Mariella gives me a pointed look, jerking her head toward Tom. I wait until the door shuts behind them to give Tom a wry look and say, "Wow. What a totally spontaneous and not-at-all orchestrated thing our friends just did, leaving the two of us alone on this roof."

Tom shakes his head in mild amusement. "I feel like I need to say I didn't ask them to do that, even if I'm glad they did. Assuming they didn't just lock the door behind them and leave us out here to rot."

He's sitting on top of one of the sleeping bags and sets a hand on it, gesturing for me to sit next to him. I do, even though it takes every bone in my body not to hug him as I'm doing it, if only to make up for the deeply unsatisfying one we hugged last.

"Hey," he says.

"Hey," I say back.

It feels more like coming home than walking into the apartment did. For a few moments after that we sit in silence, but it's a comfortable one. A "gathering our thoughts" kind of silence.

My eyes skim the makeshift campground as we ease back into each other, when an astronomy book by Tom's knee catches my eye.

"Is that a new one?" I ask. The cover is sleek and shiny and doesn't look anything like the ones with the dog-eared corners and beaten-up spines on his desk.

He picks it up and flips through a few of the pages. "Yeah. It came this morning, right before we were supposed to leave."

"Another dispatch?" I ask.

Tom nods, staring down at the book and then at me with the slightest wariness in his face. It occurs to me that it's not just me wondering if Tom has been sending me dispatches. Tom might be wondering the same thing about me.

"You don't know who's sending them," I say out loud, just to confirm.

Tom swallows. "I thought it would be weird to check."

I can't decide in that moment whether to tell him that it isn't me, because I can't tell whether he'd think it was a disappointment or a relief. I don't think I could handle interpreting either of those from him right now, so instead I let the unasked question hover between us until it gets swept up by a breeze.

I wonder who it is, then. If Tom has a sense for who it could be. If it's someone he knew from school or the dispatch service or traveling with Vanessa, someone Mariella might not have known about. Someone Tom has already held the face of in his hand, someone Tom has already wrapped an arm around the waist of and danced with and fallen asleep beside, same as he's done with me.

"Anyway—I guess it would have been handier for stargazing out in the woods," he says. "But maybe we'll see a few stars tonight. It's been a while since I bored everyone to tears with astronomical facts."

I feel a knot in my throat. When we initially were going

camping it was going to be at a grounds halfway between Virginia and New York the spring of junior year. It was meant to be an all-around reunion of sorts—not just for me and Tom but a cluster of our friends, too, Jesse included. I was so excited that I scraped some money together to buy a used telescope and spent the weeks leading up to it learning all the constellations Tom had memorized long before we even met, the ones he was always so excited to tell me the names of and the stories behind whenever we found ourselves out at night.

Ultimately I had to bail because my mom thought Vanessa would be chaperoning, and when it became clear she was in an uninterruptable "creative flow" and wouldn't be leaving New York, my mom said I couldn't go. I was devastated but told everyone to go on without me. Then Tom dropped out of it, too, so we missed out completely, stargazing and all.

Now someone else appreciates Tom enough to know his stars, someone I've never even met. I was planning on telling Tom about the constellations I'd learned, the maps of them I'd scored into my head, but the thought of it is almost humiliating now. Like I'd be showing too many of my cards when Tom's plans have already scattered the whole deck.

Tom nudges his shoulder against mine lightly and says, "You okay?"

I purse my lips. "You're leaving," is all I say back.

Tom gives a slow, quiet nod, staring out at the city past us. No matter how many times I see this view from his apartment it doesn't lose the ability to take my breath away. The strange infinity of it, how you can see forever and still see so many individual parts—every single one of those twinkling lights leading to a room full of people living lives just as complicated and exciting and routine as ours. It feels like holding entire worlds in the palm of your hand. It seems impossible to me that Tom would let it go.

"I feel like I should explain more why I didn't say anything about that either. The thing is, there's no real hard out for me going to North Carolina. I was worried if I told you that I planned to go that you'd feel like you couldn't stay. And I love having you here. I just wanted it to go on as long as it could. So I hope—I hope you're still planning to stay through August like you planned."

His voice is so unsteady by that last sentence that I understand this is what he's been worried about all day—that I wasn't just spending the night at Jesse's, but might decide to clear out entirely.

"I'm not going anywhere," I say sincerely. "I just don't understand why you are."

Tom nods, and I can feel the weight of his relief as he leans back so he's lying flat on the sleeping bag, looking up at the sky. I do the same. It's a familiar gesture from childhood. I lived in an apartment complex in the middle of town, but Tom's house was a few miles out, free from enough of the light pollution that we could make out planets and constellations, that during meteor showers we could pick out shooting stars.

"I remember the first time I looked up at the sky from here," he says after a few moments. "Realizing it wasn't my sky anymore. That everything was all—murky and unknown." He gestures upward, where we can faintly make out a few loose stars winking back at us. "Everything about this city has felt like that ever since. Like there are so few things I recognize in this place or even myself. And I want to be settled like I used to be."

"Tom," I say quietly. "I don't think anyone gets to be settled at our age. The whole point is everything being murky and unknown. I don't know if leaving is going to change that."

I feel Tom nod next to me. "Maybe it won't," he admits. "Maybe I'll go out there and it'll be even worse. But I won't know unless I try."

I'm thoughtful for a few moments, or as thoughtful as I can be with all of these conflicting thoughts tangling in me, each one trying to outmatch the others.

"I guess the reason it's so hard to wrap my head around this is—you've always been the one with everything figured out. Do you not want to go to Columbia anymore? Or study psychology?" I ask. "You've talked about getting into an Ivy League and majoring in that for years. Like way before any adult was pestering us about it."

"I do want those things still. But I also don't. I just—" Tom lets out a sigh so deep it borders on a shudder. "That's what I wanted, is the thing. But I haven't felt like myself in so long that I don't know if it's still what I want. So maybe I leave and I want to come back. But maybe I leave and—I find out I want something else entirely."

"Jesus," I say with a laugh. "You sound like me deciding to come to New York."

"So you get it," says Tom quietly. "Why I have to go."

I do and I don't. There's something about the way Tom's talking about this that doesn't sit right with me. In my mind it feels like New York was me running toward something, and North Carolina is Tom running away. But I feel like I can't say so without sounding like a hypocrite.

Or worse, without wondering if maybe I've got it all wrong. If maybe I just have that sense because it's convenient for me. Because it would be an easy way to justify convincing Tom to stay when I have too many reasons to want him to, every single one of them more selfish than the last.

"It just seems wild to me to walk away from a sure thing. I've never had that," I admit. "Like my whole life I've had no idea what I'm doing, and you have, and now you're just—choosing to be like me, when I'm just a big mess."

Tom is quiet for a moment, then slowly rises to prop himself on his elbows, staring down at me so deliberately that it's impossible not to look at him. I don't rise to meet him, stunned by the depth of brown in his eyes now that they are this impossibly focused on mine.

"Riley fucking Larson," he says, "if you're a mess then everyone on earth should want to be one, too."

My cheeks aren't just flushing but searing. I feel like he just held a match directly to my heart.

"Yeah, yeah," I mutter, moving my head to the side.

Tom doesn't let me, gently pinching my chin between his thumb and his finger, redirecting my face so it's right in his eyeline again. There's something else brewing in his eyes now. An intensity that punctuates every word that comes out of his mouth, that makes them impossible to dismiss even when every instinct in my body wants to try.

"You know what the real issue is?" Tom tells me. "You have too much potential. You're curious about everything and have a knack for a lot of it. It's why you survived all those ridiculous clubs your mom put you in and why you're confused about what comes next. But I'm not worried. No matter where you are, your energy is infectious. Not a single person can feel it and not want to be a part of it. The problem isn't what you're going to do in this life, because it's going to be amazing. There's just the challenge of you deciding what's going to make you happiest, because you've got way too much to choose from."

"Tom," I say, trying to shake my head. I'm quivering at the impact of his words, at the faint pressure of his touch, so on the verge of being undone by them that I'm almost terrified by it. That if this goes on much longer Tom won't just see me the way he always has, but *see* me. Down to the feelings I'm realizing I've spent more than this summer denying. Down to the core of me I'm still too scared to look at myself.

He tweaks my chin, still holding it there. "I mean it. Not

that it matters what I think, because it's just a fact either way. You don't need stars, Riley. You are one. You have your own gravity and I cannot fucking wait to see what you do with it."

My eyes well up then, unbidden. I want to tell Tom that's not true. That all the years we were growing up, that was *him* — the person people wanted to orbit around, the warm light that grounded all of us. That if I'm a star in Tom's made-up galaxy, it's because he taught me how to be one first. It's because he showed me how life could change when you let yourself shine.

Tom goes very still, lifting his hand to my cheek. "Riley," he says quietly, the *are you okay?* implied.

I'm not. Just as much for his sake as for mine. Our lights have been dimming all these years we spent caught in other people's forces. Maybe I am flickering back, but it does nothing to quell the worry that Tom won't. That once he's gone, he'll slip through my fingers again.

"I'm staying in the city," I say. My voice is steady, despite the crush of everything else. "I was planning on telling you last night."

Tom's eyes well up, too. "Good," he says. "See? You'll get wherever you need to be. I'm glad you found it here."

I shake my head into his palm. "I'm worried about you being so far away."

Tom hears what I'm not saying, and I'm more thankful for it than ever. This proof that we still know each other best, even when something rocks us to our cores.

"I promise I won't let it get the way it was again," he tells me. "We'll talk on the phone every day. I'll text like a regular human. We'll be fine. You'll see."

I believe that he believes that. But I also know that wasn't true a month ago. I also know that whatever has happened in the last few weeks of my being here isn't near enough to fix whatever has been broken in him. I don't want him to make promises like that for my sake; I want him to be able to make those promises because he's feeling like himself again, someone who doesn't feel so out of place that they can't even reach out to people they love.

Maybe that's what North Carolina will be for him. If it is, the last thing I want to do is stand in his way.

"When are you leaving?" I ask.

"Mid-August. I'm waiting for my mom to come back so we can still spend the week with her. I'm sure she'll want to take you all over the city." He shifts his hand off my face and there's more of a strangeness in it leaving than it being there in the first place. "I'm sure you already know this, but you're welcome to stay with us even after I go. I feel like I can very freely speak on my mom's behalf about that."

"I know," I say. "But it's like you with the app, I guess—I have to know I can do it on my own."

He nods knowingly, then slowly shifts himself onto his back beside me, both of us looking at the sky again.

I know any moment now that the others are going to spill back onto the roof, and there's still so much I want to say to him. So much I feel like I can't, without being the most selfish person in the world. So instead of saying any of that, I ask, "Can I tell you something ridiculous?"

Tom's voice is wry. "I'll allow it just this once."

The stars in front of us are faint but feel so strangely stark despite it that I realize Tom's right. This might be the first time we've seen them all summer. Like the sky was only waiting for this night to split the clouds and light just enough for us to have this moment now.

I point at the sky but tilt my head so I'm talking into his ear. "I know that's Orion's Belt," I say.

Tom's lips quirk immediately, his eyes still trained on the sky. "Alnitak, Alnilam, Mintaka," he says, naming the stars in it with that same cadence he did when we were kids, each of them like tiny touchstones on his tongue.

"And I know that moon up there is currently waning," I tell him.

Tom hums in agreement. "Not unlike the pizza we're about to inhale."

A beat passes before I pull in a resolved breath. "Actually, I know most of the constellations in your nerdy book," I confess. "I learned them two years ago, when we were supposed to do this the first time."

Tom turns his head toward me then. "You did?"

"Yeah," I say, nudging his shin with my foot. "Couldn't have you shouldering the burden of being the only nerd on the trip. That's what best friends are for."

Tom leans his head in closer, just close enough that I turn my head, too. That I can see the faintest spray of freckles on his nose, the ones he gets every summer despite his diligent sunscreening. I resist the urge to lift a finger and tap them each in turn the way he pointed up at the sky, and have the strangest sense in that moment that he's resisting something, too.

"This is going to sound so cheesy," says Tom. "But that makes me so happy. The idea that we know all the same stars. That we'll always have that in common even when we're far away."

It doesn't sound cheesy. It sounds heartbreaking. *Fuck stars*, I want to tell him. *Every single one of them. I'd rather have you.*

Tom does something that knocks that thought right out of my head, though. He inches his hand toward mine, interlocking our fingers and squeezing tight.

"I'll miss you," he says. "Same as I did all these years. But I'm happy you found your place here. I really am."

I want to be able to say the same for him, but I can't. Because I won't miss him the same way he misses me. And I'm not happy for him. I'm uneasy. I still can't say why.

But I'm spared from having to say any of that, because the door to the roof creaks open again. Just before Jesse and Mariella and Luca clamor back onto the campground Tom squeezes my hand one last time, quick and reassuring, then lifts himself up from the sleeping bag and diligently fishes out the paper plates and napkins.

Maybe there's some other version of this summer where the five of us took that train upstate and settled out in the mud and trees like real campers, but if there is I wouldn't want it. We spend the rest of the night so high up and insular that it feels like Manhattan's our kingdom and the rumpled sleeping bags are our thrones. We polish off the pizza while looking at the videos we took of our more epic karaoke moments last night, including the one where Luca and Jesse jumped on the couch so aggressively to a One Direction song that it's frankly a miracle they're both intact today. Jesse whips out the Reese's for his famous "s'mores hack" and starts lighting marshmallows on fire with his pocket lighter. Luca tells a ghost story about a kid who haunts the F train that's somehow so unexpectedly frightening that we make Mariella describe every cute dog in her building to recover from our mutual terror. The others indulge me and Tom when we go off on a tangent about "star hopping," a sport in Tides of Time where pilots in the distant future operate tiny ships that go a hundred times faster than light speed in a Space Olympics.

The tent turns out to be more of a prop than anything, because in the end we all decide to lie out on the roof under the open, cloudy sky.

"We can make wishes on pigeons," jokes Mariella.

Luca turns his head to look at her and says earnestly, "I always make them on planes."

Mariella reaches out and pats Luca on the hand like she's just too overcome by the cuteness of that to say anything else.

I don't miss the quiet moment when Luca lifts his hand to briefly squeeze hers. They don't hold hands, but they hold each other's eyes for a long beat before looking back up at the sky with identical close-lipped smiles.

Over the course of the night we wish for a whole lot of things between us, including and not limited to all our hopes and dreams coming true, more pizza, and the rumored Tides of Time prequel to come out faster. We wish until we start running out of silly things to wish for and start dropping off one by one, until I'm pretty sure I'm the only one still awake, Tom breathing even breaths on one side of me and Mariella on the other, Luca and Jesse lightly snoring on the other side of her.

The faint stars are fully blotted out by clouds by the time I finally shut my eyes, but I like the idea of wishing on planes better. Knowing that half the ones overhead might be leaving this city, but they'll eventually come back again.

# Chapter Nineteen

"I can't believe I've just been existing in the human world all these years without having read these books," says Luca, who is currently crouching in the YA section of the Strand's Upper West Side location, digging for the fifth Tides of Time novel. "No wonder you and Tom are so obsessed."

"Just wait until you finish and don't have to worry about spoilers. Tumblr and the Archive are a black hole of fan art and fic," I warn him.

"Good, because I'm not sure what I'll do with myself when I'm done."

I walk back up the stairs to the register with him, a heck of a lot more at ease than I was two hours ago when Luca and I met up. A few days after we went "camping" he messaged me outside of the group chat to ask if I wanted to get lunch in Riverside Park, which I was familiar with both from my dispatch routes and because my mom and I have watched *You've Got Mail* no less than sixteen times. Because I'm primed to think of that park as "the famous kissing spot" and because I know Luca sent me something through the dispatch, I was worried that maybe he was inviting me for romantic reasons.

A worry I felt particularly silly for having when Luca immediately busted out a flyer for a short-story contest he saw at the library and started talking a mile a minute about how we had to had to had to enter it, calling me "dude" about ten times in the process. We spent the afternoon swapping each other's Google Docs links for potential contenders for the contest. Once we'd exhausted our brains with plot points and prose we popped into the Strand on our way to an ice-cream truck to reward our efforts.

It's there, standing over the shelves of all these published books that used to be nothing more but ideas floating around in authors' heads, that I know how I want to use the notebook I was sent. I've been so hesitant to write in it, worried I wouldn't be doing justice to the pages that felt so much more permanent than a Google Docs tab. It feels almost like stage fright, as if the notebook itself would be watching me, making sure I was writing something worthy of it.

But a short-story contest is something else entirely. For the first time, other people would be reading and critiquing our work. For the first time I wouldn't just be pulling out a piece of myself and putting it into words, but giving it to other people to see, too. That feels notebook-worthy. That feels *big*.

And scary. Scary enough that I can't decide whether or not I'll actually submit anything. But whether I submit it or not, I know exactly where I want to start.

"Thank you for this," I say to Luca, feeling strangely but happily overwhelmed.

Luca looks up from the shelf he was staring at. "For what?"

"I just—never imagined writing this much at all, let alone

sharing it with other people. I thought that would be terrifying. And it still kind of is?" I say. "It's just that I don't feel that way swapping things back and forth with you."

Luca gives a sheepish smile. "Yeah, well. Probably because I'm the least intimidating person on the planet."

"No. Because you're supportive and nonjudgmental and give really, really good writing feedback," I tell him.

Luca blinks like he'd been expecting us to banter back and forth like we usually do, and the sincerity of the compliment doesn't know how to land. I feel a sympathetic twinge thinking that Luca probably doesn't have a lot of people in his life who talk to him that way, at least when it comes to writing. From what I've gathered his family is really tight—enough so that they all work at his family's restaurant—but aren't quite on his same literal or figurative page about this.

"Seriously," I say as we make our way out of the bookstore. "There's no way in hell I'd be considering something as big as a contest if I didn't have you to talk writing with like this. Getting to toss ideas around with you is always one of the best parts of my day."

Luca is uncharacteristically quiet for a few paces. In the silence I realize how ridiculous I've been, being disappointed at the idea that the notebook might have come from Luca. Here's this whole person who is not only as eager to start from scratch as I am, but is so open about it that I don't even have to think twice about texting weird ideas to him in the middle of the night, that I can already feel our writing styles starting to shift and grow as we feed off each other's excitement.

"It's been really nice to have someone to talk to about writing at all," he says. "I'm so relieved you're staying. Seriously. You have no idea."

I grin. "Yeah. Manhattan's sure having a hard time getting rid of me this summer, huh?"

I made this announcement the morning we all woke up on the roof. Jesse let out a celebratory howl and got lawless flickering his lighter in every direction. Luca leapt up and hugged me like I'd just declared second Christmas. Mariella was entirely unsurprised and deeply smug, whipping out the calendar on her phone and saying, "Ugh, it's about time you made it official. Now I can stop pretending I didn't factor your face into all the plans I made this fall."

Tom didn't immediately tell the others he was planning on leaving, but I nudged him into telling Mariella. I figured if he was going to leave someone else the app it should probably be more her decision than his, which he agreed with immediately.

I can't say any progress has been made on finding anyone, though—not only was Tom not looking all that hard in the first place, but Mariella processed this task by patting Tom on the shoulder and saying, "No."

"No?" Tom repeated.

"No," said Mariella. "You were planning on running it remotely until you found someone, right? Just do that. This is your baby. So, no."

I don't know if they've actually worked any logistics out between them since, but I'm secretly grateful that Mariella and I feel the same way about it, at least.

All this to say, Luca and Jesse still don't know about Tom's imminent departure, so it only makes sense for Luca to ask, "Are we still going to try to get through the Getaway List this summer?"

"Yeah," I say. "We've only got two things left. One is a road trip, which I guess we'd better figure out."

I feel like the pressure is a bit off on that one, though. At some point or another Tom is going to have to leave the city. If he's hoping to do that in relative peace and quiet, well, tough luck. He's got too many friends who will want to see him off for that.

"I hope by 'we' you mean you and Jesse, because I think it's safe to say none of the New Yorkers can drive," says Luca. "Where is the road trip supposed to be?"

I shrug. "When we were freshmen Tom and I always said we'd take a road trip together when we graduated. It was the first thing we put on the Getaway List, actually. But we didn't have any place in mind."

It was like that in the old days. Meeting up with no plans for the day, no idea where it was going to lead us. As long as we had each other it didn't matter where we went. Safe to say that neither of us imagined when we made the plan to road-trip together that we wouldn't have seen each other in the four years in between.

"Well, what's the other thing?" Luca asks.

"An oddly specific but easily achievable one," I say. "You know that famous brownie place a few blocks from here?"

"Not Brownie Bonanza?" Luca asks, the pitch of his voice unexpectedly high.

"Yeah. That's the one. You get to make your own brownies on the premises, right? With all those different secret-recipe brownie batters and fillings?"

"Right," says Luca, who is suddenly very interested in looking at the holographic ocean on the cover of his new Tides of Time book.

"Well, you know Tom has a thing about desserts that are actually ten different desserts at once, so that place is kind of his white whale. He really wanted to go when it blew up, must have been—"

"Around Christmas," Luca supplies.

"Yeah," I say, recalling all the very delicious-looking Tik-Toks and "I went to Brownie Bonanza" foodie-influencer articles that went viral a few months ago. I was grateful for them at the time because they gave me an excuse to bombard Tom with links, some of which he'd actually responded to. "The reservations were basically impossible to get."

In fact, that's why it got added to the Getaway List in the first place—once it was clear that supply was absurdly smaller than demand, we agreed we'd just go together the next time I was in the city, when the hype calmed down. Besides, someone needed to make sure Tom didn't dive headfirst into all the toppings and frosting options and refuse to leave the premises. It would have made for a very strange mark on his arrest record.

"Yeah. The place is, uh—pretty popular," says Luca.

I wince, wondering if I've already blown it for this summer. "I should have booked something earlier, I just meant to look into it first because of Mariella's peanut allergy."

"Oh, it'll be fine. It's a peanut-free facility."

Luca sounds strangely distant, enough that I stop a good block from the ice-cream place and tilt my head at him.

"Do you not like brownies or something?" I ask.

Luca lets out a breathy laugh. "I'm not a sweets fan, really," he says. "But, uh—we won't have an issue getting in."

"How come?"

"I know a guy," says Luca. Which would be an objectively very cool New Yorker thing to say if Luca didn't deliver it with the enthusiasm of someone about to walk into a five-hour SAT test.

"Only if you don't mind asking . . . the guy," I say carefully.

Luca shakes his head. "The guy would be thrilled," he says. "The guy will hug me and make a big deal out of the whole thing." Then he sighs deeply and clarifies, "The guy is my mom and dad."

"Sorry, *what*?"

Luca looks at me miserably. "My family runs Brownie Bonanza," he mumbles.

I stop dead on the street. "Excuse me, and you were going to tell us this *when*?"

"Never. I'm the black sheep of my whole family," says Luca, whose puppy-dog face is close to crumbling. "A monster who doesn't like sweets."

"Then why the hell are we getting ice cream right now?" I demand.

"I don't know!" Luca blurts.

I pivot us away from the ice-cream shop abruptly. "All right, I'm not your writing friend anymore. I'm your self-advocacy friend. Stop letting people drag you places you don't want to eat."

Luca laughs and says, "No, you can still be my writing friend. I already got this lecture from Mariella a week ago."

"Well, apparently she needs to give it again if it didn't stick!"

Luca laughs out loud, following me down the sidewalk, pink-cheeked and pleased.

"So you and Mariella are hanging out?" I ask.

I have no intention of stirring the "Luca and Mariella" pot here, only because Mariella might have taken it off the stove. But it's clear from today that if Luca had any feelings for me early in the summer—enough to send something from the dispatch—those feelings are only writerly enthusiasm now. I can't help but wonder if that means other feelings have developed in the meantime.

Luca nods. "I keep waiting for her to get bored of me, but I guess there's a lot of crossover on places she wants to photograph that also make for good places to write. Plus I think she doesn't like taking photos on her own."

This is getting less and less true as the summer goes

on—while Mariella took me up on the offer to be her emotional-support bystander a few times, she's confident enough to hold her own in the wild now. I feel like I need to impress this upon Luca, so I turn to him and put both hands on his shoulders.

"Luca. You are very good company. That's why Mariella asks you to go places. You're an exceedingly kind human being with a giant, ridiculously amusing imagination and apparently no taste in dessert, which is just a tribute to how good of a friend you are that we're all willing to forgive you for it."

He wavers for a moment, like there's something he wants to say but isn't quite sure if he should.

"Thank you for saying that," he says in the end, with enough finality that I know he wants me to drop it. "Even if I'm not sure that dessert thing is true for Tom."

"Valid point. The rest of us will go to the grave with your secret," I vow. "Now, where are we going to get a snack around here?"

Before Luca can answer, my phone lets out a loud ping.

"If you've got to pick up a dispatch, I don't mind," says Luca.

I sigh. "It's not a dispatch. It's my mom."

With yet another text indicating that she is still living in the reality where I'm coming home mid-August as planned, and that my "I'll think about it" was in fact already thought out and decided. Last week it was a photo of the back-to-school section of Target: Anything you want me to grab before classes start? Today it's a reminder that class sign-ups are next week, if I want to take another look at the roster.

I'd put a stop to it, but I'm so grateful that we're on speaking terms at all that I can't seem to do it just yet. Talking to Mariella made me realize we were long overdue for a discussion, but I wasn't accounting for this—the relief of having some normalcy with my mom back, even if it's just a shade of what it was before.

Luca peers at the text over my shoulder and winces. "Okay, then. I'll be your self-advocacy friend for the afternoon, too. Tell her to keep dreaming."

This wrestles a smile out of me if only because the mental image of Luca marching up to my mom and saying that to her face is more amusing to me than all of the short stories I've written this summer combined.

"I'll get there," I say reluctantly.

Luca pats me on the back with adorable authority for someone who hasn't wielded much of it in his life. "She'll get on board. And one day we'll go back to that bookstore and have books with our own names on them, and disappointing our dessert-loving, New York–hating parents will all have been worth it."

I smile at him, because the idea of that has an impossible kind of magic. I just hope I have enough courage to reach for it, knowing I might not have my mom's support or Tom at my side when the time comes. Knowing that this is a kind of magic I'm going to have to make on my own.

## Chapter Twenty

"We should also take out the trash to make sure all the wrappers from the freezer burritos are out of sight, so she doesn't think she's coming home to two deeply advanced cases of scurvy," I say.

Tom looks up from the fridge we're cleaning the leftovers out of and says, "Trust me. The hallway could be littered with empty vodka bottles and I don't think my mom would bat an eye."

"We're putting that on the list of things we're never saying to my mom, ever ever," I say, widening the trash bag I'm holding out for him.

We're not really cleaning for cleaning's sake, because Tom has assured me that a house cleaner always comes and scrubs the place from top to bottom the day before his mom gets back to town. But the closer we get to Vanessa coming back the antsier Tom seems to be, like he can't focus on a task for more than a few moments to save his life. I figured cleaning might be a constructive, Tom-friendly way to work out whatever it is that's eating at him, so we're going through the motions of being responsible apartment dwellers and not two people who have mostly subsisted on Pop-Tarts the entire summer.

"You never told me what your mom thinks about the whole 'leaving New York' thing," I say, wondering if that has something to do with his unease.

Tom shrugs. "She just said it would be nice to catch up with my aunt."

My brows furrow. "She does understand that you're like — *moving* moving. That this isn't a social call."

Tom just shrugs again. "I'm not sure if she'll notice my being gone either way."

I'm not sure what's more concerning, the words coming out of Tom's mouth or the casual way he says them. Like he's come to terms with them in such a permanent way that they don't have nearly the effect they should.

"I feel weird eating up the last of your time with your mom when she gets back. I can leave earlier," I tell him. "Really. The sublet starts in two days. Plus, then I can establish myself as the alpha of the apartment and whip the boys in line."

In a disappointing turn of events to all the Craigslist bots I accidentally messaged looking for a sublet, it turns out that Jesse and the band found a permanent apartment to lease that has a little alcove up on a ladder with just enough room for a mattress and a makeshift bedside table. While it's not strictly *legal* for me to move into it, it sure is cheap, and comes with the added perk of roommates who are definitely not going to cut off my hair and sell it in my sleep. (Some of Luca's ghost stories the other night were a little *too* specific for my taste.)

"I don't want to keep you from your *New Girl* self-insert fanfiction, but if you don't mind staying — I don't know," says Tom. "She's just . . ."

"A lot?" I supply. It may have been years since I've seen Vanessa, but that doesn't make the impression she leaves any less deep. From what I've heard from Tom these past few weeks, her tendency to act like a human pendulum—distracted and disengaged one second, and then shining a spotlight brighter than the sun on you in the next to make up for it—has only gotten more pronounced.

Tom shifts uncomfortably. "It's weird. It's like I never feel like I'm—interesting enough for her."

I turn my eyes to him, slowly setting the trash bag down. I had a feeling that cleaning might lull Tom into opening up a bit, but I didn't expect him to say something this grim.

"What do you mean?" I ask.

Tom gestures vaguely at the space in front of himself. "I just mean—she hardly ever wants to know what's going on with me. And then suddenly she does, and she has all these questions about, like—my friends and my classes and what I'm up to in the city. And even when I tweak the truth to make it sound like I'm not a total loser, she just zones out again on me anyway."

My heart feels a little bit more like it's splintering with every word. That anyone as clever and kind and genuinely passionate as Tom could ever be made to feel *boring*. Especially from the one person who is supposed to know and love him best.

He lets out a breathy, self-conscious laugh and says, "Not that it matters. She doesn't even remember half the things I tell her. I tried telling her about Mariella once and she's called her 'Gabriella' for, like, a year."

There are a lot of things I want to knock into Tom's head right now about how this is anyone's fault but his. But first I look him square in the eye and say, "Tom—does your mom not have any idea how much you've been struggling here?"

His eyes immediately skim the floor and I feel my stomach churn.

"I talked to her about it when we first got here. She tried to help, but she just sort of—started taking me everywhere with her. Like she could feel like she was doing something about it if we were in the same place." He looks at me ruefully. "Surprise, surprise. She basically had no time for me then, too."

I don't even know where to start. I knew things weren't great between Tom and Vanessa, but in my head it was just that she was too busy to notice Tom floundering. Not that she was actively part of it by making him feel like he wasn't important enough to listen to in the first place.

"Have you talked to her about . . . all of this? Like not the part where you were struggling. But the part where she's not listening to you at all?" It's a struggle to keep my voice steady, the anger licking under my ribs. "Because shit, Tom. That's fucked up."

Tom's eyes get glassy. "It feels like it's a bit my fault, too. Like maybe if I were different—" He shakes his head, and the pain that streaks across his face stops the protest that's about to fall out of my mouth. "Or if I were the same as I was before. Back in Virginia. She wasn't like this back then. I've changed. You've seen it. You know."

For someone so tall he looks so breakable in this moment that I'm almost afraid if I reach out to touch him he'll splinter like glass. He looks more like his little-kid self than he ever has, not because he's on the verge of tears, but because he's on the verge of something worse—a soul-deep uncertainty. A basic human need to love and be loved in return.

I reach out and pull him into me. It's not like our usual hugs, where we're practically competing over how many bones we can crack. It's soft and steady. I feel him let loose a shuddering breath against me, easing into it.

"Tom, you didn't change," I say into his ear. "You adapted. You had this whole new life thrown at you and you tried the best you could with the support you had, which apparently was pretty close to zero." I press my hand into the back of his neck as if to press the words into his spine, to help him hold himself up again. "Your mom is the one who changed. Into someone I kind of want to scream at right now, to be honest."

Tom laughs, but I don't. There's nothing funny about this. I'm so angry on his behalf that even as I hold him to me, the heat rising in my chest makes me feel like I'm about to breathe fire.

Tom lets me go and says with red-rimmed eyes, "We're not doing so well on the mom front right now, are we?"

This giant chasm that exists between Tom and his mom makes whatever is going on between me and my mom look like a hairline fracture. I feel freshly upset with myself for putting off the conversation with her, because yes, it's going to suck. It's probably going to involve some tears and some yelling and plenty of things neither of us wants to hear. But I know there will never be a single moment of it, during or after, that I'll have to question whether or not the things I say matter to her. Whether *I* matter to her.

My mom might have gone about things in the wrong way, but I've never had to question whether she did them out of love.

"Tom, my mom and I aren't seeing eye to eye. Yours isn't seeing anything at all."

Tom tries to shrug this off, but it's disjointed like a puppet. "Yeah. Well. It kind of snuck up on me. I just don't want the same thing to happen with you and your mom. You two have always been super close."

This is something Tom and I haven't talked about much, even if it's been one of the thickest threads that's tied us together our whole lives: being kids who only ever had a mom and nothing else. Not just that, but being kids our moms actively chose on their own, without anyone else's input. Tom because his mom used a sperm donor, and my mom because she chose to have me in a position where a lot of other people wouldn't—something I'm only starting to understand the depth of now that I'm close to that age and know for a fact I wouldn't decide it for myself.

"You don't have to worry about us," I say. "It's you I'm worried about."

Tom looks like he's about to shrug again, but it stops before it can reach his shoulders. "I always worry about you," he says. "That's our deal."

I take a small step toward him, only because we're already so close that there isn't much distance left to take.

"It is," I say. "Which is why I really think you should let me clear out before your mom gets here. I'll come to dinner or sightsee. But I think before you go you have to have a real talk about it. You said when she gets back she's all hyperfocused on you—maybe that'll make it sink in more."

On the heels of that is another thought that's only just occurring to me, one I didn't know enough about the situation to form before. That maybe it isn't New York Tom is trying to leave; maybe New York isn't the problem at all.

It feels selfish to ask it because there's no denying I've got my own stake in this, but it feels even more like it needs to be said. "Do you think maybe this has something to do with why you want to leave? Less New York and more this stuff with your mom?"

Tom hesitates for the slightest beat before shaking his head. Even then it doesn't seem like he can commit to it, like the thought is weighing him down.

Neither of us says anything for a moment, and I feel more

useless than I ever have—torn between what Tom probably needs a friend to say to him right now, and knowing that I might be saying it for the wrong reasons if I do. There's no way to pretend that digging into this isn't just another way of asking, *Can't you just stay here?*

Tom twists his lip to the side and says, "I'll talk to her. I will. But it's really just everything, you know? I need a clean slate."

There's a finality in his tone, the kind bordering on pleading, so I drop it. I nod and clear my throat and say, "All right." I can't dismiss the unease in my chest, the anger still churning in my stomach on his behalf, but I can pretend for Tom's sake.

"All right," says Tom back, as if he's bracketing the conversation. A neat and tidy close.

Except neither of us moves, and Tom says suddenly, "At least keep your key to this place, will you? If things ever don't work out living with the band you can always crash here."

I resist the urge to roll my eyes at his mother-henning, because he's offered this no less than five times since we finalized my knockoff-sitcom living situation. "As much as I'm going to miss the fancy trash chute and chatting up the doormen, I'm sure we'll be fine," I assure him.

Tom's still watching my face carefully. It feels like we're suspended in motion here—by now all pretenses of cleaning have been abandoned between the two of us, but we're both standing very, very still, like we know something is inevitable about this moment even if we don't know what it is yet.

"This might be a weird question," he says slowly. "But I guess the reason I'm wondering about you living with the band is—it seemed like maybe there was still something between you and Jesse when you got here?" I open my mouth, a laugh bubbling up my throat that stalls when Tom's cheeks flush all the way to his hair. "What I mean is—the way he was so happy to see you, and—I don't know. I wondered for a bit if the flowers were from him."

"Oh." I suppose there's no reason to keep it a secret anymore. More than anything I'm surprised the flowers are still on Tom's mind. "Actually, they were."

"Oh," says Tom back. His expression doesn't change, but something under it goes static. Like he's bracing himself for whatever I say next.

"It's not like that, though. We just had some loose ends to tie up. Like, really old ones," I say. I try to smile just to emphasize how un-big of a deal it is, but there's something about the way Tom is watching me right now, like he's trying to test the weight of every word I'm saying, that makes me feel unsteady. "But we had a talk about it the other day. We're friends, is all."

It takes a moment for Tom to consider this. "Like you and me?" he asks.

Only then do I appreciate just how close we're standing to each other. In the heat of my anger at his mom I got right up in Tom's face, which is still inches from mine, to a degree that suddenly makes me very aware of my own heart beating in my chest.

"Yeah," I say. The word comes out a little choked, but I'm steadier by the time I say, "Like you and me."

Tom's eyes skim my face, lingering on my lips, settling on my eyes. I try not to shiver, try not to lift myself up to my toes to exactly meet his gaze.

"You know," he says quietly, "when we were trying to determine that—you and I never actually kissed."

"That we did not," I say. My heart's not beating anymore so much as slamming, because Tom doesn't just say the words; he leans in closer so there's barely any air between us for them.

"So is that—really ruled out?" he asks. "Without a thorough check, I mean."

Oh, shit. Oh, *shit*. I stare up at Tom almost as if to call his bluff, but he's staring at me so intently that I understand at once that there isn't one. That he's giving me room to play it off if I want to, but this isn't like it was last time, when it felt more like we were agreeing to a dare than a kiss.

I have to swallow hard before I say, "I guess not."

There are a thousand reasons not to lean in and cross the distance between us right now, but one reason is louder than all of them: I want to kiss him. I want it so badly that it feels in this moment like the only thing I've ever wanted, like it's such a natural impulse that it would go against the laws of nature *not* to.

In the end it isn't me who leans in, but both of us. It's different from last time, when it felt like we had something to prove. From the moment our lips touch, the noise of the whole summer goes to static—this is something that is immediately and unmistakably *ours*. It's in the hitch of surprise in my throat at the honey-warm taste of him, the way I'm shaking with the satisfaction of it before it's even fully begun. The way we're reaching, stunned with the impact of each other, pulling each other in with rushed, needy hands and arms that only have one objective, which is to somehow, impossibly, be even closer than we already are.

This is unmitigated chaos. This is Tom and Riley, Riley and Tom.

We pull apart and we're both breathless, both flushed and disbelieving but somehow not surprised at all. For once we're not reading the story—we are the story. Like this was written in the pages all along, and was only just waiting for us to reach it.

Tom presses his forehead into mine, his hand just under my jaw. "Riley," he says.

And something in me thrills just as a stone settles against my chest. He's never said my name like that before, but I can hear everything in the tone of it so clearly that he might as well have said it out loud.

He loves me, too. Not the way we've always loved each other. But in another way entirely, one that binds us deeper than I thought my heart could go.

"We can't," I croak.

Tom doesn't move and neither do I. We're still pressed together, but suddenly rigid as statues. Almost like neither of us wants to go forward or back, just wants to keep being the people we were five seconds ago, when reality didn't matter on either side of that kiss.

"You're leaving," I say. "And if we—if we ever—Tom. I need you to understand. You're too important to me."

"I'll stay," says Tom immediately.

I shake my head so hard that the tears I didn't even realize were forming in my eyes spill out with it. "Fuck. No. Don't—" I swipe at my eyes with the heel of my hand, furious with myself. "I can't let you do that."

"You wouldn't be. I'm deciding."

I shake my head again, pressing my hands to his chest. I have every intention of pushing him away, but I can't bring myself to do it. I'm leaning into him and he's leaning back, the two of us in such a perfect balance that it feels inherent.

"You've spent your whole life worried about everyone else. Making friends with outcasts like me. Taking care of everyone with your giant backpacks of supplies. Being worried about what your mom thinks when she's the one who's being shitty to you." I reach up and cup the hand he has under my jaw, lacing my fingers through it. "But I won't let you do that for my sake. I love you too much for that."

Tom swallows hard, his eyes searching my face. "You want me to go?"

Fuck, no. I want him right here, wherever *here* is. I want

him at my side the way I have every moment since he left, the way I will until the day I die.

"I want you to be happy," I tell him.

His voice cracks enough that it almost cracks through my resolve. "I'm happy with *you*."

I take a deep breath. I shake my head again. It feels like the hardest thing I've ever done.

"That's not—I don't think that's how it's supposed to work," I tell him. Every word feels like sandpaper on my tongue, but they need to be said. I love him too much to say anything less. "You need to be happy with yourself. And if I stand in the way of you doing that—I'd never, *ever* forgive myself for it."

A true fucking choice of words, because I'm not sure if I'll forgive myself for saying them, either. For brushing up so close to something I want more deeply than anything I ever have, and letting it slip through my fingers. For saying these words with the hope of preserving him and knowing that I'm hurting him just the same.

"I'm sorry," I blurt, for lack of anything else to say.

Tom comes back to himself then, in a way that breaks my heart because I know he's only doing it for my sake. He presses a kiss to my forehead and says, "Don't be. You're right. I want—if we ever do this, I want to do it right."

I didn't think relief could hurt until he said those words, but there it is—a warm knife pressed against my ribs just before it slides into my heart. Something that somehow heals but opens up another wound, one I don't know the shape of yet, or if we'll recover from it.

We pull apart. It feels strange to be in command of my body again so suddenly and so easily, like snapping the rubber band of myself back into place. A painful, instant happening.

"How's this?" says Tom, his eyes steady even as his voice is wobbling. "You have your talk with your mom. A real one, airing the whole high-school thing out. And I'll stay here on my own an extra few days to talk it out with mine."

This is a deal I can make. A deal that should be easier than any I've made in my life. But I'm stuck on the feeling that something else has already been broken, something neither of us had any power to prevent.

"Yeah," I say. "And if you need me for any of it—I'm right here."

Tom nods. "I know," he says, like he means it. Not like the times we texted back and forth these past few years, when I'd reach out and he'd pull back. This time he's meeting me there. "Thank you for that. For all of it."

I smile and say, "You're my best friend. If you thank me for that kind of shit again, I'll kick your ass."

Tom smiles back, even if it's every bit as weary as mine, and says back, "I'd expect nothing less."

# Chapter Twenty-One

"Oh shit," says Jesse candidly, staring at the line around the block as Luca guides us toward the side entrance of Brownie Bonanza. "I feel like we just cut past the bouncer in a club."

Sure enough, every single person in line stares at us like they want to chuck brownie batter at our heads. Luca closes the door behind us fast, like he's practiced in this and not so sure they won't try.

He leads us into a hallway just off the main entrance with bright purple walls full of giant blown-up pictures of brownies hung up in neon frames. From Tom's intense dessert chronicling I know that Brownie Bonanza has four mainstay flavors and two that rotate out every week, so I recognize more than a few of them in this brownie hall of fame—a giant, rainbow-sprinkled one I know is stuffed with cookie dough, one with piped-on frosting roses that's full of passion-fruit jam and coffee, another with a spicy-sweet salt crust filled with caramel.

234 • Emma Lord

Tom is gaping at the wall like they're signed posters of his favorite celebrities. He's wearing an expression not unlike the first time he tried that Pop-Tart at our apartment and Tom the Dessert Person was born.

"Aw, look at you in your own personal Disneyland," I say.

Tom pulls in a breath as if to soak it all in. "I can't believe I'm going to peak at eighteen."

I flash him a quick grin instead of ribbing him like I usually might. It's been two days since the "surprise, it turns out we had mutual and deeply intense feelings for each other the whole time" kiss, and ever since then it's like we've been playing friendship on safety mode: unfailingly polite and avoiding touching each other whenever we can.

It's all well and good except for the part where I'm possibly losing my mind being in constant proximity to Tom knowing what it feels like to have *all* of the proximity to him. But that's what throwing myself into my attempts to come up with a short-story idea and cold showers are for.

"Wait. I know this place," says Mariella.

"I should hope so," says Tom, seemingly indignant on the brownies' behalf.

"No, I mean—wasn't there a different bakery here?" Mariella peers up and down the walls with scrutinizing eyes. "One that didn't do interactive stuff or anything, just a regular storefront."

"It's the same bakery," says Luca, who is back in mumbling mode again. He's been in and out of it since we all met up at Tom's an hour ago to line our stomachs with lunch as a dessert pregame. "It got a renovation a few years ago, just before it went viral."

Mariella opens her mouth as if to protest this when two tiny, enthusiastic humans who can only be Luca's parents spill out from a side door, followed by even *tinier* enthusiastic humans who can only be Luca's siblings. In all the commotion I hear snippets of "so nice to meet Luca's *friends*" and "you must be Riley!" and one distinct, pip-squeaking voice aimed in my and Tom's direction that says "they're so *tall*." Somehow in this commotion we are all hugged in turn by Luca's parents, poked by at least one sibling, and ushered into one of the back rooms where parties can design and bake their own brownies.

The chaos does nothing to lessen the impact of what feels like falling directly into a room in Willy Wonka's factory. The side walls are streaked with a glittery-gold-painted list of all the available brownie-batter flavors, fillings, frostings, and unexpected combination ideas. The back wall is lined with a big table full of vats of different chocolates, candies, and sprinkles you can stuff into your batter. Toward the middle are five workstations, each of which have a little name card with our names written in giant, childish lettering dusted in glitter that can only be the handiwork of one of Luca's many mini-mes.

I glance over at Tom and decide even if we'd ended up bungling every other item on the Getaway List this summer, it still would have been worth it to see the Christmas morning–level bliss on his face right now.

The door closes and Mariella turns to Luca with wide eyes and slightly askew curls, looking as windswept as I feel. "Um, was that hurricane the *entire Bales family*?"

"Yep." Luca takes a grounding breath, picking up the one purple apron on the counter laid next to the white ones. "And I'll be your Brownie Bonanzer this afternoon."

Mariella laughs, but when Luca continues to go through the motions of tying it around his waist, the Brownie Bonanza logo unmistakably embroidered on the chest, she says, "Wait a minute—you work here?"

Only then do I realize that we were so busy talking about what kind of brownies we wanted to make at lunch that neither Luca nor I bothered to explain *how* Luca was able to sneak us in, accidentally leaving Mariella and Jesse in the dark.

"Yeah," says Luca to his feet, still in Mumble Town, population: him. "My whole family does."

"Even when it was the old bakery?" Mariella asks.

"Yep," he says again, and then so fast that Mariella can't get another word in edgewise, he says, "Anyway, the basic gist of the whole thing is—"

"Wait, that's *wild*," says Mariella excitedly. "I used to come in here all the time after school. I can't believe we never crossed paths before now."

Luca mumbles something so indistinct that if his mouth weren't moving I wouldn't be entirely sure it came from him. Even Tom goes still in his brownie reverence.

"Sorry, what was that?" Mariella asks wryly.

The playful smirk slides off her face when Luca looks up with wary, almost apologetic eyes. "Well, our paths did cross? Like, crisscrossed and crossed and crossed again," he says. "I worked at the register so I saw you, like, all the time."

I feel my own jaw start to loosen from surprise as Mariella's full-on drops. "That can't be true."

Luca is still fidgeting his apron strings as if he's never tied a knot in his life.

"You always had a bunch of friends with you, so," he says, as if this is a complete thought.

A rookie mistake with Mariella, who is the last person to let him get away with it. "We've been hanging out the whole summer and you never said anything?"

Jesse and Tom have enough wherewithal that they're both pretending to be very, very interested in the list of fillings on the wall despite Tom having it memorized to the point of it being tattooed on his eyelids, but I'm just gaping like I accidentally fell into a reality show.

"I took your order every other day and you didn't even recognize me," Luca says, shifting uncomfortably.

Mariella's cheeks flush. "Maybe not, but I definitely felt like *something* was familiar about you. Why on earth wouldn't you say something? I'm sure I would have remembered then."

"Because I had a big embarrassing crush on you," Luca blurts.

"Oh shit," says Jesse, who is doing a very bad job of looking distracted now.

Between Luca's bright red face and Mariella's gobsmacked eyes I'm expecting the room to come to an excruciating halt, only it doesn't, because Mariella fires back without a moment's hesitation, "Well, that's ridiculous, because I've spent the whole summer with a big embarrassing crush on *you*."

Luca blinks. "What?"

"What?" Mariella shoots back.

And there's the beat of excruciating silence I was expecting, one that Tom scoops up as easily as brownie batter. "Oh. Well. That was an easy fix."

Jesse nods, popping a stray chocolate chip from the toppings bin into his mouth. "You can have tiers of brownies at the wedding."

Mariella waves a hand, stubbornly not looking at any of us when she says, "Luca *had* a crush on me, past tense. He likes Riley now."

Before I can slowly peel out the window to remove myself from this narrative, Luca's brows pucker in confusion. "Says who?"

"Says you sending her stuff from the dispatch!" says Mariella. "And yes, I'm an asshole for knowing that, but the fact is I do, so no point in beating around the bush anymore."

Luca looks genuinely offended, but not personally so. "What are you talking about? If I had a crush on Riley, I wouldn't have sent *cheese*."

"Hey," I protest.

Luca turns to me in mild panic. "No, I mean—not that you're not—you know, great and all—"

"That was in defense of the cheese, not myself," I say, gesturing for him to proceed.

"So that was you?" Tom asks.

Luca looks between me and Tom like we all just drop-kicked him onto another planet. "You guys were discussing well-crafted faux-marble cheese plates so intensely. I thought it would be like a fun 'welcome to New York' thing. You didn't realize it was me?"

Tom chokes trying not to laugh, but I don't have even that much self-control. Luckily both Luca and Mariella look too mutually stunned to be upset with us for it.

"We did not, but it was deeply appreciated," I tell him. "You have impeccable taste in random cheese deliveries."

"Thank you," says Luca, who seems genuinely out of breath now, like this conversation is a gym class he didn't mean to sign up for. He glances around at all of us in turn, settling somewhat defiantly on Mariella, and adds, "Now can we please get to making these brownies? I have a professional reputation to uphold."

Words that might have held more weight to them if Luca hadn't tied his apron to the part of the chair behind him, and subsequently knocked over a small vat of edible glitter that created a cloud that dusted us all in turn, so the group of us were immediately sparkling from head to toe. In the ensuing distraction I almost miss the sneaky smile curling on Mariella's lips and the faint blush under Luca's freckles when she aimes it right at him, but not quite.

"All right, Brownie Bonanzer," says Tom to Luca as he pulls a glittery apron over his equally glittery shirt. "Show us what you've got."

The next hour is as deliciously lawless as we were all anticipating, and then some. After some deliberation, we each decide on our flavors largely based on what occasion they're for. Jesse is taking Dai out to see live music in the park tonight, so he opts for a combination of their favorite flavors, regular batter stuffed with Rolos and toffee bits with cookie-dough filling, plus bright blue and black sprinkles for the band's signature colors. Mariella and Luca appear to be in some kind of face-off making brownies for *each other*, which is a pursuit I wash my hands of considering Luca's aversion to dessert (Mariella has opted for a blondie base and a *not*-small amount of some kind of chili-lime jam) and Mariella's aversion to chocolate (I decided not to ask too many questions after watching Luca start fileting gummy worms).

My heart twinges a bit when I notice Tom filling his with raspberry jam and honeycomb and nothing else, because those are Vanessa's favorite flavors, not his. But she's back tonight and he's been nervous about it all day. If he needs someone else to protect his true brownie agenda, I am more than happy to be the one to create an *actual* Tom version, which I have precariously stuffed with cookie dough, sea-salt caramel, crumbled frosted animal cookies, pretzels, chocolate chips, and marshmallows, and topped with rainbow sprinkles and sea salt on his behalf.

Luca has to dispense the dough and fillings for each of them to make sure the ratios won't obliterate their ovens—probably smart, considering the batter I made could easily take out the entire Upper West Side unsupervised—which he's in the middle of doing when Tom gets a call on his phone and ducks out.

Mariella walks over to Luca, her face solemn. Jesse and I busy ourselves to give them some space, Jesse with sending glittery selfies to Eddie and Dai in an attempt to convince them it should be part of the band's next rebrand, and me with washing an entire sticky Halloween haul worth of candy off my hands.

"Hey. Just so you know—the crowd I was with back then—they were assholes," says Mariella.

Luca's lips twitch into a sympathetic smile. "Yeah. I got the gist of that at karaoke."

"What I mean is I was probably too busy trying to impress them to notice people *actually* worth impressing," she says, scooting closer to him. "People who are deeply informed about the proper filling and batter ratios of brownies and how to optimize oven temperatures based on them."

Luca doesn't blush or get self-conscious like he usually does. Just stares at Mariella and says sincerely, "I'm sorry I didn't tell you earlier. I guess it was sort of like—a second chance at a first impression, maybe? Or just a first one at all, since I didn't make one the first time."

Mariella shakes her head. "I'm the one who needed a second chance at that impression," she says.

Luca just smiles and says, "Nah. I liked them both."

I stare down at my hands only so neither of them catch the grin I'm trying to bite down. The two of them banter back and forth about who is going to like the other's brownies more, long enough that I frown at the door, wondering what's taking Tom so long. I'm about to poke my head out when Mariella turns to me abruptly, with a triumphant look on her face.

"I just realized—now that we know who sent the flowers and the cheese, the mystery of your summer rom-com trope is solved," she says.

Jesse mentioned the flowers to Mariella at lunch today,

since I'd ended up pressing them between some of Tom's gigantic textbooks to preserve them back when I didn't know who they were from. They made for an eclectic addition to Vanessa's otherwise bare room.

Off my expression, Mariella raises her eyebrows and says, "Unless it's *not* solved?"

I towel off my hands, my eyes still focused on them. "There was one other thing," I confess.

Mariella slaps an enthusiastic palm on the table. "Wait, what other thing?"

I'm not sure what makes me say it. Maybe it's just the comfort of seeing everyone else look settled in this moment, or at least on the verge of it. Jesse's planning on telling Dai how he feels tonight. Mariella and Luca are clearly about to peel out of here and un-crush their mutual crushes on each other. They've got closure, and really, so do I—Tom's leaving. We know the exact measure of what we are and what we could be, know exactly what's going to happen next.

But this summer still has one loose end, and suddenly I can't resist the urge to tug it. As if unraveling it could stop the summer from ending, even if it's just a few seconds more.

"Someone sent me a notebook."

I look at all three of them in turn as if one of them will give themselves away, only their expressions are unchanged— Jesse's curious, Luca's confused, and Mariella's oddly determined.

"What kind of notebook?" she asks.

"Just—a blank one is all," I say, feeling the heat creep into my face. "It's nothing."

Mariella's eyes fixate on me slyly. "Your face looks like it's something."

"My face is the same face it's always been."

"Goopy recognizes goopy," she says, which makes Luca's

head tilt in further confusion, and prompts Mariella to pull out her phone. "And enough is enough."

I blink. "Wait—what are you doing?"

"Abusing my power," she says.

I cross the room to her fast. "Are you going into the backend of the 'Dear, Love' Dispatch again?"

"Only because at this point it feels like my civic responsibility," she says into her phone screen. "I think I can speak for everyone in this room when I say your whole 'will they, won't they' thing with Tom has gone past the legal limit. We need clarity."

"Actually we don't," I say quickly, but I'm swallowed up by Luca saying, "Wait, are we sure we want to do this?" And Jesse unsubtly chanting, "Do it, do it, do it."

It takes Mariella all of five seconds to pull it up, and the thing is, I don't stop her. I don't pull the phone out of her hands or kick up a fuss or think about any of the consequences. I let it happen so easily that I might as well be pressing the buttons myself.

"Wait—are you the one who's been sending *Tom* things?" Mariella asks.

I feel a louder version of the quick, defensive twinge of jealousy I've been trying to push down all summer. "No," I say.

"But there are all these outgoing deliveries to Tom's number, and they have the same area code as his. The Virginia one."

I glance over her shoulder, recognizing the number immediately. Tom insisted we memorize all our collective emergency numbers by the time we were eight.

"No, that's Tom's mom," I say, too bewildered to think the better of it.

"Wait, what?"

We all startle like cartoon characters at Tom, whose entire six-foot-something self walked right through the door without any of us noticing. He looks upset but not in the startled, accusatory way he probably should. He looks drained. Dull. Strangely resigned.

"What's wrong?" I ask. "Who was that?"

"Um," he manages. Whatever it was cracking in his expression, he seams it up fast when he feels the weight of all our eyes on him. "It was my mom. I guess she's not coming in tonight after all. Says it's looking more like next week."

Shit.

I step forward on instinct even knowing full well I can't pull him into my arms like I want to right now—if Tom is determined to pretend everything's fine, the last thing I want to do is call more attention to the fact that it's not. Tom finds my eyes just the same, and the hurt in them is so raw that it's like I'm seeing all of it at once—every moment in the past few years he's hoped for something from Vanessa and she's let him down.

"Why would your mom send you stuff through the dispatch?" Mariella asks. "I thought she didn't know you were running it."

"I don't know," says Tom, who is staring at her phone now, too, his voice flat. "I don't know."

There's a beat none of us are sure whether to fill, waiting to see if Tom's going to say something else.

"Well, she'll tell you when she gets back," I say firmly. I'm ready to add that I'll stay with Tom until then, ready to offer up theories for what his mom's doing with the dispatch if he wants to discuss them, ready to drop what we're doing here and leave with him so he can give me the play-by-play of what she just said to him on the phone.

Tom just shakes his head. Then he pulls in a breath so resolute that I start steeling myself for his next few words before I even know the shape of them.

"I'm just—going to leave the city early." He's talking to the group, but he's almost looking at me. Like he wants permission, maybe. Or forgiveness. "The way I originally planned. So I'll be gone before she gets back."

"Gone where?" asks Jesse.

My heart sinks not just for the clear pain Tom is in right now, but the finality of this. It's ridiculous, I know. But there was some stubborn, relentless, overly optimistic part of me that was hoping maybe fate would intervene. That Tom and his mom would have an opportunity to work things out, and it would settle this ache in him. That maybe if we just kept him here a little while longer—here with our friends and our various misadventures, here in this city he's seeing in a whole new light this summer, here with *me*—that he'd change his mind.

Tom smiles an apologetic smile, an almost sheepish one.

"I'm moving," he says, so casually that it's clear he's trying to play it off, not to let anyone worry. "I should have said something earlier. The summer just got away from me, is all."

My heart doesn't just sink then, but crash. It wasn't just stubborn hope, I realize. There was a reason Tom kept this from all of us for so long. I think he didn't really believe he was going to do it either.

When I blink myself out of the ache of that thought I realize everyone's turned to me. Expectant. Hopeful, even. As if I'm going to step out right now and say the miraculous thing that stops this from happening.

I want to. I know I'm the only one of us who can. The trouble is, given everything I have on the line, I'm the last one who should.

"Tom," Jesse starts.

But Tom pulls out his phone fast and says, "Anyway, uh— we're short on dispatchers today, so I'm actually going to go help out with a few real quick. So sorry to bounce."

Every single one of us can tell this is a lie, but nobody calls him on it, not even Mariella with the app open a foot from her face. I watch him carefully until his eyes snag on mine, until he can see the question in them. He gives me a quick shake of his head. Wherever he's going, he wants to be alone.

He leaves and it's so quiet that for a moment nobody knows what to do with it. Tom has a way of filling the nooks and crannies of a space in that comforting way of his, even when he's not saying much, and there's nothing quite as loud as the silence he leaves behind.

"Shit," says Jesse. "He can't be serious."

"He is," I say, trying to keep my voice light. Trying to keep up Tom's ruse, or maybe one of my own: that everything really is fine.

Luca just keeps shaking his head like he's confused or rejecting the idea entirely, and Mariella's eyes are on me, searching my face. She must see the grim certainty in it, because she pulls in a breath.

"Well, I guess there's only one thing left to do," she says. "Which is obviously throw a going-away dinner for him so good that he'll come to his senses and stay put."

Luca nods in agreement and also faint alarm. "Why do I have a feeling we're all going to be arrested for kidnapping before the end of the night?"

"Luca," says Mariella, reaching up to pat him endearingly on the head. "You can't get arrested if you don't get caught."

# Chapter Twenty-Two

There's a scene in the fourth Tides of Time book where the time stone cracks midmission, and Claire and one of her best friends are separated in the time stream. Several long chapters are devoted to finding him, but her time instruments just keep finding doppelgangers. She dismisses most of them easily, but eventually she starts to question herself. Starts to wonder if she should go back and make sure she wasn't too hasty—if maybe something happened in that garbled time stream to make him forget her, and she'd accidentally left him in a time where he didn't belong because of it.

By the time she does find him she's seen so many doppel-gangers, including ones that try to trick her into taking them with her, that she doesn't know if she can trust him. "Tell me something only you would know," she demands, just in case.

But he doesn't tell her. He shows her. A series of hand gestures—a collection of the ones they used to make in class together, when they were trying to talk without getting caught.

She knows instantly she's found him, and they bring him back home to the time school, where—for the next few pages before the time worms attack, at least—all is finally well.

We read that book just before the summer Tom and I were ten, the same summer Vanessa took him out to Los Angeles for a month to start meeting with producers about one of her first big scripts. It was the longest we'd ever been apart since we met, so long that it felt like the kind of time that I couldn't measure, could only dread. We'd only been friends for two years by then, and for some reason my little-kid brain was certain that a month would be all it took to unravel it. Like Tom happening to me was some kind of happy accident from the universe, but as soon as he unhappened, he'd be lost to me like Claire's friend in the time stream. He'd come back as some doppelganger of himself, someone so changed that he'd finally come to his senses and realize he didn't want me around anymore.

This irrational thought was partially fueled by the sense that us being apart didn't even seem to bother Tom in the days leading up to it. So I tried to pretend it didn't bother me either. I went out of my way to make plans with my cousins and Jesse and our other friends. I told Tom about them loudly and in great detail whenever I got the chance. I did it like I was punishing him for caring less than I did; I did it like I was trying to test to see if he really did.

I kept this whole charade of mine up until the Fourth of July, the day before Tom was supposed to leave. The fireworks started going off and everyone's heads tilted toward the sky, and with all eyes safely preoccupied, I immediately, humiliatingly started to cry. It was as if someone had turned on a faucet in me—big, thick, silent tears just dripping down my cheeks so fast that it felt less like crying and more like I was malfunctioning. Like someone had tapped the wrong button in my brain.

It didn't take more than a few seconds for Tom to wrap his hand in mine and say, "Let's get ice cream." Which seemed absolutely ridiculous until I realized he was using it as an excuse to pull me away from our moms and friends without anyone else noticing I'd become a geyser, which only made me want to cry harder, because here was Tom being *nice* to me when I'd spent the whole start of the summer grandstanding about how perfectly fine I'd be without him.

Tom found a bench away from the crowd and sat us down on it. He didn't say anything, just let me sit there and cry, which was for the best because my throat was a big knot and I wouldn't have been able to answer if I tried. The fireworks kept whirring and popping and flashing overhead, but neither of us looked up. We just watched the faint light of it streak across our faces, mine wrecked and his as solemn as I'd ever seen it.

Eventually I came back to myself just enough to realize I needed to make something up to explain. Except when I opened my mouth, all I could do was immediately croak out the words, "I don't want you to go."

Tom didn't try to do that thing adults did when they were trying to make you feel better, like tell you it won't be for long, or to think of the bright side. Instead he just said quietly, and so easily that I was embarrassed for thinking even for a second that he might have felt otherwise, "I don't want to either. I'm going to miss you a lot."

The relief might have bowled me over if we weren't already sitting down. I was still crying, but it almost felt good to cry after that. Knowing that I wasn't alone in the feeling.

"What if we're totally different when you come back?" I asked just the same. This seemed entirely possible. Tom made friends wherever he went and he didn't seem too picky about them. I held myself as perhaps the highest example of this.

After two years I was still confused about what made him care enough to wait me out so long in the first place.

Tom was thoughtful in that way he mostly was around me. He didn't take his time with our other friends, almost like he was worried about letting silences go on too long. It seemed like a shame because Tom always had something smart to say on the other end of it.

"We'll do what Claire did in Tides of Time. Make our own handshake," says Tom. "We'll do it before I leave and when I come back. And then we'll know nothing's really changed."

We spent the rest of that night coming up with our goofy, ridiculous, nonsense handshake, one that I practiced by myself every single night after Tom left. When he came back he was a little tanner, a little taller, but bursting with a grin so wide that even before we did the handshake—publicly and flawlessly and very, very loudly, much to the amusement of our moms and several bystanders—I knew everything was going to be okay.

As it turned out, we needed that handshake more than we knew. That trip to Los Angeles was the first of many. Tom would be gone for spring breaks, for chunks of summer vacation, sometimes a few days in the middle of the school year. Then one day, finally, the inevitable happened—Tom was gone for good.

It should be a familiar feeling by now, watching Tom leave me behind, but it isn't. This is the first time Tom's ever left by choice.

This is the first time it feels like he's taking a piece of me with him.

I come back to the apartment after a long walk in the park to find that same backpack I saw on my first day. Only this time it's already sitting on the chair by the door, with a duffel just underneath it, and Tom is standing sheepishly a few feet away.

I don't say anything and neither does he. He steps forward first, wrapping me in his arms. I press my face into the crook of his neck, breathing him in, teetering on this strange edge of what we are and what we might have been.

"What time does your bus leave tomorrow?" I ask.

Tom settles a hand on the back of my neck and I feel the quiet apology in it. "I'm leaving tonight."

The surprise forces my eyes open, pushes air into my chest. "Tonight?"

Neither of us pulls away, like we can absorb each other now—my shock, his apology, our mutual hurt.

"Tom, what did your mom say?" I ask into his shirt.

Tom shakes his head and says, "She didn't. It was her assistant who called. I asked if she could put my mom on and she said she couldn't find her, and—well. It's been hours now. I'm guessing she's not calling back, and honestly, I'm just—I'm done."

I'm holding him tighter, but his voice is surprisingly steady. I know better than to think he's come to peace with any of this, but it sounds like he thinks he has. That leaving like this is just enough of a balm on the situation that he can pretend.

"You're not even curious about all the things she's sent you on the dispatch?" I ask.

Tom only shakes his head again. "I bet it was her assistant, at this rate. And even if it wasn't—it's even more upsetting in a way. To know she'd be willing to do that but not actually talk to me. And I've tried. I've been trying."

"I know," I say.

I pull back just enough to see his face. His hands are still wrapped around my waist, my hands still pressed to his shoulders. It's the first time we've ever stood like this, but that's maybe the only bizarre thing about it—that it hasn't happened before now. That we can fit this well together and have spent our whole lives not knowing it.

"I'll take the bus with you," I offer.

Something still doesn't sit right with me, letting him go on his own like this. I know he doesn't want to hear it, but it seems now more than ever that he's not leaving for any reason other than to be so far from Vanessa that she can't disappoint him anymore.

But judging from the look on his face, he already knows that, too. He still wants out.

"This is your home now, Riley. Anyone can see that. And you've got plans for tomorrow and the next day and the next that are finally all your own." He says it with such pride that I find my face warming despite the overwhelming worry, despite the tangle of everything else. "I don't want to take you from here, not even for the day."

I've got one other card to play. I lean in, briefly pressing my forehead to the bridge of his nose.

"The last thing on the Getaway List," I remind him. "Our road trip. We'll make it this."

When I pull back Tom is smiling with a heaviness that could crack a heart.

"Let's make another list," he says. "Instead of that being the last one, it can be the first. We'll start new."

"I hate that," I tell him, so bluntly I can see the ghost of a smile on his lips. "I really, really hate it."

He's still smiling, soft and fond and heartbreaking. "But you love New York."

"I love you," I say. "And I'm not telling you that so you'll change your mind. I'm telling you that so you never doubt it no matter how far you go. I'm telling you that because you are someone so easy to love that it kills me to think you've ever been made to think you're not. And I'm telling you that because I'm too selfish to keep it to myself."

Tom's on the verge of crying again, but there's a smile on his face just the same. A quiet one that he only ever seems to smile for me.

"You know, Riley," he says, his voice low. "I've thought the same thing about you since the first time I saw you."

"I was an asshole the first time I saw you," I remind him.

Tom shakes his head and says, "The first time you saw *me*. I saw you before that. You were getting out of the car with your mom and telling her some story about your cousin. You had the biggest smile I'd ever seen and the loudest voice I'd ever heard, and I just—I thought I'd wait forever if it meant making you laugh like that even once."

It's strange to be this belatedly embarrassed for something I can't fully remember, but I remember well enough. How even when I was little I was aware that I was a bit *too much*. Too loud, too sharp-tongued, too curious. How even by that age I was trying anything I could not to be, because I was trying not to call attention to myself. Trying not to be different.

I haven't thought about that in a while. Not since I grew into our group of friends and all our little edges and quirks all grew to fit into each other's. And certainly not since I moved here, where I've felt free enough to be louder and sharper-tongued and more curious than I've ever been.

Tom tucks a stray hair behind my ear. "But you were so quiet around most people. I couldn't understand it. I think I do now, but back then it broke my heart, too. Because I loved you even then, I think. Before I knew what it meant, I knew what it was going to be." He pulls in a breath so steady that it feels like I'm breathing it with him, then says, "If we're going to lay it all out tonight, you should know, Riley. I've been in love with you for a long time. Since before I left for New York."

The words have a soul-deep warmth to them, the kind that settles over me like a blanket after coming in from the cold. There's that same flutter just under my ribs that I've been feeling all summer, the one I tried so desperately to ignore, and for the first time I let myself feel it. Let it spread through my body, a quiet, rippling, certain thing.

I've never felt anything like it before. It's so simultaneously grounding and terrifying that I almost don't know what to do with it, except to choke out the words, "I didn't know."

He squeezes the hand he still has on my waist, a quick and reassuring pulse. There's a gentleness in his voice that almost borders on teasing. "Because I didn't tell you." Then he adds quietly, "I didn't know if you felt the same. I didn't want to put it on you."

That's fair. I don't know what I would have thought of it either—if I'd have been ready for this kind of feeling back then the way I am now. The way I clearly wasn't with Jesse, when I thought getting together and breaking up with someone was as easy as sliding on and off a pair of shoes.

"And since it's all out there—you're the reason I came up with the app," says Tom. "I told you I had imaginary conversations with you. Well, really, it was more like—I'd write letters I didn't send. *Dear Riley. Love, Tom.* Like a journal, except I just wrote everything to you. Things I wanted to say to you so badly. Not just what was happening in New York, but how I felt about you. And I just thought—" He takes another breath to steel himself. "Maybe I'm lonely, but I'm not alone in this. In feeling like there are things you want to say to the people you love, but aren't ready to say to them, or don't fully know how. It made me think about that game we always loved to play on our friends. How we'd sneak things into their lockers without a word, so they wouldn't feel that way anymore. So I had the idea for the app. And Mariella—I saw what happened to her. I saw someone as lonely as me. I figured we'd make a good team, and well—the rest was history."

The story finally makes sense, now that I understand the roots of it. I was right. He didn't do this for the money to leave. He didn't even do it to escape. He did it so he could do the same thing he's always done, even if he couldn't do it here the same way—to help bring people together. To make people feel loved.

"I still would rather you had told me," I tell him. "Then I could have been that person for you."

"I know. I even said that to you in some of the letters. 'You'd be so mad at me if you knew about these,'" he says, with a faint laugh. "But it's like I said before. If I never sent them to you I could still be the Tom I was when I was with you."

"You're always that Tom, you dope. You always have me."

I say that even though I know I've done a version of the same thing to him. I came to New York for a lot of reasons—to start over. To make my own choices. To figure out what kind of person I wanted to be. But every one of those reasons was buoyed by the idea of coming here to find my old self before I could be someone new. A self I could only find in Tom, who knew me as I was then, who still held that version of me in his heart like she never left.

We were never going to preserve those old selves for each other. We're both very different people now, for better and for worse. I wish so badly I could change parts of the past that made us this way—that I could rewrite Tom's loneliness, that I could give myself the control I didn't realize I'd lost until it was too late—but then maybe we wouldn't have this clarity we have now. This understanding that we don't have to be our old selves to fit, because this love will always change shape with us.

"I know that now," Tom says. "I hope you know it, too. That you always have me."

I see it in his eyes then. Something wavering. Something I

could press right now and bend to my will if I wanted to, and all it would take is one word: *Stay.*

I press the word back into me, sealing it like an envelope, like my own "Dear, Love" letter unsent. I don't think there's a way for me to say that word without making it the most selfish one in the whole world.

"I'm worried," I admit instead. "With you leaving like this. Without even saying goodbye to our friends. It all seems really fast."

Tom's eyes flit to the floor. It happens quickly but not before I see the flicker of disappointment, almost like he was hoping I'd say something else.

"And not to sound like my own mom right now," I say, trying to keep my tone light, "but do you even know anyone there aside from your aunt?"

When Tom looks up again that waver in his eyes is gone, his expression soft but resolute. "I know it seems sudden, but I've been thinking about this a long time. And saying goodbye to everyone—I don't want this to feel like a big beginning and end. It's just a change, is all. I'll be back to visit. No big deal."

He caps this off with a slight smile, one that I know is meant to reassure me. But I'm not Tom's mom or our cluster of old friends or any number of people who were close enough to get that smile from Tom and fall for it.

But I nod, because he needs me to be reassured. I nod even though he sees through me just as easily as I see through him. I nod because I love him and maybe this is his chance to be happy the way he deserves; I nod because I love him and I'll be here for him if it isn't, the same as he'll always be there for me.

He pulls me in again and I understand that this isn't just a hug but a goodbye. I feel those old words creeping up in me the same way they did so many times as a kid: *What if we're totally different when you come back?*

Only this time it's not a matter of *what if*. We're already different; we'll always have this just the same.

We don't kiss. We don't do our handshake. For a moment it almost feels like Tom said—not an ending or a beginning, just something that's happening for now. But then he pulls me in a little tighter, tells me he'll text me when he gets in, and the moment he's out of my reach I can feel my heart taking a reluctant snapshot of this moment. The split and excruciating second between before and after; the last moment I have to say his name or let him go.

The door closes behind him, a strange bracket closing the summer with the two of us on opposite sides of this wall. I stand there, entirely unsure of what to do with myself for a few long minutes, only to realize there's only one thing I can do. I pull out my phone and call my mom.

"Tom's leaving New York," I blurt.

Inexplicably, impossibly, my mom says, "I know."

I don't ask how on earth that could be true, because in this moment it almost doesn't matter what she says. I just need to hear her voice, and know she can hear mine. "Also I'm in love with him."

Her voice is softer. "I know."

And then finally, with an unbearable crush of disappointment and relief, I start to cry.

# Chapter Twenty-Three

I spend the next day outrunning the absence of Tom, and at first it's easy. I have to meet up with Eddie and Dai to help move a used couch into our new place while Jesse's working a shift at his new gig at a guitar shop. I have to pack up the last of my things strewn around the apartment. I have a final job interview as a barista at a charming little hole-in-the-wall spot in the East Village where Mariella's been going since she was a kid.

I should be nervous for the interview, but being in the shop is the most settled I've felt all day. It's not just that it's cozy and homelike, with the maroon walls and worn-out lounge chairs and warm yellow fairy lights on the wall. It's that everyone here knows each other—what they do for work, how they take their tea, what the names of all their pets are. There's a back wall so littered with flyers you can't even see the wallpaper behind it, advertising upcoming shows from indie bands, creative work-shops, odd jobs in the community. The longer I'm in New

York the more I get the impression that it isn't the shiny new universe I expected it to be—it's just the home of a hundred thousand little universes like this one that all exist rubbing up against each other, sometimes never touching, sometimes spilling to make something new.

I look at that wall of flyers and it feels like a manifestation of all the Rileys I could be here, that I'm going to get a chance to try on. I walk into the interview with a bright, settled smile. I show off all the tricks I've learned from being my mom's shadow at the coffee shop back home. I walk out not just with a job offer, but the sincere question, "How soon can you start?"

I open my mouth to say *tomorrow*, but instead I say, "Would it be okay if I start next week?"

A few ideas seize me in that moment. I'll take a road trip on my own; eight and a half items out of nine is still better than eight. I'll take the train upstate to where we were going to camp and walk around the small town outside of the camping grounds. I'll book a bus ticket to one of the *Tides of Time* shooting locations I always wondered about seeing outside the city. I'll take my blank notebook somewhere to try to drum up ideas for the short-story contest that's kept me awake every night this week, still trying to decide whether or not I want to go for it in the first place. I'll take a subway, a train, a bus, just for a little while, just to get out of my own head, but that doesn't stop my head from doing exactly what it did last night. It takes me right back around in a circle.

I have to go home.

This probably should have been clear during the brief, mostly one-sided conversation I had with my mom last night. She stayed on the line with me as long as she could, but she was the closing manager on duty so mostly what I did was blurt it all out: that I'd been determined not to fall for Tom, but I fell for him anyway. That she was wrong about him being the one to push things, because he was the one keeping an eye out on everyone all summer. That I was scared for his sake because all these years nobody was keeping an eye on him, and now he was gone.

My mom didn't try to fight me on any of it—she wasn't even upset. She just said a lot of "I know" in that comforting way moms do when you're not sure if they really do or not, but it doesn't matter because they know *you*.

She tried to stay on the line longer but I told her to go when I heard people calling for her from the front. I promised I'd catch up with her tomorrow. But now that I've talked to her, the ache of missing her is too deep to ignore. Like hearing one "I know" from her let me finally pull in a breath deep enough to feel how far it went down.

I need to talk to her face-to-face. Not just about everything I told her last night, but about everything I've avoided talking to her about all summer, and long before that. Everyone around me has already been brave this summer, following their passions and having hard conversations and starting fresh from them. I've been cheering them on through it all, but I've been a hypocrite. It's time for me to take their cues and be brave, too.

My bag is already packed, so it's really a matter of figuring out which bus from Port Authority will get me back to Virginia the earliest. My nose is buried in the transit schedule when I open the door to leave Tom's apartment, only to find my mom on the other side of it.

For a moment we're too stunned to react, like we're both recovering from the uncanny sensation of almost running into a mirror. Then it really *is* like running into a mirror, because both of our expressions wobble at the same time, our arms stretching out so fast that they're tangled before I can even croak out the word "*Mom*."

She hugs me fiercely, smelling like coffee and lavender shampoo and home. We stand there in the open doorway for so long that we might have just been reunited from a millennium apart, from separate edges of the world. It feels like enough of me has changed that we might have been, but also like there are some things, comfortingly, that could never change if I tried. This feeling between us we've always had, one that I recognized the shape of before I had the words for it—the two of us are a team. Maybe we've wanted different things these past few years, but we are still the same in our cores. We still want the world for each other, because for so long we've been each other's worlds.

She pulls away from me but keeps her hands on my arms, looking me up and down as if to account for me. Only then does she see the backpack on my shoulders, her eyebrows lifting in question.

I look her up and down, too. At her familiar bright red floral top and her faded jeans and her hair every bit as wavy and recently sun-kissed as mine, the same way we get every summer.

"I missed you," I say. "It's a good thing you showed up when you did or we'd be passing each other on I-95."

My mom pulls me in for another hug then, one that eases the backpack off my shoulders and has us headed back into the living room. She hasn't been here before but that somehow doesn't stop her from seamlessly figuring out that the hidden door in Vanessa's kitchen is in fact the fridge, and pulling out two seltzers. She hands one to me as we stand at the ceiling-high window, staring out at the lush green of Central Park, at the expanse of downtown Manhattan beyond it, at the whirring traffic of the street down below.

"Wow," says my mom. "It feels like being on top of the world."

I want to smile but there's something in the way her eyes

are skimming the view, hushed and reverent, that weighs on me. The understanding that I was right. That for all my mom's "do as I say, not as I do," we're still the same—I can recognize everything I feel about this place reflected back in the lights in her eyes.

Neither of us moves to sit. We just stare out at it.

"Nothing compared to the back-alley brick wall view of the new place with the band," I quip.

"Yeah, I bet not," she says wryly. Her shoulders soften a bit, a resignation in them. "You were never planning on coming back for good, were you?"

A beat passes where I'm still scared to answer. I can tell she's already come to terms with it, but it feels like it's deeper than that even. The way Tom was insisting his leaving wasn't a big beginning or an end—telling my mom face-to-face would make this decision finally feel like one, once and for all.

"No," I admit. "I should have said something earlier. I just—I missed you. I didn't want to drive you away again."

My mom shakes her head. "You didn't drive me away. I was—trying to give you space to let you make your own decisions. I've been wrapped up in the ones I made at your age. But I know that's not fair to you."

"Well," I say, glancing at Tom's empty bedroom. "You can still have an 'I told you so' moment about falling for Tom."

I'm partially saying it to break the tension, but also so she doesn't have to say what I know has probably been on the tip of her tongue since the moment she took my call last night. Instead she waits until I meet her eye and says carefully, "Maybe. But we've talked enough these past few weeks that we both know that what you're trying to do here isn't about him."

The relief of hearing her say that is like cool water through my veins. Tom's being here had nothing to do with the real problem I've been running from, or the future I've been running toward. Loving Tom is something that exists separately from that. I'm learning that's a lot of what love is—stepping aside for the sake of each other's futures. The way Tom wouldn't let me come with him. The way I wouldn't ask Tom to stay.

But I've been missing that same resolution with my mom, because it's not the same. She's already lived a version of this life I've chosen. I've thought of it as a sticking point the entire time I've been here, but now that she's actually here, I'm understanding that it never should have been. It should have been common ground.

"I was wrong to assume you and Tom would get into trouble up here, but you have to understand where I'm coming from, too." My mom's eyes fall from my face and toward the view in front of us, and for a moment I don't think we're looking at the same New York at all. "I know you've heard some of this over the years. But when I came up here I was the exact same age you are now. I had all these big dreams about performing, but I never made a plan to pursue them. I got caught up in a person, one I thought I could trust. He felt like my best friend, too. It didn't take long for me to get caught up in his world instead of mine, because that was how he wanted it to be. Everything was about his music. The partying. The shows. The travel. Before I knew it, I was burnt out and broke and spending more time trying to support him than myself. I lost track of myself before I even knew who I was."

There's so much of this I want to ask her about while this unexpected door to her past is open, but I'm still too tangled in the present. The bruise of that conversation we had earlier in the summer still hasn't faded. I need to press down on it again before it can start to heal.

"And then I came along," I prompt her.

My mom shakes her head, turning to me and saying firmly,

"I'd lost track of my plans before that. I hadn't even been to an audition in months. I know we haven't talked about this much, and it's mostly because I didn't want you ever thinking you had anything to do with why I gave up on those dreams. I need you to know that I left New York before I found out I was having you."

She waits me out like she's expecting to see the relief in my face, but I don't feel any yet. I press on the bruise harder.

"You were still so scared I'd make a mistake and get knocked up, too," I say pointedly.

My mom sets down her seltzer and puts her hands on my shoulders, waiting for me to meet her eye. "That's what I should have made clear from the start. That was never the mistake, Riley. It was losing sight of myself for the sake of someone else. I don't need you to go to a certain school or live a certain place. I just need you to live your own life, on your own terms." She squeezes me lightly, her eyes misting. "I'm lucky that I figured out a way to do that back home after my time here, but I just—you're so spirited and so much like I was back then, and the last thing I want is to see that spark of yours blown out by someone else."

My own eyes are watering, my voice thick with frustration. "That's what I don't understand, though. You watched Tom grow up. You know he's not like that."

She nods carefully. "But you two still had a bit of a track record for trouble. And maybe it was harmless, but it was hard to think about that when the rest of this threw me for a loop— you moving so suddenly, and practically moving in with him. It was like watching my past self in a time machine. Especially at the start of this, when it felt like you didn't have much of a plan, either. There were just too many parallels. It scared me."

"It scared me, too," I tell her, my voice suddenly unsteady, my cheeks warm with the strange relief of the confession.

"Being here without you. And thinking—thinking you were mad at me for it. That maybe I was the thing that wrecked this for you, if you wanted it as badly as I do now."

My mom wraps me up in her arms fast and says fiercely into my ear, "I regret a lot of how this summer was handled, but if you ever thought for a second that you weren't the best thing that's ever happened to me, that's the worst regret by far." She pulls back to look me in the eye again, holding me there. "You are my everything, and I'm grateful for every second of the life we built together."

It's nothing I don't already know, nothing she hasn't told me in other words before. But it hits me sideways in this moment, I think, because it's the first time she's said it not just as mother and daughter, but as two fully grown people. Before I know it we're both blinking back tears.

She lets my shoulders go, her voice as choked up as mine when she says, "I was scared of losing you, and you have to know that's never going to stop for me. But I know things have to be different now. You're your own person, no matter how much you remind me of the old me."

"Mom," I say wetly, trying for a laugh. "I would never, ever wear rhinestone Ugg boots."

This earns me a wry smile. "Don't knock them until you try them."

We move toward the couch then, sitting side by side, still facing the sprawling city view. The way the lights from the city cast over her face, I have that same sense of being displaced in time. Like I'm looking at some version of my mom from before I existed, one who must have felt the same magic in the glow of those lights, walked the same streets and felt the same kinds of dreams.

"We're the same but we're not," I say quietly. "Because you're right. I came here without a plan. I'm still not sure if I have one. But I want to find out who I am, and I think—that's what the city does for me. Gives me the space to figure it out. To make a plan someday, even if I don't have one now."

My mom nods slowly, taking this in. I brace myself for her objections. For her to remind me that I don't have her or my aunts or cousins here. That as of tomorrow I'll be living in a glorified cabinet drawer paid for with the exact job I could get at home and could be saving the money from.

Instead she says, "When did you get so grown up?"

I feel my face flush. "Funny how the passage of time works."

She sinks farther into the couch, and then so do I. There's something about reaching this point in the conversation that already feels like a relief before it's over. This feeling that we can say whatever needs to be said right now, and whatever we're opening up in ourselves will find a way to seam itself together again.

"I'm sorry I didn't hear you out on this sooner," says my mom, shifting her head to look at me. "I'm going to try to be better about it. But it's a two-way street, Riley. You have to talk to me, too. I had no idea you were so upset about your schedule."

It takes a moment to answer her, only because for all I've resented the past few years, I've never actually imagined a conversation about it. It didn't seem like one we'd ever have.

"It wasn't just being upset. It was that—I hated having everything decided for me. I hated not having any time to do what I wanted, like write or explore or even just—be with my friends." Now that I've said it the rest spills out of me, almost faster than I can keep up. "It felt like you were rejecting all those parts of me, and it felt even worse when I realized you were using it to keep me from Tom, too. Like you didn't trust me to stay out of trouble or even pick my own friends. But I didn't say anything because I thought you knew how I felt and just—didn't care."

That last part is only half true. The other truth is that I didn't want to rock the boat. Becoming friends with Tom as a kid gave me a new perspective on single parenthood, because he and Vanessa were always so comfortable. I don't think I appreciated just how hard my mom had to work to give me the same things Vanessa gave Tom until then, and the last thing I wanted to do was make it harder on her.

But I can't say that. I think she must already know, because there are plenty of things she's done in turn to hide it from me, to make it so I'd never have to worry. So much of this, I'm starting to realize, is less that we don't understand each other, and more that we understand each other too well.

"I'm your mom. I always care," she says. "But we've both been busy these past few years and I just—I'm sorry if it seemed like I was rejecting you, and if you felt like you had to do any of that to make me happy. All I wanted was for *you* to be happy. But I've always thought of that more in the long term, and for me that meant keeping you out of trouble, and I thought that meant keeping you from Tom. All that structure seemed like the way to do it. Something I didn't have with my own parents, to the point where it seemed a lot of the time like they didn't even care. It upset me so much that I felt like I had to kick up a big fuss and go to make a point."

My throat tightens in that moment because it reminds me so painfully of Tom that I feel the ache for him all over again, only deeper this time now that I'm feeling it for my mom, too.

"I never knew that," I say.

"I didn't tell you, and I wish I had. Especially now that I know your aunts sure gave you a mouthful," she says, rolling her eyes.

I choose my next words carefully. "I think it might have helped me understand where you were coming from on this if I knew. I wasn't—I've always known how much you care," I tell her. It feels important that she knows that.

Sure enough, she ducks her head for a brief moment, like maybe that really had been one of her fears. Like maybe it was the one that was driving all the overscheduling and helicopter parenting of the past few years. It starts to shift the narrative in my head, enough for me to understand how deep this conversation needs to go before we can come out to the other side of it.

"I've always known I can count on you. But the way you were involved—too involved—it felt like you didn't trust me," I tell her.

"Sometimes I didn't," she admits. "I've always trusted your intentions. But your judgment—well. I didn't tell you what I did at your age because I worried it might just give you incentive to get into more trouble than you already had."

She's said variations of this before, and they're a snag that can't let go of me. I never needed ideas. I had plenty of my own, and they came from an entirely different place than she thinks they did.

It feels scary to challenge her on that, even in this moment when we've been more receptive than we've ever been. It's less that I'm worried she'll be upset, but more that it feels strange to point out the differences between us, the disconnect.

"I've never wanted to get into trouble, though. I've just wanted to explore." I think of what Tom said to me on the roof the other night, about having so much potential because I'm curious. It didn't know how to settle in me then, but I'm starting to see the truth in it now. "All those things we snuck off and did as kids—it was just because we wanted to learn things, wanted to see what we were capable of. We've been doing a lot of that this summer, too."

"I know," says my mom. Not reluctantly, but confidently, the same way she did last night. As if she knows a whole lot more about the summer than the bare details we discussed over text.

I watch her carefully. "You do know," I say, the *how?* very much implied.

My mom nods. "You were right about Tom. He really is looking out for you. When you and I weren't texting as much, he'd fill me in on what you two were getting up to. He said he didn't want me to worry."

I go very still, only because this is a lot to digest at once. The idea that Tom was keeping yet another secret from me, the way he did with the dispatch service.

"I hope you're not mad at him," says my mom quickly. "I get the sense that he was worried about us because of his own relationship with Vanessa."

I'm not angry. If anything I'm a little bit sad. Understanding that Tom's way of keeping secrets is just another quiet way he's trying to protect the people around him, whether it's the best way to go about it or not. He didn't want my relationship with my mom to go the way of his, and this was the only way he could think of to intervene.

It's a very Tom thing to do. Another way of isolating himself, of taking on other people's problems. It makes me worry even more now that he's about to be in the middle of nowhere, more isolated than he's ever been.

So I shake my head. "I'm not. But yeah, things with Vanessa—well, for lack of a better way to say it, have gone to shit."

"I gathered that." My mom's voice is tight. "Vanessa and I were briefly in touch, too. I had her old email and got her attention with a less-than-polite subject line about you two being up here unchaperoned and her just being okay with it. I always hated how the two of you could slip right out from under her nose when you were kids."

I bite down the urge to smile, because Tom and I counted on that for all our adventures. But the urge fades just as fast knowing that the same way we used to slip out from under her, she let Tom slip out completely.

"Then as the summer went on and I was in touch with you and Tom separately, I kept emailing less out of worry about what the two of you were up to and more worry for what was going on between Tom and Vanessa," says my mom.

"Did you know she was sending him things through the dispatch?" I ask.

My mom tilts her head. "What dispatch?"

"There's this app where people can anonymously send gifts," I explain. "They deliver all over the city. And for some reason Tom kept getting them every time we were going on one of our Getaway—our, uh. The activities we were doing with our friends."

"For the Getaway List," says my mom.

My skin prickles, so unprepared to hear those words come out of her mouth that the guilt of it doesn't even know where to land. "You know about that?"

Her backpack is still at our feet. She unzips it and produces something I sure as hell never thought I'd see again: my graduation cap. She flips it to show the inside, where my version of the Getaway List is taped and still very much intact.

"Oh," I say, and then before I can think the better of it, "Shit."

"You never told me about this," she says. I'm relieved to hear some bemusement in her tone, even if mostly she just sounds sad. "Why not?"

And here comes the bit I was avoiding; the truth we can't quite skate around anymore. "I didn't want you to feel bad. I know some of it was you keeping us separated, but I also know some of it was because we were on our own."

She settles the cap into my lap and doesn't speak for a few moments, but there's no tension in the silence. Just a quiet understanding.

"I think every parent feels that way about their kids. Wanting to give more to them than they can." She lowers her eyes just enough that I know better than to look away. That these are words she needs me to hear most. "But you don't have to protect me from that kind of thing. I'm your mom. I'll always want more for you. And I'll always be here for you no matter how old you get."

I lean in and she pulls me into her arms again, and I'm grateful in that moment not just to be the eighteen-year-old Riley I am—the Riley who has dozens of Google Docs tabs of writing and lifelong friends and a whole future to dive into—but all the iterations of Riley I've ever been. The ones that have always, always known that this is my soft place to land.

We pull apart, both a little weepy again. It feels like there's going to be a lot of that today. I cast my eyes on the graduation cap I thought I'd never see again, skimming a finger through the unchecked boxes on my list that are all mostly checked now. All of them save one—the same one that is somewhere in North Carolina right now, farther than he's ever been.

"If Vanessa knew to send things to Tom before you did any of your adventures it was probably because I was telling her about them," says my mom. "She said she was hoping to repair her relationship with him. I thought maybe if I kept her in the loop she'd take the time to reach out on her own."

I open my mouth to ask how on earth my mom kept in touch with Vanessa when even Tom couldn't manage it half the time, but a lot of old memories well up and answer for me. There was a time my mom and Vanessa were friends, too. A time that predated me and Tom being friends. When Vanessa was like another older sister to my mom, and my mom must have felt like the funny, judgment-free friend Vanessa never had at her big corporate job before she quit to write.

They were close once. Close enough that it seems strange to me looking back on it that they grew as far apart as they did. But I suppose Tom wasn't the only one Vanessa let fall to the wayside in this climb of hers. It gives me some new context for all the times my mom didn't want me coming up here, for why she was so upset Vanessa wasn't here to "supervise" me and Tom when I eventually did. She understood Vanessa was disconnecting from the people she loves before I did, before Tom could even fully comprehend it. I wonder how many times before this my mom might have tried and failed to pull her back.

I draw my knees up on the couch, leaning into her. "She picked a weird way to go about it."

My mom nods. "I didn't hear much back from her, but when I realized how bad it was I told her she should call Tom more often. Learn what's actually going on in his life." She leans her head onto the top of mine. "Maybe that was her way of starting."

My eyes well up again, partially because of Tom, but mostly because there's something overwhelming about knowing that my mom and I spent the summer quietly on the same team. It feels like some measure of order has been restored, knowing that we both still think the same way, hope for the same things.

"I don't want you to think I'm running away from you," I tell her, choked up again. "Leaving home was the hardest thing I've ever done."

She runs a hand through my hair and says it again. "I know." Then she adds, "And I know it probably doesn't sound that way, from the stories. But it was for me when I left, too."

My mom has always been close with my grandparents, but

I spent too much time in the collective bubble of my family not to know there's still some lingering tension between them. Tension that I'm sure came to a head when she struck out on her own that first time.

The words pile out of me then, because all my bravery about New York still hinges on one soul-deep fear. "If I stay—we'll be okay, you and me?"

"*When* you stay," my mom corrects me. "And Riley, of course. I'm sorry it's taken me some time to adjust to this. It's new territory for us both."

"I'll visit," I promise her.

"Good," she says. "And if I won't cramp your style too much with the ghost of Ugg boots past, I'd love to come up here and visit you, too."

The distant lights have been gleaming through the window the whole time, but they feel like they're casting a new warmth now. Like something is finally settled between us, and now the weight of it is off our shoulders, giving us room to breathe.

"You can show me all your old haunts," I say with a sly smile.

"I can show you a very narrow margin of them," says my mom, "and not because I don't trust you, to be clear. I just cannot look anyone in the eye who might remember what I looked like with bedazzled bright green hair."

"You didn't," I say, delighted.

"I did," she says grimly. "You can disregard the rest of my advice if you want. But let me warn you, my mini-me, that you and I cannot pull that look off."

I burrow in then, feeling a flicker of mischief, one that I haven't felt in a conversation with my mom in a long time. "Are you finally going to tell me about your time in the city then? I didn't even know you wanted to act."

My mom does something then that I haven't seen her do

since she had a crush on my fifth-grade teacher, and genuinely blushes. "That was a long time ago," she says. For a moment I think that's the end of it—that I've finally pressed on the boundary of how far this conversation will go—until she adds, "But yes, I will tell you. Under the condition that you only make fun of me a little. And that you tell me about your best hijinks here, too."

I hold my hand out. "I can mostly agree to these terms."

My mom lets out an exasperated laugh, taking my hand to shake. "You're lucky you're my favorite daughter."

I beam. I am lucky. Lucky that no matter where I go, I have two places to call home—one wherever my heart leads me, and one right here that I've had from the start. Lucky that no matter how much time passes and no matter how different a person I become, the comfort of both feels exactly the same.

# Chapter Twenty-Four

My mom stays for the rest of the day, the two of us swapping New York stories and walking around Central Park and grabbing dinner at a café in the West Village where someone does, in fact, recognize her as "Genny with the green hair!" so loudly that my mom momentarily looks like she might die on the spot. But I can't help but notice how undeniably pleased she looks when the bartender leans in and tells me conspiratorially, "Nobody could tear it up at karaoke like your mom over here. Shania Twain was shaking in her boots."

By the end of the day she seems almost transformed—like the shine I've always seen under the surface is working its way out of her with every street corner we pass, with every sweet and wild and downright bizarre memory they bring up along the way. She practically seems electric when she's hugging me goodbye to go home on the same bus I almost got on last night. It's a strange role reversal for a moment, being the one to wave goodbye on the curb and watch her leave, but one that suits us. One we'll grow into over time.

Tom's true to his word. He texts me when he gets in, and a few times a day. We talk on the phone in the evening. He tells me about working on his aunt's online presence for the winery, about helping out ringing up customers at the front after they go on one of the hourly tours. I tell him about the deeply lawless group chat I've been added to with the band as we cobble together a bunch of cast-off furniture from random curbs and flea markets for the apartment. I tell him about my mom coming up, and he seems so genuinely, painfully relieved that I gently call him out on having texted my mom these past few weeks.

"I'm sorry," he says sincerely. "I only started doing it when you said at the beginning of the summer how upset you were not to be talking to her. I guess I just—I don't know what I thought."

I know what he thought, but I do something I've been doing a whole lot of with Tom lately, even if it makes me hate myself a little bit. I avoid the truth right along with him.

In the meantime, everyone in our little group is so busy—Mariella shopping with her cousins for outfits for their trip to Puerto Rico, Luca working extra shifts for his parents with one of his brothers out of town, Jesse and me with the move—that two days pass before we're all together again, and the others realize Tom is already gone.

At first we're all too startled to fully let it sink in—me because I assumed Tom just told the others individually, the others because they're confused that I let it happen at all.

"You had one job, Riley. One job!" says Mariella. "And you somehow let Tom leave this city without us throwing a goodbye-party-slash-kidnapping?"

"Unfortunately Tom has something called 'free will,'" I say, without making eye contact with anybody.

"Fuck free will," says Mariella, loud enough to make Dai flinch mid-pancake flip.

"This ugly one is yours," Dai informs her, when it lands halfway out of its ring mold.

Since moving in, pancakes are pretty much all we have consumed, thanks to buying a bunch of flour and sugar in bulk. It started with my mom's buttermilk pancakes, then Eddie's dad's Swedish crepes, and now Dai's mom's fluffy Japanese pancakes. I cannot emphasize enough how disastrous all our collective attempts at cooking these evenly on our ancient stove have been, making it all the more hilarious that Dai would dare refer to any of these pancakes as "the ugly one," but at least they have all been delicious.

"Incorrect. I'm too cute for ugly pancakes," Mariella says right back. She scans the rest of the new apartment, which is not hard considering it is the size of a shoe, making eye contact with the rest of our friends. "Are we really going to let this whole Tom thing stand? I mean, shit. He Irish-goodbye'd the whole city."

There's an uncomfortable silence that I'm pretty sure I'm supposed to be the one to fill, because without Tom here I'm the closest thing to a representative Tom has. I'm so torn that I don't know what to say—what I actually feel, or what I know Tom would want me to say to put everyone at ease.

That's just the thing, though. It's Tom who always knows the key to putting everyone at ease. It's me who yanked this group together, trying to give him something he gave me when we were eight—a group of friends he could rely on. But it's Tom who's held us together. Who eases the tension away with a few choice words or an easy laugh. Who always has the practical solution or a bright side to any setback. Who sometimes just sets people at ease with his presence, that grounding, non-judgmental way of his.

It's only been a few days, but everything feels stilted with him gone. Like we're all struggling to find a new rhythm with each other, since Tom was the steady bass beneath us. I feel a pinch of guilt. For all I've been worried about how Tom leaving will affect me, I didn't think much on how it might affect the others, too. Jesse, who's known Tom even longer than I have, so far back that Tom must be like an anchor for him in this new place. Mariella, who has been Tom's mutual lifeboat. Luca, who is always the first to put himself down, a habit he's gradually started breaking out of with the easy, small ways Tom will build him back up.

I used to think of Tom like the sun, pulling all of us into his orbit. But it's not necessarily that people follow Tom. It's just that he helps steady them. He's the quiet matter in between that holds us together.

Evidently I've taken too long to decide what to say, because Mariella's lip twists to the side. "I've watched Tom for the past four years, and well—he's been a completely different person this summer. But until then he was, like, such a loner that we were all this close to spreading rumors he was a vampire. And now he's off at some winery full of stuffy adults that seems like loner on advanced mode."

Jesse walks the half step from the kitchen to the couch, a similarly worried look on his face. "Yeah. I texted him a bunch of times after he moved here and got pretty much nada. I only knew he hadn't been recruited for a Mars mission because he sometimes talked to Riley. And I feel like the same thing is already starting to happen," he says, lifting up his phone to hold up the group chat. It's full of memes and pictures of cute dogs we've seen, but noticeably absent of one thing, which is any texts from Tom.

Luca, who is sitting close enough to Mariella on our scavenged couch that they're practically squished together, looks at me thoughtfully.

"Well, Riley's his best friend," he says. "If she thinks it's okay, then—it must be, right?"

Jesus. Luca could have sharpened a knife to fit exactly under the grooves of my ribs and not have hit a point as sore as that one. It must be written all over my face, because Mariella narrows her eyes at me, leaning in.

"Does Riley think it's okay?" she asks, even as she makes direct eye contact with me.

I'm sitting on the floor for lack of chairs, but I'm still decidedly in the hot seat. I feel everyone shift slightly to look at me—Luca and Mariella from the couch, Dai and Jesse from the stove that is probably way too close to the couch for comfort, even Eddie from deep in his laptop screen.

"I . . ."

My throat's gone dry. Tom isn't here, and it makes me realize that he's not the only one of the two of us who has been keeping things from the other. I might have told him the truth of my feelings about him, but I didn't tell the truth of my feelings about what he was doing. I grazed the surface, maybe. But I avoided the core.

"I don't know," I confess. "It all just kind of happened so fast. This whole thing with his mom—it's really been messing with him. But he was planning to go the whole time, so it's not like he didn't think it through. So I don't know."

Hats off to what might be the worst, most muddled answer to a question in history, because if anything I've only made the unease in the room all the more pronounced.

Mariella seizes on it, leaning in. "Do I have permission to blow up your spot in front of this entire assortment of boys?"

I'm almost relieved at the question. Like I already know

she's going to give me some kind of permission to say what my loyalty to Tom has stopped me just short of saying.

Except when I nod, she unexpectedly leans in and grabs the tote bag I had at my feet, yanking out the blank journal and holding it up.

"You have been carting this all over the place like a security blanket, but you haven't written a damn word in it yet."

I resist the urge to snatch it back like it is, in fact, a security blanket, and ask, "What's that got to do with anything?"

"You did the brave things," says Mariella, with a firmness that tells me that she's about to use that praise as a buffer for when she digs in deep. "You moved here and you finally talked to your mom, but you're still just way too in your own head. So you're not writing a short story and you're putting off starting your coffee shop gig and you haven't done what we've been waiting for you to do all damn summer, which is tell Tom Whitz you're head-over-sneakers in love with him."

My mouth falls open, but Mariella's gaze stays on mine steady as ever.

"I'm not—I mean, that doesn't have—" I take a breath that feels like only half of one, because my lungs are betraying me just as much as my flaming-hot cheeks. "However it is I feel, it's got nothing to do with Tom leaving."

"Sure it does," says Mariella. "Don't you dare pretend I didn't have front-row seats to the 'Riley and Tom are in love with each other' show all summer. I've got all my ticket stubs to prove it."

Everyone's eyes are on us now, clearly expecting me to either get mad or fess up. We all know there's no point in my denying it when we've been about as subtle as two teenager-shaped bricks.

"I'm not saying that I don't feel that way about Tom," I say carefully.

Jesse points a fork at me, like he was waiting for just enough of me to bend before he says, "You have to tell him the truth about how you feel then. I'll bully you the way you bullied me."

"Thanks for that, by the way," says Dai. "If it weren't for you I wouldn't be able to do this."

Dai ducks forward so his face is mere inches from Jesse's, so Jesse's lips curl into an expectant, bashful smile, but just before Dai is supposed to kiss him he ducks farther down and swipes the bite of pancakes Jesse had poised on his fork instead.

"Thief!" says Jesse, indignant.

Dai grins through a mouthful of stolen pancake and obligingly kisses him. My heart cinches at the quick ease and intimacy of it, at the few moments like that I had with Tom before he walked out the door with them.

"I don't need bullying," I say with a sad smile. "He knows. I told him."

Now it's Mariella's turn to be stunned, her eyes widening and brows furrowing at the same time in an expression so distinctly Mariella that I'd laugh under any other circumstances.

"That can't be true," she insists. "There's literally no universe in which you told Tom you were in love with him that he'd still go to bumfuck nowhere."

My voice is small when I answer. "Actually there is." I swallow thickly, the pancakes I've already eaten churning in my stomach. "Because I told him to go."

Mariella lifts a flat, open palm toward Dai. "Give me the ugly pancake. I'm throwing it in her face."

"Wait, why would you do that?" Jesse asks me.

"Because I—because I don't want to be the reason he stays," I blurt. "Not when I have every ulterior motive in the world for it. Not when it would mean standing in the way of his chance to be happy somewhere else that he didn't get here."

"Riley," says Mariella slowly, as if she's afraid it won't register otherwise. "Tom *is* happy here."

I shake my head, feeling my eyes start to sting because I don't want to have to fight her on this. I wish more than any of us that it was true.

She hands the notebook back to me. She's right. I have been carrying it around like a security blanket. Tom never even told me for sure it was from him, but I think I knew from the moment I held it in my hands. It's just that knowing made it scary, because it meant that suddenly I had more of him than I've ever had; suddenly I had so much more to lose.

"I see what's going on here. You're in your head about this. You're too close to Tom to be objective," says Mariella. "But none of us have been making googly eyes at Tom all summer, so we *can*, and trust me. Tom's been happy here."

I've got my knees hiked up so close to my chin now I might as well be in a human knot. "He doesn't think so."

"Because he's all up in his head about this shit with his mom, maybe," Mariella counters. "But you already knew that."

I bite the inside of my cheek. "Yeah. I think he does, too. But it still felt wrong to try to stand in his way."

Mariella nods, seeming to visibly recalibrate. "For noble reasons, sure. But the rest of us are not beholden to that, and we've got more than enough proof of how happy Tom is here to make him see sense. Exhibit A."

Mariella produces her phone and opens up the shared file where she's kept all the photos she's taken of the group this summer. She swipes her thumb through them in big, bright, colorful clusters—the day we spent in Central Park, the times we met up for pizza and cheap Tuesday movie tickets, the night we spent camping. It's a blur of buildings and limbs in motion and wide smiles, including Tom's, over and over again.

She lingers on one that has my heart in my throat. It's me

and Tom the night we all went to Jesse's show on that hotel roof. Tom has an arm around my waist. I'm looking straight ahead—embarrassed, I remember, to be feeling as intensely as I did at his touch. But Tom is staring down at me with a smile so soft and bright that it reminds me of the way his face looks when he's talking about constellations, so awed by the expanse of the universe that his eyes get misty with it.

My own eyes are misting now, but even then I'm reluctant to let myself be swayed. "What are we going to do, scrapbook him back to the city?" I ask.

I mean it as a joke, but Mariella jolts to attention like she's already grabbed the idea and run a mile with it. Before I can even think to talk her down, Jesse says, "If we did that, I kept all of the ticket stubs and flyers from places we went."

Mariella and Luca nod enthusiastically, but I still don't move. Even if we wanted to do that, we've hit a snag—one that's hard to define, but I can sense we're all feeling in the next few moments of quiet. It's all well and good to document all the fun we had this summer, but life can't always be like it was these past few weeks. We're all hurtling into our own versions of the city right now, separate from each other, and Tom has seemingly rejected his.

"But Tom was already here for all of that," says Luca sadly. "He knows."

I feel a tide of something starting to well up in me, a sadness I've tried to tamp down the past few days bubbling up to the surface. It's one thing to push it down for my own sake. It feels impossible to do it when everyone around me is feeling it, too. I can't help but start to write the whole idea off.

Then my phone buzzes next to me, reminding me of my afternoon dispatch shift, and of something else entirely.

Tom didn't reject New York. He only thinks he has. But he took part of it with him, maybe the most important part—despite swearing upside down and backward he was done with this place, he never found a replacement to run the app. In fact, the more I think about it, the more I think he never planned to—he wouldn't have really hired someone without running it past Mariella. If he'd been serious about it, he'd have told Mariella from the start.

"The 'Dear, Love' Dispatch," I say. "As soon as Tom started telling me about it I was obsessed with the whole idea. I was always looking up cute stories about it that people were posting online. Like tweets and TikToks and even reviews in the app store."

I look up, feeling oddly self-conscious in front of everyone, now that it seems like I'm all in on this, too. Now that we're committing to something, knowing there's a chance it still might not work.

I clear my throat. Mariella's right. I've been brave, but now I'm on the other side of that. Now I need to figure out how to harness it—not just for Tom, but the friends who need me to be right now. Someone has to lead the charge, and for the first time in my life, I feel ready. Like even after all these weeks I've spent here discovering new things about myself and what I can do, I'm still shifting into someone stronger, someone new.

"Maybe if Tom read the stories and saw everything he's done to connect people here, it would help him feel like he really belongs," I explain.

For a moment nobody speaks, but I don't feel the flicker of doubt I'm expecting. Instead I feel a measurable difference between the Riley I was when I got here and the Riley I am now. One that's still figuring things out, sure. But one I couldn't have imagined the day I was sitting in that graduation hall, trying desperately not to cry as it felt like everyone I knew was leaving me behind.

It was easy to blame that feeling solely on high school, on

my mom's scheduling and all the things that kept me distracted. But it was also that I just hadn't grown into this person yet. One with confidence. One with clarity. One who has taken charge of enough of her life to take charge when it matters most.

"Well, fuck," says Mariella. "That's beautiful."

Jesse nods. "I love that."

Luca looks up nervously, and I worry he's about to work himself into a state about not having an idea of his own to contribute, but then he says, "If you guys all want to send everything to me, I can be the one to arrange it all. Turn it into an overarching story," he says. "If there's anything I've learned this summer, it's how to structure a plot."

Mariella kisses Luca on the temple. "That's genius."

Luca's lips press into a smile that makes his entire face look like a sunbeam. I raise my eyebrows at Mariella, who has yet to update me on her situation with Luca. She gives me one as unsubtle as she can possibly give when she answers my eyebrows with a cheeky wink.

"All of this is great," says Jesse, "except what do we do once it gets sent in the mail? Four-way call him and yell at him to come home?"

The idea that's forming in my head right now is a Riley classic, because if we follow through with it, it will be exactly on brand: unmitigated chaos. But if there were ever a time for it, it's right now.

"Well," I say slowly, "there's one more thing on the Getaway List we haven't checked off."

Mariella looks between me and Jesse, eyes gleaming with delight. "Which one of you suburban clowns knows how to drive?"

# Chapter Twenty-Five

As it turns out, nobody in their right mind will rent a midsized car to a bunch of eighteen-year-olds with an armful of Sour Patch Kids and a mission. In the end we all take the bus down to Virginia, where my mom meets us with the car and finally meets all of my new friends. We grab a quick bite at my mom's coffee shop for lunch, and any lingering nerves I have about us taking this trip are pushed aside by the pride of watching my mom start to take a shine to my friends the way I knew she would when she got to know them. By the time we've polished off our sandwiches and lattes, Mariella and my mom have swapped enough true-crime podcast recs to warrant both their arrests, my mom has all but adopted Luca, and Jesse has finally gotten her to tell him the real stories behind her few tattoos he's been pestering her about since we were kids (most of which involved friends and Fireball).

My mom hugs me on our way out, squeezing me tight. "I trust you. But be careful."

"We will," I say into her ear.

She pulls back without quite letting me go, then glances to make sure the others are out of earshot. "I think I'll be nervous every day you're up in the city on your own," she says. "But I feel better knowing you've got your little pack here. It's clear you all care about each other a lot."

There's a wistfulness in her tone then, the kind that makes me wonder if that's what was missing from her New York experience—people who would look out for her the way all of us have. I know she has that here with my grandparents and aunts, but I can't help but feel an ache for the version of her that didn't.

She hands me the keys. "Also nobody is allowed to drink. But obviously all of you owe me a bottle of Tom's aunt's wine for loaning you the car."

I salute her, and then we're off on the open road. The rest of the drive takes four hours, a heap of gas station candy, and nearly all of Taylor Swift's discography, but before we know it we're rolling into the parking lot of Ornery Bitch Vines, the sun starting to dip over the large hill of the gift shop and visitor center.

"Oh shit," says Mariella, perking up just enough at the sign that Luca, who was sleeping with his head propped on her shoulder, startles awake with an endearing snuffle. "You guys might have to leave me here. This lady is my people."

I cut the engine and put the car in park, but for a few moments nobody moves to get out. Jesse turns to me from the passenger side where he's been playing navigator/Swiftie DJ for the last few hours, searching my face with a solemnity that I rarely see.

"Maybe Riley should go in ahead of us," he suggests. "Just to make sure Tom is ready for the full force of our combined friendship."

I smile at him gratefully. The more we all talked about it over the past few days, the more we agreed this wasn't necessarily a trip with the intention of retrieving Tom—more just a trip to let him know that we're here for him, whether he wants us to be here for him from the city or come back to the city with us. We rented an Airbnb not far from here to crash for the night, figuring we could still turn it into a fun night when we give Tom a proper send-off with a combination of all the Getaway List items we ticked off--we'd watch *Tides of Time*, roast s'mores, sing to karaoke tracks, and eat brownies made from the batter I created for Tom that Luca re-created and brought with him in a cooler in the back.

All this to say that none of us want to pressure him. We've all had enough of our decisions made for us to force ours on anyone else's. But in the event Tom wants to come back and needs a nudge to do it, there is a spot for him in this car and all of our collective Sour Patch Kids–filled hearts.

I walk into the gift shop of the winery, where it seems like things are just starting to wind down for the day. There are a few stragglers still talking merrily at the little counter that serves as a bar, a few more squinting at the wines on the racks, the rest in line to check out at the register. Only it isn't Tom at the other end of it, but his aunt, looking just as dour and—for lack of a better word—*ornery* as ever.

I wait in line to talk to her, but her eagle eyes spot me immediately. It's been five years since she last saw me, at least ten inches of height and a full set of braces ago, but that doesn't seem to stop her from recognizing me.

"If you're looking for Tom you better step on it," she says, more growl than not.

The woman checking out looks a little miffed to be interrupted, but in that moment neither of us cares.

"Why?" I ask.

Tom's aunt jerks her head toward the visitor's center. "Kid's headed out for god knows where."

My blood runs chillier than all the fancy wine fridges I just passed. I'm not even sure how to process what she's said, only that it can't be good. This was supposed to be Tom's escape. If he's escaping the escape, well—I'm not even sure what the contingency plan is for that. Only that I'd better move, and fast.

I clamber out of the gift shop, not without noticing a shelf full of angry-looking teddy bears wearing DO NOT TEST AN OR-NERY BITCH T-shirts on their fuzzy bodies, and spill into the visitor's center. The place is empty with all the tours wrapped up for the day. The only signs of life are coming from a slightly ajar door with a thin stream of light coming out of it, one so unassuming that I almost dismiss it for a supply closet.

Then a shadow crosses over the stream of light, and the shape of Tom appears in the doorway.

We both startle at the sight of each other. It's almost like the start of the summer, when I showed up every bit as unexpectedly at his apartment door, only it's nothing like that at all. This time there isn't a flutter in my ribs, but a hammering. This time there isn't a thrill, but a bone-deep, impossible relief.

This time when Tom sees me, he bursts out laughing, so hard that it doubles him over before I can even reach him. Then suddenly I'm laughing, too, without even knowing what the hell we're laughing about, especially because Tom's got his backpack slung over his shoulder like he's about to jump into a getaway car and leave his life all over again.

He pulls me into him for one of our bone-crushing hugs, somehow the least stunned of the two of us despite the fact that I just party-crashed his new life from eight hours away. I'm so relieved to see him in his corporeal form that I can't even make a Tides of Time joke about it; I'm still laughing but somehow trying not to choke on the well of emotion working its way out of me at the same time. I'm so grateful I caught him before he left. I'm worried to think where the hell he was planning to go.

But when he pulls back he doesn't look like a guy on the lam. His eyes are shining with amusement, his lips curled into a wry smile. "What on earth are you doing here?" he asks.

"That depends," I say.

"On what?"

I press my lips together. "On how kidnappable you are today," I quip, trying to keep it light. "Also I should warn you there's an entire carful of our friends in the parking lot."

I'm prepared to play the whole thing off as a joke. To let him know we're totally fine to just spend the night goofing off in the Airbnb and reminiscing and bullying Tom into being more active in the group chat before rolling off with the sunrise tomorrow. Except Tom's smile goes soft, his eyes warm. He's looking at me the same way he did in that photograph of us on the roof—like I'm something cosmic and bright, and he can't believe I'm here.

He nudges the backpack on his shoulder. "Is there room for one more?" he says. "If we're headed in the same direction, that sounds way more appealing than another cramped bus."

My eyes flood with tears, my entire being threatening to spill over with the relief of it before my brain can fully catch up with his words. I pull enough of myself together to point a firm finger at him just the same, the words coming out choked: "You better not be fucking with me right now, Tom Whitz."

He takes my hand between the two of his and squeezes it lightly. "Nah. It turns out I'm extremely kidnappable today."

He has to pull his hands apart because I'm leaning in to hug him again, this time without our usual bone-crushing pressure. Like we're melting a bit, so grateful to see each other and be on the same page again that we've got no choice but a complete bodily reset.

"Oh thank god," I say into his neck, "because logistically, you are way too tall to put into a trunk."

I feel his soft laugh rumbling against my own chest and close my eyes for a moment, breathing him in. I want this to be real so badly that I don't want to ask, but I know I have to if I'm going to believe it. If I'm going to be sure he's coming back because he wants to, and not because he feels like he has to.

"What made you change your mind?"

Tom nudges his chin into my temple. "You did," he says, as we pull apart again. "And I did. Part of it was hearing about you having that whole conversation with your mom. It made me realize that I still need that conversation. Maybe it won't help the two of us as much, but I think it will still help me? To have some kind of closure, if nothing else."

He sounds more sure of himself talking about it than any other time he's brought it up, but I can still see the way he's waiting for me to respond before he feels fully settled in it. I nod firmly and say, "Good."

He nods back, satisfied. Then he shifts his weight between his feet, his expression thoughtful but not guarded. "And I think the other part of it is—I've never known New York with that closure. You were right about this thing with my mom sort of changing my perspective on the city," he says, meeting my eye meaningfully. "I don't think I realized just how much that started to shift until I was watching the group chat these past few days and thinking about all the things I was missing out on. I think if I can start working through all this I'll be able to give the city a real chance. Maybe find my own place like you guys are."

I take Tom's face in my hands, the gesture both affectionate and teasing. "Tom, you absolutely ridiculous if not very handsome human," I tell him. "You already have a place there. Not just with us, but with— Oh, shit."

Tom's brow quirks in amusement. "What?"

I abruptly take my hands off his face to root around in my tote bag. "We didn't even get the chance to lure you back with this. You have to lie to the others and say you begged and kicked and screamed to be left alone until you saw it. For dramatic effect."

I pull out the notebook then, one with a brown leather cover and delightfully blank pages that made for a perfect canvas for a story of the summer.

"But this is yours," says Tom worriedly.

I smile wider than I mean to, because it's the first time Tom's said as much about sending me the notebook through the dispatch. It took me half the day to find an identical one for him, but it's worth it. It's the perfect size, beautiful and hardy and built to last.

"It's not," I say. "Mine's preoccupied with another project. But this one is all yours."

Tom opens it carefully, skimming through the pages, his eyes already welling before he's taken any of it in. Each of the pages crinkles with old memories, carefully chosen by me and Jesse and Mariella and artfully arranged by Luca. I open my mouth to tell him so, but I figure I'll let the group tell him. That, and Tom seems too overwhelmed to hear much of anything right now.

He comes to a slow stop on the front page, where there's an insignia in the same place where he put one for me. The call-back to the time-stone mantra. "'From the home where you're known,'" he reads out loud. He looks at me with a fondness that makes me feel known, and I feel a shiver of happiness in my bones. "This is beautiful. I can't wait to read every page."

"I'll wait until we get to the others so we can go through it," I tell him. "But just—I hope you'll read the stories all the people shared from the dispatch. Little ways it turned people's days around or brought them together or made them laugh. You don't just have a place in New York, Tom, but all over it, in all these connections you made."

Tom's throat bobs as he carefully hands it back to me, eyes steady on me. "If that's true then so do you," he says. "I never would have made the app without you in my life, making sure I still had a connection of my own."

My face burns from the depth of what those words mean to me. Of what that connection has always meant to me, and how lucky I am to have it. If I let myself think about it too much I'm going to start crying all over again, and I've spent enough time the past week doing just that.

So I clear my throat and say, "I know talking to your mom is going to be tough, but—it'll be different this time. I'm a subway ride away. We all are. You've got every single one of us on your side."

Tom nods quietly, his eyes misting again. "I can't believe you're all really here."

"Of course," I say. "We've got each other's backs now. Even when each other's backs have abandoned polite society to sell a wine varietal called Get Off My Lawn."

"It's a popular one," Tom admits, pulling in a breath to collect himself. On the other side of it he asks, "So where is your notebook?"

"Right in here," I say, patting my tote bag again. I smirk, feeling almost shy about it, and add, "You didn't tell me it was from you."

Tom smiles with satisfaction, seeing the outline of it in the bag. "It didn't matter who it came from. Just mattered that it got to you," he says. "Even if you don't end up writing,

I think it's clear you're a person who was meant to create things."

I think of the way the notebook came to me when I needed it most, in a moment of doubt when I needed an extra nudge to believe in myself. Tom's right that it mattered that it got to me, but wrong if he thinks that it doesn't make it any more special, coming from him.

"I finally started writing in it," I tell him.

Tom's brows lift, happy to hear it. "Writing what?"

"My submission for that short-story contest," I say.

"You're entering it?" says Tom, positively beaming.

I nod, feeling a new kind of pride in the decision now that I'm actually saying it out loud. After all the second-guessing about what on earth I could submit, it came together in my head so fast that there was no room for doubt anymore. Or maybe I was finally feeling brave enough to make room for the idea in the first place.

"I figure I've done a lot of scary things these past few weeks. What's one more?"

"You're going to knock it out of the park," he says confidently. "What will it be about?"

It's not really a matter of what it will be about so much as what it already is; I drafted it in a frenzy, first jotting down notes and errant dialogue with such fervor that I felt like I was briefly possessed by Vanessa. It was easy, once I started reading through all those stories of the "Dear, Love" Dispatch I'd collected over the years, the ones I'd coveted and lived through almost as if I could put myself in Tom's shoes in New York and see it in real time. They weren't just individual stories in my mind, but a larger, moving story that gives them all one important thing in common: the need to love and to be loved. The universality of it, and the beauty in all the different and wild and unexpected ways we express it.

So the story will start the way my time in New York did: with disjointed, separate journeys between the characters that all slowly, satisfyingly start to converge. It won't end with four teenagers crammed into a beaten-up sedan littered with candy wrappers outside of a winery none of them can technically legally enter, but it will end in the same satisfying way: with love bringing everyone together, despite all the circumstances that keep them apart.

"How about this?" I say. "You can be the first to read it when it's done."

Tom smiles. "Sounds like a good deal to me." Then he takes an abrupt step back. "You know what this reunion calls for?"

I grin, squaring my shoulders and planting my feet in preparation. "Let's go."

There's that familiar Tom mischief in his eyes when they meet mine.

"Just a heads-up," he says, "I might improvise a bit at the end."

We haven't even touched yet and I feel electric, that same current we've had since we were eight that's taken on new rhythms with time. One we'll always know the shape of as uniquely *ours* no matter how it changes over the years. Tom extends out his right and I clap it into mine and we're off, clapping and spinning and snapping, pulling each other in and out, putting our thumbs to our noses, and just as we're about to burst into our usual laughter Tom pulls me in firmly by the waist and presses his lips to mine.

I'm breathless, near boneless with the effect of it—this kiss that isn't just a kiss, but the kind we get to keep. A kiss that doesn't come with conditions or consequences. A kiss that's sweet and slow and simmering, and distinctly our own.

We're both flushed and grinning when we pull apart, taking a few beats to collect ourselves, staring into each other's eyes.

"You should know that if you're coming back with us to the city, I'm going to want to do that to your face a whole lot," I tell him.

He reaches up and pushes a stray lock of hair behind my ear, this time his fingers lingering on the shell of it, sending another tingle up my spine.

"That's exactly what my face was hoping for," he says back. Then he extends his hand, wrapping it around mine so our fingers intertwine. "Let's go home."

By the time we reach the parking lot the rest of the gang has already spilled out of the car and managed to scam free cheese from Tom's aunt, who is apparently not as much of an ornery bitch as she'd like her clientele to believe. They all spot us at the same time, but it's Jesse who lets out a *"Fuck* yeah" before either of us has said a word, evidently reading it all over our faces. Luca lets out a cheer and Mariella rolls her eyes at the theatrics but noticeably swipes a tear with the heel of her hand.

We converge on Tom in a group hug that would bowl anyone else over if it weren't for his height and sturdiness, and the rest of the night is a happy blur from there. We head to the little Airbnb with our Getaway List–themed treats and activities, reading through all the pages of the scrapbook one by one. We're back in the winding paths of Central Park; in the pounding bass of Jesse's shows; in the greasy, delicious heat of pizza between our teeth; in the fragile quiet of the sunrise from Tom's roof. In the excitement and unpredictability and fear and doubt and hope. In the bond we've all formed together, and the bonds of the strangers whose stories are intertwined with ours through the app. In the stories that have yet to be told because now we have so much more time together to make them.

The next morning we pile into the car, me driving, Tom on the passenger side, Luca and Mariella and Jesse in the back. Tom, of course, has snacks. Jesse's got the aux cord. Mariella's got the map. Luca's got road-trip games, each more ridiculous than the last. I've got the steering wheel in both hands and my heart all over the car. When we finally complete the last item on the Getaway List, there's nothing but open road ahead.

# Epilogue

"Laptop down, nerd."

I blink away from my screen and up at Mariella, who is party-ready in a tasseled dress with glitter streaking her cheeks. Even with her crouching a few inches from my face it takes me a moment to recalibrate myself from the story I was working on back into the real world, or at least this cramped version of it in the back office of Brownie Bonanza.

Mariella leans over the desk where I'm perched. "Fic, fan-fic, or fuck-for-all?"

Which is her way of asking if I'm working on original fiction, fanfiction, or am free-writing whatever comes into my head the way Vanessa encourages us to do. A fair question, because these days there are so many Google Docs tabs full of works in progress open on my laptop that my brain feels like it's trying to access a fourth dimension.

"Fic," I answer. "That short-story contest Luca and I entered last year is doing another round."

A contest that we predictably lost, being two inexperienced newbies running mostly on enthusiasm and one writing class between us. But the rejection was almost too exciting to feel like one, because of the novelty of it all—it was our first experience with someone in the industry actually reading our work and giving us personalized feedback on it. And sure, while it wasn't exactly a picnic to hear I had pacing problems and that I "overexplain" plot points, it ignited something in me that felt almost like the Getaway List. It gave me new challenges to meet. Ones that I could keep reaching for over and over again by writing and rewriting and improving a bit more every time.

Odds are despite all the workshops and classes I've taken since then, I'm going to lose this contest, too. But that's more than all right. If the past year and the thousands of new words under my belt have taught me anything, it's that writing is a marathon, not a sprint. I'm not in this to win anything, but because I love every second of it—the parts where I get to know myself and my abilities a little more with each draft, and the parts where I collect new friends along the way.

"Well, that explains why Luca put enough plotting index cards on the back of his bedroom door to look like a crime-scene investigation," says Mariella. She waits for me to stand up from my perch and unceremoniously drops a gigantic pan of brownies into my hands. "But we've got to get a move on."

I blink again and look at the clock by the door. As usual, time has just slipped out from under me. Thankfully I'm already in my nicest jeans and a flowy green top Mariella loaned me for the occasion, so I'm ready to go.

"Can you believe we fully launched an app together just so your boyfriend could drown himself in brownie batter tonight? We really went above and beyond for him, huh," says Mariella once I'm on my feet.

I follow her to the back room of the shop, where we're

currently setting up for our app's Saturday-afternoon launch party. Everything is mostly set up, but Luca insisted on pulling out even more stops for the shenanigans by doing an "insurance bake" of extra brownies. This seems overkill, seeing as this party is mostly for a collection of our parents, friends, classmates, and the few investors we've managed to snag, but Luca takes his parents' dessert reputation seriously, even if he doesn't work here anymore.

"Yeah. But I'm pretty sure all roads would have ended in Tom's brownie agenda anyway," I respond.

Mariella blows a stray lock of hair out of her face. "Ain't that the truth."

We take a step back and look at our handiwork for the party—the purple and yellow streamers, the array of desserts and mini appetizer bites we used the Brownie Bonanza ovens to heat up, the little framed QR codes that lead people to our website where they can download the app. We're as ready as we'll ever be, and quite possibly as tired as we've ever been.

Still, when I hold up my hand Mariella high-fives it without breaking her stride and says, "Let's go kick some technological ass."

Truth be told, this party is just the tip of our workload iceberg. Setting up a new app with Mariella took a whole lot out of us—on my end it was all the field research and hiring and user-experience testing, and on Mariella's it was coding and tweaking and debugging for months. No easy feat to balance between my writing classes and shifts at the coffee shop, or for Mariella to balance with helping corun the "Dear, Love" Dispatch with Tom, especially now that they're starting to test it in two other cities. But after many tireless nights, plenty of dollar slices of pizza, and a lot of blue-light strain on the eyes, our little baby is ready for its debut.

We carry the brownies to the front, where the app's name

is hung on a banner spanning across the room: THE GETAWAY LIST. Mariella elbows me. "Looks pretty snazzy, huh?"

She's got more license to be excited than I do, maybe, because her last app was soft-launched in the dark and never got the initial fanfare ours is getting. In fact, the only reason we're getting this much fanfare in the first place is that Tom opted to go public with the "Dear, Love" Dispatch and its creators. When he caught wind of Mariella's issues with her parents about quitting school to work independently in app development, he figured the best thing he could do for her was make sure she'd be able to put the app on her resume as loudly as possible.

What we weren't expecting was for investors and advertisers to start scrambling for Tom and Mariella's attention the minute they went public. At first I was worried they might be overwhelmed—Tom had just started at Columbia, after all, and was loving every minute of it, and Mariella was still deciding on whether or not to commit to school. But it turns out I worried in vain.

"If this isn't the universe saying 'fuck that' to paying another dime of tuition, so be it" was Mariella's official stance on the matter. Tom was happy to follow her lead, especially since the app's extra boost in publicity meant they were hiring more dispatchers, enough that all of us working for the app were starting to become a tight-knit unit of our own.

"Yeah," I agree with her, helping myself to one of the insurance brownies. "Pretty fucking snazzy."

Jesse swoops in, late as ever—a full year into our time in Manhattan and I'm never *not* waiting for a call to say he accidentally took the train to Queens when he was supposed to be home at the apartment—and squishes us both into a hug. As appreciated as the gesture is, it is slightly less appreciated that he's holding two large bags of ice in each hand as he does it.

"So proud. Wish I could stay the whole night. Mostly wish I could drop these before my hands freeze off?" he says.

"Over there," says Mariella, pointing to the buckets where Tom has artfully arranged a bunch of sodas and seltzers. We don't really need *that* much extra ice, but Jesse insisted on being helpful despite the Walking JED doing their first headlining set at the Milkshake Club tonight. At some point we just let him elect himself as the ice guy so he'd feel useful.

Jesse dutifully starts filling the buckets as Mariella and I do another sweep of the place, joined by Luca, who has his arms full of so many things I'd be worried he's going to tip over if he didn't have so much experience in food service.

"Oh. Right on time," says Luca, handing Jesse a smaller pan of brownies. I know from the crispy edges and telltale black and blue sprinkles that it's made up of the same batter Jesse made for Dai on their first date. "These just finished baking."

"Bless your brownie-baking soul," says Jesse, carefully taking it from him. "We're too busy with gigs to do much for our one-year, so this is perfect."

Mariella rolls her eyes at the cuteness, despite her and Luca's official one-year anniversary coming up next week. "We're not going to be cheesy about it," she's told me multiple times. (That said, Luca has written no less than ten drafts of poems for her, and she has been learning to cook his favorite kind of lasagna on and off for the past week, which is both the figurative *and* literal definition of cheesy.)

I'm not sure what Tom and I are doing. For all I know we'll bandwagon Luca and Mariella's plans—something that happens often enough, considering Tom moved in with Luca in a little apartment above Brownie Bonanza a few weeks after he got back to the city last summer. But I'm not worried. These days Tom and I are so busy running around every inch of this city together that it feels like a mini celebration every damn day.

Right on cue, Tom comes in from the back with a few cartons of iced coffee. He gives me a quick kiss on the lips, then looks immediately and hilariously scandalized.

"You told me no brownies until the guests had a chance," he says, clearly having tasted it on me.

"Did I?" I say, licking my lips. "Sounds irresponsible of me."

Tom leans in and kisses me again, deeper this time. I can feel his smile against my lips as he skims his tongue over my teeth as if to get a better taste.

"Happy?" I ask him wryly.

Tom nods, cheeks endearingly flushed. "You decided to go with the toffee bits after all, huh?"

Mariella makes a gagging noise and says, "We're launching an app here, folks, not the world's most insufferable Hallmark movie."

Tom obligingly starts setting up the spouts and the cups for the iced coffee, a smirk still playing at the corners of his mouth. I glance around the room, and when I figure there isn't much else left to be done, lean into him, grounding myself.

Tom presses his chin to the top of my head for a brief moment. "Nice of the shop to give you these for free," he says about the iced-coffee boxes.

I nod, still lazily using him as a human lamppost. "And very much on theme."

The thing is, if it weren't for the coffee shop, I'm not sure if this app would exist in the first place. As it turns out, the shop got a bit of hype when Luca came on board and helped consult on some of the desserts—despite his aversion to sweets, he has an undeniable knack for creating them, and his caramel-gouda-stuffed croissants and chocolate-chili donut holes put us on the map. Before long tourists were making it one of their first stops in the city and then had no idea what else to do in our neighborhood. As a native New Yorker and someone who had recently moved to the city myself, Luca and I became the designated idea generator for these folks, to the point where we started posting handwritten lists of places people could go.

For a few months we didn't think anything of it. We'd just started organizing weekly write-ins for writers in the neighborhood, and were polishing up more short stories to submit to workshops and enter in contests, the same way we'd been doing since the very first one we both lost. Soon enough those handwritten lists Luca and I were making were getting so long that the truth of it was hard to deny.

"Shit," I said to Luca one day. "These look a hell of a lot like the Getaway List."

Within the month Mariella and I were plotting to make an app version of it, something we could share not just with the tourists from the coffee shop but anyone visiting or living in the city to use. It started out as something we were half joking around with. I guess now that we've locked in real live investors and have a launch date in a few days and T-shirts with our logo on them, it's anything but a joke now.

Tom hands me a cup of iced coffee. "Liquid courage," he says.

I take it from him, grateful, then toss back half of it like a shot. Which is naturally the moment my mom walks in the door, Vanessa in tow, both of them watching me overcaffeinate myself with mild alarm.

"Hey, kid," says Vanessa, pulling Tom in for a hug.

My mom does the same to me, even though I only just saw her at the coffee shop this morning. Of all the plot twists of me coming to New York, maybe the biggest came six months ago, when my mom finished her degree and decided to move up here, too. She's been working for a small advertising firm and doing community theater in her spare time. She settled into the city so quickly that it reminded me of what she said to me when she was trying to convince me to come home: that the city would still be there waiting for me later. It's clear from the way she's enjoying every minute of her time here that it was something she needed to hear herself.

"Looks great in here," says my mom, an unmistakably proud gleam in her eye. "Anything else we can do to help?"

I shake my head. "You've done enough already."

In fact, aside from helping plan this party, both my mom and Vanessa have helped as scouters for the app—my mom to help keep it updated with things going on in the theater scene, and Vanessa with writing and art. It's been a fun way for all of us to reconnect again, particularly for my mom and Vanessa. They didn't quite pick up their friendship where it left off, but they're finding a new version of it now.

Vanessa says something that makes Tom laugh. She pats Tom on the back as she releases him, a little too emphatically, but Tom doesn't seem to notice. He just seems happy to have her here in the first place.

I wish I could say things were perfectly fine with Tom and Vanessa, but at the very least I can say they're working on it. It turns out Vanessa had been sending things through the dispatch knowing that Tom created it. She'd known since the start, for better or for worse—the worse being that she assumed when Tom was being withdrawn or distant from her, it was because he was throwing himself into the app. She also assumed Tom knew it was her sending the items since he was in charge of it, not taking into account that Tom would try to protect the anonymity of it across the board. It was basically a mess of misfires and miscommunication that all came to a head during a series of long talks Tom had with Vanessa last summer.

I think being around my mom has helped to some degree. Seeing the way my mom and I have navigated this new version of our relationship—one where we're close by, living independently, but still checking in with each other—gives her a template for how she should handle Tom. By actually talking with him and being present, instead of keeping tabs on him from afar and assuming he knows that she cares. By actually listening to what he needs from her instead of finding a way to solve his problems with convenient trappings of their new life.

It's a work in progress, but Tom is happier. Genuinely and actually embracing the city, now that he's living separately from his mom and making friends with his fellow Ivy League nerds at school. Plus he's taking a more publicly active role in the app he made, so he can see the joy it's spreading firsthand. He feels settled again—not into his old self, but a happy medium between the two. The Tom who draws people in and the Tom who knows precisely the feelings that make people pull away in the first place.

He catches me staring at him and smiles so easily that, as usual, I can't help but smile back. It's the kind of smile that grounds me. That makes this big moment in our lives feel like it's just one of many: nothing to worry over, but plenty to get excited about.

The party starts in earnest a few minutes later, a whirlwind of shaking hands and explaining the app and running around to make sure we've got enough drinks and small bites going around. I'm not nervous for any of it. We've worked damn hard this past year and know exactly what the app is capable of—through both Tom's and Mariella's experience and all the rigorous testing we've done. The afternoon slides into early evening and we're all feeling triumphant and exhausted as we clean up what's been left behind (or rather, eat up what's been left behind).

Once we're finished I flop back on a lounge chair and say, "That was a lot of extroverting even for me. I'll be happy if I never have to speak to another human again."

"Well, it was nice knowing you," says Mariella, flopping into the chair next to me. She reaches out a fist and I bump it with my own, the two of us exchanging a look that says all the sappy things I know better than to say to her in front of an audience: that we're so damn proud of what we've done here, and prouder still to have done it with a best friend.

Once we have our moment I sink in deeper and say, "If anyone needs me, I'll be on the moon."

Then Tom is standing over me, offering me his hand.

"Actually," he says, "I have an idea in that vein. If you're up for it."

I glance over at him and see a shade of that conspiratorial look in his eye he'd get when we were kids and about to go off on some half-baked adventure. Only that look has shifted these days. It's grounded and deliberate and suits Tom well. New York is an adventure that has no end or beginning, and we've spent the entire past year going on as many as we can—not a Getaway List anymore, but one that plants us new roots here every time.

"You got a spaceship parked out back?" I ask.

"Next best thing," he says. "But it will involve a train."

It turns out I was wrong about us not doing anything to mark our one-year anniversary, because next thing I know Tom and I are heading up to spend the night at the campground we never made it to last year for the rest of the weekend. My mom's in on it and has my bag packed for me. Actually, turns out almost everyone's in on it, because Jesse let her into the apartment to do it and Mariella picked a hiking outfit with the best "Instagram potential." All I have to do is follow Tom and enjoy the view.

The sun is just starting to set when we find a spot to pitch our tent. We make a mess of it at first, laughing at each other through the whole thing, but figure it out together the same way we always do. Tom pulls out sandwiches from a deli we love and the fixings for s'mores, and once we've made our fire and roasted them up and relived the mutual horror of Luca's newest ghost stories (honestly, Stephen King better watch his back), we sit leaning into each other in happy silence, watching the last of the embers flicker out.

"We should make this a tradition," says Tom. "Do it on our anniversary every year."

It's a given that Tom and I will have lots of years ahead of us, but I feel the warmth of those words and the assumption behind them just the same. I turn and burrow my head into the crook of his neck.

"Yeah," I say. "Only next time I'll help pack. We didn't bring you near enough candy."

I can feel the smile in Tom's voice when he wraps his arm around me, pulling me closer to him. "Maybe. But I've still got everything I need."

Not long after that we lie back under a curtain of black night and gleaming stars, the summer air balmy and sweet, and stare up at the sky. Neither of us points out the constellations now that they're a quiet, shared thing between us. I silently account for them all just the same, reveling in how strangely close they seem now that I know them by name—how something that always seemed so far from me suddenly feels near enough that I can reach out and skim it with my fingertips.

The longer we sit in that feeling the more I recognize it. The unknown becoming known. A strange place becoming home. It's something I'm appreciating every day that I spend in New York, watching new homes build themselves all around me—that home has never been a place, but a feeling. It's in the cluster of Columbia students Tom rounded up for Tuesday-night study groups at a cafe near campus. It's in the network of bands Jesse and the Walking JED are slowly coming up with a little more with each season. It's in the bikers for the "Dear, Love" Dispatch and the scouts for the Getaway List app that Mariella hosts karaoke and bowling nights for. It's in the writing workshops Luca and I have started taking, and all the writer meetups we've arranged. It's in my mom and Vanessa finally reconciling and meeting each other in the middle from very distant shores.

It's right here next to Tom, in the warmth of his hand in mine. It's anywhere I want it to be. It's in the family I know, and the ones that I found, and ones I don't even know yet. It's in the power to choose, one that I love testing the boundaries of every day.

I came to New York a year ago with one directive—to get away. To find somewhere to belong. Maybe New York felt like the place to run to, but really, that *somewhere* was in me this entire time. I just needed the space to discover it, and people I love to help me along the way.

There isn't a single shooting star in the sky tonight, and I'm glad for it. I don't need to ask for wishes now; I have choices all my own. Ones that will always be built on love, on hope, and on infinite, daunting, beautiful realms of possibility.

# Acknowledgments

My first thank-you is to an inanimate object, which is my favorite bench in Central Park, where I wrote most of this draft in the summer of 2022. I made so many new friends and ran into plenty of old ones sitting on that bench. Most of them human. A lot of them not! Some I only knew for a few minutes, and some I hope I'll know for life. I will never make sense of the strange magic of this city, but that's probably why there are so many good bakeries here—ingest enough serotonin and we won't break our brains thinking about it too hard.

Thank you to Alex and Cassidy for all the love and care and "!!" you infused into this story, and as always to Janna for being the reason I get to write these stories at all. Thank you to every single person at Wednesday Books for helping bring this to life in all the big and little happenings going on behind the scenes. I will never get over how lucky I am to get to work with and learn from such a hardworking, passionate, talented team. I promise I am not just typing that to butter anybody up for more

ARCs from other Wednesday authors and/or sticker sheets (she typed, while impersonating the smiling imp emoji).

A sweeping "I love you" to all of my friends. There is so much of that love woven into this book in all the adventures we've taken and ones we've yet to plan. I am so grateful to be smack-dab in the middle of them in this very wacky good lawless life with all of you.

Thank you to New York City for always kicking my ass and making me laugh about it, and for giving me the most magical moments of my life and making me cry about it. Equilibrium is for squares.

As always, my last and largest thank-you to my family. I made plenty of lists growing up, but none of the getaway variety—I am one lucky human to have you in my corner believing in me for every harebrained, ridiculous, often dessert-based item I've checked off along the way.

Enjoy an excerpt from

# The Rival

Available January 2025

## Chapter One

"Why do you sound like you're being chased by a zombie horde?" Christina asks in mild alarm.

"McLaren Hall," I gasp into my phone. "Where is it?"

"Uh—I'm assuming not where you are?"

I can count the number of times I have been late on one finger. The day I was born—end of list. Ever since I came into the world a week overdue, I have been so reliably on time that I wouldn't be surprised if clocks started resetting themselves around me.

Turns out I'm making up for it now, because I'm not just late, but *late*.

Thankfully, Christina's gorgeously manicured nails are clacking on her keyboard on the other end of the line, where she is no doubt still starfished on her bed in our dorm where I left her ten minutes ago. "So there's a McLaren Hall and a McLaren Hall II across the street from it. Do you know which one you're looking for?"

No, because it did not occur to me that somewhere in the universe there exists a college campus architect nefarious or lazy enough to do such a thing. "Shit shit," I squeak.

"According to my good friend the internet, the zine meeting is in the OG McLaren, which is the one next to the fountain," Christina informs me.

I do an absurd pivot like I'm auditioning for a musical, finally spotting the fountain across the street from me. "Angel human," I wheeze gratefully. "Goddess among mortals."

"Okay but like. Sadie. Take a beat, okay?"

"I'm out of beats," I say, looking both ways for cars and booking it across the street. "I'm so late I have negative beats to take."

"It's an interest meeting, those always start late. And this is like—your big dream zine, right? You can't go in there looking frazzled."

"I'm not—" I glance down at myself and see that not only is one of my sneakers untied but my carefully chosen floral blue first-day-of-college dress has pit stains deeper than most emotions. The first building I was trying to get into was locked at every entrance, but that sure didn't stop me from sprinting multiple laps around it to make sure. "*That* frazzled looking," I concede.

"One beat," Christina insists.

I take a breath and stare at the wide brick building, a small thrill working its way up my spine—not fear, but anticipation. I earned this opportunity. Every test I pulled all-nighters studying for, every school newspaper deadline I raced the clock to meet, all so I could get into Maple Ride University and have a chance to try my hand at getting a staff position on *Newsbag,* arguably the most famous college zine in the country.

Maybe I should be scared. It's taken me years to get this close to the thing I want most, but now I have to prove myself all over again.

"You're at your dream school. You're finally away from your family drama. You're hot as hell and have the best roommate in the world." I roll my eyes at Christina's pep talk but bite down a grin. "And you—how did you phrase it? 'Vanquished your nemesis at long last.'"

By "nemesis" she means Sebastian Adams, whose favorite and only hobby growing up was one-upping me at every turn. It only got worse in high school when we both clearly took an interest in journalism. I'd get the editor position on the school paper, but he'd become the school's most beloved writer. Seb would get a coveted recommendation from our recluse of an English teacher, and I would win the year-end student departmental award. The competition was so absurd that we started competing in every other way we could, forcing the school to declare the first-ever tie for salutatorian—our GPAs and mutual accomplishments were such a dead tie that nobody could decide who won.

But I broke the cycle. I got into Maple Ride. Seb didn't.

I breathe back out, decidedly grounded again. "You're right," I say, nodding into the phone. "Thanks. You're right."

And she is. At least until five seconds later, when a boy rounds the corner at top speed, lets out a surprised, "Shit, sorry, shit!" before colliding right into me, depositing half his smoothie on my human form.

Naturally, I open my mouth to say "sorry" right back, a re-flexive smile already poised on my lips. Avoiding conflict is quite literally in my DNA. Or at least I assume it is, since my sisters seem to have absorbed all the conflict-creating genes, leaving me to play family peacekeeper more often than not.

But then I glance up into the wide, apologetic brown eyes directly in front of mine and realize this is not just any boy. This is the aforementioned archnemesis, looking distinctly unvan-quished in the late August sun.

"Sadie!"

A grin cracks across Seb's face—that trademark wide-open-sky one that somehow only got more dazzling in the last few days.

There's a dusting of new freckles on his newly tanned skin, and his dark-brown hair is even more tousled than usual, like it's still salty from the beach trip I know he took this past weekend. He looks like he should be recruited for a billboard for an all-inclusive, family-friendly resort.

Unfortunately for Seb, I'm immune to every inch of it.

Clinton B. Photography

**Emma Lord** (she/her) is a digital media editor and writer living in New York City, where she spends whatever time she isn't writing either running or belting show tunes in community theater. She graduated from the University of Virginia with a major in psychology and a minor in how to tilt your computer screen so nobody will notice you updating your fanfiction from the back row. She was raised on glitter, a whole lot of love, and copious amounts of grilled cheese. Her books include *Tweet Cute, You Have a Match, When You Get the Chance, Begin Again,* and *The Break-Up Pact.*

# From *New York Times* Bestselling Author Emma Lord!

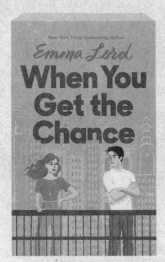

"If you haven't read a novel by Emma Lord before, you've been missing out on something spectacular." —*Paste*

W WEDNESDAY BOOKS